CHILDREN

of

ISAAC

PJ Connolly

Ockham Press

Entia non sunt multiplicanda praeter necessitatem.

Paperback ISBN: 978-1-909154-90-2
ebook ISBN: 978-1-911131-99-1

A CIP catalogue record for this book is available from the National Library.

Front cover art by Trisha Fitzgerald.

First published in Ireland in 2015 by Ockham Press, in association with Choice Publishing, Drogheda, Co. Louth, Republic of Ireland.

www.choicepublishing.ie

To Dara, Yuko, Niamh and Ciarán

Acknowledgements

Special thanks to Joan McKenna, without whose unstinting support this book might not have seen the light of day.

The author also wishes to acknowledge invaluable editorial advice received from each of the following:

Imelda Mc Donagh, Jackie Morrissey, Jane Ryan, John Maguire, Pat Talbot and Ellen Kelly.

The author would also like to acknowledge the contribution of all whose memories and anecdotes were to find their way, in one form or another, into the finished story.

Back cover photograph by the late Paddy Coffey is reproduced with the kind permission of Martin Coffey.

One

No one disputed that it was Victoria herself who had asked for a childrens' party as a special treat for her future loyal subjects in Ireland. What seemed less clear was the question of whether the twins were in the Park to see the Queen or the Queen was in the Park to see the twins. Annie liked to think it was the latter and stuck to her guns in the face of Isaac's scoffing. She insisted on telling anyone who would listen that her two children had been the star attraction for the Sovereign.

What happened was that the teachers in St Paul's were in the middle of selecting a group of children to participate in the event when Annie appeared in the school hallway, to see about having David and Becky enrolled the following September. When Miss Morris, the head teacher, caught sight of the three and a half year olds she decided there and then that they would have to be part of the school contingent. 'You simply must allow them,' she begged Annie.

As Annie, with her two toddlers in tow, arrived in the Park and tried to find the St Paul's pupils among the hordes of excited and noisy children she thought there must be several thousand youngsters already there, all dressed up to the nines, corralled for the most part by teachers or parents determined to make an impression on the monarch. She guessed that most of them were from Protestant schools since the Catholic schools were openly boycotting the event from notions of nationalism and religion. Right now she didn't concern herself with such contentious issues. Like everyone else in the Phoenix Park on that April day in 1900 she was hoping the Sovereign would decide to stroll through the

Polo Ground while the children were picnicking there.

The Queen's arrival was announced by a great cheer which grew and spread across the open spaces of the Phoenix Park in a swell of fervent excitement. She appeared in style, driving out through the back gate of the Viceregal Lodge, the gate nearest that part of the zoo which held the lions' enclosure. The lions chose that moment to emit a mighty roar, whether of approval or its opposite no one would ever be sure. Indeed, Annie overheard one spoiled brat explaining to his sniggering classmates that the hungry lions, waiting for their dinner, had sniffed the air and detected the makings of a tasty royal snack. She was not too surprised at such sentiments for there were some amongst the Irish population who would have considered it no bad thing at all if the Queen's open carriage had been redirected into the lions' den.

A wave of excitement rippled through the crowd when it was seen that the Queen had been assisted down from her carriage and was beginning to walk among the crowds of curious children, many with little flags in their hands. Who would have dreamed that Becky and David would be singled out by the Queen for her special attention? She seemed to spot them straight away amongst the swarms of older children and turned to walk right over to where they sat on the grass guzzling all the goodies they could get their greedy little paws on.

How or why she came to pick them out was a mystery although the way Annie had kitted them out must have had a lot to do with it. She had gone to a lot of trouble for the occasion, dressing them in almost identical little sailor suits with white blouses and navy blue collars. David had navy trousers and Becky a skirt of the same material.

'Aren't they adorable!' the Queen said, stooping low to bring her face almost to their level.

'Stand up and greet Her Majesty,' said Annie. She had been teaching Becky to curtsy, though never imagining she would have occasion to do so. Becky remembered and made a passable effort while David just stared at the monarch with a look of suspicion and distrust.

Her Majesty seemed enchanted by the similarity of brother and sister. 'Are they identical twins?' she asked Annie in very upper class tones.

'Everyone thinks they are, Ma'am. But no, they're not.'

'Well, they are as close as can be,' said the Queen reaching down to touch Becky's blond curls. David, instead of the regal touch, only received the benefit of a benign smile. In that instant a strange idea pushed its way into Annie's mind. What if the touching of Becky's hair conveyed some kind of blessing? Where did that leave David who had missed out on the royal benediction? Did it mean he would grow up less loyal than his twin sister who was sanctified by a queen's touch? Common sense reasserted itself then and she dismissed the thought as so much silly nonsense.

The whole affair had been promoted as a party for *patriotic children* and the children for the most part were too young to know or care that priests were fulminating from the pulpit against parents who permitted their children to be used in such a shameful display of boot-licking towards a Protestant monarch. There could be no doubting the loyalty and allegiance of the twins, however. Nine months later when the news came through that the Queen was dead they told their mother and each other that they would never ever forget the Queen nor all the lemonade and biscuits that made a magical appearance for her visit on a sunny April afternoon in the Park.

In the front parlour — for there was a light dusting of snow on the ground outside — the twins re-enacted the royal funeral. One of Becky's dolls stood in for the Queen and a shoe-box made do for her coffin. The morning paper carried a photograph of Her Late Majesty lying-in-state so they had a reliable indication of how things should be arranged. Annie, pottering around in the dining room, was listening through the open doors.

'You have to kiss her, David.'

'Why do I?'

'Because we'll never see her again.'

'Oh, well, it's only an old doll anyway.' And he gave *the Queen* a quick reluctant peck on the forehead. Together they placed the lid on the box and slid it behind the sofa there to remain until the angel's trumpet should sound on the Day of Judgement.

'Mamma says we're going to get a king next,' Becky said. 'He's *Edward the Seven.*'

'That's a funny name.'

'And there's going to be a coronation,' she said.

This was a new word and David repeated it over and over, savouring the tripping feel of it along his tongue. 'What's it mean, Becky?'

'It's something they do to a king.'

There were other words too which Becky had heard her father read aloud from the paper. They sounded like *oats and legions.* She asked her mother. 'What's *oats an' legions,* Ma?'

Annie believed in answering all her children's questions. She never shooed them away with a *go ask your father.* As far as Isaac was concerned, children were a woman's responsibility and he didn't have a lot of patience with their childish chatter. Some people, Annie explained – important people – had to swear an oath of allegiance. It was a way for them to acknowledge that the king was above everyone else, up there at the very top, higher up, even, than the Prime Minister.

'Who's the Prime Minister, Mamma?' said Becky. 'Will he swear *oats an' legions?*'

'Lord Salisbury, and I'm certain he will, love.'

Becky pondered this in silence. Then she said, 'I'm going to swear *oats an' legions* to David. He'll be the King and I'll be the Prime Minister and I'll swear *oats an' legions* to the King.' And so, there in the parlour and within Annie's hearing, David and Becky acted out a ceremony of their own devising. David had to promise to look after his sister, while she gave her solemn promise never to let anyone say a bad word against him. This, she told him, was what was meant by *oats an' legions*. Such love, such devotion, thought Annie. Please God it will always be so. At this point in their young lives how could they even begin to grasp the reality that anything might happen to test their loyalty. Life is strange, she thought. You just never know what's waiting around the corner.

Who could have foreseen, for example, when she set out on a lonely train to take up her first position in a remote Wicklow town that before that school year was over she would end up married to a man she scarcely knew? It hadn't taken her long to discover that she had tied herself to a man of sullen moods and violent outbursts. A man as incapable of love as he was of grasping any viewpoint that differed from his own. Isaac Townsend, she decided, carried some awful secret that caused him to convulse in the middle of the night and cry aloud for God's mercy.

He was a man so different in every way from that gentle boy she had truly loved. Who could explain why God had seen fit to spoil her chance of real happiness? For when Rory was snatched away from her, all her dreams had gone with him. There are those who will tell you that man proposes but God disposes, and yet she wondered how things might have been if it hadn't been for one little medal slipped inside a hopeful envelope.

Two

Never in her wildest dreams did she expect to have a reply by return of post. When she sat down at the little table in her bedroom to pen her job application she had stuck closely to the template handed to her by Mother Oliver, who taught music and singing to the trainee teachers. It was her own idea, however, to put in something about her two years' experience teaching the babies back in her school at home.

Mother Oliver had given her one word of advice. 'Slip a miraculous medal into the envelope while asking Our Lady to intercede for you.' In Lourdes as a young girl, Mother Oliver had seen with her own eyes the cripples throw away their crutches and walk.

But Annie had forgotten to take out the medal before sealing the envelope so she was more than surprised when her letter produced the offer of a position in a two teacher school in the South of County Wicklow. The letter was signed, *Monsignor J.P. Liddy, PP, Drumboley.*

***

Annie stood looking after the train as the guard's van disappeared around a bend in the track. She watched the only other passenger to have stepped down pass through the picket fence barrier and walk to a waiting gig where she was assisted onto her seat by a liveried servant. The sound of the horse's hooves soon faded and silence descended on the railway platform and the street outside. She looked all about her but the place was deserted. Even the ticket office was empty.

There will be someone there to meet you, the letter had said. As Annie emerged from the station she saw a shop some way up the street and made her way in that direction. Fruit, vegetables, footwear, hardware—every kind of merchandise—competed for space on the cluttered pavement outside Drumboley General Stores. She stepped onto the roadway to get past.

She was about to go inside and ask for directions when a man emerged through a wooden gate next to the shop and flung some empty crates onto a cart outside. His hand went to the peak of his cap, acknowledging her presence. Seeing as he was the first person in this place to have noticed her existence, she moved to where he now rested against the side of the cart. His eyes never left her as she approached. He seemed older than she by three or four years, though not quite as tall. 'I was meant to be met,' she said.

He took some time to absorb this information before answering. 'I'm ready to wager you must be the new school mistress,' he said. 'To take the place of Mrs Fay. Would I be right in thinking that?' The whole town must have known she was coming, yet not a soul had come to the train to meet her or show her the way to her lodgings.

'Could you tell me the way to Miss O'Connor's?' If she could get rid of her case she might then try to find the schoolhouse and get acquainted with its layout. She might even find someone who could fill her in on her duties.

'Miss O'Connor's?' he said. 'I'll take you. Here, let me give you a hand up.'

He took her trunk and threw it easily onto the open cart where it found a place among the empty crates. She marvelled at his strength. Then, pointing at a step on the side of the cart, he said, 'Foot there, Ma'am.' She caught the brown eyes peering at her from beneath sandy brows, penetrating eyes that seemed to search inside her head. With his hand gripping her elbow he guided her over the side and onto the loose wooden plank that served as a seat. His firm grip on her arm sent a shiver through her, a sensation she found not at all unpleasant. He climbed up beside her.

'Hup,' he said, sending a ripple along the reins as the mare moved off. 'Isaac's the name. Isaac Townsend. I run a small bit of a farm out the road.' Annie smiled to herself for she had heard her own father use those exact words to describe his smallholding back in Cavan. 'I'm Annie Brady,' she said and then wondered if she had been too forward in giving him her Christian name. The children in her charge and the townspeople would come to know her as Miss Brady.

As they came around the bend into the town's main street she got the impression of a busy market town with people coming and going about their business. Carts and traps stood outside shops and offices while their owners pursued their business within. He did not speak except to point out places of interest and then only in brief announcements.

'Saint Mary's,' he said nodding in the direction of what Annie guessed must be the Catholic Church, since the doors were wide open and there was a grotto in the grounds.

'That there's our own church,' he said as they passed an austere building built around a solid square tower, its doors closed and the whole area submerged in the deep shade of sycamore trees. Annie had been told this town was evenly split between Protestant and Catholic, so she was not surprised to learn that her guide was of the opposite persuasion to herself. She spoke little, feeling no need to be anything other than polite with a man she had just met. She confined herself to looking where he pointed and nodding her head when he spoke.

'There you go,' he said jerking the reins and pointing.

Number Ten was written in white letters glued to the glass above the front door of a two-storey house opening directly onto the pavement. He helped her down and again she felt the strange pleasurable sense of being held in his strong assured grip. He put down her case on the pavement beside her and turned back towards the cart. 'Good luck to you, ma'am,' he said before climbing back up. 'Hup there.'

She stood looking after him but he gave no backward glance in her direction. She turned to the house and rapped the knocker twice. She heard a movement on the inside before the door was dragged inwards by a girl in a white apron and solid-looking boots.

'Miss Brady you must be,' said the girl. 'We were watching out for you. Come on in.'

***

On Monday mornings he brought potatoes and vegetables into town. Carrots or leeks, or whatever else was ready for the market. He had a good relationship with Taggarts, who would take whatever was in season, knowing as they did that Isaac's produce was of a consistently good quality which they and their customers had come to trust. It had been his own idea entirely, to turn the haggard over to vegetables, a handy side-line that saw him with ready coins to rattle around in his pocket and get him out from under the thumb of his father. The old man seemed happy enough to see him taking more responsibility for the farm which—now that his older brother Adam had taken himself off—would become his inheritance.

Those extra shillings gave him the independence he needed to enjoy himself at weekends, to have a pint with the lads and afterwards if there was a dance on in the local hall to take a look in there, his courage boosted by the beer. He hoped he might court some nice lass, someone he could settle down with, a strong reliable woman to give him children and continue the Townsend name on that stretch of Wicklow hillside his people had farmed for generations.

Isaac found himself thinking about the young teacher he had given a lift to at the end of August. He hadn't seen much of her since. She hadn't turned up at any of the dances and no one seemed to know much about her or how she spent her time. He hoped he might see her in Taggarts. There was every chance she went there to buy something for herself, a bar of Fry's chocolate, maybe, or some sweets to hand out to the little kiddies she taught.

The days were already shortening when he again ran into her. It was more or less as he had imagined it, himself in conversation with Mrs Taggart about what he was owed for last week's delivery. Somehow he sensed who it was the minute she walked in. Instead of going to the counter, to the young girl who helped out on Saturdays, she came over to where they were talking. Mrs Taggart saw her and broke off the conversation to see what she wanted. The two women spoke in lowered tones before he heard Mrs Taggart say, 'Try the chemist. They're your best bet.'

Before she left, Miss Brady turned to Isaac. 'Excuse me for butting in like that,' she said. 'I just needed a word with Mrs Taggart.' Her hand touched his arm in an apologetic gesture, as if they had known each other for ages.

Later he saw her emerging from the chemist's and taking his courage in his hands he crossed over to where she stood fumbling with her purse. 'Good morning, Miss Brady. I haven't seen much of you since you came.'

She gave him a shy smile. 'Oh, I've been busy. Settling into the job. You know the way.'

'Getting on alright with the locals? People treating you okay, I hope.'

'I can't say I've any complaints.'

'There's a dance in the hall tonight. Any chance you might be thinking of going?'

He caught her amused look, a look that seemed to say she could read every thought in his head. 'I wouldn't find it much fun, to tell you the God's truth.'

'I don't much like it meself, the dancing. A rough crowd does be there sometimes. I do often go walking down be the river, just on me own, like. You might like it if I was to show you the waterfall and the salmon pool right next to it.' He didn't know why he said that—it came from nowhere.

'I might like that right enough.' She seemed to be studying his face.

'Tomorrow, maybe?'

'I'll be going to eleven mass. I can wait for you near the bridge if that's alright.'

'Fair enough, so. Well, I better be getting along. I'll see you tomorrow then.' He felt a singing in his heart he couldn't explain for he had never known anything like it before.

***

Annie taught the junior classes while Mr McGrath took charge of the older children, preparing them for the day they would put new nibs in their pens to face an examination which could determine the course of their future lives. McGrath was easy to work alongside, seldom interfering, except for the occasional friendly word of advice born out of his experience and which she accepted with grace. From day one he had addressed her by her first name which could have been his way of marking out their respective positions – headmaster and teacher. She for her part would never dream of addressing him as Gerry which she had heard the Parish Priest do.

In February Master McGrath brought up a subject that Annie felt was nobody's business but her own. 'I hear you're friendly with a young man of the Townsends,' he said as they waited in the teachers' room at the back of the schoolhouse for the children to trickle back after dinner. Annie was taken aback and not sure how to respond. She had been walking out with Isaac Townsend for the past five months, true enough. Usually on a Sunday morning when Isaac could get away from the farm for a few hours. Never at night though when Annie liked to stay in her bare upstairs room and prepare lessons.

'Isaac you mean?' She had nothing to hide.

'Isaac Townsend, that's who I mean right enough. You do know he's Church of Ireland don't you?'

'He goes to the Protestant church. It doesn't bother me a bit.'

'The trouble is, Annie, it might bother some other people.'

'No one ever said a word to me about it.'

'Maybe not to your face.' He paused, as if unsure how to proceed. 'Father Liddy tells me there's been talk.'

'Father Liddy?' So that's where all this was coming from. McGrath was simply passing on the PP's message.

'I would love to be able to reassure him, Annie.' The headmaster picked up a pencil and stared at its point. 'If you could just—. I mean if I could let him know there's nothing in it.'

'If you have to tell him anything at all you could just say I know what I'm about.' She felt a sudden surge of anger. She wasn't going to be bullied or dictated to. It was a trait she brought from her mother's side of the family. But she remembered that the priest was her employer and held all the cards, so she just said, 'He must have little to bother him.'

McGrath did not seem reassured. 'At least now you know what people are thinking,' he said and stood up to go into the classroom where the children were already making a din.

***

Annie and Isaac became more circumspect. They no longer met at the salmon pool where they had exchanged their first tender kiss. Their new meeting place was a spot which Annie discovered on a solitary excursion at the end of a tiring school day. Four crumbling walls of an early-Christian church slowly collapsing under a thousand years of voracious ivy. The heavy covering of green served at once to soften the stark outline of the walls while at the same time endowing the place with an atmosphere of soft luxury and quiet seclusion. Annie brought Isaac there to tell him what she knew of the monks who must have built this little church as a place of Christian worship in days long gone.

'At that time,' she said, 'there was no such thing as Protestant or Catholic. Saint Patrick belonged to all the people. But sure what am I talking about? You must know all that yourself.'

'I heard tell of something like that, right enough, but sure it all went in one ear and out the other.'

'Were you not fond of school?'

'I'll tell you now the way it was. The teacher would be talking away at the top of the room. As for me, me mind would be out in the fields, rounding up the sheep maybe, or mucking out the stable. The farm's all I ever thought about.' It was then he confided in her how he looked forward to the day his father would hand the land to him to manage. And then, when the sad day came that his father passed on, he, Isaac, would be master of his inheritance, head of the Townsend family, with children of his own to carry on farming those hilly fields for another generation. As he mentioned children Annie was aware of his quick glance in her direction. Who did he have in mind, then, as a mother for his future children? Herself? Maybe.

***

Annie planned to go home to her family for the summer holidays. She was going to miss Isaac for she had grown fond of listening to his talk of sheep rearing, barley growing and market gardening. He foresaw a time when the population of Dublin would be crying out for potatoes and fresh vegetables. When he talked like that his eyes shone. She was fascinated by Isaac's ambitious plans for the future. Now they weren't going to see each other for six weeks. She thought they should meet at their trysting place and be together away from prying eyes and gossipy townsfolk.

He was waiting for her at the ruined church. When she arrived he put a strong arm around her neck and she felt the rub of a bristled chin against the soft skin of her cheek. Knowing they would not be disturbed, they sat together on the grass, their backs against the ivy-clad wall and their faces to the sun. He kissed her. She liked when he kissed her like that for he had long since shed his initial inhibitions. She liked the thrill that ran through her, like a shock from a battery, when his strong arms pressed her against his body. She often wondered if this is what people meant by being in love. By now, though, she was convinced that what she felt for Isaac Townsend was real love and she wondered sometimes if he felt the same about her.

At first she tried to resist when she felt him tugging at her frock for she had a deep-seated sense of modesty, instilled in her from an early age. She felt his hand on her leg seeking the inside of her thigh and made a feeble attempt to push him away. In spite of all the nuns had said about *going too far* she found her will to resist melting before his fierce urgent embrace. Maybe it was the bird-song, maybe the warm sun, maybe the remoteness of their hideaway, but Annie gave in, prayed that things would be alright, and allowed Isaac to do as he wished.

Afterwards, as she straightened her clothes, she felt sore and dishevelled and could not shake off a nagging sense of guilt that could only have stemmed from her Catholic upbringing. As Isaac lay back in the warm sun he appeared utterly content but it was impossible to know what his thoughts were.

***

Annie was already back at her teaching post six weeks or more when her worst fears came to pass. She had never missed periods before now and there could be only one explanation. With the knowledge that she was pregnant came the realisation that her whole life was about to change. Before her condition became plain for the population of Drumboley to see and gossip about, she would have to offer her resignation and leave the town for good. There was nothing to be gained now by putting it off. She wondered should she write to the PP or ask to speak to him. She decided to do it in writing. More formal and less embarrassing.

There would be questions too at home. Her mother's disappointment at her daughter's fall from grace would be grievous. Annie, the qualified teacher, had been her great pride and joy. How she was going to explain things she had no idea. Her one hope now lay with Isaac, that he would offer to marry her and so make her respectable.

His reaction took her by surprise. She had hoped he would be happy when she told him. He had talked often about his desire for children to continue his line into the future. Now he was a different man altogether. Instead of showing any sign of welcome for the new life growing inside her, his attitude was one of recrimination and blame.

'You could have stopped me,' he said.

Though shocked at this answer, Annie was not about to give in so easily. 'This child is our child, the start of what we talked about – the next generation of Townsends.'

'Will you hold on there a minute,' he said. 'Are you saying I'm going to have to marry you? Is that what you're saying? Because if it is you're going to have to put it right out of your head.'

'What way is that to be talking, Isaac Townsend? Of course we're getting married. It's the only way. A child has to have a father. Besides, it's what you always said you wanted. So what's come over you?'

'This whole thing's a mess. It's all wrong. They won't allow it.'

'Who won't allow it Isaac, who?'

'I don't know, I don't know.'

'It's because I'm a Catholic, isn't it? Isn't it, Isaac? Answer me.'

'You don't know me ould-fella, Annie. He won't stand for it. And me ma's just as bad. She'll back him up to the hilt.'

'So you're running scared of your ma and da? Well I don't give a tinker's damn about your ma or your da. Listen to me here, Isaac Townsend. You're the baby's father, no two ways about it. You're going to face up your responsibilities like a man. You and me is getting married and the quicker the better. Do you hear me now?'

Three

Mrs Harold was still trying to get over the loss of her husband, who died when the face of the quarry where he worked in Greenhills collapsed and buried him. She liked them the moment she opened the door, she said, for she could tell straight away they were country people like herself and Isaac had the build and bearing of the man she had lost.

For their part they counted themselves fortunate to have found clean furnished upstairs rooms that were far enough from the squalor behind Patrick Street and the Coombe, yet still only a twenty minute walk from the city centre. For Annie, though, the main thing was that they had a roof over their heads at a rent they could afford. Mrs Harold said the shilling she got from them would go a good bit of the way towards her own rent. They could use her kitchen downstairs for cooking and eating. She would keep out of their way when they were there. All in all it was an arrangement that suited both sides.

St Catherine's was the obvious place to get married since it was just a short walk away in Thomas Street and the minister there was not the sort to start asking questions. He had children of his own and could hardly avoid noticing Annie's state as she grew round with the baby within her. He understood straight away that they wanted a quiet affair. There was no one else in the church on the morning they were married apart from Thomson, the verger, and a Mrs Scully, who happened to be passing and came in when she saw the doors open. Both were roped in to act as witnesses. Once she had added her own name to the register beneath that of Isaac, Annie felt an immense sense of relief. Now at last everything was right and proper, their union legitimised and recognised. Now at last she could tell her family at home that she had moved to Dublin and got married. As for telling them about her pregnancy—well, everything in its own good time.

Back in the house after the informal ceremony they found that Mrs Harold had prepared a special breakfast of fried eggs, rashers and black and white puddings. It was an act of kindness they had not been expecting. 'For the bride and groom,' she said as she led them into her own little dining room at the back of the house. 'You shouldn't have done this,' Annie said. 'You're too good altogether.'

***

'Any luck?' she said as Isaac arrived home at the end of another day of job hunting. She turned away in case he noticed the anxiety she felt inside.

'No need to fret.' he said, 'I'm telling you, there's no shortage of work out there. Besides I'm not going to grab the first thing someone fires at me. I know my own worth. But she didn't miss the look of disappointment on his face. They both knew he needed a job and needed to find it soon. Only weeks after arriving in Dublin, the prospect of running out of money was a frightening possibility. Having to leave home in disgrace with only the clothes on his back and the small amount of money he had been able to collect from the shops he supplied, Isaac was now breadwinner for both Annie and the child she carried within her. Between them they had barely enough cash left to put some food on the table and pay the rent for another week or two. She managed to put by some savings from the teaching but she knew they could not go on much longer without a steady wage coming in.

Isaac had been asking around for over a week now – coal

yards, building sites, even Dublin Corporation – anywhere he thought they could use a strong pair of shoulders. He tried the Lucan Dairy, thinking his experience with horses would stand to him but there too jobs were like gold dust. He had been putting on a front to hide his failure but the façade slipped one evening when he asked her did she think God was punishing him for leaving his aging parents with no one to help them.

She reminded him it wasn't like that at all. His father and mother had demanded that he renounce the young teacher he had made pregnant. They even offered money for her to go away and keep the whole thing under wraps. Their disgrace was compounded when Annie stuck to her guns and insisted that Isaac marry her. It was the parents who suggested that he take her away to the city. No need then for Isaac to feel guilty. A vengeful God was not part of her upbringing. And yet it continued to trouble him. He told her the home place would now pass to his little brother, John. Meanwhile Annie hoped her husband wasn't being too choosy in the kind of work he was prepared to take on.

A few days after that conversation, Isaac struck gold. The huge sprawling brewery a few streets away from where they lived is where he got his lucky break. He arrived home to tell his new wife he had been offered a start as a general labourer.

'Thanks be to the Lord.' She threw her arms about his neck and hugged him. He pulled away from her, probably afraid Mrs Harold would appear in the hallway and find them embracing.

'Well, that's one thing settled anyway,' he said, but he couldn't hide the pride in his voice. Although the work he was given was menial unskilled labour like cleaning the yard and being at the beck and call of the skilled craftsmen, both he and Annie considered this the luckiest break in their life together so far. She asked him about the work – was there a lot of lifting, was it dirty?

He rolled up his shirt sleeve. 'Look,' he said. 'I didn't get muscles like these from sitting around. Anyway, with a little nipper on the way,' he poked her gently in the abdomen, 'we'll need every penny.' She knew then that nothing about the new job would bother Isaac, accustomed as he was to the hard graft of the farm.

'A job is a job,' she said and to back up that sentiment she set about finding some work for herself. She began to do the rounds of the local schools. It wasn't long before she realised there was a problem. Her pregnancy was starting to show and she was quick to notice some sort of taboo against employing a woman in her condition. A po-faced headmistress took it upon herself to lecture Annie about a married woman's place being in the home – or, in Annie's case – preparing for her baby. It would, she added, be quite unseemly, scandalous in fact, for a woman in Annie's condition to parade herself in front of a classroom of innocent and impressionable young children.

'So where, I wonder, do these little children think they came from, if not from their pregnant mothers?' Before the scandalised woman could recover from her shock Annie turned on her heel and marched out. She persevered, though, and at last came across a school principal who took a liking to her and asked many questions about her background and experience.

'I've been teaching since I was fifteen,' Annie said.

'Really?' said the headmistress, looking at her with renewed interest. She went on to explain that she sometimes found herself in a fix when one of her teachers was out sick. She asked Annie if she would be willing to step into the breach next time something like that cropped up.

'Send for me any time you're stuck. We're over there just off Marrowbone Lane. Here's the address.' She hoped her eagerness wasn't too obvious.

Annie had booked herself into the Coombe Hospital, where she was going for her check-ups. Arriving home after one hospital visit, she marked the calendar in red ink at the week they said her baby was due. She began to spend hours running her fingers through the baby clothes in Frawleys and wishing there was some way of knowing if it was going to be a boy or a girl. She was convinced it was a boy, in part because of the way he kicked and in part because Mrs Harold downstairs said it was definitely a *he* and claimed never to have got it wrong.

Annie told Isaac she wanted to call her son *Rory*. It was a good strong-sounding name, she said, the name of the last High King of Ireland. She kept to herself the true significance of the name, a sacred memory she had chosen to treasure forever in her own breast.

'I wanted a name from the Bible,' he said.

'Like what?'

He thought for a moment. 'Like – . Something like –. A good old name like Saul.'

For the first time her husband was attempting to assert his authority. She didn't answer. Where was the point in arguing over something that would only arise if the baby was in fact a boy?

Annie was resting on her bed one morning when she heard knocking on the door downstairs. She hadn't been feeling well – a general sense of malaise hung over her. Mrs Harold must have been out since the knocking persisted. With some difficulty she made her way down keeping a tight grip on the handrail.

'You're to come as quick as you can, Missus. Miss Sheerin said to tell you she's stuck.'

Annie stared at the child, a little redhead with no socks in her worn out sandals and a rip in her hand-me-down dress. She debated in her mind whether she felt well enough to face a class of energetic youngsters. Then she said, 'Tell her I'll be there as quick as I can.' The child scuttled off while Annie struggled to get herself presentable and put on her coat which she left unbuttoned.

She took charge of one of the classes and did her best to keep them engaged up to the dinner bell. It was at that point that the pain in her lower abdomen became too much for her.

'I'm very sorry, Miss Sheerin, but I really have to get back home.'

'Off home with you, Mrs Townsend. You're just as well not to take any chances.'

***

As Isaac approached the house his mind was troubled. He had tried and failed to rid himself of the sight he had seen as he came out through a back gate of the brewery onto one of the little streets of dilapidated houses and ragged urchins. There, at the street corner, he saw something the like of which he had never seen or expected ever to see again. It was a living figure no bigger than a child but with the wizened head of an old man, a misshapen mockery of humanity. The unfortunate creature was perched on a low wooden trolley, on four miniature wheels. He was surrounded by a bevy of excited boys who made great play of pushing the trolley round and round on the roadway while shouting, 'Hold on tight there, Billy, we don't want you falling off and getting yourself killed.'

Isaac stood and stared, at once horrified and fascinated. The man on the trolley possessed head, shoulders, arms and hands but little else. No legs or feet that he could see. An aberration born to be the plaything of generations of boys in the grotty streets that surrounded the brewery where Isaac worked. The creature on the trolley saw Isaac staring and gave him a nod of acknowledgement.

Embarrassed at being caught gaping, Isaac moved away and set out for his home. He was troubled by questions for which there could be no answer. Why, for instance, had the Lord played such a cruel trick on some unsuspecting mother? Was this the work of a vengeful God determined to punish the transgressions of the parents or even, like in the bible, the sins of the parents' parents? He found himself praying that his own child would be born healthy and fully formed. Attempting to dismiss the image of the deformed creature whose very existence disturbed him so much, Isaac quickened his pace and headed for home.

***

All day Annie had tried to ignore the pain, believing that sooner or later it would go away. Instead, it grew steadily worse. Now, when she could bear it no longer, a sudden convulsion in her abdomen made her shriek for help.

Mrs Harold came rushing up the stairs. One glance was enough for the older woman to take it all in. Amidst the blood and sticky mess Annie could see something pulsing on the bedroom floor. She lay back on the bed and turned her face to the wall. She lacked the strength to strip off her blood soaked dress. She couldn't bear to look as Mrs Harold rolled up her sleeves and set to work. She kept her eyes closed while her landlady, with bucket and rags, made several trips up and down the stairs and outside to the lavatory in the yard.

***

There was no sign of Mrs Harold as Isaac stepped into the hall and saw that the door leading to the kitchen was closed. There was no welcoming smell of cooking as he dragged his tired feet up the stairs. He found his wife sitting on the bed fully clothed, looking pale and drained, her expression empty. Everywhere the strong smell of disinfectant. He read on her face a look of abject apology and knew there was something very wrong.

'What's up, Annie? Are you feeling sick?'

'I'm sorry, Isaac. I'm terrible sorry.' She seemed unable to say any more but pointed at her belly and it was then he realised what it was she was trying to tell him. He wanted to say something to her but his thoughts were in turmoil. He might have told her it was alright – except that it wasn't. He went into the front room where the window overlooked the street. Happy laughing voices of children at play carried up to him in the dying day. He pulled over the curtain to shut out the sight of those children for they served only to sharpen his pain and confusion. There in the gloom they sat apart in separate rooms, unable to communicate, each lost in their separate thoughts.

He had agreed to marry Annie, even though it meant turning his back on all he had lived for. He couldn't have known then that this is how it was going to turn out. It had to be that some Angel of Vengeance was at work in his life.

A deathly stillness filled the house.

Four

The brewery held in high regard the men who made the barrels. Isaac saw this from the first day he was assigned to the cooperage, becoming a general dogsbody for the coopers. In and out of the workshops all day long, hauling the oak planks or rolling the finished barrels to the storage yard, he saw for himself the way those skilled craftsmen were respected and cossetted. Double the daily beer allowance, a free pint in the morning and another in the afternoon. He often watched them swallow it down as he looked on parched.

'I can tell by the look on your face that your tongue is hanging out for a sup.'

He looked around to see who had addressed him and recognised him right away from the incongruous starched shirt and silk scarf visible above the long cooper's apron. A small wiry fellow called Morton.

'I could do with a sup of the black stuff right enough,' said Isaac. 'Are you not drinking yourself?'

'I'm off the liquor for good. The wife never laid off nagging till she got me down to the Temperance Hall in Abbey Street to take the pledge.'

'God, that's a fierce big step, altogether, Mr Morton, and you working in a brewery of all places.'

Morton moved closer and lowered his voice. 'There's fellas here, Isaac, naming no names, that's not a bit content with the two pints they do get for their daily ration. Helping themselves, unofficial like, and there's ways and means for them that knows the ropes. I was one of them meself. There's drinking goes on in this place I can tell you and not all of it above board either.'

Isaac had heard some of the coopers saying there was no way they could work full belt in the heat and noise if they didn't have the beer to keep them going.

'So what were you planning on doing with your own allowance, Mr Morton, now that you're gone on the dry? It seems a terrible shame to let it go to waste.' For Isaac this was a pertinent question.

'Seeing as you're a damn hard worker, Isaac, I'll let you have it and welcome. No one need be any the wiser.'

Isaac believed that the lubrication of his throat found its way into the muscles of his arms and thighs. He was convinced he worked twice as hard when he had one of those pints inside him. Morton, on the other hand, claimed his work had improved no end since he went teetotal. And since he was on piecework the increase in his output meant more money to take home to the missus. Sticking close to Morton and watching his way of working, Isaac began to think he would welcome the chance to have a go at this barrel making business himself. He mentioned as much to Morton and Morton began to treat him as a kind of unofficial apprentice, explaining everything, revealing the tricks and techniques he had developed for himself over the years.

So while Isaac continued in the employ of the brewery as general labourer, the coopers came to recognise that he was to all intents and purposes apprenticed to Morton. Even Jackson knew about it but did nothing to interfere. The workshop overseer saw it as his job to keep everyone happy and productive.

***

A crisis arose in the cooperage. Isaac watched it all play out. It began when a cooper called Jones was found tapping a pipeline in

Vat House Four. He was brought before a senior manager, accused of *pillaging the company's property* and fired on the spot. By way of compensation for his instant dismissal the man's wife was given five pounds, amounting to a month's pay. Jones refrained from implicating any of the others and his loyalty to his fellows was to yield dividends. He recruited half a dozen others to join him in setting up in business on their own. They rented premises in the neighbourhood of Smithfield, on the other side of the Liffey, and founded a cooperage, hoping to cash in on the demand for barrels from the nearby distillery.

With the sudden loss of these skilled workers, new men had to be drafted in to fill the gap, men from other parts of the brewery, men judged to be quick learners and good with their hands. Barrel-making, however, was not a craft you could master in a week and it would take years for these new men to attain the level of skill of those who were gone.

For Isaac it was a question of being in the right place at the right time. He had learned a lot from Morton, who stayed on after the others left. Having watched and learned under the tutelage of his master he was ready now to try his hand at the making of a barrel on his own. That first barrel took him a long time, measuring, cutting, carving and banding but Isaac never doubted the outcome. Morton kept a friendly eye on his efforts, offering a word of advice now and then.

When at last it was finished Isaac went in search of the overseer. 'Have you got a minute to spare, Mr Jackson? I'd like to show you my handiwork.' Jackson ran expert hands up and down the freshly banded staves searching for any fault that would render the barrel unfit for purpose. When he failed to find any he turned to Isaac with a look of admiration in his eye.

'Well, Mr Townsend, I think I just found myself a new cooper. Never have I seen a man pick up a trade in a year the way you've done. May I wish you the best of luck in your new job.'

'New job, Mr Jackson?   Are you saying I can call myself a cooper?'

'Starting tomorrow morning, Isaac, you'll take your proper place in this here workshop. You'll have your own bench over there and a full set of tools that no one else can lay their grubby hands on. '

A grin spread across Isaac's face. A cooper was *somebody* – somebody to be looked up to and respected. Now he, Isaac Townsend would command that same respect. He was a happy man. When Jackson was gone another cooper called Ward came over to shake his hand. 'You'll come and have a few pints after work, Isaac. You're one of us now. This calls for a celebration, what do you say?'

'I'm tempted, sure enough, Mr Ward, but I've got to be getting on home. It's the missus, you see. It looks like it's going to be twins and she's finding it rough going.'

'Ah, sure what difference will an hour or two make? She'll soon get used to it, they always do. Besides it doesn't do them a bit of harm to know their proper place.'

'Not today, Mr Ward.'

'Charlie. Call me Charlie. Charlie's the name.'

'See you tomorrow, Charlie.'

Isaac couldn't wait to tell Annie his good fortune. They would now have more money coming in, which meant they could start looking for a bigger place to live. With twins on the way they would need more space and with the standing of a trade behind him he owed it to himself to find something better than two cramped rooms in the upstairs of a redbrick terrace house.

Walking home he reflected on his good fortune. To have found himself placed alongside older, more experienced men in the cooperage was beyond anything he could have dreamed. The distinctive aroma of the oak timber was something he would look forward to in the mornings. It might make up for the incessant din of iron hoops being bashed into place. And there was the sense of pride he would feel every time he stepped back to look at a finished barrel and realise that here was something he had created with his own hands, his own skill. He knew it was something that would never pall for as long as he continued to work there.

A month after his promotion he was late getting home. He had gone with Charlie Ward for a couple of pints in the staff bar. They had stayed longer than he had intended. He quickened his pace when he remembered that Annie hadn't been feeling well when he left that morning. He let himself in and found Mrs Harold waiting for him in the hall.

'She went in this morning.'

He looked at his landlady, not knowing if he could believe his ears. 'But it wasn't supposed to be till after Christmas,' he said. 'That's what they told her.'

'She thought she felt something stirring and asked me to call a cab. I told the cabbie to take her to the Rotunda. With twins, you know, the Rotunda's your only place.'

'I suppose you're right.'

Realising there was no one now to cook for him at home, Isaac remembered that there was always food in the canteen bar. Without changing out of his working clothes he turned around and headed back to the brewery.

He might get some news in the morning.

Five

It was snowing outside, they told her. The cobbled surface of Granby Row lay beneath a full five inches of virgin snow as the twins came into the world in the early hours of the eighth day of December, 1896, a Tuesday. Annie gave thanks to the Immaculate Conception, whose feast day it was.

The girl was the easier of the two while her brother, who lay crosswise in the womb, had to be turned by a doctor and midwife working together pulling and pushing in the hush of the night. 'He's just being awkward,' said the Doctor, 'but don't you worry, we'll get him right way round.' And sure enough the baby emerged after much painful and protracted pushing on Annie's part as the first wintry rays of sunlight made magic of the icicles that dangled outside the hospital window.

The safe birth of the twins was a considerable consolation to Annie, a glorious Christmas gift, conceived as they were so soon after her miscarriage in January. The little girl weighed only five pounds and two ounces while her more robust brother was a larger six pounds. Though exhausted after her ordeal, she asked to hold both babies together for a few moments, before collapsing into a deep healing sleep. When she woke she saw that the babies had been placed in basket cradles on either side of her bed. She marvelled at the utter perfection of their little limbs and faces and made a solemn promise to the Virgin Mary to raise them in the love and honour of her Divine Son.

Isaac arrived that evening. He said he had asked one of the girls in the office to telephone the hospital at lunchtime.

'Did you get a bite to eat?' She noticed the whiff of beer as he approached her bed.

'I called in for a sandwich and a pint on the way down here.' She guessed he would have needed more than one pint to fortify himself for the occasion. She knew how awkward most men were when faced with the reality of child-birth. Some of them never went near their wives in the hospital. He looked at the sleeping infants and nodded his approval. She wondered did he feel proud of his achievement in siring not just one but two healthy offspring.

'What are we going to call them?' Annie said. She knew well how things were usually done. A female child would be named after the wife's own mother or one of the aunts while the father would want to see the eldest boy getting a revered name from his own side of the family. She knew, though, that this question would be decided by Isaac.

'We always get our names from the Bible,' he had said. She had seen him with a bible on his knee, opening it at random as if hoping for divine inspiration. 'My father called me after the son of Abraham. And his father before him did the same. Jacob – straight out of the Holy Book. That's the way we always do it.' He could see no reason why Annie wouldn't want to go along with this Godly custom.

Now that they knew they had a boy and a girl, it was time to decide for definite.

'David,' he said. 'What do you think?'

'David? I like it well enough.'

Annie thought it was time to assert herself by proposing a name for the little girl. 'Rebecca for the girl.' She uttered the name in a tone which suggested finality. She was well acquainted with the bible stories she had read aloud to the little children in her care in Drumboley. 'In the bible Rebecca drew the water for

Abraham's camels and he chose her as a wife for his own son.' Since God had blessed them with a little girl, she wanted her to be as sweet and helpful as Rebecca in the bible. It would make her a happy mother indeed. Besides, her mother had always spoken with great fondness of her own Aunty Becky.

As for *David*, the name struck her as a good strong name and she prayed that he would embody all the strength and doggedness of her own father, a hardworking, gentle giant of a man who, even as he grew old, continued to wrest a living from a few scrawny cattle on the gravelly hills that constituted his little farm. Although her husband had taken the naming of the boy out of her hands she found she was more than happy with the names they now had, *David* and *Rebecca*.

She had mourned the loss of her first son, the child she had miscarried and had secretly named *Rory*, and now God had seen fit to repay her on the double. She had a son to step into the shoes of the little lost boy and a girl to be her constant companion.

***

Her sister was smaller than Annie but fuller in the figure with a round face on which was embossed the trace of a smile with twinkle lines that radiated from her eyes. A suggestion of laughter which never left her even in her more reflective moments. Her face though didn't tell the full story, for Rose had come to Dublin in search of a husband and though she had put many a worthy prospect through her hands, somehow had never felt sure enough to commit herself and was now considered by herself and others to be a woman with rapidly diminishing prospects.

Because Rose worked in the cake shop down the street from the Rotunda she was first to lay eyes on the twins when she dashed up to the hospital during her lunch break, even before their father who might still be unaware of their arrival. She came in clutching a cream sponge cake which would later be shared out among the other mothers in the ward.

'I don't think you believed me, Annie.' She beamed. 'I told you it was twins'.

'Get away outta that, Rose, sure the world and his mother knew, with the size of me an' all.'

Rose had been fretting for her sister after the way her previous pregnancy turned out. She needed to see for herself that Annie and the twins were safe and healthy. She stooped to pick up one of them, the little boy, making her own goo-goo noises while a couple of smiling nurses came over to join in.

When the nurses had gone away Rose said, 'I asked Miss Whiston to let me have a couple of hours off in the morning so I can pop around to Gardiner Street with the twins and get them baptised.'

'She's a Methodist, isn't she, Miss Whiston? What did she say?'

'Not a problem. She knows the way we like to get them baptised as quick as we can just in case anything happens, like.'

Isaac had made it clear he wanted them baptised in the Protestant church. 'We'll get them baptised in a few weeks,' he said. 'I'll talk to the minister about it. All in its own good time.'

Annie had said nothing to that, letting him think she was agreeable. She knew by now how he would want to stick to the way things had always been done in his own family. She chose not to mention any of this to her sister.

On the following morning with the snow outside churned to slush and the twins as yet but one day old, Annie watched a young nurse, a Catholic girl from Annie's own part of the country, wrap them up in warm woollen shawls and, accompanied by Rose, take them the half mile or so up to the Jesuits in Gardiner Street.

When they got back an hour later Rose told her they had been baptised by a Father Coyle who had welcomed them with several other babies into membership of the One True Church.

The twins were now baptised Roman Catholics. Annie with the connivance of her sister Rose had seen to that. They suspected—no, they knew—there would be trouble if Isaac were ever to learn the truth.

'This is between you and me, Rose. No one need know a thing about it.'

Six

Not long after Annie took the babies back to the upstairs flat in the Liberties, Isaac's sister came to visit. With only one bedroom there was no question of Hannah staying over, something Annie was grateful for since she found Hannah a little on the bossy side. Though Annie had been hoping to avoid any talk of religion, Hannah was only an hour in the place when she asked Annie straight out if she had been in touch with the minister about christening the twins.

'Isaac will want to look after that,' Annie said. 'I'll let him deal with it.'

'Isaac, is it? You'll be waiting.' It was clear Hannah was intent on taking matters into her own hands.

Isaac came home later than usual saying he had paid a quick visit to the staff bar to avail of the brewery prices. He had barely taken off his coat when Hannah asked him what he had done about getting the twins baptised. 'What's the mad rush, Hannah? There's many a one leaves the christening till the kids are walking and talking. I heard tell of a man once...'

'Don't bother me with your tall stories, Isaac. Get yourself down to St Catherine's on Saturday and talk to the Reverend about fixing a date.' Annie marvelled that Hannah, even if she was his senior by a couple of years, would talk to Isaac in those terms. It was clear now that this visit from her straight-talking sister-in-law had no other purpose than to make sure the twins were enrolled in the Church of Ireland, the church to which the Townsend family for hundreds of years had given their allegiance.

Isaac had brought disgrace on his family, not just by getting a girl in trouble but getting involved with a young Catholic teacher in the first place.

Unlike Annie's own sister Rose, small, round and soft-hearted, Hannah was tall, straight as a pine, with a lean serious expression that never left her face. Often when Annie said something intended as a joke, Hannah would stare at her with a quizzical look. Hannah's world was a literal world – you said what you meant and you meant what you said. Still, for the few hours she was there, Annie found Hannah a big help. Hannah saw what needed doing and did it. If they had the room she would have insisted on staying longer. She would have made herself useful with the washing, hanging things out the back to dry and letting Annie get on with the never-ending task of breast-feeding two ravenous infants.

'It's time you thought about getting a bigger place,' Hannah said, looking around at Mrs Harold's kitchen.

'Money doesn't grow on trees,' Isaac said.

'Rubbish, Isaac. Porter might be cheaper in the brewery but it still has to be paid for. So don't try giving me the poor mouth. Father always says *where there's a will there's a way.*'

Isaac ignored her rebuke. 'How's young Johnny getting on?'

'A boy trying to do a man's work. But there's no one else to do it since Adam took himself off to England and you, Isaac, decided to do a—.'

There was silence as both Isaac and Annie looked at Hannah. *Do a runner.* Annie knew what she had been about to say and thought how unjust it was. It would be closer to the truth to say Isaac had been run out of the place. Isaac stayed silent but Hannah had said enough to let them both know how they were regarded in Drumboley.

Hannah thought it important that the minister know the full story. After she left the house she made her way around to the rectory. She was fortunate to find the Reverend Ryder at home. He said he didn't have a lot of time to spare but he could give her perhaps ten minutes. Hannah got to the point. 'We're talking here about a mixed marriage, Reverend. You know yourself how tricky that can be.' He didn't answer so she continued. 'We shouldn't delay the twins' baptism. You just never know what notions the mother might get into her head, being a Roman Catholic and all that.'

Reverend Ryder didn't seem to be listening. The sense of urgency was lost on him. Like Isaac he seemed to think there was plenty of time. However he promised to call by the house *one of these days*. 'We can discuss it then,' he said.

'I'm afraid I have to get back to Drumboley, Reverend. With Mother and Father getting on in years and young John talking about joining the police—.'

'I understand perfectly, Miss Townsend. I hope you'll get back up to Dublin for the christening, whenever that is.'

'And in the meantime? I'm worried my sister-in-law may come under the influence of the priests and try to make the children Roman Catholics. That's my concern.'

'Try not to worry yourself, Miss Townsend. Now that I think about it, there are two other children in the parish in need of christening so we'll see if we can combine them all in a single ceremony.'

Although Hannah thought she had been wasting her time, her efforts did bear fruit a couple of months later. On a sunny Sunday morning in the spring of '97 she helped Annie carry the twins to St Catherine's to be christened in the faith of their Protestant forebears and baptised in the waters of salvation.

Hannah was a happy and much relieved woman that day.

Seven

The Reverend made it sound like they would be obliging both himself and his Aunt Beryl by taking up the offer. It was a Saturday afternoon when Annie led him up the stairs and into the pokey room they called home. The twins were protesting, for Annie had lifted them back into the cot before going down to answer the door. They stood now against the bars of their pen, howling against the injustice of their imprisonment. Isaac had gone into the bedroom to change out of his work clothes.

Rev. Ryder admired the toddlers in the cot, saying, 'They'll be needing a lot more space from now on.'

'They're getting to be a right handful. They turned two last month.'

'Let me explain why I called around, then.'

Isaac came into the room as he was saying, 'She's looking for some place smaller, now that Jeffrey's passed on.' Standing up to shake Isaac's hand he said, 'My aunt Beryl has asked me to find a responsible family to look after her house.'

Annie thought it sounded very attractive when he said the rent would be only half a crown, something she knew they could afford since Isaac started bringing home a cooper's wages. No one needed to remind either of them how cramped their accommodation now was with a pair of boisterous two-year-olds to keep amused.

Moving to Orkney Street would mean a longer journey to work for Isaac but he told her he knew lots of men who crossed the Liffey every day and it wouldn't take a bother out of him. She began to think how fitting it would be to have settled into a spacious new home for the start of the new century with all its promise of peace and prosperity.

***

Annie made the move on foot, with the twins sitting in a pram lent to her by a kind neighbour. She found Isaac, who had gone ahead on his bicycle, waiting with the front door open. The cart carrying their few bits and pieces of furniture hadn't yet arrived.

Her mouth widened in wonder at the sight of the two storey house with a cement path crossing the lawn to their own front door. Her eyes were drawn upwards towards a double row of chimney pots standing proud against the blue June sky. *Eight*, she thought, and then realised that four of these belonged to the house next door. Still, four chimneys meant four fireplaces and such luxury was almost beyond her comprehension. When she stepped inside the front door and tried to take in the amount of space that was now theirs, she felt like she had arrived in the hallway of Paradise.

Isaac told her they were now only ten minutes' walk from the Phoenix Park, which would be great for the children. She didn't mention the pleasure she felt on finding the Catholic Church was only a short distance down the street.

Isaac came into the house carrying a couple of chairs, for the cart carrying their furniture had arrived. 'I don't know how we're going to fill this place,' Annie said. He must have taken her up wrong for he looked sheepish and she could not help laughing at his blushes. In spite of two miscarriages so far, she knew there would be more children. Isaac was a man who enjoyed his beer and he liked to come home from the company of the pub to the comforts of the marriage bed.

From an upstairs window Annie gazed across at the empty

cattle stalls on the opposite side of the street. She had not anticipated that they were going to be so close. Still, it all looked peaceful right now. She would have to wait for a market day to find out how it might impinge on their lives. She tried to convince herself that stories of crazed cattle crashing through people's front gardens were invented by locals to impress those who dwelt in the more sedate areas.

'Annie! Come here, I want to show you something.' He stood on the return of the stairs looking through an open door. She stepped down after him into the room he had found.

'Oh, God bless us and save us, Isaac. What are we going to do with this mess?' Her mouth hung open at the sight of a mountain of rubbish that must have accumulated over many years. Broken old furniture and mounds of musty books and papers.

'That'll be going out for the binmen,' Isaac said. 'And we don't even know what's behind the other door.' She saw that there were indeed two rooms in this part of the house, extending out over the kitchen. As they sat down for their first ever meal in their new house, Isaac pointed his knife at the ceiling over their heads. 'It's a crime to let them two rooms go to waste.'

'We've more than enough space as it is.'

'We can rent them out and make some cash.'

'You think so?'

'I reckon they were servants' rooms at some stage. There might even be a tap and a sink up there.'

'What about old Mrs What's-her-name?'

'What she don't know won't bother her.'

Annie began to warm to the idea when he said they could get enough to pay their own rent. 'We could be living rent-free,' he said.

***

Mrs Mattis was a widow from County Mayo who worked as a cleaner in the offices of a provisions company in Hawkins Street. She moved in early in the first year of the new century when the twins were three and after Isaac had transformed the former rubbish dump into a habitable space with sink, draining board and gas cooker. He mounted a gas-lamp on the wall of one room. A gas meter went in downstairs near the back door, for the flat was reached by an outside stairway at the back of the house.

'I'll let you have a key for the back gate,' Annie said to the new lodger, 'so you don't have to come through the front door or use the main stairs.'

'That'll do me fine,' Mrs Mattis said. She settled in and took an immediate liking to the twins who had no inhibitions about visiting Mrs Mattis in her rooms any time the mood took them. When she started to bring home chocolate bars from work she had made friends for life. She worked afternoons which meant the mornings were her own and it did not take her long to develop the habit of coming uninvited into Annie's kitchen, expecting Annie to put on the kettle for tea and sit down for a long chat.

Mrs Mattis was hardly a year in the house when she delivered her bombshell announcement.

'I found someone.'

'Found someone?' Annie was puzzled.

'Yes, me cousin. He's landed a job above in the abattoir. There's big money for a skilled butcher I needn't tell you.'

'That's great news.' Annie still did not know where this was leading.

'He'll be able to get to work in five minutes on foot.'

Suddenly it hit Annie what she was saying. This cousin of hers was planning to move in.

'I've got oodles of space up there and God knows I could do with someone to share the rent.'

'You're bringing in a lodger, you mean? So when exactly were you— is he—'

'Tomorrow, if that's alright with the man of the house and yourself.'

'I'll talk to him when he gets home and see what he says.' Annie was not going to be steamrolled into anything.

'Tell him he needn't have the slightest worry, Missus. You couldn't meet a finer gentleman than me cousin, Plinny.'

'Plinny?'

'And a scholar at that.'

Eight

She could tell the minute he came in that he was bursting to tell her something. He heard all about it in the pub, he told her, from a fellow who saw the whole thing with his own two eyes. Nothing about it in the papers, mind you. It's the sort of thing they don't want you to know about. The pub is the place you get the real news. Isaac sat down at the kitchen table, picked up a potato with his fingers, stuck it on the end of his fork and began to peel. Annie eased her heavy bulk onto a chair. She felt another twinge of pain. The twins were already in their beds recouping their energy for tomorrow.

Annie hoped that Isaac's news would take her mind off the pain in her abdomen. He told her what he had heard, that the Viceroy and his wife had been jeered at outside the gates of the Castle as they arrived for the first anniversary of the Coronation. Their carriage had been forced to a halt while the police attempted to drag the trouble-makers away. 'I only hope them louts got a night in the cells,' he said. 'Cool their heels for them.'

'Harmless drunks, I'm willing to bet.' Annie tried to pretend interest although her main concern was that she might be going into labour.

'Drunks me eye. A bunch of Fenians and Gaelic Leaguers, that's who.' All for the Union, Isaac. He had no time for the Celtic dreamers. But Annie had her own ideas. She had nothing against Edward the Seventh but she thought the government should listen to politicians like John Redmond who wanted Ireland to have a bigger say in its own affairs.

She looked in on the twins and found them asleep. She went to the big bedroom to get ready for bed. Daylight had faded early that August evening as she pulled down the blind and closed the curtains before climbing into bed beside her husband and blowing out the candle. He was already asleep. She knew he wanted to rise early and get to work an hour before his usual eight o'clock start. The extra few shillings would be very welcome right now with another child about to make its entrance. He was already snoring. He had given no indication whether he would prefer a son or a daughter but in her gut she knew he wanted a son for he sometimes let slip his misgivings about little David. The boy was too tied to his sister. He didn't want him growing up a namby-pamby, playing with dolls instead of learning to mix it with the other young lads on the street.

Maybe, too, he was afraid of her own influence on the twins. She hoped he would never find out she was taking them to mass on church holy days when he was at work. What he didn't know wouldn't hurt him. Neither did he have to know she was planning for them to make their First Communion next year with the other seven year olds. She would swear the twins to secrecy and pray that no busybody would start carrying stories.

They had told her that her baby was due the first week of September. Today she had felt those pains, pains that reminded her of her first pregnancy and the awful way it had ended. She hadn't said a word to Isaac seeing as he needed to get his rest tonight. Now he was snoring while she tossed around, worried about what was going on inside her.

It must have been well after midnight when she screamed. Isaac jumped up in the bed. 'What in God's name is the matter with you?'

'I think it's coming.'

'The babby you mean?'

'Get me to the hospital before it's too late.'

Already he was pulling on his trousers and shoes. He got out of his night-shirt and into his working shirt and waistcoat. He helped her down the stairs to a chair in the hall. 'Wait here till I get a cab.' He pulled his bicycle out through the front door and headed off down the street. The moment he was gone the door on the return opened and Mattis, her dishevelled hair about her shoulders, was standing there looking down at Annie. She guessed straight away what was happening.

'You're going in, Missus?'

'Himself is gone for a cab. Look after the twins, will you, if I'm not back by morning.'

'You're not to worry about a thing, now.'

'You're an angel, Mrs Mattis. I'll know they're in safe hands.'

In less than five minutes Isaac was back. 'Not a cab to be had. They're all gone off for the night.'

'What am I going to do? We can't chance it happening here. Think, Isaac, think.'

'Come on, so. I'll get you there on the bike.'

She didn't have the energy to argue. The bicycle was the only option they had. His stout arms were around her as they set off, freewheeling all the way down Orkney Street and into Manor Street. Stoneybatter was deserted. Even the drunks who lie propped against the pub walls till they're sober enough to stagger home, even they were gone. The narrow crossbar cut into the flesh of her bottom but she could not change her position. She tried to blank out the pain and discomfort. Another ten minutes, fifteen at the most, would get them to the Rotunda where there would be doctors and nurses who knew what to do. She had good memories of that hospital with its green space outside, the grassy patch that had lain covered in a blanket of snow six years before when she laboured through the night to bring her two lovely children into the world.

All along North King Street the cobble-stones were worn and chipped, broken by the constant movement of the heavy-laden drays that moved up and down here every working day of the year. A sudden jolt brought her back to the present. The front wheel had hit a rut in the road. The jolt hurt her and she bit down on her lower lip to stop herself crying out. The bike's front wheel took the brunt of every bump and depression of the cobbled surface. The pain was getting to be unbearable and she thought of asking Isaac to stop and let her off so she might sit on the edge of the pavement for five minutes to recover.

Annie gave an ear-piercing shriek and threw herself off, prevented from hitting the pavement only by Isaac's arm firm around her upper body. He let go of the bicycle so he could lower her onto the pavement. Looking around her she saw that they had almost made it. She sat propped against the locked doors of a shop on the corner of Great Britain Street and Granby Row. Just across the street was the outline of the Rotunda maternity hospital.

'It's coming,' Annie gasped. She pulled up her skirt to reveal a tiny head already visible between her legs. 'Good God Almighty,' said Isaac. 'Who's going to help us now?'

His prayer was answered almost immediately. Two women who had been standing on the opposite corner were coming across the deserted street. 'She's having a babby,' said one, taking in the situation straight away. 'Move over there, Mister, and give us a look,' said the other, the older one, in her middle forties. Isaac moved aside to let the two women in. Annie's nose was assailed by the sickening smell of perfume.

'You'll be alright, love,' said the woman. 'I've been down this

- 48 -

road a few times meself, as you might well imagine.' Annie was too exhausted to answer. 'When I tell you to push, you push like the divil, d'you hear me? You can make yourself useful, Mister. Get someone out of that Mammies and Babbies Hospital over there to give us a hand.'

Isaac took himself off at a trot and disappeared through the iron gates leading to the hospital. Meanwhile Annie got on with the exhausting task of pushing when told to push by the woman claiming to have previous experience in the childbearing business. Her efforts were rewarded a lot sooner than she expected. Five minutes after Isaac had gone in search of help and ten minutes before that help arrived the little girl was in her mother's arms, eyes squeezed tight and an expression of contentment on her little pink face.

A nurse took charge, dismissing the two unofficial midwives who had played a vital role in the birth of the baby but who seemed happy enough to return to the street corner opposite, to continue their wait for whoever it was they were expecting. Another nurse had brought a wicker-work wheel-chair and once they had snipped the cord they helped Annie into the chair and handed her the new-born infant, enveloped in a soft baby blanket. She pressed her face down on its tiny body as they were wheeled – mother and baby – across the wide empty street to the warmth and safety of the hospital.

Nine

Annie didn't mind at all that the twins had taken to visiting Mrs Mattis when they came in from school. Mattis seemed happy to have them now that she had given up her cleaning job. She would always offer them a slice of cake and a glass of lemonade. When Plinny was out at work she allowed them to go through his books. Annie for her part was delighted to see them develop an interest in reading. She saw Plinny's books as their gateway to a whole new world.

They told their mother that since Plinny didn't have any bookshelves you had to rummage. On top of the dresser was a good place, but under the bed could also yield good results, except that under-bed books you had to wipe with your sleeve to clear away the fluff. On Plinny's side of the bed Becky found a worn copy of *Nicholas Nickleby* while David turned up the 1901 edition of Pears Shilling Cyclopaedia. Mattis said they could take the books downstairs. Plinny wouldn't mind as long as they took care of them. This is how the seven-year-olds began their quest for knowledge. The twins, of course, never questioned that Mattis and Plinny slept in the same bed. To them this was the normal state of affairs in any household.

David became immersed in the Cyclopaedia with its tea stained hard red cover and its filmy pages packed with information. At the back it had an English dictionary which Annie told him would be useful for reading Dickens. The Atlas section made plain the reach of the great powers, the British, the Austro-Hungarian, the Russian and Ottoman Empires. David would set up wars between these realms, the Germans against the Austrians or the British against the Russians, pushing their borders around for the sheer fun of it. The British always came out on top, of course, for Isaac had told him they could be proud to belong in the Empire and live in its Second City.

Becky put Dickens to one side when Annie arrived home with the new baby. She couldn't wait to get home from school in the afternoon so she could take charge of little Ruth. When they asked Annie why she called the new baby *Ruth* her answer was, 'Go look in the Bible and tell me what you find there.' Plinny didn't possess a bible but Isaac did. They eventually found the story of Ruth and how she refused to abandon Naomi after their husbands died. *Entreat me not to leave thee, or to return from following after thee: for whither thou goest, I will go; and where thou lodgest, I will lodge: thy people shall be my people, and thy God my God.*

They liked that story and it made them see their baby sister in a new light. Little Ruth would grow up to be a loyal supporter of her brother and sister, ready to follow them to the ends of the earth. Becky spent much of her time rocking the pram and singing little Ruth to sleep.

David made an important discovery, namely that Plinny seemed to know even more than the Cyclopaedia and liked nothing more than to share his knowledge. Father knew an awful lot too but hated being asked questions. 'You'll find out when you're older,' was his usual answer. Plinny on the other hand loved to be asked questions. When he sat outside at the end of the week it was as if he were setting himself up as a dispenser of wisdom, to be questioned by anyone seeking knowledge. He was different in other ways, too. He was never afflicted by thirst in the way their father was, never went near Hanlon's pub, up the road from the abattoir. And another thing, you would never hear any raised voices coming from the part of the house Plinny shared with Mattis.

On a bright Saturday morning in February David came out the back door to find Plinny sitting on the wrought-iron seat that was missing a leg and leaned against the boundary wall for support. The book in his hands had a cracked cover. Near the door Becky was rocking Ruth in her pram while chatting away to her. David thought he would like a chat with Plinny.

'What language is that you're reading, Plinny?'

'Latin. Classical Latin.'

'What's it about, the book?'

'The biggest disaster to hit the ancient world.'

'What sort of disaster?' His curiosity was aroused.

'A whole city and all its citizens suffocated and buried in ash before they knew what was going on.'

'Who wrote it?'

'A young man saw the whole thing happening and wrote it down afterwards. A man by the name of Pliny.'

David studied Plinny's face to see if he was making it all up.

Plinny laughed. 'You're wondering if I'm related to Pliny the Younger. It's a special relationship. We've got the same name but different spelling.'

'Who called you Plinny?' David wanted to hear the full story.

'Dead Man Walkin'.'

'Who's he?' David was baffled. Dead men don't walk, that much he knew.

He's the one that taught me to read the Latin. Taught me everything I know, except for the butchering. It was my own father taught me that. *Latin is all very good*, my poor father used to say, *but it'll never put bread on the table*. He was right, I suppose. The butchering trade gives me a living right enough. But real food, the food of the soul, is to be found in books. A man needs sustenance for his mind as much as for his body. Never forget that, son.'

'Who's Dead Man Walkin'? It's a queer name.'

'A quare name right enough but a fitting one for all that. I'll tell you now how he came by that name. As a young man he used to take himself off for a ride on his pony, most times down by the river that flows through the lower part of the town. One time, after torrents of rain, he tried to take his pony through the swollen stream. The pony lost his footing in the flood and got swept away and your man with him. The pony somehow got himself out of the water and found his own way home but there was ne'er a sign of your man. Not till the next day was he found, caught in a branch he was, and him stone-cold dead.

'Well, they waked him that night and the next morning they bolted down the lid of his coffin and carried him to the graveyard, three men either side of him and his poor widow mother behind and she wailing her heart out. When the priest was finished praying over him he nodded for the grave-diggers to let the coffin down into the grave. And that's when they heard it, the knocking from inside the coffin. The lads dropped the coffin down on the edge of the grave and all the people were looking at one another, wondering were they dreaming or what. But no, there it was again, only louder this time, a lot louder. There was nothing for it then but to prise the lid off the coffin, which they did. And if they did what do you think they found but the dead man trying to sit himself up for to get a better look at his surroundings. In the heel of the hunt he made a complete recovery and was well known as a travelling teacher walking the countryside, ready to teach anyone who had the price of a pint to hand him. *Dead Man*

Walkin'. That's all he was ever called.'

'Did you ask him to teach you Latin?'

'No, but me mother did. You see, nothing would do her but to make a priest out of me. She sent me up to Maynooth College for the interview and the college Rector asked me did I believe in the resurrection. I told him I was personally acquainted with a man who was sealed in his coffin but rose up again on the third day. That answer, I have to say, was enough to stymy any chance I ever had of becoming a priest.'

'Did Dead Man Walkin' tell you his real name?'

'No. After being dead so long, you know, he must have had trouble remembering who he was. At any rate he seemed happy with his new name.'

'Did you call him *Mr Walkin'* or just *Deadman* for short?'

'*Dead Man Walkin'* is a bit of a mouthful so I just called him *Sir.'*

'And what did he teach you?'

'He taught me to read Virgil, Livy, Cicero and Ovid. Above all else, sonny, he taught me to question everything and take nothing on faith.'

Ten

'You'll never have a rat around the place if you've got a good terrier.' Joey Patterson wasn't interested in wrestling or any of that rough stuff that went on in the school-yard. He had other interests, mainly to do with the fox terriers his father bred and sold. 'They're great ratters, so they are.'

Joey and David sat together in the schoolyard eating their lunch. David envied Joey his jam sandwich while Joey longed for a bite of David's rosy apple. Joey said David could have the crust of his sandwich if David gave him the butt of his apple, a fair exchange, David thought. Joey couldn't stop talking about the terrier pup his father had given him for his last birthday. Straight after school he was taking the pup to have him inoculated against distemper. David wished he could go with him but his mother expected him to arrive home at the same time as his sister. She didn't like the idea of him wandering around the back streets that surrounded the school.

'What's he called?'

'Drac. It's short for Dracula. You should see his teeth.'

'What will you use him for?' David's interest was mounting.

'He's going to be a ratter.'

'What's that?'

'A ratter catches rats, you eejit.'

'How do you know he'll catch them?'

'He's going to be trained, that's how.'

After school David walked home with Becky. 'Joey asked me go and see his dog getting ratted.'

'Getting ratted? What's that?'

'His Da has a rat in a cage and they're waiting till Sunday to let the rat out so that Drac can get him.'

'That's horrible. I hope you said you couldn't go.'

'I wouldn't miss it for a hundred quid.'

'Sunday morning we'll be at church.'

'I've got a plan.' David explained to his sister what he had in mind. He would go to church with Becky and their father for the eleven o'clock service. As the congregation got to their feet for the first hymn he would slip out of the church and dash around to the street where Joey lived hoping to be in time for the ratting. If their father noticed him gone Becky was to say he felt faint and went outside for a breath of air.

All went according to plan. Their father didn't notice him slip away. As David approached the street where Joey Patterson lived he saw a group of boys and men at the street corner. He ran faster in case he missed anything. He wasn't a minute too soon. Joey held the terrier on a length of rope tied around its neck. A caged rat sat in the centre of the roadway, surrounded by the noisy crowd. David had to push his way through. 'You barely made it in time,' Joey said.

'They've all got their trousers tucked inside their socks,' David whispered.

'They're afraid the rat will run up their leg and bite their thing off.' The thought sent a shiver through David who was wearing short trousers, no protection at all, but it was too late now to do anything about it. The excitement built amongst the onlookers, while inside the cage a terrified rat surveyed the scene. *Weighing up his chances*, David thought. They eyed each other, rat and dog, dog and rat, before the rat resumed his fruitless search for a way out.

One of the men, a big fellow with his flat cap on back to front, stepped forward, picked up the cage with one hand and released the catch with the other so that the door swung open and the rat spilled out onto the ground. A cheer went up from the onlookers, reminding David of the roar in the boxing stadium when the bell sounded for the start of a bout.

The rat crouched for a moment considering his options. The dog looked up nervously at Joey who was fumbling with the rope, trying to release the slip-knot. 'Let him off, will you,' someone shouted. The rat, though, had no intention of waiting around. Spotting a gap between the legs of one of the bystanders he made a bolt for freedom. The gangly youth whose spread-eagled legs had offered the rat a welcome escape route howled in terror when he saw the rat making for him. He threw his arms about his neighbour saying, 'Holy jaze.'

The rat's hopes of escape were dashed when a quick witted old-timer got his boot to the creature just in time and with a vicious kick landed the animal right back in the centre space only feet from the startled terrier. The dog's natural responses may have been slow in waking but then some deeply embedded instinct kicked in. He bounded forward, grasped the already stunned creature by the loose skin of its neck and began to shake. The harder he shook the bundle of flesh and bone the greater grew his frenzy. Roars of encouragement filled his ears, confirming for him that this is what he was born to do.

David's pulse raced. He experienced in his veins the primeval instinct of the hunt, the capture and the kill. Yet, when the initial excitement had cooled, he began to see it had been an unfair fight, that in any encounter the opponents ought to be equally matched. As he took one last glance at the rat's lifeless form where it had been kicked into the gutter, a trickle of blood trailing from its mouth, it seemed to him the rat hadn't been given a proper chance.

Later, as he told Becky what he had seen, he admitted he didn't want a terrier after all. In fact he had a new respect for the rats that scurried in the back lane when there was no one around at night. Their father always maintained that they wouldn't have a rat problem if the neighbours would only keep the lids on their bins. Becky, though, agreed with her twin as she did about most things. She too was on the side of the rats.

'Tell you what,' said David. 'Why don't we get a pet rat instead of a terrier?'

'How much would it cost, do you think?'

'I saw them in Billy King's for a shilling.'

'You're going to need a cage and I don't know what we'll feed him on.'

'They'll eat anything. Left-overs, anything.'

'Wait till I tell you. Sally Downes took a mouse into the class one day. Didn't the mouse get away and Miss Rodgers had to jump up on her chair. We were all in stitches with the laughing. '

'What did she say, the teacher?'

'She made Sally catch the mouse and bring it back to the shop.'

'Did she get her money back?'

'They told her she could have a rat instead, but she said her Mammy would kill her, so they took back the mouse but they only gave her three pence for it, the meanies.'

***

Billy King's white hair hung loose about his neck and his

moustache curled downwards at the ends, reminding David of two rat's tails. He held a white rat with practised grip right in front of the twins' faces.

'It's a young one this, barely six months but mature for all that. You'll want to feed it lots of grub to keep it growing.'

David and Becky looked at each other before David plucked up the courage to ask the all-important question. 'Is it a boy or a girl?'

They had been discussing the topic of procreation on their way to the shop. They knew baby rats needed a mother and father. Not sure why or how but it was clear to both that in order to have baby rats you had to have mammy and daddy rats. David was thinking ahead.

'What do you mean?' said the pet shop man with a startled expression.

'We want to know is it a he or a she,' said Becky. 'We want it to have babies.'

The pet shop man stared in disbelief at the two ten year olds.

'I'm sorry, kids, but you'll just have to take pot luck. What you see is what you get.'

'Alright' said David fishing in his trousers pocket for the coins that would make himself and Becky the owners of this rodent of uncertain gender. They watched as the shopkeeper placed the animal in a box bearing the words, *Lucas Bicycle Lamp* in large letters. It had a number of air holes roughly punched in the sides.

'I suppose it doesn't really matter,' David said as they carried home their prize. 'It doesn't matter till we get the money to buy another one.'

'I'm sure Plinny will know which it is,' said Becky. 'If he doesn't we can look it up in the Cyclopaedia.'

Eleven

For ages their mother had been promising to take them to Sandymount Strand. All she wanted was a fine sunny day and they would all go, the twins and little Ruth. They would get on the tram at Nelson's Pillar with a basket crammed with towels, swimming togs and sandwiches for the picnic. They would have bought a kettle full of boiling water from one of the houses across from the beach. The new baby, wee Sammy, could be left at home to be looked after by a willing Mrs Mattis.

For some reason it never happened. The weather was never fine enough, or there was some other objection. Sea and sand remained in the realm of things to be dreamt about. Meanwhile they had to listen to other kids in their class who were brought not just to Sandymount but even as far as the fabled sand-dunes of Portmarnock.

Their hopes of ever getting to see the seaside had waned when something extraordinary happened. Instead of the twins and Ruth going to the seaside, the seaside came to them. One sunny Saturday morning Becky stepped outside the garden gate to find that a huge mound of sand had appeared, piled up in one great providential heap at the top of their street. Two red and white painted barrels stood in the roadway as a warning to traffic.

The news of a sand bonanza must have run wild amongst the youngsters of Cowtown. Already they had begun to arrive. Becky knew well how word spreads, up and down the little narrow streets like it had a life of its own. She rushed back into the house to tell what she had seen and David ran outside to see for himself. The twins couldn't wait to get up to the corner to take full advantage of such luck. They set up a chorus of special pleading to cajole their mother into letting them out to make the most of this bonanza. 'We won't get dirty, Ma, we promise.'

'I'm worried there might be a rough crowd there. You could get hurt.'

'Please, Ma, we won't go near the rough crowd. We'll come straight home if there's any fighting. Promise.'

She gave in with obvious reluctance, letting them go with a strict warning to come straight home if they saw any rough play. Now little Ruth began jumping up and down, tugging at her mother's skirt, begging to be allowed to go as well. 'Take me, take me,' she wailed.

'Let me take her,' said Becky.

Their mother gave in on the strict condition that Becky hold her little sister's hand and keep her safe. 'She's only a baby, Becky. Any sign of trouble and you take her home straight away. Is that clear?'

'I'm not a baby,' squealed Ruth, stamping her foot for emphasis, 'I'm four.'

'Just hold your sister's hand and let her mind you.'

***

On the pavement stood a sort of sentry box, a narrow wooden hut painted red. The watchman was missing from the watchman's hut, although there was a barrel with holes punched in the side and a heap of charcoal to make a fire.

Children swarmed all over the sand-hill, digging and scattering, attempting to make sand castles and as quickly having them demolished by someone else. One or two of the children had brought brightly-coloured seaside buckets and spades. This was Sandymount at home. It was quite obvious that most of them, like

Becky and David, had never been to the sea or seen a sandy beach. Though Becky kept her eyes open for anyone she knew, all the faces were unfamiliar. They must have come from far and near. Those who had no spades, the majority, raided a heap of sticks stacked against the watchman's hut.

While some of the more creative children attempted to mould miniature streets and buildings in the sand, there were others who could think of nothing more constructive than whipping up sand into other kids' faces. Becky saw how things might turn ugly. With little notion of how to occupy themselves in this unfamiliar setting it was to be expected that some might try to stir up trouble. And sure enough things began to look bad when one young fellow decided to create a lake in the sand. Having scooped out a hole with a flat stick he proceeded to urinate into the hollow, right in front of everyone, boys and girls, with no notion of shame or modesty.

A stout girl with her hair in a pigtail and older than the twins began to scream, 'Hey, youngfella, watch where you're spraying your friggin piss.'

The surly-faced offender turned to face the pigtail girl. 'D'you want a dig in the kisser?' To emphasise the point he kicked up a shower of sand in the girl's face. Everyone stopped what they were doing to see how the confrontation was going to develop. David, however, did more than watch. 'Leave that girl alone,' he shouted at the bully. Becky was horrified. Their mother had warned them to stay clear of trouble. 'Shut up, David. It's nothing to do with us.' But she was too late. The young tough forgot all about Pigtail and turned to face his new challenger.

He took a few steps nearer David, who was clearly no match for the bigger boy. He pushed his face close up to David's while grabbing him by the shirt collar. With a foot placed to trip him, he gave David a push, sending him headlong to the bottom of the mound. The ruffian's pals raised whoops of approval and took David's humiliation as a signal to create havoc. They charged up and down the sand-heap, trashing all the innocent efforts of the little boys and girls who had made careful constructions of their own.

Becky knew it was time to get herself, David and Ruth away from this dangerous carry-on as quickly as she could. Just then she noticed a little girl, not much older than Ruth, sitting on the ground, sobbing great sobs and snuffling for breath.

'Don't cry,' Becky said going down on her knees beside her. 'Do you want me to take you home?' The child raised wet eyes to look at Becky, unable to say anything. A long green sticky drip trailed down her upper lip.

'What's your name?' said Becky.

'Bridgeen,' sobbed the child.

Becky raised the hem of her own dress and used it to wipe away the tears and snot from the child's face. 'Go straight home, Bridgeen, and get your mammy to make you some hot cocoa.'

Bridgeen refused to budge. 'I don't want to go home. Me Mammy's dead and me sister's out.'

'Where do you live?' The child pointed in a vague sort of way. 'Here, Bridgeen. Take my hand.' They all made their way in the direction Bridgeen had indicated. They found the house, the last in a street of single-storey terraced cottages. The front door was wide open. There was no one at home as they took Bridgeen inside. The remains of the breakfast were on the table, dirty cups and saucers sitting there unwashed. Flies fed on the sticky residue. An open room door revealed a bed with the bedclothes scattered on the floor. Becky had never seen anything like this— such disorder and neglect—in the whole of her young life. Bridgeen promised to wait there for her sister to come home from work. She was still snuffling and the thick mucus was again evident on her upper lip. They left her there on her own to get back to the cleanliness and order of their own home.

The moment they came in their mother knew that something had happened. David's shirt must have been the give-away with its dirty pawmarks and missing buttons. Becky was careful not to say that David had instigated the attack by intervening on behalf of the pigtail girl. Always loyal to her brother, she portrayed it as an unprovoked attack by a gang of hooligans. She made sure to add that she had taken David and Ruth away from the scene as quickly as she could.

'I knew it, I knew it,' their mother lamented. 'I don't know why I let ye up there at all, at all.'

'Becky dragged me away before I could get a proper dig at him,' said David. 'I would have given him a good doin', I would,'

'I don't want you getting involved in any fights. There's enough fighting in the world as it is.'

'I've decided I want to be a boxer.'

'We can talk about that when the time comes.'

When their father heard later that David wanted to be a boxer he squared up to his son and said, 'Let's see you land a punch, boy.' And when David fell in with the game and tried to get past his father's guard, his father gave a roar of approval. 'That's the way to do it, boy. I'm telling you, we're going to have another Tommie Burns right here on Orkney Street. A world beater, by God!'

***

A week went by before people began to suspect it had started on the sand. Annie herself was convinced the sand-hill was the source of the epidemic. Some sneezer scattering the germs that were now sweeping the neighbourhood. Every child who developed measles over the following ten days had either been playing at the sand or been in contact with someone who had. The sand was the single common factor.

Six days after her spell at the sand little Ruth was cranky and out of sorts. She was off her food and coughing. That night her forehead was blazing and her nose ran like a tap. 'Me eyes is sore,' she whimpered over and over.

'It'll not be for long, lovey. You'll be better soon.' Annie hoped and prayed that the illness would pass without leaving any permanent damage. She kept the little girl in bed and plied her with hot drinks. That night Ruth was soaked in perspiration. Annie stayed awake through the night in spite of Isaac telling her not to be fretting. 'It's only the measles,' he kept saying. 'They all get it. It has to run its course.'

Mrs Mattis, though, wasn't so casual about it. The minute she heard how sick Ruth was she insisted on taking baby Sammy into her own bedroom. 'You just can't be too careful,' she said. She and Plinny managed to squeeze the cot in at the end of their bed. Annie put up only a half-hearted resistance for she knew in her heart that Mattis was right – little one-year-old Sammy had to be protected from getting whatever it was Ruth had caught.

She was aware of course that Mattis had a particular soft spot for the little boy she had helped into the world. When Annie was caught out and there was no time to get to the hospital it was Mattis who had come to the rescue. Isaac and Plinny were both at work when Mattis, with such presence of mind and steady hands acted the part of midwife to deliver little Sammy, Annie and Isaac's fourth living child.

The following day little white spots appeared in Ruth's mouth and Annie knew for certain it was measles. Soon the little body was covered in a blotchy red rash. It was when she noticed pus in both ears that Annie knew they needed the doctor.

Considine shone a torch into each ear in turn and nodded. 'Ear infection,' he said straightening up. 'It's not at all uncommon with measles. It should clear itself up. It usually does.'

'And what if it doesn't?' Annie felt a cold fear clutching at her heart.

'Let's not talk about that now. Only time will tell.'

He called in again the following day saying he just happened to be passing. 'I'm getting real worried, Doctor.' Annie said, 'She never stops whinging about the pain in her ears.'

He examined both ears again. 'My advice is to keep her warm and keep giving her lots of that stuff.' He indicated the lemonade syphon on the dressing-table. 'I'll call in again tomorrow.' Annie was convinced the doctor hadn't told her the full story. She could see for herself the infection was worse and Considine must have suspected an awful lot more than he was letting on.

'Would you like a drop of lemonade, pet?' she said. Ruth didn't answer. She gave no indication she had heard. Annie filled a glass and helped her into a sitting position. Ruth took a few sips before handing the glass back.

'Can I get you anything else?' The child just gazed at her. 'How about an ice-cream? Becky or David can run down to Hickeys for a wafer. You would like that, wouldn't you?' Ruth didn't answer. Her eyes were fixed on her mother but she said nothing.

'Ice-cream, love. Ice-cream. What do you say? Yes or no?' Ruth continued to stare at her mother's face but seemed unable to take in anything her mother said. It was then, at that moment, that Annie realised her little daughter hadn't heard a word she had said. It was obvious she could hear nothing whatsoever.

***

When Annie took Ruth down to St Paul's to have her enrolled in the same school as the twins, the headmistress bent low to address the little girl. 'Hello Ruth. Thinking of coming to school, are you?' At first the only answer was a shy smile but when Annie prodded her Ruth said *Hello* and offered her hand. Several more efforts to elicit a response confirmed for the teacher that the child was indeed completely deaf. Her decision was that although the little girl was clearly intelligent beyond her years it would not be in her best interest to put her in with a class of normal children. 'I'm afraid it might give her a severe inferiority complex.'

Annie, herself a trained teacher, did not see it like that at all but nothing she said could change the woman's attitude. Visits to other schools in the vicinity produced the same result. No one would take her in. She was left with little option but to keep Ruth at home and teach her herself.

Mother and daughter developed a way of communicating with each other, a system of signs, nudges and facial tics which worked well for Annie and Ruth but which Isaac lacked the patience to bother with. If he asked Ruth to bring him something – the newspaper, say – and she didn't respond, he made no further effort, calling instead for one of the twins to get him what he wanted.

Not so with Becky and David. The twins spent hours with Ruth teaching her to lip-read. They all enjoyed it, it was like a game. They would write a word on her slate and make her watch their mouths as they exaggerated the shape of the word. Ruth was getting lessons in reading, writing and lip-reading all in one.

'Ruth,' Becky said, holding her face straight in front of her sister's and prodding her finger in Ruth's chest. 'You. Are. Ruth.' It always ended in fits of giggling, yet that's how it came about that the very first word Ruth learned to read, write and lip-read was her own name. The result of all this attention was that Ruth was way ahead of her age in reading and writing. David preferred a more physical approach. His tickling and wrestling contributed in its own way to his little sister's development, turning her into an extroverted and bubbly individual.

Though unable to hear, Ruth retained her ability to speak, using the childish vocabulary she acquired in her four years of normal development. It was when people heard her using this *baby-talk* that they began referring to her as *poor Ruth.* In time the epithet stuck and she became known to everyone as *Poor Ruth* and nothing else. Even Annie herself used the name.

Poor Ruth's home education continued for the next two years or so until it came to a point where Annie felt she could do no more. It wasn't that she found the whole thing a burden – she would never have thought of Poor Ruth in that way. In fact she found the little girl a huge help with household chores and running errands. Annie often sent her around the corner to Beatty the butcher with a note saying what she wanted for the dinner. What worried Annie, though, was that Poor Ruth was going to fall behind in her education.

The education of a little girl with a profound hearing problem was starting to prove too much for her. Poor Ruth was intelligent, a quick learner, voracious for knowledge. The problem was that neither Annie nor Poor Ruth knew any sign language apart from the nursery mode they had developed for themselves. It became increasingly clear that without a means of communication Poor Ruth was destined to fall behind. Yet Annie baulked at the idea of sending her child away. In spite of the advice coming at her from all quarters, she was reluctant to let go of her special child. Then the Parish Priest became involved. Fr Kingston met Annie outside the church after mass. 'You really ought to have a chat with Mother Eusebius. You'll find her a most understanding lady.'

Isaac was at work when the nun arrived on the doorstep one morning. The head of the Institute made a compelling case to have Ruth educated in the company of other children similarly afflicted. 'Wouldn't it be a crying shame,' she said, 'to deny the child the opportunity of a formal education?' Her pupils were as well qualified, if not better qualified, than normal children in normal schools.

'I'll have to talk it over with himself, Mother. Mr Townsend is Church of Ireland, you see. He might have a small problem sending her to the nuns. I'll let you know what we decide.'

Isaac gave his consent. At least Annie took it for consent when she told him about the nun's visit and he said nothing. She had no idea what was going on in his head but she was well aware of the distrust he harboured towards the devious workings of the nuns and clergy of the Roman Church.

She suspected he had never really come to terms with the notion of having a handicapped child, different from others, an object of pity, maybe even an object of curiosity and mockery amongst the more ignorant elements. She asked him if the men at work ever mentioned Poor Ruth. 'No,' he said, 'never a mention.' She guessed from this answer that Poor Ruth's existence was an embarrassment. It wasn't that he didn't love the child, just that he found it hard to relate to her.

At any rate Annie took the reins into her own hands and went ahead with the arrangements for Poor Ruth to be accepted into the Institute. Not only did Isaac not oppose it, but as far as Annie could tell, seemed quietly relieved. He must have decided that even if Poor Ruth ended up praying to statues it was the price he had to pay for placing her in the hands of the professionals.

He seemed to believe he still had the minds and hearts of the twins. He had done his best to pass on to them his own Protestant faith, far removed – in his view – from the superstitious nonsense his wife clung to.

Annie said nothing to disillusion him.

Twelve

A tall skinny nun with bony fingers and icy eyes marched her down the corridor and into a large room full of girls. Poor Ruth stood there, petrified, and tried to take it all in. Most of the girls were older, some a lot older, but she spotted one or two who might be her own age. Everywhere she looked the room was alive with the animated waving of hands, wiggling of fingers, grabbing of shoulders and the fierce screwing up of faces and blazing of eyes. Some girls, sitting on the floor, amused themselves with their dolls while others sat at tables playing draughts and other games. It was at once a place of frenetic activity and deathly silence.

Through the open doorway she caught a glimpse of her mother dabbing her eye with a handkerchief. She was about to run back to the only person she knew she could trust when the bony fingers tightened their grip on her arm and she felt herself being propelled across the room to where a couple of girls her own age sat cross-legged in front of a doll's house.

With the front of the doll's house wide open she could see the furnishings of the miniature rooms, tables and chairs, beds and wardrobes, everything in perfect proportion. She looked back towards the door to see if her mother was still there but the door was closed and she realised she was in the total control of the nun with the bony fingers. She screamed but her scream went unnoticed by anyone but the skinny nun, who tightened her grip while attempting to introduce her to the two girls sitting on the floor. Not only was Poor Ruth weeping for herself but she wept for her mother whom she knew was crying too.

The skinny nun pushed a rag doll into her hand as if that could make up for anything. She flung the silly thing on the floor and tried to make a dash for the door now closed on the world she had left behind. She found herself trapped. Her legs were off the ground, swinging and kicking to no avail. The bony fingers were hurting her arm and she had no option but to let herself go limp and wait for the nun to set her down again. It was futile, she realised, to try and follow her mother who must have left the building by now.

When the nun had gone Poor Ruth tried the door but found it locked. A wave of panic took possession of her and she gave vent to a piteous scream. She tried the door handle again, rattling it with all her puny strength. In that whole room full of contented children not one soul was giving her as much as a glance. Her screams were having no effect. They could not hear her any more than she could hear herself.

With her tears at last exhausted she began to take in what was going on around her. She noticed there was something not right about that doll's house. The sofa was in the same upstairs room as the bed. You couldn't let people away with such stupidity. She set about putting things right, moving the furniture around, returning everything to its proper place.

The two girls watched with interest and curiosity. When she was finished they began to make funny shapes with their fingers. She screwed up her face in puzzlement and it was then one of them picked up a slate and wrote with chalk, *ME MAY, SHE JOSIE*. She guessed they had been trying to tell her their names with their finger language and she decided there and then to learn this kind of spelling for herself. She reached for the slate and wrote her own name, *RUTH*. From that moment on she was firm friends with May and Josie, both six and a half like herself.

It was Josie who informed her that the nun with the bony fingers had two names. Her official name was written, *Aoibhinn*.

Her other name, known only to the girls, was *Evil*. Josie drew a sketchy image of a wicked witch complete with pointed hat. Then she leaned over and gave Poor Ruth a pinch on the arm. Poor Ruth squealed with the pain but her companions giggled and made her understand that the pinch was something she would come to associate with Sister Evil.

When it was time for tea the older girls herded the younger ones into a room where there were three long tables flanked by long wooden benches. Poor Ruth counted thirty eight girls altogether ranging from babies all the way up to young women. She soon figured out that each of the big girls played Mammy to two or three younger ones.

Ruth's *Mammy* turned out to be a rosy cheeked girl with red hair woven in two plaits which swung about on each side of her face. Her round cheeks gave her a soft motherly look and Ruth decided she was happy to have this big girl as her protector. The big girl wrote her name on Ruth's slate. *MARY KATE*. Mary Kate would be her guardian angel in this new world where Sister Evil was seen as a presence to be avoided.

***

Annie walked home alone. She had deposited her little girl in a grim forbidding building on the outer fringe of the city, delivered her into the hands of black-robed nuns to be handled in a manner over which she had no control. No one had told her it would be as hard as this. Not one had warned her about the guilt she would feel, having abandoned her child into the care of strangers. She hadn't expected to experience pain like this. It was like some part of her had been torn away leaving a gaping hole that could never be filled, a wound that would never heal.

She walked past fields and occasional roadside cottages to the spot where the road crossed the railway. She paused to lean on the parapet for a few minutes to reflect on the enormity of what she had done. It was peaceful here on the bridge and peaceful too on the line below with just the sound of birdsong rising from the scraggy brush bordering the tracks. As her eyes followed the line stretching off into the distance in the direction of Dublin Port, she fought the impulse to turn around, retrace her steps, find her little girl, wrap her arms about her and tell her the whole thing had been one terrible mistake.

At that moment she heard a long shrill screech from the direction of the Park as a train emerged from the tunnel beneath the Wellington monument. In a matter of minutes the train would pass below her. She decided to wait and allow herself to be enveloped in the smoke and steam, to lose herself in the noise, and sympathise with the moaning complaints of the laden waggons. She stepped back to avoid the belching rush of black smoke that welled up from below. She turned her head aside, shielding her eyes with her arm and waited for the shuddering monster to move away. Then it was gone, the great black beast , chugging away into the distance, followed by an endless line of sighing railcars. The stinging in her eyes, the moisture on her cheeks, could have been caused by smuts, by smoke. Or maybe by the distant memory of a quiet deserted railway platform in a little town in County Wicklow. Which is where it all began.

***

Classes in the morning, play in the afternoon, study and homework in the evening. That was the regime Poor Ruth had to adapt to. There were two kinds of classes, formal and informal. The formal ones were given by two teachers who came in every day. These outside teachers dressed in ordinary clothes but Ruth had no idea whether they were married or not. One taught geography with a pointer which she aimed at maps showing countries, counties, cities and towns. The other taught sums and wore a severe expression as though her subject was a continuous source of pain for her.

Poor Ruth was greatly relieved to find that neither of these women ever used a strap or a cane. She remembered David and Becky telling her about beatings they received in their own school. Though Sister Evil carried a swishy bamboo cane into the classroom and though she often pointed it threateningly at some girl who was looking around her, she had so far not used it to dish out punishment. However the mere pointing of that cane was enough to bring a girl to instant attention.

The most enjoyable classes were the informal ones given by an older pupil for the younger ones. They took the form of conversation, with new words being brought in all the time. Ruth noticed how her classmates loved to use the new signs they learned each day. It was like a game for them. She found she need have no fear of this new way of talking and chatting and promised herself to become the most proficient of anyone there when it came to the use of sign language.

At home Poor Ruth had slept in her own little bed in Becky's room while baby Sammy slept in the smaller of the two front rooms with David. He had inherited the little cot with protective rails that had once been hers. Here she found herself in a dormitory with twelve beds. Her bed was at the end of the room furthest from the door and closest to the cubicle where Sister Angel slept. She was right next to her friend, May and opposite her other friend, Josie.

She felt cosy here, up against the partition which formed one side of Sister Angel's cubicle. It was the one spot she would have chosen for herself. There was comfort in being so close to Sister Angel and comfort too in the fact that when you couldn't stop yourself crying for your mammy in the dark you could try to convince yourself that Sister Angel was sobbing for her own mammy, far away down the country somewhere.

Thirteen

The street outside was gleaming and fresh, a total transformation from the Wednesday scene with its masses of cattle and sheep, its noise and slobber. The sun played hide and seek among the scudding clouds as Annie left her house to make her way on foot to the Institute where her unfortunate child was waiting to see her. There was no question of bringing the twins. The nuns were adamant about that. Visits from family had an unsettling effect on the morale of the children. As for Isaac, he preferred to leave it to his wife, saying she was better able to communicate with the deaf girl.

At the corner of the North Circular she stood back for a few minutes while a tram went whirring by, sparks shooting from the overhead cable as the swaying vehicle headed for Phibsboro and the city. She never bothered with the tram unless the weather was really atrocious. She liked to walk the more direct route from Hanlon's Corner along the Old Cabra Road, past the fields and farmyards that reached all the way over to the wall of the Park.

This morning, with the sun shining, she would take Poor Ruth for a walk in the grounds, away from the forbidding edifice that somehow reminded her of a prison. They would find a secluded spot with a bench where they could sit and face each other to converse more easily. For it was with their faces they communicated – with their eyes, their lips, the full toolbox of facial muscles. And not just with their faces, but with hands and arms in constant motion. She had grown fond of Ruth's constant waving and flailing to emphasise what she was saying. She told herself again that she would have to make the effort to master the signs and language of the deaf.

As she made her way up the drive and past where the children were housed – where they studied and played – she saw young faces pressed flat against the window panes looking out at her. One of the faces, she could have sworn, was Poor Ruth's. Annie waved and all the children waved back. Some of them were from the country and she knew from Poor Ruth that they never got a visit from anyone.

The nun who opened the convent door wore a doleful expression and seemed taken aback at the sight of Annie standing there. Annie explained that she had come to visit her daughter. The nun said there could be a problem. There was, she said, a *general confinement* in operation. All the children were being kept indoors for the weekend.

Annie was taken aback and felt the anger rising within her. 'I've never heard such rubbish, Sister. I've come to see my daughter and I've no intention of leaving till I get a chance to talk to her.'

'We can hardly make an exception for one child.'

'I want to talk to Mother Eusebius. She's a sensible woman. I haven't walked all the way here to turn on my heel and walk all the way home again. *Confinement* my eye.'

'Mother Eusebius is away. Would you like to talk to Sister Aoibhinn? She'll be able to explain things.'

'Anyone who can talk sense.' Annie was fuming.

'Wait here, please.' Sister Doleful scurried off down the hallway.

When Sister Aoibhinn arrived she was all smiles. 'I understand how inconvenient it must be, Mrs Townsend. And I'm quite sure your little Ruth had no hand, act or part in any bad behaviour, but discipline is important for children. They have to understand that insubordination carries consequences. It's just unfortunate that you should have arrived this morning while sanctions are in place.'

'If my little girl had no part in whatever it was, then she shouldn't be punished. Anyone could tell you that. Now, are you going to let her out or are you not?' Aoibhinn must have seen that Annie was in no mood to take a refusal. She seemed to hesitate but then she said, 'I suppose we can make an exception, seeing as you've come this far. I would ask you to limit the visit to half an hour, though. That way the others won't feel too peeved. If you want to wait outside in the sun I'll send Ruth over to you.'

Without answering, Annie stepped out onto the granite steps and down onto the gravel driveway. After what seemed like a long interval she saw the figure of a little girl coming towards her. Poor Ruth spotted her at the same moment for she began to run and when they met she threw herself into her mother's arms and Annie made to lift her but quickly realised the seven year old was no longer a baby.

Annie was curious to find out what was this whole hoo-ha about bad behaviour and punishment. Through signs and gestures Poor Ruth did her best to explain and eventually Annie believed she had got the gist of it. Bad behaviour in the dormitory. Sister Aoibhinn, arriving to check that the lights were out, with every girl in her own bed, bumped into something suspended from the electric lamp. She shone her torch on a Halloween witch complete with pointy hat, black shawl and sharp nose. Pinned to the effigy was a card with the words, *Wicked Witch*. There could be no room for doubt about the meaning of the message.

Annie was aware that Sister Aoibhinn had the unflattering nick-name *Evil* and knew that the children's behaviour was grossly disrespectful. At the same time she harboured a secret admiration for their daring and ingenuity. In front of Poor Ruth, though, she made sure to show disapproval even if she were laughing inside.

When their pitiful half-hour together was up and she told Poor Ruth she would have to go back to her friends, the child began to cry. Poor Ruth threw her arms about her, cradling her head against her mother's breast. She looked up at Annie and made a gesture which couldn't have been clearer. *I hate it here. Take me home.*

Annie took her by the hand and walked her back to the door of the building where her envious friends were waiting. She kissed her at the open door before turning her back on her child and walking away. Instead of going home, though, Annie took the tram to Glasnevin.

In Glasnevin Cemetery there was a damp shady corner beneath the high boundary wall, a spot where they buried the tiny bodies of babies born dead, or who died before they could be baptised. Everyone knew that such babies were barred from the joys of heaven. Their little eyes would never, ever, gaze on the face of God, a privilege reserved for those souls who had received the saving waters of baptism. They had as little hope of salvation as the pagans of darkest Africa or the heathen infidels of the East.

Annie could not forget that her miscarried son, Rory, had never received the sacrament. In common with the unknown millions of unbaptised babies he had been consigned to some dark part of the Underworld, a place she knew as Limbo. He was lost to her forever. She could never hope to see him or hold him in the world to come when at last, with God's grace, she entered the Kingdom of God.

And what of his body? The flesh and bones that had grown within her, grown to a point where she could feel the beating of his heart and sense the stirring of his living limbs? On that terrible day she had been too ill to know or care what was happening as her body disowned the interloper and flushed it out – a reject refused and repulsed. What had happened then? She tried to remember but could not. Mrs Harold had looked after everything, cleaning up the bloody discharge, putting everything back as it should be, restoring the order of the universe.

She had never been able to ask the supremely practical Mrs Harold had she put it out for the binmen or had she consigned it to an even more ignoble fate, floating away down the deadly drains that ran beneath the streets of Dublin for a final sluicing into the insatiable waters of the Irish Sea.

It was a question that would not cease to trouble her, in spite of the four fine children God had bestowed on her in the succeeding years. Grieving mothers were not supposed to ask these questions. *Don't think about such things – just get on with it.*

Now Annie knelt at the edge of a bare patch of grass, with no individual graves marked out, just an occasional wooden cross pushed down into the ground or a child's doll left on the surface for little hands to fondle during the night when there were no eyes around to see. She had come here to mourn the lost souls in her own life. Two Rory's. That first Rory snatched from her on the verge of manhood. That second Rory who never got to open his eyes on the light of day.

As she stood there in the deep shade of an overhanging sycamore another sorrow took possession. For was not the present plight of her helpless little girl due entirely to Annie herself? If she had put her foot down and refused to allow Poor Ruth to play on the sand-hill that summer day in 1907, the child might never have contracted the disease that took away her hearing. And if she hadn't allowed herself to be swayed by the Parish Priest and the head nun, Poor Ruth would not now be locked up in her gloomy prison at the mercy of women in flowing habits interested only in the smooth running of their Institute. Standing now at the damp, grassy edge of the Angels' plot in

Glasnevin, Annie made the decision to take Poor Ruth away from that awful place of confinement. Whatever the consequences she would bring her home to her own family where she would once again be loved and cherished.

Fourteen

If they were enforcing strict discipline at the Institute, Isaac said, that could only be a good thing. He didn't have a high opinion of nuns in general but in this instance he was behind them all the way. 'Don't interfere, I'm telling you. A little bit of discipline and obedience won't do her the smallest bit of harm.'

'But she's only a child. She's only seven, remember. It would break your heart to see her so distressed. I'm thinking of bringing her home and taking care of her myself. I'll fight them all the way to get her home again.'

'You don't have to fight anyone. If you say you want her home there's not a damn thing they can do to stop you. But if you want my advice you'll leave her where she is. You can't be expected to cope with a dummy child around the place, not knowing the least bit about how to deal with her.'

'She's no dummy and I don't want anyone calling her that. We have long chats, the two of us, and she's as well up as you or me. That child has more brains than a lot of them that passes for normal.' In spite of her husband's clear opposition Annie was more determined than ever to get Poor Ruth away from that awful place. She would bide her time, though, waiting for the right moment to make her move.

***

St. Brigid's dormitory, up under the roof, was an icy place that winter, the second one Poor Ruth was to spend in the Institute. From late October onwards stripping off your warm clothes to put on a flimsy nightdress called for courage and endurance. The sheets were so cold that waiting for your bed to warm up took forever. There was a solution that the little girls had discovered for themselves. It meant creeping into the bed of your neighbour or inviting her to creep into yours. As a way of getting warm and staying warm it was hard to beat yet it was fraught with danger. For those caught in someone else's bed the punishment was guaranteed and instant. Both visitor and host were held equally at fault and equally deserving of what was coming.

There were two kinds of chastisement and you could debate which was worse. The more usual one was a sharp slap on the backside with the small leather strap that Sister Evil carried with her all the time. Both occupants of the bed were punished and you never knew who was going to get the sharper crack of the strap.

There were times, though, when Sister Evil didn't bother with the strap. Whipping off the covers she would drag one of the little girls from the warmth of the bed with one hand while giving her a painful pinch with other. The pinch could be on the bottom but more often it was on the arm. The blue-black mark from one of Evil's pinches would last for days.

One cold night in November May slipped out of her own bed and squeezed in beside Poor Ruth who was very glad of the extra warmth and cuddled in close against her friend. It soon became a regular thing for the two to spend a good part of the night together in each other's beds. No need for any prior arrangement, just whatever way it happened. Being at the far end of the dormitory, furthest from the door, meant they were pretty safe. When the light from Sister Evil's torch began to dance in great circles about the ceiling the visitor knew it was time to creep across the floor and back into her own bed before the inspection reached their end of the room.

Always Poor Ruth was able to get back to her own bed in time and pretend to be asleep. It was not until early December in her second year that her luck ran out. That night, the top of the house where they slept was as cold as the Alpine peaks where the snow never melts. Poor Ruth had crawled into May's bed for warmth and comfort. The lights were out and everyone else was asleep. She pushed her back in against May and felt May's arm wrap itself around her. They tried to keep very still for Sister Angel was only feet away in her bed on the far side of the partition. At any rate they were both ready for sleep.

The first thing Poor Ruth saw was the light of a torch shining on her own empty bed. Evil was there. Far too late now to make a dash for her bed. She froze where she lay, unable to move a limb. A swirl of cold air as the covers were whipped away. She felt herself being dragged by the arm in the direction of her own cold bed. Struggling to climb in she felt a painful pinch on the bottom. In a world of silent retribution the pinch said it all. *Serves you right,* it said. *Just let me catch you one more time and it's the strap you'll get.*

There would have been furtive dashes for safety in other parts of the dorm – she knew that. But by the time Sister Evil had turned to swing her torch in a wide arc across the other beds she would have been met with a scene of total conformity. Ten model little girls in separate beds and wrapped in peaceful dreams.

Poor Ruth could not sleep. She hurt too much. There was a tender weal on her behind where Evil's sharp nails had dug in. And another bruise on her arm. There was, too, a different kind of pain – the realisation that the world was a hard place for a little girl torn from the bosom of her family and thrown amongst strangers. It was these thoughts of abandonment and desolation that made it impossible for Poor Ruth to sleep. Instead of sleep came wrenching sobs, silent in a place where no one could hear. Then she remembered. On the other side of the partition there was a pair of ears that could hear everything.

Poor Ruth detected a movement of the bed covers as a larger hand found her own little hand, urging her to leave her bed and come. In the dim light from a little red lamp beneath the Sacred Heart, through the tears that blurred her vision, she recognised the figure bending over her in a long white nightdress. Sister Angel. Gentle caring arms raised her up and she found herself being carried inside the cubicle and into the comfortable bed warmed by the body of the young nun. She snuggled into the cosy curve of Angel's body and there she slept, more soundly than she had slept since the day she arrived here more than a year before.

It was still dark when Angel woke her with a gentle shake and with the cubicle door held open pointed the bleary-eyed little girl back to her own bed. She saw Angel slip into the bathroom, imagined her splashing water on her face and neck and saw her return to her cubicle to emerge minutes later fully clothed in her habit before making her way between the beds to the door at the other end.

***

Poor Ruth trusted Sister Angel to know when it was safe to fetch her from her hard little mattress and carry her to her own soft bed to comfort and console her. She discovered that Angel was someone who understood what it was like to endure feelings of abandonment and isolation. Sometimes when it was Angel's turn to supervise playtime she would take Poor Ruth aside to confide secrets of her own. The man she thought had loved her had left to marry another whose existence she had not even suspected. She had run to the religious life thinking to find there some meaning in her bitter disappointment. Angel tried to make her language comprehensible to the little girl whose own loneliness she understood too well.

Locked into a situation that grew daily more unbearable, Angel felt nothing if not strangled. Caught between the older women on the one hand and the children on the other, she now realised she had made a serious mistake. All of this Poor Ruth picked up from the quick movements of Angels fingers and hands whenever they had a chance to be together.

After a year and a half in the Institute Poor Ruth could converse with all who lived or worked in the place. She embraced the language of facial expression, hand movements and finger spelling. It's how the children communicated with each other and with their teachers apart from the odd few words scribbled on blackboard or piece of paper.

One morning in the early Spring, as she was leaving the warm comfort of Angel's bed to return to her own, Angel used the sign which asked, 'Are you happy here?' Poor Ruth wrinkled her nose, shook her head and whispered, 'No.' Angel drew her close to herself so that Poor Ruth could see straight into those sad grey eyes. Then Angel signed, 'Me neither.'

In the nights that followed, or whenever the two unhappy souls could snatch a few forbidden moments, a plot was hatched. They agreed that since neither was happy where they were it was time to do something about it. It was Angel who came up with the plan but in Poor Ruth's eyes it had been the obvious course of action for some time now.

They decided to run away.

***

When Sergeant John Townsend took the call he could tell straight away that there must be near panic at the Institute. Two gone missing, the one a nun, the other a young pupil. Since they were found to be missing on the same morning it was a near certainty that the little girl was in the company of the missing sister. The nun at the other end of the telephone line was giving such a garbled account that he decided he would have to cycle up to the convent to find out for himself what happened.

The head nun brought the Sergeant into the visitors' parlour and gave instructions they were to be left undisturbed. There she gave him as full an account of events as she was able to put together. She had been slow to report the incident, she said, thinking there might be some perfectly reasonable explanation. Sister Angel might have decided to treat the girl to some kind of outing. The child was known to be a favourite of hers. They could have gone to the Zoo, for example. However the Zoo had telephoned back around dinner time to say there was no sign of a nun, with or without a child.

Then one of the workers, a woman who came in every day to do some cleaning, discovered her coat and hat were missing from their usual spot. Their worst fears were realised when nun's robes were found rolled up in a ball and hidden in shrubbery under the perimeter wall.

He watched her face as she spoke and noted her evident anxiety. He wondered briefly if he would get a chance to see his little niece before he left the premises.

'I suppose,' she said, 'we have no option now but to inform the child's parents.'

'Of course,' he said.

'I'll send Sister Ethelbert. She's young and a fast walker.'

'Where do they live?'

'Orkney Street. Townsend is the name.'

'You're talking about Ruth Townsend?'

'That's right. Ruth Townsend, seven years of age and deaf mute. '

'Poor Ruth Townsend is my niece.   Isaac Townsend is my brother.'

Mother Eusebius seemed bewildered – at a loss how to handle this development. Then she said, 'I'm sorry you had to learn it like this.' She paused a moment. 'Do you think you could send out some kind of police alert?'

'You can leave all that to me. I'll get back to you the minute I have any news. Right now I'm going straight down there to let Mrs Townsend know what's happened.'

Seventeen minutes later Sergeant John Townsend of the DMP wheeled his police bicycle through the front gate of the Townsend house in Orkney Street. He gave a sharp thump of the knocker. When the door opened he found himself face to face with his sister-in-law. Annie's mouth opened in surprise.

'John! What brings you here in your uniform?   Is there something wrong, tell me?'

'Let me in, Annie, will you. I can't talk out here on the doorstep.'

Annie stepped out of his way and he marched straight down the hall and into the kitchen. The sight that greeted him there made him think for a moment that he had taken leave of his senses. Sitting on the floor with her little legs crossed, a book wide open on her knee and a look of supreme contentment on her face was Poor Ruth. He was on the point of asking his niece what she thought she was playing at when he remembered that she would not hear a word he said. He turned to his sister-in-law. 'Where did *she* come from?' he said.

Annie went back to washing the potatoes at the sink. 'Poor Ruth, you mean? She's come home to her mother, can't you see that?'

'She's been declared missing. They're searching for her all over the city.'

'Just tell the whole lot of them she's at home with her mother.'

'How did she get here anyway?'

'I haven't a notion how she got here. I heard the banging on the front door this morning. When I asked her how she found her way home she laughed and spelled, *Angel*. It was her guardian angel alright, but I don't suppose you believe in such things yourself, John, do you?'

'Guardian angel me backside. She was abducted by a runaway nun by the name of *Angel*. That's who brought her here. That's who left her on the doorstep.'

'Runaway or not, I've a lot to thank her for if she brought my little girl back home to me just when I was on the verge of going up there myself and taking her away by force.'

'You mean you're not sending her back?'

'Divil a send. She'll stay where she's wanted and loved. The devil possessed me to let her out my sight in the first place.'

'In that case I better get back to the barracks and see about calling off the search. Will I tell those nuns you'll not be blaming them for what happened? For letting the little girl run away like that.'

'They can set their minds at ease on that score. I'll not be pressing no charges for negligence. You can say that to them, John, and they can sleep easy in their beds tonight. For I'm counting it a blessed day that brought the dear child back home where she belongs.'

John was on his way out through the front door. 'I'll drop in on yourself and Isaac one of these evenings for a bit of a chat.'

'You're always welcome.' He knew he was, even if he always brought his shirts and socks to be washed.

***

When John was gone Annie went down on her knees in front of her daughter and drawing her close gave her a tight hug. She had taken the trouble to teach herself the finger alphabet. She would now go the whole hog and teach herself the sign language which her little girl had mastered during her stay in the Institute.

She went back to the sink to get on with preparing the potatoes. In an hour or two they would all be in for their tea and she wanted to have the lamb stew ready for her hungry family. This evening there was special cause for celebration.

Fifteen

Up to now they had gone nowhere without each other. Inseparable. It wasn't easy for David to accept that he was no longer a little boy reliant on a devoted twin sister. He was being forced to grow up against his will. Now that they were in separate classes, with Becky in the big girls' class, and he with the boys, she had taken to staying back after school with a bevy of young-ones, giggling at the sort of things that girls giggle at and beginning to look at boys in a whole new way. He just had to get used to it, walking home from school on his own. Still, he missed his sister's company.

David had no interest in girls. They were silly in the extreme, not to say boring, rarely worth a second thought. He couldn't figure out what fellows like Hewson and Pratt saw in them. His own pal, Joey Patterson, had embarrassed the hell out of him one day by wolf-whistling after a couple of lassies. Nor was he able to follow the sniggering insinuations or double-meaning jokes traded in the classroom when the teacher was gone outside for a smoke.

He dawdled in Stoneybatter, gazing in the window of the shoe-shop which for some reason had been turned over to a display of sports items. There were singlets and shorts for boxing, jerseys and knicks for football or hurling. He had an old hurley stick at home with the tip broken off and the sight of a new hurley in the window made him wish he had money of his own to buy whatever he wanted, whenever he wanted. Depending on grown-ups for what you want is a killer. Thank God he would be leaving school for good at the end of July to start his apprenticeship. Independence! For the first time in his life he would be his own man.

What really caught his eye now was a beautiful pair of boxing gloves. With those gloves he would be the envy of his pals. With those gloves he could learn to box like the army boxers his father followed. With gloves like those he might even begin to earn his father's respect.

Meanwhile, he had no boxing gloves and no training. He dreaded having to run the gauntlet of the thugs who hung around Lucky Lane. *Lucky Lane*, indeed! He would be very lucky to get by there without being seen and accosted. If he took the short way home he was almost certain to run into them. On the other hand he could continue up Prussia Street to the North Circular and get home the long way round. But the last time he tried that he had been waylaid by the enemy at the back of the Church.

If he spotted the thugs in time he would duck into the church and let on to be saying his prayers. That was the great thing about having two religions. You could go into either church and not feel out of place. Something about the Catholic chapel appealed to him. There were statues around the side walls that you could pray to. There was a shrine with Mary and Joseph and the boy Jesus. St Joseph holding a saw so you would know he was a carpenter. He felt an affinity with Joseph, since he himself was going to train to be a carpenter.

He often sat looking at them – the Holy Family – wondering just how holy they really were. Did they never have a row or an argument? Did Mary never give the young lad a clatter for dragging mud in all over the house? Did Joseph never swear when he cut himself with the saw? Did he ever come home drunk and punch his wife? Did he ever take his belt off to his son for not telling the truth and whack him till he cried?

Joseph never did any of these things or he wouldn't be called a saint. He wished his own family could be like that – a holy family.

Then he would never have to listen to his father shouting at his mother, accusing her of trying to double-cross him, of conspiring with the priest to proselytise his children. There would be no sulky silences that went on for days on end.

David decided to try his luck with the short way home. Whichever way he chose, the streets and pavements were awash with slippy cow dung. It was always like that on a Wednesday. Though it was late in the afternoon he still met the odd herd of cattle coming from the market in the direction of the quays. He headed for home, dodging from one dry patch to another, trying to keep his shoes and clothes clean.

As he came close to the front of the church he thought it wiser to stay on his own side. It meant he could dive into Harty's shop if the need arose. The coast seemed clear so he would skip the church and keep going. He could visit the tabernacle another time. Once past the entrance to Lucky Lane he would make a dart for his own front door and the safety of home.

He caught sight of the bullies. They had seen him. They must have been crouching behind the wall, waiting for their chance to pounce. 'Hey, Paudge, it's yer man Townsend. We need a little word with him.'

On any other day of the week you might just get away if you ran for your life but not on a Wednesday. There was no way you could run and dodge the cow dung at the same time. Since path and roadway were covered with the stuff you were bound to slip and if you didn't get it from the thugs, you got it from your ma for coming in covered in cowshit. He decided to keep on walking and let on he didn't hear the taunts and insults.

Gorman had fuzzy red hair, a puffy face and the mean beady eyes of a bulldog. He and his sidekick Dunleavy stepped out to block his way and David came face to face with his tormentors. They were older than he, kept back in school for lack of brains or application.

'Hey, Townsend, I didn't see you blessing yourself passing the chapel. What kind of a way is that to be treating Holy God?' Dunleavy, the one with the black hair and blank eyes, sniggered at his pal's wit.

'What'll we do with him, Paudge?' said Gorman. 'A skinny Prod showing disrespect for the chapel.'

Dunleavy came to life. 'I'll hold him, Gormo, and let you get a dig at him. He needs a lesson.'

David had been through this before. Always one pinned him from behind while the other punched him hard in the stomach. There was no use protesting. How could he begin to explain that he was half Prod, half Catholic? They would say that was even worse. All they wanted was to give him a beating. They enjoyed making his life a misery. They didn't care that they were older and stronger. They got their kicks out of picking on quiet kids.

Paudge Dunleavy pulled his arms behind him, twisting them in a painful knot. David was seized by a sudden surge of fury. He lashed out with his heel at where he figured the bully's shin should be. A howl of agony behind his ear told him he had connected and with his arms suddenly free he sprang at Gorman, his fist smashing into the slob's fat nose. Gorman's face contorted in pain. However, he succeeded in grabbing David by the wrist and with brute strength swept him off his feet. He lifted him up and carried him in his arms to the middle of the road. He held him a moment above a pool of liquid manure before dropping him face down in the slurry. The thugs then made off amid hoots of derision. David rolled over on his back ensuring he was now covered back and front with sticky excrement.

His mother let out a screech. 'Jesus, Mary and Joseph, will you look at the cut of you. Get them filthy duds off you and I'll boil the kettle for the bath.' She put the big copper kettle on the gas while David took off all his clothes, including his drawers, and threw them into the washtub in the yard.

'My heart is scalded with you,' she said as he stood there shivering while she pulled out the old zinc tub from under the sink. There was no way she was going to let him use the upstairs bath. She handed him a fresh bar of carbolic soap and made him scrub every inch of his body under her critical eye.

He decided not to tell her about being ambushed by the bullies. He didn't want her going around to their houses and berating the mothers for their sons' carry-on. She would end up telling them she was as good a Catholic as any of them, bringing up her family better Catholics than a lot she could name. He decided to take the blame on himself and said he had been messing around with some chaps from school when he skidded and landed in a pool of you-know-what.

'Just you wait till your father hears about this. He'll give you a good talking to, if he doesn't take his belt to you and it'll be good enough for you if he does.' She was ripping mad. He hadn't expected this. His mother usually covered for him. Now she was about to involve his father, which could have serious consequences. Becky arrived home in the middle of all this and their mother said that if she had stayed with her brother it might have kept him out of trouble.

'He's fourteen, Ma. I can't go around holding his hand for the rest of his life.' Poor Ruth started to snigger and David felt isolated. It just wasn't his day.

When his father came in you could tell he had been drinking. You always knew from the smell of his breath. You tried to gauge his mood. Bad mood and you kept out of his way, good mood and you could get anything if you asked him right. He seemed in good form this evening. David was relieved. His mother held off telling their father until he finished his food and was drinking his tea. Then she said, 'You might like to hear your son's been acting the hooligan with some yobos from the back streets. Came in here covered head to toe in cow-dung.'

'What's this I'm hearing?' His father glared at him. David froze. He didn't know how to answer. Whatever he said would only make matters worse.

'Get yourself into the parlour and wait for me there.' He did as he was told. It wasn't looking good. He heard his mother talking, probably giving the version of events he had concocted for her.

When his father came into the parlour David was relieved to see he hadn't removed his belt. 'Now, tell me the whole thing from start to finish. Who started it?'

David made an instant decision to tell the truth. 'Dunleavy and Gorman. They jumped me at the corner. I tried to get away but I couldn't.'

'You did nothing to provoke them. Is that what you're saying?'

'They called me a dirty Prod and started to beat me up. I tried to give as good as I got but I hadn't a hope against the two of them. I ended up flung in the dung and them running away laughing.'

'And all because of your religion. For once in my life I'm proud of you, son. We need men who'll stand up for what's right.' His father's eyes had a rare twinkle. It wasn't often you saw him like this.

'I only wish I knew how to box right.'

'Well son, I've just the man for you. Jimmy Behan. Matter of fact, I ran into him this evening. He dropped in for a quick pint when I was in Mulligans. A great boxer in his day, Jimmy. Could've been another Tommy Burns if he got half the chance.'

'Will he show me?'

'He tells me he's trying to find a room or a hall somewhere to start a club for young fellas like yourself. He thinks the army might let him use the gym in Arbour Hill.'

'Will you ask him to put my name down?'

'That I will, son. I wish we had more like you, ready to stand up for their king and their church. There's far too many of the other sort around – sleeveens, ready to put a knife in your back.'

Sixteen

Mr Behan seemed to recognise him for he came over the minute he saw him and shook his hand. 'Your father tells me you want to be a boxer, is that right?'

'If you'll take me on, Mr Behan. I'm willing to learn.'

'That's the spirit. Call me *Coach*.'

'Alright, Mr Behan.'

Behan's six-foot-something frame towered above the dozen or so young hopefuls who turned up that first night. He pencilled David's age and details into a dog-eared notebook and when he held out his hand for the two pennies you could see his oddly twisted thumb. 'Now get yourself into your togs and we'll see what you're made of.'

Before allowing anyone into the ring Mr Behan got the boys to form a circle around him while he ran through the more basic moves and postures. He began by demonstrating what he called the classic stance, sideways to the opponent, left shoulder leading, with the chin tucked in. After showing them how to stand he showed them how to move. 'Footwork is important. Keep moving. Never stay in the one spot. Keep your mitts up and your face covered. Don't let your guard down – that's what your opponent is waiting for. Footwork and defence are just as important as attack.'

Despite his giant frame and crooked nose, Behan was a gentle and understanding coach who clearly enjoyed passing on his skills to a bunch of young hopefuls. Soon he had them paired, roughly matched for size and weight and got them sparring and shadow boxing. He moved around from one pair to the next, intervening here and there to show a boy how to keep his guard up or skip out of his opponent's range. He kept them at it for the best part of an hour, with short breaks where they changed partners and started over.

There was a single boxing ring in the tin-roofed building. It had a raised floor with a springy surface. David had been eying the ring and wondering when he would get a chance to use it.

'I'm going to put two of yous in the ring and see how yous get on. The rest of yous are to watch and be ready to answer questions afterwards.' Behan scanned the eager faces, his eyes skimming and skipping until they landed on David. 'You, Townsend. Into the ring with you.' Next his eyes came to rest on a short stocky fellow with thick arms and legs. His black hair was brushed back from the front. 'Brennan! Let's see how you get on in the ring. Hop to it.' David had never laid eyes on this Brennan before and knew nothing about his boxing ability.

'Remember what I said, lads. This is a defensive workout. No hard punches, no rough stuff. Defence and movement, nothing more, do yous hear me?' They both nodded. As David understood it, they were to keep on the move, always just beyond the reach of the other, deflecting any blows that came close. He would try to remember the techniques he had been taught and put them into practice.

They touched gloves before stepping back to take each other's measure. Then the sparring began. David tried a volley of quick jabs, three, four, five. Brennan had no trouble pushing them aside. David wondered if Brennan was really a newcomer to all this. Now Brennan stepped up and his blows came fast and furious. David did as he had been instructed, keeping his gloves up to shield his face. Something told him, though, that Brennan was intent on getting through.

Brennan's punches were all aimed at his head but he succeeded in blocking or deflecting them with the techniques Coach had shown him, fast footwork, moving around the ring and parrying some of those punches with one or two of his own. Out of the corner of his eye he noticed the coach moving away towards two small lads sparring at the other end of the gym. Brennan must have noticed too for he straight away changed his tactics.

Something in the way he started to dance and skip, moving in fast from different angles, made David uneasy. His opponent was just a little too eager in what was supposed to be a friendly sparring session. With the pace increasing David began to tire. His level of fitness was far from what he would have liked.

When it happened – and the way it happened – took him completely by surprise. He had turned aside for a moment to wipe the perspiration from his brow. He dropped his guard for a few critical seconds. A left swing caught him in the face sending him reeling against the ropes. He was dizzy with pain. He leaned against the corner post for support while he drew his arm across his mouth and nose. It came away streaked in blood. He felt tears welling but in that humiliating moment he knew that if he was ever to be a boxer he must be a man and grown men don't cry.

He was certain that the sneaky punch was no accident – that this brute had, for whatever reason, set out to hurt him. Instead of indulging in tears, he would channel his pain into vengeance. Somehow, somewhere, he would get his own back on the little bastard.

'Sorry pal.' Brennan was beside him with a conciliatory glove on his shoulder. 'You dropped your guard and it was too late to swerve.' His *sorry* sounded hollow to David whose nose still bled. He hoped he wouldn't end up with a nose like Coach.

Mr Behan came over to investigate. He took David to the sink and handed him a sponge to wipe the blood away. 'Don't worry, son, you'll survive. Dropped your guard did you? Learning the hard way. Just keep your mitts in front of your face like I said. Now back with you to young Brennan there and tell him there's no hard feelings.'

David did as he was told, touching his gloves to Brennan's, but it was a false gesture and his heart wasn't in it. That rogue punch was no accident.

***

David kept himself in the shadows. He saw Brennan emerge from the gym, cross the street and turn in his direction. As he came abreast David jumped out and grabbed him by the collar.

'Okay, smart guy,' said David, his courage bolstered by the pain in his still stinging nose. The element of surprise was on his side and he managed to drag Brennan around so that their faces were inches apart.

'Hey, what's all this?' said Brennan.

'That was a sneaky punch and you meant it.'

'Hey, hold on there, mate. It was an accident, I swear. Let go, you're choking me.'

'Say sorry like you mean it.'

'Like hell I will.'

'Say sorry.'

Brennan's response caught David unawares. He brought up his knee and caught David in the crotch. David screamed with pain. 'Jesus, Brennan, what did you do that for?' The surprise move allowed Brennan to break free. He came in low, his head down and butted David in the chest knocking him off his feet. As David went down Brennan threw himself on top of him punching with both fists.

'Get off, you madman.' David screamed. Brennan's stocky frame was impossible to shift.

'Beg for mercy,' said Brennan. 'Beg.'

'Shag off,' said David. Brennan took a tight grip of both his ears and began to twist. David gasped with the pain. 'Beg,' said Brennan. The tears in David's eyes were tears of agony. 'Alright, alright.'

'Say, please.' He twisted tighter.

David had no option. It was suffer or surrender. 'Alright, alright, I give in. Please let me up.' He reckoned that once on his feet he could catch Brennan off guard. Maybe get a kick at his shin. It wasn't to be, however, because right then he heard a familiar voice booming.

'Get up outta that the two of yous and stop acting like animals.'

They struggled to their feet to face their coach.

'Townsend,' he said, 'I'll bet any money you're the one that started this. You're a disgrace, Townsend, a disgrace to the club and a disgrace to your father. I'm inclined to think we'll be better off without the likes of you. There's no room here for thugs. D'you hear me, kid?'

'Yes, Coach.'

'Talk up, I didn't hear you.'

'I said I'm sorry, Coach.'

'I'm giving you a week to come up with a proper apology and then we'll decide whether we can take you back. Get off home now with yous. I'll talk to the two of yous next week.'

David and Brennan set off in different directions but curiosity got the better of David and he turned to follow Brennan in the darkness. Brennan's route took him onto Stoneybatter and then towards Manor Street. David saw him disappear up a dark alley known as Piggery Lane. The people who lived in the lanes behind the main street raised chickens, pigs, goats and other livestock. The lanes were noisy, smelly and covered in animal excrement. The people who lived there were shunned by respectable folk who saw them as dragging down the tone of the place. David knew all this for he and Becky had been cautioned by their mother and father to steer clear of those people with their flat *common* way of talking. If you had any dealings with them at all you might end up being labelled as one of them.

David now knew where Brennan came from. As his enemy disappeared up the lane he found his aggressive feelings towards Brennan starting to subside. Foremost in his mind now was a new fear, the fear of being barred from the club before ever getting a chance to learn anything about self-defence.

The mirror in the hall showed him a face that was swollen and smeared in blood. 'Jesus, Mary and Joseph,' his mother said. 'Stand over here in the light till I get a proper look at you.' She took him into the kitchen and wiped his face with a damp cloth while an admiring audience looked on.

Becky, Poor Ruth and little Sammy had a new hero. David, their boxer brother, back from the wars.

Seventeen

Like everyone else who worked in the cooperage, Isaac accepted noise as a necessary part of life. The sawing, paring, cutting and shaping as staves were fashioned from raw boards. The hiss of steam as the great metal bell was lowered over each new barrel to soften the wood. The piercing ring of metal on metal as rivets were flattened on the hoops that would keep the barrels watertight for years to come.

The men worked in the knowledge and assurance that something important was going on here, that their efforts were valuable and valued. He was one of a privileged class and he knew it. Their knowledge and skill was a part of them and informed every aspect of their work. What they did here week after week, month after month and year after year was essential to getting the product of the brewery to every corner of the island, across the water to the neighbouring island and around the world to wherever people had acquired a taste for the stout black beverage.

'Jackson wants to see you.' It was Willie Salmon at his elbow. He never quite knew what to make of Willie who had a habit of winking whenever he said anything, as though everything in life was some kind of joke. He winked at Isaac now as he said, 'He wants to talk to you. He's in his office.'

'You mean *now*?'

'Right now.' Another wink.

He threw down his tools with a groan. He hated to be interrupted in the middle of something. Jackson was smiling when he went in. 'How're you keeping, Isaac? Sit down a minute and take the weight off your feet.' Isaac did just that. He had been on his feet since eight this morning and hadn't bothered to stop for the tea-break when the others had trooped over to the canteen.

'I hear you're turning out barrels to beat the band, Isaac.' Jackson seemed in good form.

'I do my best, Mr Jackson. When you get a run at it you just keep going.'

'Your output last week beats anything I've seen, and I've been in this job, what, fifteen years? That's saying something.'

Jacob looked down at the floor. He wasn't comfortable with this kind of talk. 'I'm making a lot more money with the piecework. Nearly double what I was earning before.'

'It's a good feeling to be able to look after your wife and kids the way you would want to.'

'That's it. I try to do the best I can for them. I count myself damn lucky to have good money coming in when a lot more is on the breadline.'

'How're the kids getting on, by the way? They must be nearly finished school by now.'

'Becky's starting commercial college in September. Clever girl, too. David, the other twin, is getting a start at the carpentry with Shires the builders. I happen to know the foreman there. The two younger ones is doing fine, thank God.' There was no need to discuss Poor Ruth's handicap with Jackson. None of his business.

'It's good to see them being brought up with the right values. That's something the company takes very seriously – honesty and respectability. I remember a chap we had here a few years back. Everyone thought he was one of our own. How he got away with it for so long I've no idea, but he did. When the truth came out he was sent packing. Not for being a Catholic, mind, but for the deception. That's something the company won't tolerate, any kind of deceit.'

'Absolutely.' Isaac wondered where all this was leading.

'Your wife is Roman Catholic, I believe?'

Isaac shifted his position in his chair. 'It's not something we talk about. She goes her way and I go mine.'

'A regular church-goer by all accounts. Even on weekdays.' Isaac wondered how Jackson could know so much about his family. He waited.

'She brings the children with her, I'm told. Dublin is a small town. Everyone knows everyone. You can't pick your nose without it being talked about. I don't have to tell you this.'

'I'm afraid you've got it wrong, Mr Jackson. The children are being brought up in the Church of Ireland. I see to that. They're right there beside me in St Paul's, singing their hearts out most Sundays.'

'Listen to me a minute, Isaac. I can tell you for a positive fact your children are being brought to mass. Maybe not on Sundays when you're around, but other times when there's some holy-day or other in the Catholic chapel. You can't know everything that's going on, can you?'

The sudden relevance of the worker sacked for deceit flashed in Isaac's brain. 'Mr Jackson, if there's even a glimmer of truth in what you've just told me, you can trust me to get to the bottom of it. You've got my word for that. Any truth at all and I'll see to it that it stops. You've my solemn pledge it won't happen again.'

'Isaac, old chap, I never had the slightest doubt you would do the right thing.'

'Leave it to me, Mr Jackson.'

***

The wind and rain were in his face making it hard to push against the hill. He got off his bicycle outside the Blue Coat School to walk the rest of the way. He had driven himself like the devil to make up for time lost listening to Jackson threatening him over his failure to control his wife and kids. He still didn't know how he was going to deal with the situation. He hated arguing with his wife. Obstinate as hell she was. He might as well be talking to the wall, telling her how to bring up the children. She always got her own way in the end. He would be wasting his breath trying to tell her how serious it was this time. Other men knew how to handle their women. How often had he heard them boast to their mates? 'Gave her a smack in the gob. That soon learned her who was boss.' He hoped it wouldn't come to that. Maybe he could talk some sense into her.

What he needed right now was something to prepare him, something to bolster his courage. A couple of pints inside him would not go astray. He would ask her first if there was any truth in what he had heard, that she was bringing the children to the chapel behind his back. And when she told him the truth, for she would hardly lie to his face, he would give her the bald facts of the case. Either she fell in line or he risked losing his job. And where would they be then? No money coming in and quite likely nowhere to live. That was hardly what she wanted.

The noise from inside told him it was business as usual in Cotters and sure enough they were all there, the regulars. He knew every one of them. Scully was there, the drover who worked two days a week at his trade and spent the rest of the week propped against the counter in Cotters putting the few shillings he had earned to good use. 'How're doing, Isaac? Move up there, men,' Scully said, and they pushed aside as Isaac approached for it was known that he needed a couple of scoops of beer before he

- 107 -

was in any position to join the general palaver. The great thing about the Cotters crowd was that they understood each other and each other's needs.

Scully was the centre of a circle of men waiting to hear what he came out with. A great man for the stories was Scully, some true, some pure fairy-tale. You could always tell the latter when you heard him add, *'and that's the god's honest truth.'*

As Isaac took the first cautious sip of the froth on his pint Scully had gained the rapt attention of his audience. He had found a way to beat the bookies hands down and he was more than willing to share it with his friends. 'You start off by putting a tanner on the favourite in the first race,' he said. 'If he gets beaten, you double your bet with a shilling on the second race. Always the favourite, mind. If he goes down, you double up with two bob on the next race. And so on and so on. You must stop betting though when you have a winner. Nothing simpler and you can't lose.' A respectful silence descended while the men attempted to absorb this revolutionary approach to winning.

First to speak was Quinlan. 'And what happens if all the favourites is bet?' This was a pretty sharp question for a man who had already consumed more than half his daily bottle of whiskey. Mickey Quinlan had achieved a well-deserved notoriety as the only man they knew who could consume a bottle of whiskey in the course of a single day and still walk home unaided. Many a man there envied him his happy ability to hold his drink.

'Yeah, Scully, what happens if it's all outsiders that wins?' This was Foxy, behind the bar.

'No problem, fellas. Just take it up again next time that there's racing. You start where you left off and double up each time.'

'Ah, now, Scully,' said Quinlan, 'will you hold on a minute. Go on like that and you end up putting a week's wages on a single horse. And if he came in at odds-on where would that lave you? '

The men were now paying close attention to their pints, which spoke volumes about their sudden loss of faith in Scully's *invincible* system. Scully had no chance to retrieve the high ground before the air was pierced by a shrill female voice. 'Yous are all a shower of eejits with your stupid systems. Yous don't know a thing about it, sure yous don't.' There was silence for a moment before the men realised where the voice had come from. Somebody shouted in the direction of the snug, 'Come out of your hidey hole, will you and let's get a gawk at you.'

The door of the snug swung open and a woman emerged clutching a near empty glass of porter in her right hand. With her other hand she held her shawl tight beneath her chin. Though still in her forties, she had lost most of her teeth which gave her the look of an older woman. As she sauntered to the middle of the floor it was clear that this was the moment she had been waiting for. Women were tolerated in Cotters just as long as they stayed in the snug and didn't show their faces in the male only bar. Biddy was the exception to this rule for she knew how to wind men around her little finger and cadge a pint into the bargain.

Biddy Schicker ran a kip-house in Benburb Street, catering for the women who worked by night and slept by day. She was held in high esteem by those who knew her for she had never been known to turn anyone away even when a girl didn't have the couple of coppers for the price of a bed.

'I backed the winner of the National at twenty to one,' she announced. 'And I'm willing to tell yous all how I done it.'

'Let's hear it, Biddy. Give us your system.'

'The night before the National I was standing here in this very spot when wee Timmy Finlay sang *Down by the Glenside*. A lovely little singer he is too, Timmy. Next day I hears that *Glenside* is running in the big race and I put every last penny I had on him. I don't have to tell yous he left the rest of them standing and I collected a small fortune in winnings. Try beating that for a system if yous are able.'

'How about giving us your beer dance, Biddy?'

'No beer, no dance.' She held her empty glass up for Foxy to see. He responded by drawing a full pint and passing it back in Biddy's direction. Biddy allowed her shawl to slide to the floor revealing an ample bosom beneath a flimsy blouse. She took the brimming glass and placed it with admirable dexterity on top of her head.

'Now,' she said, 'who's first up for a waltz?' There was a marked reluctance among the men to dance with a woman balancing a glass full of beer on her head. Isaac felt a push from behind. 'Isaac's looking for a dance. Let him through, there, will yous.' The cry was taken up and Isaac, though shy of the limelight found himself in a position where he couldn't pull back. He had already swallowed down a glass of malt whiskey and his normal reserve was in retreat. Someone started to hum the Blue Danube and others took it up in discordant keys. It was enough, however, for Biddy to place one hand on Isaac's shoulder while attempting to slide the other inside his waistcoat.

Isaac's natural caution prevented him getting too close to his partner. He could not ignore the beer balanced on the woman's head. Any false move and they were both soaked.

'Go on, Isaac, give her a twirl.' The men were enjoying the show, probably praying for the very disaster that he feared. The woman too was enjoying herself. 'Come in closer,' she taunted him. 'What are you afraid of? I won't eat you.' She drew him right in against her chest to bawdy shouts of encouragement from the men. Isaac didn't want to be seen as a spoil-sport. The whiskey and beer were combining to make his head swim.

Whatever hope Biddy had of balancing the beer on her head dancing alone it was folly to imagine she could do it with her arms around a reluctant male. The glass toppled, drenching them both on its way to the floor. Ignoring her own predicament, Biddy began wiping Isaac's clothes with her sleeve, down the sides and down the front. 'You'll be all right, luvvy. Just fine.' The watching men were enjoying themselves. 'You missed a bit there, Biddy. You need to rub harder.'

***

He was unsteady on his feet and found himself sometimes against the railings, sometimes in danger of stepping off the kerb. He had left his bicycle in the pub. His bladder was bursting and he relieved himself against the side-wall of Turner's sweet shop. It was taking him longer than usual, the short journey from pub to home. There was something on his mind, something niggling away, some sort of confrontation ahead that he would rather not have to face.

'There's a stink of porter off you,' she said. 'You're jarred.' He didn't need to be told the blooming obvious. They were alone in the kitchen. The children must have gone to bed.

'Where's me tea?' he said.

'It's in the oven. We got tired waiting for you. I was about to go up myself.' She was eyeing his wet clothes.

He sat down at the table to see would she hand him his food. After a while she got up, opened the oven door and dropped the plate in front of him. There was boiled cabbage, a couple of thick slices of bacon and four large potatoes, the skins burst open. He felt the edge of his plate and found it cold. He prodded the cabbage with his fork and found it rubbery. He cut a lump of bacon and brought it to his mouth. She was watching as he spat it onto the floor. 'It's stone cold,' he said.

'So what do you expect? Your food was piping hot two hours ago. I kept the oven going until I decided you weren't coming home at all this night.'

He wasn't getting much respect in his own home. He fought to control himself but eat this cold mess he would not. He took up the plate and threw it at the wall opposite where it smashed and scattered across the floor.

'Wipe that up,' he said.

'You can wipe it yourself. I'm off to bed.'

'Oh, no, you're not.' He jumped up, grabbed her by the arm and swung her around to face him. 'There's a little matter you and me has to talk about.'

'And what might that be?'

'A small matter of deception.' He maintained his grip on her arm.

'You're hurting me.'

'You're bringing my children to your chapel and trying to make Roman Catholics out of them. That's deception of the worst kind and it's going to stop. Do you hear me, woman?'

'I'll take them where I want and no one will stop me.'

He slapped her across the face for her impertinence. 'You'll do what I tell you.'

Annie screamed and there was a rush of footsteps on the stairs. The kitchen door burst open and little Sammy came in followed by Poor Ruth in their night clothes. The two children threw their arms around their mother from different sides as if to protect her and Isaac stepped back. Blood trickled from her nose.

'Your mother and me is having a little talk,' he said. 'Go back to bed. It doesn't concern you.'

Annie slid to her knees and pointed to her face. 'He boxed me in the nose. Take a good look now and never forget what you saw tonight.'

'It was an accident,' he said to Sammy. 'Tell your sister *accident*.' Sammy made a half-hearted attempt to convey the message. There were footsteps on the stairs and David came in. 'I heard the commotion,' he said. 'What's going on?'

'Look what your father's after doing to me,' Annie said, turning her bloodied face towards him. Fourteen year old David turned to face his father. 'You've no right to hit my mother.'

'I'll take no cheek from you, boy. Better watch your attitude or you'll get more than a bloody nose.' Before David could reply Becky burst in in her nightdress. Without a word she threw her arms about her mother.

Isaac knew he had lost the battle. The children had rallied to their mother. How was it possible for a man to be so misunderstood and vilified? You work your behind off to provide for your wife and children and what thanks do you get? You discover they are all conspiring against you. To your face they are one thing, behind your back they are something else. He asked himself how he could have got it so wrong, how he could have allowed this whole fiasco to develop.

Right now, though, he was far too tired to think. His head was throbbing and he wondered how he could face into work in the morning.

Eighteen

'He's our father,' Becky said.

'He's a drunken bully.' David was still angry after last night. He would never forgive his father for raising his fist to his mother. 'If I had a gun I would have shot him dead on the spot.'

'I hate when you say things like that,' Becky said. 'Guns never solve anything.'

'Just wait till I'm as strong as he is. He won't get away with it then, I'm telling you.'

Honour thy father and thy mother. Remember that.

'I've picked up a few moves at the boxing and I intend putting them to good use.'

'Keep that for the boxing ring.'

'There's another thing. That brat Brennan split my nose with a sneaky punch and it ends up Behan takes his side and wants me to say sorry. Would you believe that? Where's the justice?' He noticed the twinkle in Becky's eye. 'So what you want me to do? Grovel? I've had it up to here with Brennan, Behan, the whole lot of them.'

'If you want to be a boxer you'll have to learn to take the knocks.' Becky always managed to sound so *grown up*.

'I'll tell you this much, Beck, if there's blood spilt next time, it's not going to be mine.'

'I knew you would go back. Wild horses won't keep you away now that you've got a taste of the boxing ring.'

David gave a grudging grin.

***

The air was alive when David walked into the iron-roofed hut just inside the wall of the army barracks. Young fellows were already paired off and squaring up to each other. He walked straight down to where Mr Behan was showing a pale skinny little fellow how to hold his fists up.

'I'm sorry, Coach,' he said. 'I must have lost my temper.'

Mr Behan barely gave him a glance. 'Find yourself a sparring partner, Townsend. I'll be along to you in a minute.' David looked for someone his own height and build. Some kids were still arriving and changing. Some came with their togs on under their clothes so that they had only to slip off their pullovers and trousers and they were ready. A few new ones hung around inside the door waiting to be enrolled. He felt a punch on his shoulder and swung around to find Brennan there wearing a lop-sided grin.

'Well, how about it?' said Brennan. 'Fancy a return bout?'

David did some quick thinking. This could be the chance he had been waiting for – an opportunity to settle the score and teach this smart-alec a lesson. 'Okay, Brennan. Go get your gloves laced.'

The boxing ring was unoccupied but it was out of bounds. 'We can't go in there,' Brennan said. 'Beanbag won't let us. There's a bit of space down at the far end, come on.' He seemed eager. It looked like they both wanted the same thing, a chance to settle the argument once and for all. As his gloves were being laced up David reviewed his strategy. Keep Brennan under pressure, tire him out, wait for the moment his guard slipped and move in like lightening to let him have a taste of his own medicine. He had been working on this all week.

When the sparring began he saw straight away how Brennan was trying once more to penetrate his guard. He took good care to offer him no such opportunity. He had learned his lesson, he had learned it early and he had learned it the hard way. Though Brennan kept moving around he wasn't as light on his feet as David who was more athletic and managed to keep just out of range. His chance would come – all he had to do was wait.

When it came it came quickly. In the split second it took for Brennan to raise an arm to wipe his brow David bounced in and delivered a smacking left jab to his opponent's face. It was a carbon copy of the punch he himself had suffered the previous week. He saw the blood spout from Brennan's nose. It was the moment he had been waiting and planning for. He saw Brennan grab a towel and collapse onto a stool. The sight of blood however failed to give David the satisfaction he expected. Instead, all thoughts of resentment and revenge evaporated. Sitting there with his face in a towel Brennan cut a pathetic figure. You could almost feel sorry for him.

The coach was at the far end of the room, occupied with a couple of newcomers, and hadn't seen what happened. Though David had evened the score, which gave him an undeniable sense of satisfaction, at the same time he was sorry it had to end like this. He had joined the club to learn how to defend himself, not to inflict pain. Life sure is complicated. A thing can be right one minute and wrong the next. He wished to God he could figure it all out. He decided he didn't want to think about it.

What happened next took him by surprise. He expected that once Brennan managed to stop the bleeding he would be up and at it again, intent on exacting revenge. Instead, he stood up, and with a grin on his blood-smeared face put a gloved fist on David's shoulder. 'Nice one that, Townsend. You're smarter than I thought.'

They resumed their sparring and shortly afterwards the coach came by. 'That's right, Townsend, keep your guard up, keep on the move. Nice footwork there, Brennan.' He didn't appear to notice anything amiss and the two observed an unspoken agreement to keep it like that.

***

'That's the fellow you were calling a thug last week,' Becky said. She could see the change in David as he gave her a blow by blow account of the boxing session. His sense of grievance had evaporated. 'Seems like Brennan is not such a monster after all. You must be glad you went back.'

'Brennan? I suppose he's not such a bad sort when you get to know him.'

'Will you bring him home sometime so I can get a look at him?'

'It could be tricky, that.'

'No one's going to eat him.' She seemed eager.

David leaned close to his sister's ear. '*They* wouldn't like it.' He nodded towards the parlour where their father was reading and the kitchen where their mother was getting things ready for the morning.

'Why not?' she whispered.

'*Common.*' Becky understood. In the Townsend household it was a word laden with meaning. It meant Brennan was *the wrong type.*

'Where's he from?'

'Piggery Lane.'

'Oh!' She fell silent and they didn't pursue it any further. But her interest had been aroused, maybe even sharpened.

***

On a chilly night in November David walked home with Brennan after training. At the entrance to Piggery Lane Brennan said, 'Come on up and meet me Ma and Da.'

David found it hard to see where he was going as he picked his way across the rough cobbles. He barely avoided stepping into an open drain in the darkness. The air was heavy with the smell of animals and loud with the snorting of pigs. They stopped outside a low white-washed cottage with weeds and grass growing out of the rotting straw on the roof. Brennan gave a rap on the door and without waiting pushed down the latch and stepped inside. He beckoned David to follow him.

The space inside was lit by an oil lamp. Children sprawled all over the floor. In a chair on one side of the fire sat a middle aged woman with a soft round face which lit up when she saw that her son had brought a companion. On the other side of the fire a man in a wheel-chair glared at David with a look of suspicion. Beside the man was a heap of smashed up crates and he was in the act of throwing a handful of broken pieces on the fire as they came in.

'Me ma and da,' said Brennan. Without raising her bulky body from the chair his mother drew the palm of her hand across her abdomen and reached out to shake David's hand. 'Come in and sit down will you.' David looked around the cramped space for somewhere to sit. 'Get off that chair,' the mother said, pushing a girl the same age as Poor Ruth. The girl gave up the chair with a look of sullen resentment.

'I can't sit down,' David said, 'me ma's expecting me home.'

'She won't mind one bit. Sit down let you. Sure you must be famished with the cold.'

But David had already decided he had to get away from the screeching and squabbling of the children that would make it impossible to have any conversation. Brennan's father still hadn't uttered a word. He looked like a man who had surrendered to his fate, condemned to live out his life feeding the fire in a madhouse crammed with squalling children.

'Thanks all the same, Mrs Brennan but my mother will be wondering what's become of me.'

'Alright so but don't forget now, you're welcome any time in this house.'

Walking home he thought about what he had seen. Another side of life. An eye-opener. He was sorry in a way he had not made time to sit down and learn more about Brennan's chaotic situation. He had counted seven younger children, ten people in all, crammed like piglets in a pen in that tumbledown cottage. With the father in a wheelchair it was a miracle they managed to survive. He felt ashamed that he had so much while they had so little. He, Becky, Poor Ruth and Sammy. They had so many rooms, so much space. So much of everything, really.

Nineteen

Becky heard her mother call out for someone to see who was knocking. She opened the door to find a stocky youth about a year older than herself standing on the step looking at her. He seemed taken aback to see her there and it took him a while to say what he wanted. 'Is David ready?' he said. She could see he was blushing.

'He's rushing to go out.'

'I'll just wait for him so.'

'You're one of the boxers?' He nodded. 'You might as well step in. He'll be ready in a tick.' He looked ill at ease standing there in the hall. 'You're not Brennan, by any chance?' He fitted the image she had in her mind.

'That's right. Eamon Brennan. Tell him I'm here, will you?'

The kitchen door was slightly ajar and Becky caught a glimpse of her mother taking a quick peep at the visitor before going back to preparing the tea for their father who hadn't yet come home. Poor Ruth and Sammy both came into the hall to stare.

'How're yous?' said Brennan, more relaxed with the two youngsters than he was with Becky.

'Are you a boxer, Mister?' said Sammy, adopting a boxing pose for Poor Ruth to follow what they were saying. 'My big brother's going to be a boxer.' Right then David came clattering down the stairs and skipped the last two steps. 'Let's go,' he said to Brennan.

It came to be a regular occurrence after that, Brennan calling for David. Becky could see they had become firm friends, although what they had in common she had trouble making out. Boys were strange like that. It was hard to figure them out. One thing she did know about Brennan was that he didn't harbour grudges. Having made friends with her brother he was proving to be a loyal friend.

She learned from David that Brennan's father had been crippled when part of a crane fell on him at work and he was trapped for hours while they worked to free him. His spine was shattered. He would never walk again. His wife was forced to find skivvying work to help her family survive. David told Becky they depended on charity, with help from the neighbours. He told her the children were running wild while their mother was out scrubbing the floors of the well-to-do. The father, helpless in his wheelchair, could only roar at his offspring, something they had learned to ignore. All the crippled man could do was watch helpless from the side-lines. He must have felt a total failure in his own household.

Becky could only admire a lad from such a background who had managed to get taken on by the Post Office as a telegram boy.

Twenty

Brennan said a lot of the fellows who worked alongside him in the Post Office were joining the Fianna Boys and he was planning to do the same. He wanted David to go along with him and David said he would go just to keep him company. It was never David's intention to join but somehow when they got down to Rutland Square and saw all the young fellows queueing up to enrol it was too easy to get caught up in the buzz and excitement of it all. He allowed his name and details to be entered beneath Brennan's in the membership book. The recruiting officer, a Limerick chap by the name of Heuston, told him he could always change his mind later. So it was a case of no harm done if he decided to pull out.

Nothing much happened that night except for an interesting talk from a woman that someone said was a countess. She was dressed in a sort of scout's uniform with green jacket and skirt, the likes of which David had never before seen on a woman. She told all the young lads there that Ireland was a nation long before the English invaded and subjected the Irish people to the rule of a foreign monarch. She told them that this new organisation was more than just boy scouts. She said they were following in the footsteps of great Irish heroes like Fionn Mac Cumhaill and his band of warriors, the Fianna of old. The time was coming, she said, when Ireland would be a nation once again.

This was a whole new slant on things. David wondered why he had never been told any of this in school or at home. Some instinct warned him that it was not something he could discuss with his father. His mother, maybe, or Becky, but not the man who professed such great admiration for the way Ireland was protected by its special position within the United Kingdom.

Though Becky, Poor Ruth and Sammy were excited to hear David had joined Fianna Eireann, his mother didn't quite share their enthusiasm. 'Them Gaelic Leaguers is all very fine,' she said, 'as long as they stick to teaching Irish and dancing. I wouldn't want to see them teaching young lads like yourself to be marching with rifles on their shoulders.'

David knew what she was getting at. He and Becky had heard their father and mother talking about what was happening in the North, how the Ulster Volunteers had declared themselves ready to fight to keep the union with England. Very few mothers would want their boys getting caught up in that kind of agitation. His mother must be sharper than he thought for after listening to the Countess at that first meeting it would not surprise him one bit to hear they were planning to set up a Volunteer Force of their own just like the one in the North.

Their father had taken to reading out the letters in the Irish Times to bring home to his family the folly that was starting to grip the country. According to him, all the men at work and most of the fellows in the pub were of the same mind as himself. They must keep their link with the Crown at all costs. David's big fear was that his father would find out he had joined the Fianna. Yet another secret to be kept from the head of the household.

Twenty One

Brennan and the twins were together in the parlour when David let slip that it was their birthday. 'What age are yous now? Sixteen if I'm not greatly mistaken. Sure yous are still only kids!' Becky tried to hide her annoyance. A few more months and she would be finished college and into a job. She was no kid and didn't like being called one.

There was no piano in the hovel Eamon Brennan called home. So it amazed the Townsends that he was able to knock out a tune or two on their own piano in the parlour – until he admitted he had picked up a few notes from his uncle in the Naul who was regarded as the best piano accordion player in North County Dublin.

Brennan swivelled round on the piano stool and began to thump out a few discordant notes before finding his bearings. What emerged then was a tune they all knew well. As he played he began to sing the words:

'I love you as I never loved before, since first I saw you on the village green.

Come to me ere my dreams of love are o'er...'

Becky experienced a wave of confusion. She did not know whether to be flattered or annoyed. But when Eamon Brennan came to the final line, *'when you were sweet... when you were sweet... sixteen,'* she felt a sudden thrill of pleasure at the idea that this song was for her. She glanced at David and saw him frowning. He was not amused. He realised of course that the words, *I love you as I loved you...* were intended for Becky and he appeared to have a problem with that.

She had no idea whether Eamon Brennan was trying to flirt or was just being his usual boisterous self. When he swung round to face them he was beaming, clearly pleased with himself.

'Stop staring at me,' Becky said to him. 'David's sixteen as well.'

'Sixteen, but not *sweet* sixteen. I think sweet sixteen deserves a kiss, don't you?' He made a grab for her but she slipped out of his grasp. When he came after her again she put her elbows up against his chest and turned her face away. She was relieved when her mother came into the room wiping her hands with a towel. 'So Becky told you it's her birthday?' she said, her eyes twinkling.

'David told him.' Becky hated this kind of thing, everyone looking at her. 'It's the same as any other old birthday. I wish everyone would stop annoying me.'

'I'm sorry,' Eamon said. 'It just came into my head, you know, *sweet sixteen* and all that.'

'I'm going upstairs,' Becky said and dashed out of the room. But she paused on the stairs to hear what they were saying.

'Don't worry, Eamon,' her mother said, 'she hates being the centre of attention.'

'It's time we were off,' David said. 'Old Beanbag will eat the head off us if we turn up late.'

'Off with you so and let you not be too late getting home, David.'

When they were gone Becky came back down.

'There was no need to be rude, Becky. The poor lad got carried away with himself when he saw the piano with the lid open. Put the whole thing out of your mind, child.'

It wasn't that simple, though. Becky couldn't put Eamon Brennan out of her mind. It was not just the words of the song. Lots of songs nowadays were about love and silly stuff like that. There was something else though, something new, a feeling inside she could not explain and it frightened her.

***

David wanted to say something to Becky. It was tricky though because he liked Eamon and did not want to be disloyal to his pal. You had to admire a chap who with no one to put in a word on his behalf had walked right into the tram sheds in Conyngham Road and asked for a job. No fear or inhibitions, Eamon Brennan. The manager he spoke to must have noticed something about him, some quality, when he asked Eamon to come back with his father. Since his father was confined to a wheelchair, his mother had gone instead and it was agreed that Eamon could start work straight away as a tram cleaner at three shillings a week. That kind of money was a fortune for the Brennans, struggling to bring up all those children on the mother's income as a skivvy. Whatever else you might say about Eamon you couldn't fault him for lack of spunk.

But David more and more felt a responsibility to look after his twin sister. A reversal of their roles up to now. Neither had forgotten their childhood vow to watch out for each other as long as they lived. *Oats and legions.* She was collecting her hockey gear from under the stairs when he broached the subject.

'Do you fancy him?' They were alone in the hall, both getting ready to go out for Saturday games. Poor Ruth had taken Sammy into the front garden to play with some new kid who had moved in down the street. Their mother would be back from the shops any minute. Their Father had gone down to Cotters to catch up on the latest news.

'What do you mean, fancy him?' She seemed puzzled by the question.

'If you could see yourself blushing when he's around!'

'Don't be stupid.'

'I'm serious, Beck.'

'I wouldn't be seen dead with Brennan. Well no, I didn't mean it like that. He's alright I suppose. He tries to be nice to me because I'm your sister. That's all there is to it.'

'I'm not sure how to say it, Becky, but I don't want you two getting involved.'

Becky gave a nervous laugh. 'I didn't come down in the last shower, David. If there was anything dodgy about Eamon Brennan I would have copped onto it before now.'

Eamon held her by the shoulders, looking into her face.

'Tell me straight, Beck. Do you fancy him?'

'He drives me batty with his silly carry-on.'

'Do you like him?'

'Like him? I suppose you could say so.'

'Just watch your step, sister. Some fellows are more worldly-wise than you might think.'

***

Eamon arrived after dinner on Saturday to go with David for drill practice in the Park. 'Come into the kitchen while you're waiting,' Annie said. 'No need to be a stranger here.' She called up the stairs, 'Don't take all day, David. Eamon's here.'

Becky stood up when he came in, gulping the remaining dregs of her tea. 'You can sit here,' she said. 'I'm off.' She went into the hall and began to rummage for her hockey gear.

'I have to go, Ma,' she called. Seeing Eamon staring at her through the open kitchen door she said, 'See you sometime.'

He winked at her, smiling. She turned and went out through the front door. A wink could mean anything or nothing. It could mean, 'You and I have something no one else knows about.' Or it could mean he was laughing at her embarrassment. He was more than a year older than she, which gave him an unfair advantage. And there it was again, that creepy feeling she couldn't pin down. A sense of not knowing whether his presence in her home was agreeable or disturbing, to be welcomed or avoided.

***

He must have been waiting for her. She was on her way home from work keeping her face down against the driving rain and paying no attention to anything except getting home and getting dried off.

'Hold your horses. Where's your hurry?' Eamon stepped out from the edge of the pavement. He seemed to appear out of nowhere. His powerful right hand on the handlebars brought her bicycle to a sudden halt.

'Oh, hello,' she said.

'Hello, Becky.' The way he said her name, laden with respect, she thought, was different from any time before.

'You've no coat,' she said. 'Why don't you get back inside the shop door?' There were one or two others already sheltering there.

'I would rather be out here where we can talk.'

'Talk about what?'

'Would you ever tell David I won't be able to make it tonight? My sister is sick and I'm giving me ma a break from looking after her.'

'I'll tell him.' She tried to move off but found the bike held motionless in his grip.

'Not so fast, Becky. There was something else I wanted to ask you.'

She felt annoyed. 'Well ask me then. I want to get home out of this rain.'

'Were you ever in the Volta? Would you like to go?'

'I wouldn't be bothered. It's nothing but Italian pictures they do be showing in that place.' She had taken Sammy to see a couple of westerns but her father had put a stop to it saying the place was a hotbed of immorality.

'There's a western on next Saturday. It's called *The Cowboy and the Lady*. I hear it's a smashing picture. I would hate to miss it. And it has Alan Hale in it. Will you come?'

'I'll have to ask me da.'

'And what'll he say?'

'Not a hope in hell.'

'So you can't come, then?'

'I didn't say that.'

'When will I know?'

'Call to the house after work on Friday. I'll tell you then.' She pushed down on the pedal and the bike wobbled away from the kerb. She did not look back but she had already made her mind up about the pictures.

All week she tossed the question around in her head trying to find some way to justify her actions. She concluded that it could not be that big a sin to deceive her father. He was so narrow-minded that he was never going to let his children grow up. If she followed all his precepts and restrictions she would be a child for the rest of her days. God would not blame her and her father need never know. It was the first time Becky had ever done anything so bad.

Her mother and brother were a different story. Not being straight with them gave her qualms, but she was sixteen now, almost a woman. She would have to start making adult decisions, learn to lead her own life. So she told everyone she had a hockey match in Chapelizod. She cycled to Mary Street and locked her bike at the side of the picture house. Eamon was waiting for her.

It was not the first time Becky had sat in the darkness of the Volta but it was the first time she ever allowed a boy who wasn't David to hold her hand. And she didn't object when Eamon put his arm around her in the dark.

She had told blatant lies in order to get here but instead of guilt she experienced a new and powerful sense of freedom. And there was the unfamiliar thrill of being held by an older boy who seemed to be pleased with her company.

Twenty Two

He knocked again. And then again. Had he guessed she was in there, hiding? Annie heard footsteps coming down the stairs. Mattis must have assumed Annie was gone to the shops. Annie stood close against the parlour door. She didn't want to miss a word.

'There's no one in,' Mattis said before he had a chance to speak.

'I'm Father Neilon, the new curate. Can I come in?'

'Like I'm telling you, Father, they're all out. God alone knows what time any of them will be back. I can leave a note in the hall if you like.'

'You live here, Mrs —?'

'Mrs Mattis. No, I don't live here. I live upstairs at the back. I came down when I heard the awful racket at the door, thinking there must be some terrible emergency with such a hullaballoo going on.'

'I apologise for disturbing you, Mrs Mattis, but seeing as we're both here now, I wonder if I might have a few minutes, a few words.'

'I would love to talk to you, Father, and I wouldn't want to be rude or anything but it's not a good time. Not that I don't enjoy a natter like the rest of them. I do that. It's just that himself will be in for his tea at six o'clock and he doesn't like to be kept waiting. He does be ravenous after his day's work, he does. Working men do have a fierce appetite altogether, so they do.'

'I'll tell you what I'll do then. I'll drop back at seven when Mr Mattis is finished his meal and then maybe we can introduce ourselves and have a little chat together. How does that sound?'

'Well now, Father, if it's Mr Mattis you were wanting to talk to you're going to have a bit of a journey ahead of you for it's beyond in Sligo you'll find him, lying cold beneath a lump of Connemara limestone.'

'I'm so sorry. Believe me, I didn't realise.'

Annie, listening behind the door, knew Mattis was relishing the young priest's confusion, mocking him as he attempted to frame his next question.

'You're not living alone, you say. It's your son, then?'

'Son, is it? No, Father, I never had the joy of a son—or a daughter for that matter. The good Lord never saw fit to bless us with wee ones to lighten our days before he whipped poor Peter away on the horns of a mad bull. No, Father, the Man Above doesn't have a lot of regard for the likes of us poor folks.'

'Forgive me, Mrs Mattis, if I had known... '

'Let you not be put off from calling again if that's what you want. Sure there's nothing would please Plinny more than a fresh pair of ears to listen to his blather.'

'Plinny?'

'Plinny's me lodger. An extra few pence towards the rent, you understand. I needn't tell you how hard it is for a woman on her own.'

'Quite.'

'Call anytime you want, Father. Just come in through the back gate and up the back steps. Plinny won't mind you one bit. Sure he'll dazzle your head with philosophy he will. A great man for the philosophy, Plinny.'

'I'll call back when Mr—. '

'Kinsella. Plinny Kinsella. But just call him Plinny. He'll like that.'

***

Annie never let on to Mattis that she had overheard her conversation with the young curate, yet she was dying to hear if the priest had come back and met Plinny. She was to find out soon enough when Mattis came into the kitchen next day bursting with the news. 'Wait till I tell you, Missus. Didn't we have a visit from that new curate last night, meself and Plinny.' Annie affected surprise. 'I never heard a thing.'

'He came in through the back gate and up the steps. Father Naysh Neilon, on a mission to save the world from sin.' Her expression conveyed layers of meaning. 'We was in the middle of our tea, when he arrived. I offered him a plate but he turned up his nose at it. Maybe 'twas the sight of the gravy that put him off. Plinny was lashing into his steak and onions with a bottle of the usual on the table in front of him. The wee priesteen had his eye on everything that was going on. You could tell he was taking it all in. I saw him looking at me when I ordered Plinny to wash his hands in the sink. You can be sure he was trying to make out how it was between Plinny and meself. You know yourself the way a young priest would be thinking, wondering if everything was right and proper and above board. Well, neither of us was about to fill him in on that score. What he don't know won't bother him.'

'So tell me, what did ye all talk about?' Annie was curious.

'Oh, he wasted no time in getting around to what took him here. The men's sodality. The sodality's on its last legs, says he. Only a few oul' fellas left, says he, booking their place in heaven. He's looking for new recruits to jizz things up and he cast his eye on Plinny, the Lord save us. It's only once a month, says he. Rosary and benediction on Friday evening, confession on Saturday, Mass and communion on Sunday. Well, as God's me judge, didn't Plinny burst out laughing in his face. *Confession is it Father? Tell me straight, what is it the likes of a hardworking man like Plinny Kinsella might have to confess?*

'Men like yourself can provide a strong example to the rest, says the priest. Plinny lets on to be thinking it over while the priest is waiting for an answer. Then Plinny says, here's the deal. We'll talk about mass, confession – all that stuff – if you put this bottle to your mouth and drain it to the dregs.

'By way of encouragement, he puts the bottle to his gob and takes a slug of it himself, wiping his mouth with the back of his hand. Full of nourishment, says he. The priest holds the bottle up to his nose for a sniff. You can see the look of disgust on his face. Then he holds it to the gas-lamp and sees that it's still half full. Funny smell, he says. What is it?

'It's the blood of a bull I killed today, Plinny tells him. He's staring at Plinny, the priest is, trying to work out is he having his leg pulled. Plinny works in the slaughter-house, I says. Then the priest pushes the bottle of blood away across the table, afraid he's going to get sick. Plinny reaches out, grabs the bottle by the neck, puts it to his mouth and drains it to the dregs, he does. *The blood of the bull for the spirit of the bull*, says he.'

Annie was intrigued by the story. 'You don't think Plinny will be joining the sodality, then?'

'When pigs spreads their wings and joins the birds.' Mattis began to cackle and next the two women were convulsed with laughter.

Later Annie congratulated herself on not opening the door to the young priest, for the word around the parish was that Fr Naysh Neilon was a man who saw only black and white. A young man with a mission to put the world to rights.

Twenty Three

There wasn't much Mattis missed. She told Plinny she knew more about the Townsends than they knew themselves. Plinny's answer pleased her – *you've the eye of a hawk, the ears of a badger and the nose of a bloodhound.* She was happy to acknowledge that description.

When you acquire intimate knowledge of a family living in such proximity you're bound to feel burdened with responsibility. You have to know what to pass on and what to keep to yourself, when to stick your nose in and when to stay silent. One way or another, you have a duty to do the right thing.

There were nights when Plinny and herself could hear the shouting coming up from below. Mr Townsend throwing a fit about his tea not being kept hot, or not to his liking. There were times when they heard the crashing of furniture and feared for the safety of the Missus and children.

'What can you expect from a drunkard?' Plinny said.

She agreed. 'That man is the devil himself when he has drink on him.'

Yet, in spite of everything, she preferred to think of Mr Townsend as a man who provided well for his wife and family. She never said a word to Missus, never gave the slightest hint that she heard a thing, even when she saw the bruises on the poor woman's face or arms. There was little, though, she didn't discuss with Plinny in whom she saw the perfect gentleman. 'Not much of an advertisement for religion,' Plinny said. 'Off to church on a Sunday, children in tow, whichever of them he manages to rouse.

The essence of respectability in front of the minister.'

The two small upstairs rooms gave Mattis a perfect view of the long back garden stretching down to the old carriage house which housed Dodd's motor repair business. To the side was the narrow wooden door that opened onto the back lane. It was the door she and Plinny used, to avoid coming in through the family's front door.

Knowing who came and went through the door off the lane afforded Mattis a valuable insight into the workings of the family. Of late she had been keeping a close eye on Becky, a protective eye she preferred to think, for she had noticed some odd things about the girl's behaviour. One evening as she sat near the window she put down the paper she was reading to see who was coming in. Becky was saying goodbye to somebody and that somebody was a young man. So Becky had found herself a boyfriend she didn't want her family to know about. She pondered whether to convey this news to Missus or keep it close to her chest for the time being. She would hate anyone to think she was spying on the children. They could easily get the impression that she kept tabs on everything that went on in the house.

She would know herself when the moment was right to say something. In the meantime she applied her brain to the question of who the boy was. She had a notion who he might be and mentioned it to Plinny.

'You know that stocky young fellow that goes boxing with young David? A rowdy sort judging the noise he manages to make.'

'That's Eamon Brennan. Himself and young David get on well. I can't say I ever seen Becky looking at him though.'

'You dote on those children like they was your own.'

'I guess they're the closest I'll ever come to having any.'

Mattis wondered what he was driving at.

Twenty Four

Becky saw the sweet disapproving look on the face of the Virgin and turned her eyes away. She scrambled over the rocky grotto and sought the slender space between the base of the statue and the pedestal on which it stood while all the time avoiding the reproachful eyes of the mother of God. She's only a statue, she told herself, carved from a block of limestone in some marble works like the one just down from the Queens.

Her searching fingers found only the crumbs of cement that said this shrine had been here since long before her own time. Every evening this week she had come, hoping for some word, some explanation why Eamon had not shown his face at the weekend. She could have asked David had he seen any sign but she was reluctant to give any hint, even to her brother, that she was interested in the boy from Piggery Lane.

As she scrambled back down she noticed a piece of paper caught in a crevice between two rocks. She bent down to retrieve it and saw it had Eamon's handwriting. At the foot of the grotto was a rail for pious parishioners to kneel and raise their eyes to Our Lady, begging for favours, asking her to keep their children safe from sin and free from harm. This is where Becky sat now as she studied the fragile damp note in her hands.

Becky love, I was not able to come up this week. I'm reely sorry. I have overtime most nights and a meeting tonight in Liberty Hall to support the union. There's no way out. Larkin will be there himself. See you this weekend I hope. I will leave you a note. Eamon.

Becky was happy. A note was better than nothing. She drew from her coat pocket a crumpled piece of pink notepaper and with a stub of pencil began to scribble.

'*Eamon,*' she wrote. She stopped to look around. The church grounds were deserted. Everyone was at home having their tea. '*Eamon, I missed you. I was worried sick there might be something up. Come around to the house so we can talk. If Father is in I'll tie a string to the railings and you'll know to stay away. Love, Becky.*'

She read over what she had written and some afterthought made her draw a line through her name and then try to black it out altogether. You never knew where the note might end up and there would be hell to pay if it got into the hands of her parents who had no idea there was anything going on between herself and Eamon. Her father had made it clear he did not want to see him around the place.

She folded the paper and balancing on the rough rocks she stretched around the back of the statue feeling for the cavity where she could leave her message for Eamon to find. The rain was growing insistent as she left the Church grounds to walk the short distance back to her house.

***

Mrs Woods on Ashford Street had been warned by Father Kingston, strictly forbidden to breathe a word to anyone. Though he did not put it in so many words he implied it would amount to a grave sin were she to tell anyone else what she had told him. That is why, when she confided in her best friend, she was careful to repeat the priest's injunction and stressed that this must be kept strictly between themselves. She whispered in the avid ear of Mrs Lewis how Our Lady had turned to look down at her as she prayed. She knew her secret was safe with her friend. If there was anything Mrs Lewis was noted for, apart from her devotion to Our Lady of Lourdes, it was her discretion. These admirable qualities were emphasised by the black she had worn ever since the death of her husband from yellow jaundice. Of course there was always the possibility that Mrs Lewis had herself been bound to silence about some similar experience in the grotto. In any event Mrs Woods knew she could trust her friend, who for as long as she had known her had never missed daily Mass.

***

Fr Kingston made his way through the church grounds after Mass. He was still fasting and looked forward to a good breakfast of rashers and eggs. His way took him past the Lourdes grotto where he was surprised to find a group of women on their knees, fingering their beads and reciting the rosary aloud. On asking the woman nearest him what was going on she explained in a hushed voice that they had gathered in hope of another miracle.

He grasped the situation straight away. The miracle of the moving statue. He might have known that old craw-thumper Woods would not keep her stupid mouth shut. It was clear she had wasted no time spreading her pious delusions around the parish.

'Alright, Ladies. Listen here to me a moment.' The praying faded to silence.   'I'm asking you all – no, I'm telling you now – to go home, all of you, and put this silly nonsense out of your heads. If there's any more of this foolish carry on you're going to leave me with no option but to have the grotto taken down altogether.'

He waited as they drifted away, slowly, reluctantly, mumbling to each other.

***

Not only was Tom Tyler physically strong, he was also the soul of discretion, a man you could rely on to keep his mouth shut. So when Fr Kingston asked Tom to lock the gates and come with him to the grotto the sacristan asked no questions. You didn't have to

- 141 -

spell things out for Tom.

'Give her a wee push there, Tom, and see if she's anyway shaky. If she's coming loose we'll have to get a job done on her before she topples on top of someone and then we would be in a right fix.'

Tom was already beside the statue and rocking it on its base. It was clear to the two men how the statue might move when the wind was in a certain direction. As the sacristan eased the Virgin back into position, wiping away the grit with his hand, his fingers touched a folded sheet of paper which he picked up and started to read.

'A letter be the looks of it, Father.'

'Give it here to me, like a good man.'

***

Through the parlour window Annie's eyes followed the priest as he closed her gate, crossed the street and headed for the opening that led to his own house. The PP's residence was hidden well back among the trees and shrubs that lent the place a degree of privacy and privilege proper to the status of its occupant.

At that same moment she caught sight of Isaac making his way slowly, with unsteady gait, towards his home, wheeling his bicycle alongside. He would have an edge on his appetite now that he had a few pints inside him. He too must have seen Fr Kingston crossing the road and going into the presbytery. Isaac reached his front gate and stopped to steady himself against the railing. The gate had been left swinging, letting him know the priest had just come out of his own house.

'So His Reverence was paying a little visit when he got me back turned? I wish that interfering clergyman would keep away and learn to mind his own business. You weren't expecting me home so early, were you?'

She studied her husband's face. She had long ago learned to gauge the amount of drink he had on board by the colour of his cheeks and the glazing of his eyes.

'Fr Kingston had one or two things to talk about.' She tried to keep her tone casual.

'Things? Things so important he didn't want the man of the house to know anything about them?'

Annie was nervous and her hand went to the pocket of her apron where she had shoved the note. 'Get in and have your tea before it's gone stone cold.'

'Not so fast. I want to hear what's so urgent that brought His Reverence to me front door.' Annie's fingers twisted the piece of paper in her pocket.

'Give it to me, whatever it is your holding onto there,' he said.

'He found this.' She pulled out the note. 'Fr Kingston found this in the grotto.'

He tried to snatch the note from her hand but almost knocked over the hallstand.

'It looks like a note from Becky to Eamon,' she said.

'Eamon? What Eamon might that be? '

'Eamon Brennan, I suppose. How am I supposed to know?'

'You mean that stupid runt our David insists on hanging around with?'

Already she knew it wasn't going to go well for Becky. She never suspected Becky had the slightest interest in David's friend. Eamon often called for David on the way to the boxing and sometimes he would come inside while David collected his gear. Neither of them showed the slightest interest in girls but you never knew what was going on under your nose, did you? As far as she could tell, the boxing was what they lived for. And, more recently, the Fianna Boys.

As for Becky, she seemed shy whenever Eamon was around, seemed to avoid him in fact. That's why this note came as such a surprise. She had planned to have a quiet word with Becky alone but that wasn't going to happen now.

Isaac ate in silence as was his habit. Nothing about the events of his day, who said what or did what. Nothing about whether Jackson was in good or bad form. No talk about how many barrels he had produced. Such tittle tattle had dried up years before, had long grown stale as their marriage had settled into the humdrum of daily existence. Tonight, though, there was a particular edge to the silence. She remembered in her childhood the ominous silence on the lake behind the house, precursor to the treacherous whipping up of waves that kept the anglers off the water till the storm had passed.

They heard the front door being pushed in and a minute later Becky stuck her head into the kitchen where they were eating. She must have noticed the dark look on her father's face and she began to explain. 'The chain came off on the quays and I had to walk the rest of the way. I'll get David or Sammy to fix it for me.'

'I want a word with you when I finish me tea,' her father said and she looked at him as though trying to discern his meaning. She went out to the hall to take off her coat. Annie stretched her arm across the table and placed her palm on her husband's sleeve. It was a placatory gesture, an attempt to soothe the simmering anger she feared so much.

'Let me talk to her,' she said but even as she said it she knew her request was futile. He had always reserved to himself the right and duty to discipline his children. It was a duty he insisted he would exercise for as long as they remained under his roof.

'Keep out of this, woman. I'll deal with it.'

She had seen how he dealt with it in the past. His approach was direct, immediate and physical. *I'll teach them to know right from wrong* was his oft-repeated threat.

When Becky came back into the kitchen for her tea she found her father waiting for her with a piece of paper in his hand. She looked surprised when he handed it to her and said, 'I want you to read this out for me.' She must have known straight away what it was for her face went white.

'Read it' he said. 'Read it out. I want to hear.'

'Please, Father. I don't want to.'

'Did I ask whether you wanted to? Read it I say. Read it. Good and loud.'

Annie wanted to intervene but the expression on her husband's face was enough to silence her. With one last pleading look at her father Becky began to read aloud her own words.

'Eamon, I missed you. I was worried –'

'Worried sick. Go on, say it.'

'Worried sick.'

'And now would you mind telling your mother and father who the hell is this Eamon you're so worried sick about? Who it is has you in such a tizzy? Anyone we might know by any chance?'

Becky couldn't answer, couldn't meet his gaze.

'Did you hear what I'm asking you, girl? What's his name?'

'It's Eamon Brennan.'

'Eamon Brennan! That low-life little scut! Well, I'll tell you something now, missy. That pup will never darken my doorstep again. I'll see to that. And as for you, you'll have nothing more to do with him. That's my word and it's final. Now get yourself into the parlour and I'll deal with you there.'

'Don't, Isaac, don't.' Annie stepped between them. 'She's sixteen and a half for God's sake. She's not a child.'

He pushed her aside. 'She's a child of mine for as long as she remains in this house and she'll obey my rules.'

'I'm begging you, Isaac.' She could feel her own tears threatening. She had seen him beat David and viciously at that. But he had not taken his belt to Becky since she was little. It chilled her to see any of the children beaten.

She was forced to stand aside as Isaac followed his daughter into the parlour while removing the leather belt from his waist. 'I'll teach that lassie a lesson she'll not forget.' Helpless to intervene, she slipped into the dining room and stood behind the folding door to watch unseen. She saw her daughter cowering against the end of the piano. Grabbing her by the shoulder Isaac pushed her down across the arm of the settee and began to lay the heavy belt across the buttocks of his grown daughter. She cried out at the first lash, her flimsy cotton skirt and underwear no protection against the biting sting of the leather. As the lashing continued she lapsed into a low moan of acceptance. The crack of each stroke echoed against the high ceiling. When at last it was over Annie had lost count of how many lashes the poor girl had received.

'Get up to your bedroom with you and don't show your face again the rest of this day.'

Back in the kitchen Annie said, 'I wish you weren't so hard on her.'

'Don't tell me how to raise my own children, woman.' When he called her *woman* it was the drink talking.

'I'm sure there wasn't a lot of harm in it.'

'No? So why would she warn him to steer clear of her father? What does that tell you? When a daughter of mine is old enough to start thinking about finding a husband she'll marry a respectable man of her own religion. Not some low-class tramp out of a mud-floored hovel in Piggery Lane. That's not what I raised her for.'

***

In her room upstairs, Becky lay face down on her bed and wept into the pillow her bitter tears of pain and humiliation. She tried with scant success to suppress the rebellious thoughts that welled up and filled her head with resentment, even hatred, for her own father.

Twenty Five

Becky had been here a good twenty minutes and expected the train to come steaming into the station any minute now. She looked up and down the platform but there was still no sign of him. She had better start getting used to his chaotic approach to time-keeping. In Eamon's book one minute before or one minute after counted as perfect punctuality.

She wasn't alone on the platform. A man in a navy suit and bow tie was scanning the pages of the Irish Times and had just now consulted his fob watch. A young woman in the attire of a domestic servant stood staring at a poster facing her on the opposite platform showing a chubby child with a cup of steaming Fry's cocoa. Becky wondered about them, guessing that the man was heading back to his home having stayed overnight in Dublin and the young woman was on her way to work in Blackrock, Kingstown or Dalkey. The morning silence was broken when a woman with a brood of noisy children arrived and collapsed onto the wooden bench beside Becky. 'They have me heart scalded,' she said to Becky. 'Wouldn't you think they would be delighted with themselves, being took to the seaside, instead of squalling and squabbling like badgers in a burrow.'

Waiting for Eamon to appear, Becky had time to ponder her situation. The rest of her class were headed for the north side of the bay to celebrate their graduation. Looking at the clock, she guessed they were already on the tram rattling its way out along the North Strand towards Sutton and Howth. The train would take herself and Eamon in the opposite direction to Killiney. She had excused herself to her classmates, pretending her mother was sick and needed her at home to look after the younger ones.

The previous Wednesday they were handed their certificates at a special ceremony in the Hodgins Academy. Miss Hodgins had handed Becky a piece of parchment proclaiming that she had achieved a hundred words a minute in typing and a hundred and fifty in Pitman's. With a certificate like that in her hand she was as good as guaranteed a position in one of the more reputable firms in the city. Miss Hodgins never tired of reminding her girls that a qualification from the Hodgins Academy was a passport to respectability.

If Becky had lied to her classmates she had also deceived her parents. She was not too worried about the girls since they probably would not miss her anyway. She felt guilty, though, at the way she had lied to her mother and father, leading them to believe she was headed for Howth with the rest of her class while she was in fact going in the opposite direction in the company of Eamon Brennan. She prayed her father would never discover her deception. She had been given a final warning, one impressed on her with a cruel beating. She felt a shudder run through her when she remembered his words. 'I forbid you to have anything more to do with that scum. Defy me and you'll have cause to regret it.' He could hardly have been more explicit.

It was not just that Eamon was a Catholic, but the only work he had been able to find was the menial job of cleaning out the trams when they came in out of service, something her father would have learned from David. And to make matters worse the tramway workers were getting mixed up with the socialist agitator, Larkin. Her father was determined that no daughter of his would have anything to do with such unruly elements. She was well aware that she could be thrown out of her home and that no pleadings of her mother would dampen her father's anger.

Her thoughts were interrupted by the sight of Eamon running

towards her just as the train steamed into the station. She dragged open a carriage door as the guard raised the green flag. They scrambled on board as the whistle sounded and the carriage gave a gentle lurch. The train was moving. They were alone except for a man in the rags of a tramp who looked as if he had slept on the train overnight and had not yet woken. A sack, which must have held all his worldly possessions, sat on the seat beside him. Becky plonked herself onto the seat next the window and Eamon snuggled in beside her still trying to recover his breath. When he motioned her not to wake the tramp she was seized by a fit of giggles. As the train belched its way past the junk filled backyards of rundown houses Becky experienced a strong sense of escape – escape from the smothering strictures of family and convention.

Passing Lansdowne Road, Eamon told Becky he once met a man who played rugby. 'I hear it's a terrible rough game,' she said. When the train stopped at Booterstown Eamon leaned across her to point out the Bailey lighthouse, red and white on the other side of the bay. 'Where did all the water go?' she said. 'We could walk across the sand to Howth.' She remembered a Sunday in summer, when her parents had taken herself and David on the train to Bray. Now there was no one with her but Eamon, pointing, explaining and making her laugh. It's what made this trip so different, so thrilling, for a young girl in love.

***

The train chugged away into the distance, hugging the curve of the coast, and they turned to see the shingle beach below glistening in the mid-morning sunshine. They set off walking in the direction of the Vico Road, Eamon with Becky's picnic bag slung across his shoulder. He kept up a running commentary. 'Killiney's supposed to be nicer than Naples,' he said. 'Did you ever hear that?'

'I heard of Naples,' Becky said. 'It's in Italy.'

'I never knew that.'

They stopped to lean over a low wall and look at the railway below and beyond the railway the shoreline. Becky filled her lungs with the salty, seaweedy tang of the air wafting up from below. Behind them, on the other side of the road, the steep hill wore a rich veneer of furze and ferns. It was into this prickly wilderness they now went to begin the slow climb that would take them to the top and the panoramic view that Eamon had promised her.

They were about half way up, picking their path through a forest of perfidious furze, intoxicated by the heady aroma of its yellow flowers, when Becky felt her knees buckle beneath her and she slid to the ground.

'Can't go another step,' she said, holding her hand to her chest and heaving great gulps of air.

'Okay so, we'll take a rest,' he said, throwing himself down beside her.

To Becky It felt strange and wonderful that you could sink into this small cocoon of privacy, your own secret space in the wild scraggy vegetation and take in the whole sea vista from Dalkey Island to Bray Head while all the time you remained hidden from the rest of the whole wide world. You could almost believe that yourself and the boy you loved were the only two people alive in the universe. Making the most of their seclusion they drew close to each other and Eamon began to sing in a low voice, little more than a whisper, a song her mother had brought home before Christmas to practice on the piano. Now he was singing it in her ear, slipping her name in among the words.

I wandered today to the hill, Becky, to watch the scene below, the creek and the rusty old mill, Becky, Where we sat in the long, long ago.

'It's not Becky,' she said poking him with her elbow, 'it's

Maggie.'

'Who gives a hoot about Maggie?' he said. 'It's for you I'm singing it.'

She snuggled closer then as he sang another couple of verses for in reality she was thrilled to hear her name each time he used it. And he wasn't such a bad singer, either. Then, as he sang the line *When I said I loved only you, Becky, and you said you loved only me,* she could not stop herself turning her face to his and kissing him on the lips. It was a long and loving kiss. It created feelings within her that were strange and new. It dawned on her that they could kiss each other forever and without shame for there was no one to see and no one to judge. They could do what they wanted here – kiss, cuddle, wrap themselves about each other. Soon he was helping her get free of the garments that only seemed to come between them.

Becky froze. The voices of children coming nearer. They both stopped what they were doing – pulled apart. The voices grew louder. Becky buttoned up her frock and peeped above the bushes. She saw a party of chattering school children coming down the slope in the company of an adult. She held her clothing closed and waited.

Two ten year old girls stopped to stare. The teacher's voice called on them to keep moving and they were gone. Silence descended again on the quiet hillside. She prayed there would be no more interruptions. Eamon was laughing. 'Aren't you glad you weren't caught?' She wasn't sure what he meant but now that they were alone again she didn't mind that he was opening her frock. She only wanted to feel his mouth, strangely sweet and moist, against her mouth and the tingling touch of his hands on her body. He had never touched her like this before and she tried to dismiss the worry that this was the sort of thing priests warned against. She grew uneasy when she felt him doing things that at once thrilled and frightened her. Yet she did not push him off or try to stop him because she did not know enough to know what was right, what was wrong. She heard herself say, *are you sure?* But it was a half-hearted protest. So she allowed him, trusted him, tried to assure herself that he would know, even if she herself was ignorant of what was happening.

Afterwards, she relaxed and could even see the funny side, Eamon handing her her drawers, saying, 'Get these on you and make yourself decent.' They both giggled at that. He came out with the funniest things, Eamon did. It's what she liked about him, his ready laugh, his easy-going attitude, so far removed from the staid set-up she was stuck with at home.

After they had rested and relaxed in the sun they resumed their climb and at last came out beside the monument on the summit. They took in the vista for miles around and spotted on the ridge of a nearby hill a strange tapering chimney stack pointing to the sky. Then in the shade of the obelisk they sat and ate their sandwiches and drank tea from a flask. Becky had never felt so free and happy in her whole life.

***

In July Becky missed her period. She did not understand much about this kind of thing and decided she would say nothing to anyone. It was September before it crossed her mind that there might be anything wrong.

Patty had been a classmate in commercial college and now worked alongside her in the accounts department at Graysons. She was the sort you could discuss anything with.

'Sounds to me like you're preggers,' Patty said.

'What's that?'

'Janey Mack, Becky, how could you be so green?' She lowered

her voice and leaned across. *'Pregnant* – expecting a babby.'

Becky's heart missed a beat. Such a thing had never occurred to her.

'But that's impossible. You have to be married, don't you?'

Patty stared at her with an expression of utter disbelief. Leaving her typewriter with its sheet of virgin paper awaiting the first tap of the keys, she came over and put her arm around Becky's shoulder.

'Becky, love. How could you be so dumb? That Eamon fella. You've been letting him fool around with you. Am I right?'

She still didn't understand. What had Eamon to do with anything?

'Where have you been hiding all these years? If you're doing it with your fella, you're going to get caught sooner or later. I mean, what did you expect? You could've tried keeping your legs closed.'

Becky laid her head on the desk in front of her. Yes, they had been *doing it.* Eamon seemed to think there was no harm in it – just a bit of fun, really. Going through her mind was something the priest had said when she admitted to having bad thoughts. He had probed further and she had admitted the thoughts were about her boyfriend. More questions. How long was she going out with her boyfriend? Nearly a year. *And what age are you, my child?* Sixteen and a half. *Tell me, child, what are the prospects of you and this boy getting married?*

Not the slightest, she told him. Not for years anyway and even then who could tell? She heard the weary pain-laden sigh on the far side of the grill before he began to warn her about the dangers of *company keeping*. Company keeping was the greatest occasion of sin there was. If she wanted to save her soul from eternal damnation she must desist from going into the occasion of sin with a young man who did not have the slightest prospect of being able to marry her. Young men have but one thing in mind and that one thing will place her soul at risk of eternal damnation. Before imparting absolution he reminded her that Christ's forgiveness was entirely dependent on her having a firm purpose of amendment.

At the time she had no notion what that priest was talking about but it occurred to her now that this was the very thing he had been trying to warn her against – the danger of damnation and maybe also the danger of getting herself pregnant. She told Mr Grayson, Senior, that she was feeling awful and he sent her home. He was the most kindly of the bosses.

Her mother was in the kitchen as she left her bicycle outside the back door.

'My God, Becky, but you look like a ghost. Are you sure everything's all right.'

'I was feeling a bit under the weather so I came home early.'

Twenty Six

No matter how she looked at it or thought about it, she was in a terrible fix. She could not simply say nothing, tell no one, for her condition would soon be plain for all to see. Nor was there any question of turning up at work with an obvious pregnancy. Her mother, most likely, would be first to notice. And once her father was told, there was going to be ructions. Already she could hear him ranting and raving, not able to lay a hand on her because of her condition. He would want to know who the boy was. She would have to tell him and he would know then that she had defied his orders to have nothing more to do with Eamon Brennan.

There was not the slightest chance he would allow her to bear a bastard baby under his roof. Neither would he allow her to marry a boy from Eamon's background, dragging the Townsend name in the dirt. If she went ahead and married Eamon in spite of him he would kick her out, write her off, write them both off. He would never speak to her again – refuse to have her anywhere near him. Not that Eamon was in any position to marry anyone. The few paltry pennies he brought home from his ticket picker's job went to help his mother find food for seven hungry mouths.

With nowhere to go then, and an infant to look after, she couldn't imagine what would happen to her if she was put out of her home. Her fear was that she would end up begging on the streets. As for Eamon, how could she worry him any further with news like this? If his bosses discovered he had joined Larkin's union he would be out of a job on the spot. Already he had said that England might be his only option. She made a firm decision.

She would keep this to herself. Not even Eamon should know. She wasn't going to place this extra load on his shoulders when he had more than enough on his plate as it was.

Becky knew she was never going to solve this problem on her own. She racked her brain wondering who she could turn to. She needed someone she could ask for help or advice. Patty Nolan in the office was the only one who knew she was pregnant. Becky wondered if she could trust Patty not to go blabbing about the place, putting her job in jeopardy. But Patty was a girl who knew about things, and seemed to have a free and easy approach to matters of morality. If anyone could advise her now it was Patty.

'Tell me Patty, is there any way out?' There were just the two of them in the office for Miss Grace had gone off to meet her brother off the train.

'I didn't want to say anything before, Becky, seeing as you're a Catholic and your crowd are so sticky about things, you know what I mean. But there are ways and means, no doubt about that.'

'Keep going, Patty. I'm desperate to get out of this fix.'

'There's this young one living around the corner from me. We all knew she was playing the field and the fellas were queuing up to take advantage of the goods on offer. I needn't tell you she got herself in the family way. Anyway her folks set it up for her to see someone who could put her right. A little money changed hands and no questions asked. It's just a question of knowing where to go.'

For the first time in this sorry saga Becky felt a load lifting off her mind. A tiny gleam of hope had appeared on the horizon.

'You're telling me it can be fixed, Patty?'

'I can make enquiries if you want.'

'Find out anything you can.' Becky managed a weak smile.

***

A week passed before Patty said anything. Then, when they were alone in the office, she leaned across and whispered, 'Her name's Patterson.'

'Who?'

'She's what you're looking for. Lives over on your side. Might even be on your street. Ever heard of her?'

'Patterson, did you say? My god, Patty, you can't be serious. *Smelly Nellie!* 'Of course I know her. '

Everyone in Cowtown knew Smelly Nellie. *Smelly Nellie on her bike, lost her saddle and sat on the spike.* As a little girl Becky had joined the other kids in their mocking and taunting whenever they spotted Nellie Patterson approaching, rigid on her upright bicycle.

Not a lot was known about her but some of the stories were widely accepted as fact. Her father had made a packet importing cigars and all his money passed to Nellie. The rumour of inherited money, though, was hard to tie in with the reality of an eccentric who lived alone in a house going to wrack and ruin. As far as Becky knew, no one, not even her closest neighbours ever stepped across the doorstep. Accounts of the squalor she lived in were whispered with more than a little relish. *A pig-sty. A dump.* Whatever Nellie had done with her inherited wealth she had wasted none of it making her house a more attractive place to live in.

***

It was with some trepidation that Becky made her way in through Smelly Nellie's back gate and picked her way past an old wooden armchair blocking the path. She had made sure there was no one about to see her approach Nellie's from the back lane. She knew that Nellie was at home for the bicycle was propped outside the kitchen window. On the wall at the back of the house the meat safe had been left swinging open and as Becky passed a swarm of bluebottles took to the air. She knocked on the door and stepped back a little. A net curtain was drawn aside and Nellie's face appeared inside the glass.

She heard bolts being drawn back and a key being turned. The door opened and Nellie stood in the gap. 'Becky Townsend!' she said. They had never met or spoken to each other before now. This woman must know a lot more than people gave her credit for.

'Miss Patterson,' Becky said, 'there's something I wanted to ask you.'

'Come in, child.' She spoke with a husky voice and it occurred to Becky that she had never actually heard the woman speak before. Nellie led the way through the kitchen, heavy with the stale smell of gas and grease, between bundles of newspapers stacked on the floor, into a back room whose heavy curtains were open just enough to allow a little light in. The sideboard was piled high with the clutter of years. The cold dusty grate served as a receptacle for various pieces of discarded rubbish. On either side of the fireplace were two old leather armchairs worn and lumpy, into one of which Nellie eased her angular frame.

Becky took the other armchair, facing her. They sat looking at each other as though they were each waiting for the other to say something.

'I'm in trouble.' It was all Becky could manage. She was only stating the obvious – why otherwise would she be here? Nellie didn't ask her what kind of trouble so she added, 'I was hoping you could give me some advice. Tell me what to do, like.'

She felt Nellie's eyes boring into her brain as though reading all that was in there. Becky didn't have to explain a thing.

'How long are you that way?'

'I didn't have the curse for a couple of months.'

'Who did you tell?'

'No one. A girl in the office told me to talk to you.'

'What do you want me to do?'

'I don't know. Is there any way –? I don't want a baby. I'm only sixteen and a half and my father is going to throw me out when he finds out. I've nowhere to go. I'm –' She felt a tear on her cheek and put her hand to her face to wipe it away.

There was silence while Nellie studied her, seeming to ponder the problem. When at last she spoke she said, 'I might be able to do something for you. At any rate we can give it a try. That's all I can promise you. With the grace of God we'll get you on the right road again.'

Becky sat looking at her, waiting, hoping for some explanation. She wondered what form Nellie's magic would take. Would she feel the presence of the Evil One in the room while Nellie worked her spells? She thought it would be bad manners, ingratitude even, to probe further, so she confined herself to a single question – just one word. 'When?'

'Next week. Same time. Saturday. The sooner we get on with it the better – and the easier, too. '

She turned and reached for a half finished woollen scarf lying flat across a low table, the long smooth knitting needles at right angles to each other amidst a tangle of trailing red and green wool.

Becky let herself out the way she had come in.

Twenty Seven

The meat safe still hung open as Becky made her way up the narrow concrete path that led to Smelly Nellie's back door. The flies had departed leaving behind a writhing mass of maggots to continue their kind into another generation. She had taken good care no one saw her coming in since she put out the word she was playing with the Graysons team in Lucan. In fact, Lorna Ebbs had jumped at the chance to take over as captain for the game. Mr Grayson's private secretary was hockey mad and more than keen to demonstrate her captaining potential.

Becky gave an involuntary start as the door jerked open and she found Smelly Nellie putting a hand on her shoulder and dragging her inside. She followed her up the stairs and into a small bedroom at the back of the house. She saw a narrow bed along the opposite wall, a crumpled sheet covering the mattress. Lace curtains flanked by heavy drapes kept the room gloomy and private. Nellie must have judged she had enough light for whatever it was she was planning to do.

A roll of oilcloth stood propped against the foot of the bed and Nellie handed it to Becky saying, 'Here, cover the sheet with this.' When Becky had rolled out the oilcloth Smelly Nellie shoved a pillow under it midway along. 'You better get your frock and under-things off you. Then lay yourself down on the bed.'

Becky tried hard to think of Smelly Nellie as nurse rather than witch, yet neither image seemed to fit. Whichever was closer the truth she had no option now but to submit and obey. So she began peeling the clothes from her body and draping them over the back of a cane chair. She lay down as she was told on the narrow bed, her face towards the ceiling where a strand of spider's web hung listless in the motionless air. Her hand felt the grubby sheet protruding from beneath the oil cloth as she tried to shift her bottom where it was raised uncomfortably on the bulge of the pillow. She kept her eyes glued firmly on Nellie whose back was to her now as she opened the wardrobe door and scrabbled around on the top shelf before retrieving a long red knitting needle, sharp point at one end and blunt stud at the other. She drew it across her skirt to wipe it clean of dust.

Becky felt her legs being prised apart. She tried to relax but sensed she was about to be probed and recoiled at the thought of it. 'You just lie back there now and I'll try not to hurt you.'

'What are you going to do?' It didn't take a lot of intelligence to guess that the needle would play a part in whatever was about to happen. It was the only thing Nellie had in her hand.

'Close your eyes and think about the waves rolling in from the sea. That's it now, nice and easy. Nice. And. Easy.' Becky felt the probing point enter below and begin its slow stop-start journey through the secret passages of her body.

'The birds in the trees,' Nellie intoned, 'say tweet, tweet, tweet. Nice and easy does it.'

Becky let out a scream. 'It hurts, it hurts. Oh, Nellie, Miss Patterson, please stop, please. Please!'

'Nearly there now. Another minute and we'll be all done.' She never paused, ignoring Becky's terror and pain as she slid the needle in further, driving it and twisting before pulling it back and pushing it in again. Becky was on the point of passing out. Her insides were churning. She felt a piercing deep in her belly and cried out for mercy. She was stabbed, she was sure of it. Then she felt her whole inside convulse and an immense heaving sensation as though her innards were about to turn inside out.

In again with the needle. 'We've got it now,' she heard Nellie say. 'Yes, that did the trick. I'm certain we've got it. Not out yet but give it time. Mother Nature will take care of the rest. You can rest your mind, dear child. Your worries are over.'

Becky hardly heard. Could hardly move.

**

The ball came off the ground in a swerving flight and caught her right in the stomach, she said. She had to leave the pitch and sit in the clubhouse. Someone had fixed a lift back into town for her in a motor car driven by a man connected to the other team.

That was her story and it must have been convincing for her mother never doubted her for an instant. Her mother saw her clutching at her abdomen and the pain must have shown on her face for she insisted on sending her up to bed. 'Straight to bed with you. I'll bring you up a hot drink of something to help you sleep.'

Smelly Nellie had assured her that nature would take over and bring a close to the whole frightful episode and so indeed it worked out. During the night there was sticky blood between her legs and she took a candle to the bathroom to investigate. Sitting on the bowl she felt something coming, a convulsive movement that ended with a blob of dark congealed blood plopping into the water. She stood for a few moments looking down at it with a mixture of wonder and disgust before she pulled the chain. As the water swirled so too did her emotions.

She should have felt a great sense of relief and on one level there was indeed relief, relief that her ordeal was over. Yet she was sad. She knew that what was now gone forever had been a part of her, something of Eamon even and an embodiment of their love for each other. In different circumstances there might have been a handsome child to grow into a lasting reminder of a summer's day on the slopes of Killiney Hill where Eamon sang for her in words that even now thrilled her when she remembered.

When I said I loved only you, Becky, and you said you loved only me.

Twenty Eight

Mattis considered herself adept at putting two and two together. 'It's a matter of keeping your eye's peeled, your ears open, reading the signs and drawing your own conclusions.' The day she spotted young Becky letting herself in through the back gate, dragging herself along the cement path towards the house and then, as though seized by a sudden need, hobbling across to the outside lavatory, Mattis could tell there was something amiss.

Shortly afterwards she heard the girl coming up the stairs, one painful step at a time, on her way to her room. A few minutes later her mother was asking her how she felt and offering her something hot to drink. She couldn't help wondering what had happened but didn't consider it her place to ask. She might hear about it later and then again she might not. Meanwhile she could only speculate. Her speculation moved onto a new level when she had occasion to visit the outside lavatory set aside for the use of Plinny and herself. It was then she saw blood stains on the seat and around the rim of the bowl.

She mentioned all this to Plinny when he came back from the library but he seemed to think it was nothing to do with him and said she shouldn't concern herself. 'The Townsends are well able to look after their own affairs.'

During the night certain possibilities suggested themselves to Mattis. Try as she might she couldn't help making a link between what she had found in the lavatory with the furtive goodbyes she had witnessed with Becky and the boy at the back gate. There was no logical connection between the two but her intuition was powerful and insistent. There were things going on below the surface that Missus probably never suspected and Mattis would be falling down in her duty if she did nothing to alert her.

Mattis lay awake wondering how best to broach this delicate subject with her landlady. Just to remind Missus how easy it is for a young girl to get herself in trouble if she's spending so much time with a boy older than herself. She had seen it happen, young lassies barely out of school being led astray and taken advantage of by scoundrels. She pondered how direct she could be, for if she got it wrong and it turned out there was nothing to it, she would end up having stained the girl's character and opened a rift between herself and Missus. She decided on the indirect approach where you say nothing and yet say it all. A much safer option.

***

'I was lying awake in bed, couldn't get to sleep, Missus. You know the way something comes into your head, going round and round and you just can't get rid of it.'

Mattis was clearly in the mood for a chat, so Annie put on the kettle for a cup of tea and sat herself at the kitchen table opposite her lodger. She could see there was a story coming so she decided to relax and listen.

'I was thinking,' Mattis said, 'of something that happened back in the days when I was a slip of a girl meself, back home where I was brought up, on the edge of Clew Bay. There was a lassie there be the name of Bridie B. What the 'B' stood for I never knew nor I suppose did anyone else.

'She was a quare one alright, the same Bridie B for she had a name for picking up with men and letting them have their way, if you get me meaning. Maybe there was a bit of a screw loose in her, I don't know. The upshot of it was that she ended up with two wee children to care for and not a man in sight willing to take responsibility. One of the wee ones, the boy, had a twist in his foot that made him walk with a limp and the baby girl had a squint in her eye that made you think she was looking at someone behind you. It wasn't long before our lassie grew tired of being saddled with a couple of children to look after on her own seeing as she knew who the boyo was that was the father of the two.

'She was living in her father's rundown cottage and there wasn't room for the lot of them. And to make matters worse her oul' mother was threatening to put her and her children out on the road, for she barely had enough food to put on the table. There was nothing for her then but to go after the children's father and tackle him about his responsibilities for he had sworn black and blue he would marry her if she had a second child. A right scoundrel he must have been for didn't he renege on his promise, thinking he could have all the pleasure and none of the pain. And he a farmer's son, a batchelor and free as the wind.

'She threatened to denounce him if he didn't keep his word and make a decent woman of her and let the little ones have a father. After a lot of arguing and fighting the boyo changed his tune and told her he would marry her on the one condition. She had to get rid of the two kids. He didn't care what she did with them. She could leave them with her mother to look after, a woman, he said, with nothing else to do. Bridie B fought him over it but there was no changing this fella's mind. It was the children or him, he said. She would have to make up her mind. He didn't give a curse what she did. She could dump them on the side of the road for all he cared.

'The quarest thing about all this is that Bridie B gave in and said she would let the children go. She couldn't have been the full shilling, could she, for wasn't it the divil's own thing to do altogether? First she tries foisting them on her people but they tell her she's a pure disgrace and it's up to her to look after her little bastards if you'll pardon the language. So off with her then to the workhouse, walking the ten miles to Castlebar, where she spins them a yarn about her husband being dead from consumption and she and the children is starving. They say they'll take the eldest, the boy, but that she has to keep the wee girl and look after her.

'So here she is on the road back home, trying to carry the crying child in her arms, when she comes across a tinker family camped on the side of the road. What does she do then but ask the tinkers if they could do with a fine healthy little girl and they were more than welcome to have her. In them days the tinkers had a lot of use for babies for a baby was a powerful help when it came to begging. They took the child with no questions asked and handed it to a sixteen year old girl with long black hair who would easily pass for its mother.

'The same Bridie B was never to have a happy day after. The boyo married her alright the way he said he would, but the story went abroad about the way she abandoned her children for a no-good shleeveen who had never in his life done a real day's work. Before too many years had passed the rogue abandoned the miserable woman the same way she abandoned her own two children, her own flesh and blood. 'Tis said, and I can't vouch for the truth of this, that Bridie B set out on a quest afterwards, searching for the children she had given up. That she travelled the length and breadth the country, from one tinkers' camp to another in search of her little girl. All she knew for certain was that the child's name was Nora when she handed her over and that she was now a squinty eyed tinker woman, most likely with a brood of her own. Maybe she's still searching if she's not resting in her grave by now. 'Tis said her little boy went off to New Zealand with no wish to meet the woman who had given him up. And sure who would blame him?'

A silence followed, each of the women lost in her own

thoughts. Annie had found the story disturbing yet she saw no reason to question the truth of it and she pondered the strange fickle ways of human nature.

'Isn't it a funny world all the same, Mrs Mattis? Will we ever know what makes people do the things they do?'

'At least you'll never have any such worries about your own family, Missus. I'll bet there's not a place they go or soul they talk to that you don't know all about it the minute they get home.'

Annie thought about this a moment before saying, 'I've a lot to be grateful for, that's true enough. Everything's out in the open.'

Mattis said she was going down to Hickeys for her fags and Annie was left alone to ponder the true significance of the story she had just heard. She was well aware that everything Mattis said had a meaning or a message.

In bed that night it came to her out of the blue that the hidden message in Mattis' strange tale might have something to do with her own Becky. Now that Becky had left college and had a job it wasn't so easy to keep tabs on all her comings and goings. She knew her daughter had been mooning over that Brennan lad, David's friend, but she would hardly have persisted in meeting him after the beating she got from her father. None of the children dared defy their father.

Yet the more Annie thought about it the more the pieces began to fall into place. David had joined the Fianna at Brennan's suggestion. So Becky had told her and Becky knew everything David did for there was nothing they didn't share with each other. Becky was able to inform her that Brennan was trying to get David into the Volunteers. How would she know that? Did David tell her or was it Brennan himself told her?

There were other things. The amount of time Becky spent in front of the looking glass dabbing her face with her mother's powder puff. She knew Graysons demanded a high level of personal grooming so Becky had to pay attention to her appearance, but she wondered now if there was more to it than she thought.

There was something else that had been troubling her. Since they shared the same pack of towels that Annie kept in the chest of drawers she was more aware of her daughter's monthlies than maybe Becky realised. Last week she found the packet nearly empty. She had meant to say something. Now she felt sorry she hadn't brought it up.

Maybe it wasn't too late for a little chat with her daughter.

***

Poor Ruth and Sammy were gone up to bed, David hadn't yet come home from the Fianna and Isaac had slipped down to Cotters after tea for a quick glass of stout. They were alone in the kitchen, on hard kitchen chairs, Annie and Becky. It was at times like this that Annie wondered why they never made proper use of the comfortable furniture in the parlour.

There were tears in the eyes of mother and daughter. Tears of guilt and grief. What Annie had just heard had wounded her to the heart. She realised now how badly she failed her daughter. 'I didn't know it could happen to me,' Becky kept saying even when Annie put her arm around her and said, 'Don't blame yourself, love. How could you have known when I never told you nothing?'

Through her tears Becky had done her best to explain that she knew nothing of the facts of life and Annie was faced with the realisation that she had let her daughter down. Becky was right. She had never really spoken to her, never explained anything except maybe in riddles that the girl had clearly failed to grasp. It cut through her to hear that Becky had gone through months of agony and anxiety confiding in no one until the problem fixed itself when she had a heavy bleed just over a week ago.

'Well you've learned your lesson, child. That's all I can say. From now on you'll know not to take chances. Guard your virtue and ask the mother of God, the Blessed Virgin, to help you.' She was glad when Becky leaned in against her, resting her head on her shoulder. The poor girl must be relieved that the whole horrible thing was over and that she had been able to tell her mother everything.

Annie's thoughts drifted back to a distant day in a Wicklow valley when she had succumbed to the charms of a man she met only months before. That sunny July day when she yielded up her virginity with scarcely a thought for the consequences. So she knew well enough how it was and she could hardly hold herself up to Becky as a model of virtue. Preaching at her daughter made her feel a hypocrite. How could she insist on a moral standard that she herself had so dismally failed to meet?

Twenty Nine

She had never seen him like this before, so down in his boots, so unlike the cheery Eamon she had come to know and enjoy. It turned out he had very good reason to be dejected. When the bosses began to sack anyone who joined the union, Jim Larkin upped the ante by asking all the tram workers to walk off the job. In Conyngham Road where Eamon worked every man had obeyed the call – drivers, conductors, cleaners and general workers. Only the office clerks had stayed at their posts although some of these expressed secret support for the strikers. Eamon was left with no choice in the matter. Either you downed tools and stayed away or you were labelled a scab and that would have consequences too horrible to mention. Trams were abandoned where they stood in the middle of the road when the drivers walked away taking the steering handles with them.

'How are you going to manage with no money?' she asked him, understanding that this must be his major concern. She knew his family depended on what he could bring home. 'They say there'll be strike pay,' he said. 'They're only waiting for the money to arrive from England.' He didn't sound too cheerful, maybe thinking that the strike pay, if and when it arrived, would be a pittance. She squeezed his hand and laid her face against his shoulder. 'It'll not last,' she said. 'They'll come to some agreement.'

She had tried to put the best face on it for his sake but there was something troubling Becky that she wouldn't dream of telling Eamon, something that had less to do with the affairs of this world than those of the soul. No matter how she tried she could not rid herself of an immense burden of guilt. She had sinned in the face of God and every part of her cried out that what she had done must be the worst kind of sin. By putting an end to the tiny life forming within her she had broken the gravest of the commandments that God had handed to Moses on Mount Sinai. *Thou shalt not kill.* She, Becky Townsend, had killed her own baby. Without God's forgiveness she ran the grave risk of dying in mortal sin and finding herself cast among the damned to burn in hell for all eternity. Until she decided to confess her crime her immortal soul remained in mortal danger. There would be no peace until she went down on her knees and confessed her shameful deed to a priest of God.

She wondered how she was going to get through the ordeal. Some sins must be too great to merit God's mercy, too shocking even to whisper in the ear of a priest in the darkness of the confession box. Terrified of what the Parish Priest might think and say, for he knew her family well, she decided she would be better off going to the new priest. He was young, Fr Neilon, and seemed to take a special interest in the young folks. He was talking about revitalising the men's and women's sodalities with younger members. He even wanted to set up a new Catholic Boy Scouts. He was full of ideas. He sounded like the type of man she could easily talk to, someone who would understand what she had gone through.

The new curate's confession box was at the back of the church with his name, Fr N. Neilon, in large lettering above it. For serious sinners it was very much to their advantage to be back there where they wouldn't be seen. Then if the priest raised his voice in exasperation or reprimand those kneeling nearby would not be able to see who emerged from the box blushing with shame.

In the dark interior of the confession box Becky found herself gabbling her story – a story she had gone over again and again in her head, rehearsing what she was going to say and how she was going to say it. There were two parts to the story, two grave sins to be confessed. First, the fornication, a word she had found out was the word for doing it before you were married. Then there was the abortion, a word she had only just learned from her friend Patty who told her it was a criminal act as well as being the blackest of sins in the eyes of the priests.

'You could be had up in court, do you know that?'

'So now you tell me! Thanks a lot, Patty.'

'You needn't worry, pet, your little secret is safe with me. I'm not going to start spouting me mouth off. Wouldn't want you to end up in jail.'

When she finished her sorry tale of sin and suffering her mouth was dry and she half expected the priest to start shouting at her. She felt she was in for a severe telling off. There was silence, however, and she thought he must be too shocked to speak. She detected a movement on the other side of the grill and guessed he was trying to get a look at her. After a long silence he said, 'What age are you?'

'Nearly seventeen, Father.' Further silence. Then at last came the lecture.

'Do you realise what you've done to that little baby?'

'Yes, Father.'

'You've killed it, right?' She remained silent. 'But you've done something worse than kill it. You've sent it to Limbo. Do you know what Limbo is? The poor little babies in Limbo will never get to see the face of God. By your actions you've sent another little innocent to join that sorry throng. That's what makes what you've done such a heinous crime. Your sins have driven the nails further into the hands and feet of our Saviour. Think of his suffering.

Think of his sorrowing mother standing at the foot of the cross and see how she weeps for her dying son. Tell her you're sorry and beseech her to ask her Son to forgive you.'

There was a long pause and he seemed to be mulling over various possible punishments. At last he spoke again.

'Your sin has been great and your penance must be proportionate. You must come to the church to be purified. That means you will approach the altar after the early mass, kneel at the rail and wait for the priest to sprinkle you with the holy water so as to cleanse your body of defilement as Christ has cleansed your soul. If there are mothers waiting there for their churching you can wait with them. Otherwise come up on your own.'

'But father I'm working every day except Sunday.'

'Sunday morning then. Seven o'clock mass. Come into the sacristy before mass to let me know you're there.'

She was relieved to get it over with and walked with a lighter step than she had in a while. It hadn't been easy confessing but she was certain now she had avoided eternal damnation. The business of getting churched was something that could wait. The priest hadn't set any deadline. She would think about it in due course. She had seen women being churched, kneeling at the altar rail to be cleansed of the Devil's touch, for in the act of giving birth the woman was contaminated in some way with evil. That is why she needed a ritual cleansing. At least that is how it was explained to her by her own mother.

Already she foresaw that if she had to kneel at the altar rail to be blessed by the priest it was going to give rise to gossip. Someone was bound to recognise her and she would become the talk of the parish. People would ask each other if Becky Townsend had to be churched where was her baby? *We don't see any baby.* The holy marys of the parish would have a field day. And then, who knows, the whole thing would come to the ears of her father. That was the one thing she just couldn't bear to happen.

Her brother David was another consideration. David knew by now that Eamon was fond of his sister and didn't seem to mind too much. He was trusting by nature and tended to think the best of people but he would expect Eamon to treat Becky with the greatest respect. In a way she had let David down, betrayed his trust. There was a special sense of guilt about that, a feeling she found hard to nail down. There were three of them, David, Eamon and herself and their three-sided relationship had a complexity all its own.

She regretted she had not made her confession to the PP after all. His years of listening to the failings and weaknesses of his parishioners must surely have inured him to anything he might hear, however horrendous. He would surely have been a lot more understanding of human nature and human weakness. One way or another, she didn't think she would be running to confession too often in the future.

The more she thought about it, then, the less inclined she was to put herself through the humiliation of the churching ceremony. *He can go to the devil, that zealous Fr Naysh Neilon. There's just no way I'm going to kowtow before him in front of the Sunday mass-goers. I might as well wear a placard announcing I'm a dirty slut. No way. No way.*

Becky was determined never to implicate Smelly Nellie. She was a strange character, no doubt about it, but she had treated her with kindness and sympathy and without any mention of reward or payment. She was left with unexpected feelings of sympathy and gratitude for the eccentric Miss Patterson.

As for her own mother, she had never questioned Becky's version of events – had accepted without question the story of the miscarriage. Hardly surprising, seeing as her mother confided that she had miscarried three babies of her own – three that she knew of and the Lord knows how many she knew nothing of.

Thirty

David could see that Duffy was on a mission. He had set himself the task of saving the prostitutes, which meant of course saving them from themselves as well as from the soldiers who in the evenings poured out of the military barracks dotted around the city and headed for the seedier streets of the town. Here he was now giving David a detailed account of his most recent success which he referred to as the case of Bridgie Tipp. Duffy and David were sitting apart from the other men, drinking their morning tea in the middle of a sea of wood-shavings.

He first came across the girl huddled in a doorway next to a pub, in the company of an older and more seasoned woman and Duffy made it clear from the outset he was not a prospective customer. He was from the Vincent de Paul, he said, and if there was anything he could do to help they had only to ask. He was met with several ribald suggestions from the older woman. 'You should have heard the language,' he said to David. 'It would make a cat blush.' This was an education for David who had led a sheltered existence under the watchful eye of his mother and the rigid control of his father. Duffy was older than him by a couple of years and knew things about the world that David was curious to learn.

This then is the story David heard from Duffy:

'Will you look at him standing there, as frigid as the North Pole.'

I needn't tell you, Dave, no man wants to hear his manhood called into question. The young one sniggering away and the two of them making a mock of me but I offered it up for my sins and told the young one I was in a position to find her a respectable position if she wanted to take it up. The problem, Dave, is she was too much under the influence of that Maisie Golden. Afterwards, I made enquiries and discovered the girl had run away from her brother who had a fine farm of rich pastureland in Tipperary. After their father died the farm passed to the brother who then came out in his true colours as a tyrant. He made use of Bridgie and her old mother as unpaid servants who were there to serve his every whim. Young Bridgie soon grew tired of his bullying abuse and ran away to Dublin.

'I decided the best thing to do was write to the brother and tell him I was ready to meet him and discuss the girl's future. We met in Wynn's hotel and he turned out to be a pleasant enough man with a firm handshake and warm friendly air about him. My fears evaporated the minute I met him. I told him she was in moral danger from the kind of crowd she had got herself mixed up with, letting him draw his own conclusions about what I meant. I was careful, though, to keep her whereabouts to myself. I hinted that he might be able to come up with some kind of financial incentive to coax her back. He gave me a solemn assurance that the girl would have everything she asked for, all her entitlements and more.

'Next day I went in search of young Bridgie to give her the good news about what the brother had said, how she was going to be properly looked after. She had disappeared from her usual haunts. Not a trace of her could I find till I caught up with Maisie Golden and it's she who told me what had happened. Bridgie's brother had found her and told her he was taking her home. She didn't want to go but he promised her the sun moon and stars and eventually after a lot of fighting and bitter words he forced her to go home with him.

'To tell the truth, Dave, I was kicking myself for giving away so much information that he was able to track her down. On the other hand I was happy that the girl had been rescued, taken off the streets and back into the bosom of her family.

'Anyway I made sure to tell Devitt the whole story. Devitt, you know, has never approved of me going near Monto. *It's not what the Vincent de Paul is about,* he keeps saying. *We're about providing food and money to those who need it.* To tell the truth Dave, I don't care if they throw me out. If the V de P won't do it you and me can set up our own mission to wipe out vice in this city. I've got the plans drawn up.'

Duffy was different. When the other men on the job, the carpenters, bricklayers, plasterers and navvies all made for the pub after work Duffy headed straight home for his tea for he usually had something on afterwards, something important like benediction or rosary in his local church. Alcohol he regarded as the devil's curse. He was an odd-bod, Duffy, fascinating in his own way. Never shy of talking about his religious convictions and not seeming to notice how it made the other men uneasy. It certainly made them curtail their dirty stories whenever he was around.

There were a few years between David and Duffy but they were close enough in age to have much in common. Duffy shared his thoughts with David who, he decided, was in tune with his way of thinking.

One night then, without telling anyone at home where he was going David met Duffy to go with him to the centre of vice and iniquity that was Montgomery Street. On the way Duffy revealed his long-term ambition. He and a few likeminded individuals had set themselves the goal of cleaning up the city and bringing the whole scandalous situation to an end. In this they had the support of some of the priests in Gardiner Street. In his head he harboured a vision where the whole Monto area would cease to exist as a den of vice and women would no longer have to sell their bodies to gather a crust for their starving children. In the meantime what they needed was a hostel for fallen women and their babies. In the safety of such surroundings they could be led back to God through devotion to Our Lady.

At seventeen David had the barest understanding of what prostitution was in spite of mixing daily with older men and trying to untangle the double meaning jokes that were the common currency of their talk. Now he was being drawn into Duffy's vision, thinking he wouldn't mind being a part of it. There was something about being caught up in a great movement for change. It gave purpose and direction to one's life.

They met another man called Norrie in Gardiner Street and walked to the corner of Montgomery Street where they stopped in the harsh glare of a newly erected electric lamp.

David wasn't comfortable. It was so public. 'Why are we standing under a lamp-post?'

'It's the best place,' said Duffy. 'We'll soon find out who Maisie's teamed up with since young Bridgie went back home.' Norrie just smiled. He hardly ever did anything else. Already David was coming to think of him as *The Smiler*. Duffy pulled out his watch and said, she should be along any time now.'

Norrie smiled and whispered, 'Here she is.' David saw two women coming down Gardiner Street, one a mere girl, the other in her forties. Duffy was peering into the darkness to see who they were. 'God almighty,' he exclaimed, 'I can't believe it. It's not possible.'

The Smiler nudged David, 'It's young Bridgie,' he said. When she was close enough to recognise Duffy, Maisie said in a voice loud enough for them all to hear, 'Keep on going Bridgie, pay no attention to any of them feckers.' Duffy however stepped into her path. 'I don't give two hoots about you, Maisie Golden, you're past redemption, so just keep going, you're not worth the effort. I only want a word with young Bridgie here.'

'Tell him to eff off with himself, Bridgie. A pious gobshite is all he is.' Bridgie stopped to face Duffy with a defiant smirk on her face.

'So what about it Mister Duffy? Is it after a bit of female flesh you are, is that it? Well don't be shy so, for I'll not charge you anything you can't afford. And your two friends here – maybe I can do a deal for the three of yous.'

David felt his face blazing. The Smiler was struggling to hide the smile on his face. It was Duffy who spoke. 'Come along with me now, Bridgie, and I'll take you to meet Fr Devane. He has a job waiting for you with a respectable family in Rathmines. Full board, time off and money to send home to your mother. You'll not get a chance like it again. How does that grab you, Bridgie?'

She considered his words. 'Not now. I'm expected somewhere. I'll go in the morning.'

'No chance, Bridgie. The family must have an answer tonight. Come on, I'll go with you. No time like the present.'

'Ah, don't listen to him and his oul' guff,' said her companion. 'Look at them there will you, three holy joes and them only gasping for it themselves. Off with yous, off home with the three of yous like good little boys and don't be seen talking to the likes of us working women. Come on Bridgie, we're late as it is.'

Duffy made one last plea. 'Respectable family, excellent job, excellent position – '

All eyes were now on Bridgie, waiting for her answer. Her answer was defiant. 'Go tell your respectable family to stuff their excellent job up their excellent positions.' She burst out laughing and her dark eyes flashed from one to the other of the three men before fixing on David.

At that moment a strange yearning gripped young David. He had only a sketchy idea what went on in these sinful encounters between men and women but right at this moment he wondered what it would feel like to be wrapped in the arms of this spunky girl with the ringing laugh, the flashing eyes and hair the colour of coal.

Thirty One

Isaac had an easy relationship with Peter Jackson. The cooperage supervisor had a tiny office where he could talk to a man in private, drawing attention, say, to defects in his workmanship or complaints about his conduct. Like most men in the brewery, he had started at the bottom. In other words he had come in as a nipper, running errands for the men, boiling water for the tea and keeping the floor swept. Even so, he had started with the advantage that his father and grandfather held positions of responsibility in their day and were regarded as masters of their trade. Beer brewing ran in their blood.

Whenever Jackson brought Isaac into the office it was for a general chat which occasionally might include some friendly advice intended to promote his standing in the company. On this particular autumn morning Jackson wanted to alert him to something the men were saying.

Someone had recognised Isaac's young fellow in a part of town no respectable man would be seen dead in. Not just that but the lad had been deep in conversation with some of the loose women that patrol the streets in that locality. 'I've said it before, Isaac, it's a small town, this is.'

'Well I can tell you straight off they're making a big mistake there, Mr Jackson. There's not a chance in hell it was my David.'

'I'm only saying what's being said. I don't believe for a minute he was up to anything, your boy, just that you might want to know where the lad was seen, that's all.'

'Someone else, someone that looks like him.'

'I'm not saying it was or it wasn't him. If I was in your boots, though, I would want to check it out. It's up to yourself how you handle it.'

'Righto, Mr Jackson. I'll look into it. I sure as hell will.'

He called into Cotters on the way home. He was badly in need of something to steady his nerves. Foxy, behind the bar, brimming with excitement, asked him had he heard? Heard what? *Asquith is after declaring war on Germany!* Somehow Isaac was unable to enter into the general excitement all around him. Right now he was far more concerned with the conflict that lay ahead in his own home.

Faced with something he didn't know how to handle, the couple of pints would help him think straight. As the frothy liquid found its way to the farthest corners of his body he began to feel more assured about how he would deal with his eldest son. First he had to establish the facts. If David had a plausible explanation he wanted to hear it. If not he would need to assert his authority. He would not be held up to ridicule in his place of work. Neither would he be defied in his own household. David was a bit on the big side now to get the benefit of his belt, but if that's what was called for he would not hesitate to use it.

***

David was late arriving home. He hoped there wouldn't be too many questions about where he had been or what had delayed him. He had gone straight from work to Rutland Square to meet up with Eamon Brennan who had signed up for the Volunteers soon after they were launched. Now Brennan was putting pressure on David to join. 'You're getting too old for the Fianna, David. This is the big boy's army.' It was that word *army* that put him off. The boys of the Fianna could pretend they were soldiers – marching, drilling, carrying hurley sticks on their shoulders like rifles. Now suddenly they were faced with the real thing – and real rifles by all accounts. When David arrived at Volunteer headquarters he found a buzz of excitement. England declaring war on the Kaiser meant there was never a better time for Ireland to push for its independence.

'There's a fight ahead, David. Now's the time to get in.' He could see the logic in what Brennan was saying but at the same time he was aware of his father's absolute antipathy to anything that smacked of nationalism. He had joined the Fianna to keep Brennan company and now he was coming under pressure to join this new *Oglaigh na hEireann.* The only thing holding him back was his reluctance to go against his father, a convinced unionist who believed Ireland's best interests lay in maintaining its link with the Crown.

The moment he brought his bike in through the front door he was aware of the tension in the air. He found Becky alone in the parlour. She looked up from her book and made a pretence of lifting a glass to her mouth while pointing to the kitchen. He read her meaning straight away. *Their father had been drinking.* Well, what was new about that? David was starving and went into the kitchen to see if there was any food left. His father had just finished eating and was gulping tea from a mug. His mother sat facing her husband as she usually did while he ate, ready to jump and bring him more if he wanted it. She turned towards her son with a look of apprehension.

'So you're home?' his father said. There was already menace in his voice.

'I'm sorry I'm late. I had to go to drill practice.'

'Drill practice me backside. Don't give me any of your lies, boy. Where were you, I said.'

'Rutland Square. Fianna headquarters. They were talking about the war.'

'You're quite sure you weren't consorting with the whores in Montgomery Street?'

David was taken aback. His father had heard something. He saw his mother look down at the table, cringing.

'I told you, Father. Rutland Square.'

'So what's this I'm hearing then? You're trying to tell me you don't be hanging around with women of ill-repute? The truth boy. I want to hear the truth.'

His father knew something and there was no way out now. His best bet, his only option really, was to come out in the open and explain the whole thing. He had nothing to hide. He was glad Becky was in the parlour and the two younger ones in bed.

'Well, boy, I'm waiting. What have you to say for yourself?'

'Alright then, we went to Montgomery Street, Duffy and me, but we were only trying to save a girl. Duffy is planning a hostel to take the women off the streets.' His mother looked up and her eyes rested on his face as if trying to discern his meaning. He saw the distress in her eyes, in her drawn cheeks.

'Don't give me any of your lies,' his father said. 'Hostel me granny. There's only one thing takes anyone down them streets, one thing, and it's not to say their prayers I can tell you.' He pushed his chair back with a scraping noise on the tiles.

'Well, David?' said his mother.

'Answer your mother, boy. Explain to her why every Tom, Dick and Harry in the brewery knows what you're up to while your own father finds himself getting sniggered at behind his back. Answer me lad. What took you down to Montgomery Street? Who were them women you were seen talking to?'

David felt his temper rise. 'I told you, I told you. Will you not listen to me?' His father hoisted himself up from the table, his fingers fiddling with the buckle of his belt.

'It was all Duffy's idea.' David was desperate now.

"Who the hell is Duffy?'

'One of the carpenters. He asked me to go and help him.'

'So Duffy is more important to you than your own father and mother, is that it?' Isaac had his belt in his hand as he moved towards David. 'You tell the truth, boy, or I'll make you.'

David raised his arm to shield his face but the belt caught him across the hand and head. The pain was like a flame, searing. He saw his father raise his arm for a second swipe. For the first time in his life David realised he was as tall as his own father. He didn't have to submit to this humiliation. He was seized with a rage he could no longer control. He grabbed his father's right wrist, immobilising it in the air. His father tried to struggle free but David continued twisting his arm to make him drop the belt.

His father made a swing at him with his left hand but David reacted with the instinct of a boxer and blocked the blow. Then hardly knowing what he was doing for it was pure animal instinct, he struck his own father across the face. His mother screamed and Becky came running in. The two, man and boy, were locked in struggle as the women tried to drag them apart. The two stepped back glaring at each other with something akin to hatred.

'I've a mind to call the police,' Isaac said between huge gulps of air.

'Do that, so. Why don't you call them? Why don't you get your brother the Sergeant down here so you can let him know you're a drunk who beats up his wife and children?'

'David, don't,' said his mother, beseeching him on one side while Becky tugged at his arm on the other.

'Get out,' said his father. 'Get out of this house. You're no son

- 188 -

of mine. I never want to set eyes on you again.'

'Don't you worry yourself, Father. I'm going. I've put up with your bullying for far too long.'

His mother threw her arms around him. 'No David, no. He doesn't mean it. There's no need to go anywhere.'

But David couldn't back down now, couldn't allow the victory to go to his father. He went to the hall for his overcoat, opened the front door and wheeled his bicycle back out onto the step. Ignoring the crying and pleading of his sister and mother he mounted his bicycle and set off - back down Orkney Street with no idea in his head where he was going.

***

They were locking up for the night when David arrived at the Volunteer recruiting office on Rutland Square. After he watched the recruiting officer take down all his details and write his name into the register of members, David asked him if there was any chance he could bed down there for the night.

'What? Got no home to go to?' The officer, a low-sized youthful-looking chap in his mid-twenties with a country accent, regarded him with renewed interest.

'It's like this, Sir, I've had a bit of a flare up at home and I daren't go back there tonight.'

The officer put his hand on David's arm in a friendly gesture. 'You can call me *Conn.*'

'It's only for the one night, Conn. I've to be at work by eight in the morning.'

'I can't let you sleep here, David. Tell you what, though, I'll take you up to my sister's place in Ranelagh. Cathy's got plenty of space and she'll put you up, no bother. How's that sound?'

David struggled to control his emotion. 'That would be grand altogether.'

***

Becky was distraught. Her whole world was collapsing around her. David was gone and Eamon's situation was dire. Out of work now for the past year, Eamon was. He had been locked out of his job for refusing to renounce Larkin's union. Then when the strike petered out and the men were forced to crawl back, starving and defeated, he was told there was no longer a job for him in the tram company. He had been reduced to foraging for scrap timber, smashing it up and hawking it door to door as firewood. He was aware that many of those who bought kindling from him were driven by feelings of charity which did nothing at all for his own self-esteem.

Now he wanted to join the army. 'It's an answer to prayer,' he said. 'No sooner has the war started than the posters go up all over the place begging for men to join up.'

'You can't be serious.' Becky said. 'If you join the army you could end up getting killed and where would that leave me?'

'And if I don't, I'll end up a beggar and then where would you be?' Becky struggled to make sense of his logic. 'Don't worry, Becky love. I've no intention of getting killed. But I could sure do with the money.'

***

David and Becky had been life-long companions, sharing everything and supporting each other through thick and thin. He had been gone more than a week when she sat and discussed the situation with her mother.

'What's going to become of him, Ma? I'm sick with worry.'

'I'm sick too, love. Sick in my soul.' Her mother's face was

- 190 -

haggard and etched with lines.

'I would go and drag him home only I don't know if Father will let him back.'

'It can't go on like this, love. I'll talk to your father and try to make him see sense.'

'David is after joining the new Volunteers and he's going to their meetings. Eamon Brennan was able to tell me that.' Her mother was aware she was still going out with Eamon, in spite of her father's injunction to have nothing to do with him. 'If you can get around Father, I'll find David and make him come home.'

***

Becky was waiting for David when he came out of the Volunteers' Dublin headquarters. A poster in the window told her there had been a lecture on Britain's colonial history.

'David!'

'Becky! What brings you down here?'

'I've come to bring you home.'

She didn't have to do much pleading. She was surprised just how easily he gave in. He must have been missing his family as much as they missed him. He admitted that he couldn't go on accepting the hospitality of strangers and his apprenticeship wage did not permit him to find lodgings anywhere. She told him their father was strangely subdued and her mother had got him to promise to say no more about the row. If David came back home it would be a case of *bygones be bygones*.

***

Plinny came home from the library one evening with a book on chess. He was determined to teach himself the game. The problem was he needed an opponent to practise on. David said he didn't have the time. His sport was hurling and he was now team captain with his club. *Fág a' Bealach* were determined to become county champions either this year or next. All David's spare time would be spent practicing in the Park.

Becky said that sitting in front of a chess board for hours would drive her bananas and it was she who suggested Sammy. Sammy jumped at the idea and though he was only eight he proved a quick learner and more than a match for Plinny. Plinny continued to bring home more books on the subject and took the time to explain the various openings and defences to his apt pupil.

Plinny had found a fellow intellectual of his own calibre.

Thirty Two

Once Eamon had made his decision to join up it was a foregone conclusion that he would be sent to join the thousands of others who had already left for France to fight the Germans. But the army paid its men – that was the big attraction. For the first time in over a year he had a real job and real money. Now he was saying that when the war was finished they could get married and settle down together to start a family.

He had been stationed in the Curragh for the past six months and they both knew that once his basic training was over he would be boarding a ship for the battlefields of France. Yet when the orders came at the end of June for the men to mobilise it came as a shock. She hadn't expected him to be going so soon but now that his departure was imminent she did some serious thinking. Eamon would arrange for half his pay to be sent directly to his mother and father who were struggling to survive. It would help put some food into the mouths of his younger brothers and sisters.

Becky thought about this. She did the arithmetic and realised that half a soldier's pay would not go very far with a family of seven growing children. She had a better idea. She knew that the wives of soldiers were paid an allowance while their men were serving at the front. In fact the *separation allowance* had just been increased to three shillings and sixpence. If she and Eamon were married the allowance would come to her as his wife and she could then pass it on, a veritable fortune, to his impoverished family.

It seemed an obvious step to take but she waited till Eamon

was home on leave before broaching it to him. He was wildly excited and said they should do it now, right away. Her common sense told her she could never tell her parents, and her marriage would have to be kept a secret in Graysons. Otherwise they would expect her to resign.

She sought out the Jesuit priest who baptised herself and David eighteen years before and found him more than amenable. He agreed to do it as discreetly as possible. On the morning that Eamon was due to report back to his barracks, he and Becky made their way to Gardiner Street church where Fr Coyle led them to a tiny oratory in the priests' private quarters. There they were joined in wedlock, becoming husband and wife. The kindly priest had arranged for the housekeeper to serve them a hot fry for their breakfast and produced a little cake which he said they should cut together. They hadn't acted a minute too soon for a few days later she got word that Eamon's detachment was to be moved out before the end of the week.

***

She found his letter sitting on her desk at eight thirty on a Monday morning. She knew straight away what it was. Brown army envelope, thousands of them dropping into people's letterboxes all over Dublin, all over the country. A hundred thousand young Irishmen had set off to fight the Germans in France and Belgium. Often she felt a surge of pride that her Eamon was among them, serving his country and fighting for the freedom of little nations like Belgium. The day he left for the war she had gone to join the hundreds gathered along the quays to cheer the soldiers as they marched by on their way to the ship.

She stood at the bottom of Blackhall Place and pushed her way to the front to get herself a better position. She saw him alright – managed to get a glimpse of her Eamon as he marched by, smaller than his mates but with head held high, a purposeful and determined look in his brown eyes. Alongside Eamon, a boy with flaming red hair who could only be Tommy Joyce, the lad he had befriended in the Curragh. Seeing her new husband heading for the front line in France, Becky experienced a storm of conflicting emotions. On the one hand she was proud as punch to see him stepping it out as his contingent marched along the Quays. On the other hand she couldn't shake off a sense of dread which clutched at her heart, suggesting the unimaginable.

Though he hadn't seen her that day, she had written to tell him how proud she felt at that moment. He was fighting for king and country and John Redmond had promised that as soon as the war was over Parliament would activate the bill allowing the Irish to rule themselves. That should keep both himself and David happy.

A full month had gone by since and Becky's feelings of pride and elation had been replaced by a sense of loneliness and fear. If Eamon thought a letter saying *'Things is grand out here. I don't want you to be worrying yourself'* was going to set her mind at rest then he knew precious little about how her mind worked. A letter from the war telling her that things were not as bad as she might think could mean only one thing. Things must be an awful lot worse than she thought.

Her father brought home the Irish Times every day. Everything about the war was positive and reassuring. The Germans were bogged down, every German offensive was turned back, everywhere the enemy was sent scurrying, no match for *our boys*. Almost a year after the Kaiser's treacherous invasion of neutral Belgium it was only a matter of time now, a couple of months at the most, till the aggressor was forced into an ignominious retreat and ultimate surrender. Already the Axis casualties were many times those suffered by the English and French. Becky had noticed however that no actual figures ever appeared in the paper, something that made her think.

Her father accepted that the Irish papers took most of their reports from war correspondents working for the news agencies. Yet he himself was only too willing to believe what he read. In the beginning the war was supposed to be over in weeks. Now they were talking about months. She was hearing about soldiers being injured or even, God save us, killed. Everyone knew someone who had got that dreaded army envelope through the letterbox with its grim message inside.

They all knew about Mrs Leahy on Ashford Street. It was only a week since she got the awful news. Her husband Jack, a train driver on the Great Northern. Only thirty one, he was, and she now left with four young children to drag up on her own. Another family on Sitric Road the week before that. An only son. Who could bear that?

Young men were dying out there and the rumours going around said they were dying in their thousands. She didn't care what the papers said, she was worried and felt she had good reason to be. She missed him dreadfully, her Eamon. She missed his wayward, easy-going, jokey way with the world. So different from her own crowd, her stern upright father, her serious minded brother all caught up with this Celtic Revival nonsense. Her mother, conniving to pull the wool over her husband's eyes, telling him the children were gone to the service in St. Paul's when she had sent them to mass instead.

She thought of Mawzer, back from the war with his brain scrambled. Wednesdays when the women and children came to their doors to hand him the buckets of slop to be thrown in the back of his little cart. Wednesdays when Mawzer entertained the street with scenes from the war.

'Show us how you shot the Hun, Mawzer.'

And Mawzer, with his donkey in the part of the enemy soldier, would re-enact his daring dash to the enemy trenches and his tussle with a Boche officer before killing him with his own Mauser pistol. He never grew weary of performing it before a fresh audience on each of the streets that made up his round. How they cheered and laughed at the witless fool.

Becky's mother forbade her children to mock the man. 'It's a mortal sin to laugh,' she said. 'Look what the war is after doing to him. I used to see him before the war, a clerk in the Corporation and a nicer gentleman you would never meet.'

'Why did he go to the war, Ma?' Sammy's eyes were wide with interest.

'It's that horrible Kitchener I blame. And them recruitment posters up all over the place enticing fine young men to risk their lives for God only knows what.'

'It's shell shock, Sammy,' Becky said. 'That's what left poor Mawzer fit for nothing better than collecting the slops for Hartley's pigs in Manor Street.'

Whenever Becky came across Mawzer she found her mind turning to Eamon. There was nothing she wanted more than to have Eamon back home safe and sound. She began to think it might not be bad at all for him to suffer some minor injury which meant being sent home to recover. That way she could nurse him back to health and the war would be well over by then.

Thirty Three

Dear Becky,

I am writing this to tell you the good news. The captain told us this morning we'll have it all sone up in a month or two. We sit here waiting for the Huns to make some move but it looks as if we'll be waiting. They must be getting ready to pack up and go home. I can tell you we won't be sorry to see the back of them. I used up all my fags. Any chance you could send me a pack? I hate cadging smokes from the other fellows. I do be dreaming of Dublin and yourself all the time. I love you Becky and I can't wait to get back there to see you again. Thank you for all your letters. I showed your picture to the other lads and they said I was a lucky bugger. Keep writing won't you.

Yours sincerely, Eamon XXX

Becky was going to be worried anyway, no matter what he told her. That's why he hadn't mentioned a word about what happened yesterday. It's a miracle he was able to write at all seeing he was still in such a state but Marnell was the devil for handing out the sheets of notepaper and nagging them all into writing home.

He even told them what to write because some of these stupos had never written a letter in their lives. The sergeant had been taught by the Christian brothers and passed his Intermediate Certificate with honours. He read the letters and tore them up if he didn't like what he saw. 'No whinging,' he kept shouting. 'Tell them how happy you are, that's what they want to hear.' Even if he wanted to tell Becky what happened Tommy Joyce, Marnell wouldn't have let him. Not that he had the words for it. Or the stomach.

It had been quiet all day. No firing from the German line apart from an early morning volley when a maxim hidden in an old barn had swept the Dublins' trenches with a hail of fire, side to side in short bursts for several minutes. A sort of early morning reminder that the Boche were still there. After that, silence. And what a glorious silence it was. The birds were singing. Larks he thought they were. That's what the know-all from Irishtown who brought up the rations said they were. Funny how there could be any birds at all when every tree for miles had been blasted by explosions. All you could see were the ghostly skeletons that reminded him of Pine Forest after it was burned. The birds were singing alright and the sun was shining. The bottom of the trench had dried out in spots and the lads were in good form. They drank tea, passed cigarettes, laughed at each other's funny stories and when the sergeant came by they let on to be cleaning their weapons. Life could be a lot worse. Just one of those slow days – one of those days when a fellow could indulge in dreams of home and the girl he left behind.

'You would be longing for a bit of action. Just to liven things up, like,' Tommy Joyce said, popping his head above the parapet for a quick scan of the terrain. 'Peaceful as the bog in Spiddal.'

'Keep your head down, bogman, unless you want to lose it,' someone shouted. 'Maybe it's a shell you want in here on top of us, blowing the shaggin lot of us to smithereens.'

'Just relax and make the most of the lull, Tommy.' Eamon felt protective towards his friend. Tommy Joyce was a full year younger than himself and didn't have a lot of savvy. Still Eamon didn't like to hear anyone calling Tommy a culchie. Although they were from different sides of the country, they hit it off from the day they met in the barracks where they had both gone to enlist, in the same regiment, battalion and company. Here they were now, together in the same trench less than two hundred yards from the German front line.

'Did I ever tell you about the night the divil showed up in Galway, Eamon? Did I tell you that one?' Tommy grabbed him by the shoulders to get his attention.

'Something tells me I'm going to hear it whether I like it or not.' He was well used to hearing Tommy's far-fetched tales.

'The mission was on and the church packed to the door and the missioner above in the pulpit and he giving out yards about the dances. That's where the divil does be in his element, says he. Ould Nick himself does be at the dances right enough and him trying his level best to trap souls for hell.

'And he told a story, the priest did, and he swore it was the God's truth, he did. He said he knew of a young lass in a place not a thousand miles from Galway city who found herself dancing with this good-looking fellow she never seen before. They stayed dancing the whole time for she was getting kind of fond of him if the truth be known. She falling for him and him asking could he walk her home after the dance like. Well she was most inclined to say yes since he seemed such a nice gentleman an' all. And sure what harm would it do like, to walk the mile or two out the dark road to where she was living?

'But anyways, didn't she happen to drop her hanky and when she bent down to pick it up what did she see but your man's feet. Except they wasn't feet at all but cloven hooves, the likes of what you might see on a billy goat. Well, up with your lassie and away out of that dance hall as fast as her two legs could carry her and away home with her to her ma and da – never stopped running till she reaches her own front door. And divil the dance did that lassie ever go to for the rest of her living days.

'That's the story the priest told the people that night in the church in Galway and ne'er a one of them doubted the truth of it for wasn't it the missioner himself that told it.'

'Ah, come on outta that,' said Eamon. 'What kind of a gomalloon do you take me for? Surely to God they're not all such suckers in the County Galway?'

A few of the boys had shifted closer, drawn in by Tommy's drole yarn. They kept an eye out for Lacy who hated any kind of time wasting. In the corporal's book the devil makes work for idle hands and there was always work to be done keeping those stinking trenches habitable.

'There was this smart-aleck down the Claddagh,' said Tommy, the bit between his teeth, 'a right boyo he was too. Wild horses wouldn't have dragged him near the mission. But he heard the story and made up his mind to go to the dance-hall in Galway just as soon as it opened again after the mission was over. He had a special pair of shoes and them for all the world like the divil's hooves.

'The very first gersha he asked up for a dance was a hoity-toity young lassie outta the Queen's University. From Limerick she was. So there they were dancing away and your man takes his comb out of his breast pocket and straight away drops it on the floor.

'When your lassie from Limerick looks down and sees your man has the divil's feet on him, she lets fly and gives him the most ferocious kick in the shin, she does. That cured him of his tricks for a while I can tell you that.' One of the boys threw a smelly woollen sock, missing him by inches. Tommy jumped up on the fire-step to take his bow before turning to glance in the direction of the German line.

Eamon never heard the actual shot or, if he did, failed to connect it with the scene unfolding beside him. Time and motion slowed as he saw Tommy's head twisting backwards and to one side, his body folding as a fountain of blood erupted from the hole in his forehead. He froze in horror. This was death close up. As he looked at the body of his friend now crumpled in the mud it seemed to him that the hole in Tommy's head was a gaping cavern out of all proportion to the bullet that had made it.

That night as Eamon pulled his blanket about him on the damp floor his eyes explored the reaching pattern in the blood-stained clay, all that remained now of young Tommy Joyce. He reached in his jacket pocket and pulled out the crumpled muddy envelope he had carried around for months hoping he would never, ever, have to use it. The address, in Gaelic script, scratched out in Tommy's lip-biting lettering.

Bríd Bean Uí Seoighe, Bóthar na hInse, An Spidéal, Gailleamh.

'It's for me Ma,' Tommy said as they swapped letters soon after their arrival at the front. His father had drowned with two others as they tried to make it back to land in their currach in a sudden squall.

Eamon remembered now that his own *last letter* was still in Tommy's pocket when they stretchered his body away to be buried. It would be found and held by Sergeant Marnell and sent on its numbing way if and when he himself met the same fate as his now silenced friend.

He was going to miss Tommy – miss him a lot. With Tommy around you could almost forget. They had stuck close together from the day they found themselves trapped in this hell-hole, encouraging and supporting each other with comradeship and talk of home. Faced with the constant threat of instant extermination they had offered each other comfort of a sort. There were times when together they had laughed at the funny side of death, at the hysterical, hideous comedy in which they found themselves. And there were times when alone they sat down in the dark silence and wept when they remembered all that they had left behind, all the tantalising promise, the hopes and dreams of their youth.

Thirty Four

Eamon hadn't bothered his brain about religion for years. Hadn't been next or near a church since his Confirmation day. But Tommy's death made him think. The suddenness of it. The random way it happened. It could as easily have been himself. That's the thing about this war lark – you're lucky or you're unlucky. You live or you die. You kill or you get killed. He thought about all the boys and men of his own company who had arrived with him in this war-mangled corner of France. All now gone. Some carted away for a makeshift burial, others left for the rats in a shell crater too dangerous to reach. A sudden realisation that he was the only one left of his original company. Around him now the recent arrivals, ruddy cheeked boys and some older men, all lined up for the slaughter. An absolute miracle he had escaped so long. It could only be a matter of time.

He found himself thinking about things that would never have crossed his mind before. Where was Tommy now, that sort of thing. Not hell, for he had just left this blasted hell for something better. If there was a Heaven, and he had been assured there was, that's where Tommy must be now.

The week after Tommy died had been hell on earth. Constant bombardment. Shells raining down, some dropping short in no-man's land, a lot of them close enough to do real damage if you got in the way of a piece of shrapnel. Like the boy yesterday who died in his arms. Half his head blown away by the explosion. The poor lad couldn't have been more than seventeen.

'I'm hit, Eamon. Is that you Eamon?' Face filled with fear. 'I'm afraid, Eamon, I don't want to die. I'm too young to die.' He saw the boy's pleading eyes and felt his finger nails dig deep into his wrist. 'Don't let me die. I'm afraid. I want me Ma. D'you hear me? Someone tell me Ma I'm hit.'

The slippery brain glistened where a shard of skull hinged loose on a flap of skin and hair. 'You're okay, pal. No one's going to die. You just take it easy till they get a stretcher up here. They'll have you out of here before you know where you are. You're going to be just fine.' What was the lad's name? Danny, that was it. Only just arrived. 'You'll be fine, Danny, believe me.' *Believe me.* His own hands, treacled red, accused him of lying. Danny's drowning eyes blinked once more before seeming to fix on something far away as he slipped into a state of blissful unknowing.

The moment was marked by another shell-burst. Another shower of rocks and earth pummelled down. A lump of rock struck him on the shoulder. The bombardment was relentless, merciless. Did they not care about the lad expiring in his arms? Did they not know what they had done to this young boy? It no longer mattered whether they knew or cared, for when he looked again he saw that Danny had passed on to some other place where the screams of dying men were the stuff of past nightmares.

As he lay awake in the still night it occurred to Eamon that he ought to make his confession. He had left it far too long. There was no way out of here alive. He believed in God. He believed in Heaven and Hell. He knew he would have to stand before his Maker. His luck could not hold out much longer. When his number was called and he found himself answering for his deeds before the throne of God it would be too late then to start thinking about the state of his soul.

Fr Deane came by about nine next morning with the usual cheery greeting for each of the men. 'Quiet so far this morning! Anything I can get you? You'll let me know now won't you?'

Always unflustered, always the part in his smart captain's uniform even if the boots and gaiters were caked in muck. You wouldn't want to be deceived by appearances though. The men knew this was no namby-pamby priest. This man was real, able to muck it with the lads, go into action with them, reach them before anyone else when they fell. Fearless in the face of fire. The men felt easier with a priest like that alongside them for courage and consolation.

'Father, I was thinking I ought to – to go to confession.' The words were out now and there was no going back.

'No bother, Eamon. Just sit there on the ledge and I'll sit here beside you.'

Eamon looked around. All the men were busy shovelling out the dirt and debris that made the trench near impassable. He saw someone toss a dead rat in a great arc in the direction of the Germans. No one paid any attention to himself or the chaplain, who had placed a long purple strip around his neck like a skeletal scarf.

'I don't know how to start, Father. It's years since I went anywhere near a church.'

'Don't fret yourself, Eamon. You've always tried to do the right thing by everyone, am I right?'

'I suppose so, Father. But I think I committed a few mortallers – sins, as well. Like when I was with Becky, you know what I mean. I didn't mean any harm. You know yourself how it is.'

'Jesus is always ready to forgive. You know that don't you? Think no more about it. When you get out of here you'll try to live a good life, am I right?'

'Yes, Father.' He felt teary and didn't know why.

'Say a wee prayer for me, Eamon, when you get a moment and

that can be your penance. How long have you been out here now?'

'Since July, Father. Over four months now.'

'You should be due for leave shortly. I'll see if I can put in a word for you.'

'I can't wait to see how things is back in Dublin.'

'Did you say you got married? Your girl will be pleased to find you still in one piece. Leave it to me, lad.'

He must be the bravest man ever lived, Fr Deane. Didn't seem to care whether he lived or died. He would rush out to a fallen soldier, some fool who had trusted too much in the shelter of a broken wall only to be laid low by the lethal spray of a German Maxim. The priest would bend over the dying man, murmur prayers in his ear and with his finger rub the holy oil on the poor devil's forehead.

A week or so after Eamon made his confession Corporal Lacy handed him the official form granting him seven days leave away from his unit. The whole thing was typed out, the date he would leave and the date he must be back at his post, as well as warnings not to discuss front-line operations with anyone at home. He was to leave the trenches on Thursday morning. In his head he rehearsed the journey, the boat to Folkestone, the train from Euston that would link up with the mail-boat at Holyhead. The boat-train waiting on the pier in Kingstown to take him into Dublin. As he scribbled a quick note for his mother and another for Becky he wondered if she would try to get out to Kingstown or whether she might be waiting for him on the platform in Westland Row.

He was wrenched from his reverie when out of the silence of the Sabbath the German big guns opened up with a sudden barrage of shellfire. He had long learned that Sundays were no different from other days when it came to slaughtering your enemies. The Germans, whether through trial and error or mathematical calculation, had found a way to place their fire exactly where they wanted it. And where they now wanted their shells to land was right in the Dublins' trenches. It started at nine in the morning and three hours later showed no sign of easing off.

The Irish were taking a lot of punishment and some shell-shocked men were fleeing their trenches altogether. They were darting out into no-man's land seeking the dubious shelter of the deep craters. It was a crazy thing to do for nowhere was safe. A shell might explode anywhere and when it did the shrapnel shot in all directions, searing pieces of burning metal guaranteed to cause deadly damage to a living body.

Eamon, crouching low behind the steep wall of the trench, saw the chaplain and his orderly go by several times that cruel Sunday morning. Fr Deane moved up and down the trench trying to give the men all the courage and consolation he was capable of. In Eamon's segment he came across a wounded man, knelt beside him, motioned Pettigrew to open the bag and pulled out wads of bandages and cotton wool to try and staunch the bleeding until such time as the medics arrived. Later he sent his orderly back down the supply trench to stock up on bandages, ointment, the various medications they would need.

Meanwhile an officer Eamon recognised as Lieutenant Trant from Rathfarnham went out into no-man's land to round up the men hiding in the shell-holes and order them back to their posts. Eamon saw him go and couldn't believe his eyes. A lot of the officers were brave men and there were stories to prove it but this had to be the height of madness. Lt. Trant was out in the open and German snipers were waiting for just such an opportunity. If a sniper didn't finish him it was likely an exploding shell would do the job.

It was a sniper that got him. Eamon heard the report of the rifle and saw Trant go down. The officer lay out there in the open, nothing to offer cover apart from a nearby mound of thrown-up earth. Often in such a situation a man was left to his fate. Bad enough one dead or dying without offering more targets for the German rifles. No point committing suicide. Eamon viewed the scene from the safety of his firing position.

Two stooping figures dashed across his line of vision. He recognised Fr Deane, closely followed by his orderly, Pettigrew, who with one hand clutched the medical bag and with the other tried to keep his helmet from slipping. From his position on the fire-step he could see part of the fallen officer's uniform and realised there must be a clear view from the German positions. German marksmen watching and waiting just as everyone on Eamon's side was watching. A bizarre drama being played out before an awestruck audience of two parts.

It was when he saw the two men trying to drag the limp body between them that Eamon Brennan went over the top. He hadn't taken any time to reflect on what he was doing. He was driven by some primitive urge to get out there and lend a hand. Tripping, slipping, several times almost falling, he got to within a dozen paces of where the two men were dragging the lifeless figure, its boots trailing the ground.

He was almost there when the shell burst.

***

It was days before Eamon heard the full extent of what had happened. The nurses refused to talk about it, shushing him, telling him to be sensible and rest. It was the man in the bed opposite, Jennings, who gave him the details, whispering. Both the padre and the officer he was trying to rescue had been killed outright. Messy beyond belief. Some limbs were found scattered, nothing else. Pettigrew had lost a leg. He was right now in another room of this so-called hospital.

Eamon lay back against the iron bars of his bed and tried to take it all in. He shouldn't have been shocked. He had grown used to violent death and injury. Dying had become a matter of daily life. And yet when he thought of the way this priest had met his death, giving himself totally in a futile attempt to help a fellow officer, he was filled with unfamiliar feelings, feelings of loss and admiration, of anger and disbelief, of pain and frustration.

Later he tried to piece together the fragments of memory. The shrill momentary whistle of the approaching shell, the blast flinging him back several yards, the eruption of earth and stones which seemed to pause a moment in mid-air before coming down on him like hell's rain. He had been oblivious of the pieces of jagged metal buried in his leg until he woke up in the field hospital.

That night, when nurses and doctors had gone to their beds, Private Jennings, propped on a pair of crutches, dragged himself across the floor and slumped onto the edge of Eamon's bed. He fumbled in the pockets of his dressing gown and dug out a packet of Woodbines. He took out two of the skinny fags and handed one to Eamon. He first lit his own and then with the flame flowering towards his coppery finger and thumb he leaned in to light Eamon's. They each drew long and hard on the life-giving, pain numbing nicotine. It was a risky thing to do, to smoke in that old wooden building commandeered as a field hospital a few miles back from the front line. It was a small act of defiance.

Jennings used both hands to lift his left leg onto Eamon's bed, the leg with the foot missing. And with eyes fixed on the space where the foot had been he began to sing in a croaky voice that only Eamon was meant to hear.

With your drums and guns and guns and drums, hurroo, hurroo
With your drums and guns and guns and drums, hurroo, hurroo

With your drums and guns and guns and drums
The enemy nearly slew yeh
Oh me darlin dear, yeh look so queer
Johnny I hardly knew yeh.

There was silence then as if the singing of that song had given each man permission to retreat to an inner space where a soul was free to think subversive thoughts that could never be given voice in the cold light of day.

'I saw a young boy, not more than seventeen he was,' said Eamon, 'and he was crying for his mammy. I held his hand while he died.'

Jennings said nothing. As if he was turning this information over in his head. Then he spoke.

'I saw a poor fella in a terrible state altogether, shaking an' all, and he walked up to his lieutenant and told him he couldn't take any more, he wanted to go home. We was all watching, you know, to see what way the officer was going to take it. "Sonny," he says, with his hand on the lad's shoulder, "you do just that." The lad said nothing for a while, didn't budge. Then he says, "You mean that, Sir? It's alright then? I can go?" The officer said, "You want to go, off with you."

'Well the young fella goes over to pick up his kit and turns to head off with himself with ne'er a glance to right nor left. This officer, he takes out his Webley – out of its holster – aims the gun and puts a slug in the back of the boy's skull. And that's as far as that poor bastard ever made it on his way home to his folks.'

Thirty Five

Annie should have known that the O'Tooles would not be there. She felt guilty about putting Mrs O'Toole on the spot, forcing her to invent excuses. The whole world knew the O'Tooles hadn't spoken a word to each other for years. Even the children in the street sensed something odd about the O'Tooles. It's why they taunted Mr O'Toole as he cycled home from work. *Old Daddy O'Toole, he never went to school. Old Mammy O'Toole, she married the old fool.* If only he ignored them they would soon grow tired of their game and find their amusement elsewhere.

As for the McEvoys, on the other side of them, they needed no invitation. With or without one, they would be there. Like the O'Tooles they were childless but unlike them they socialised with neighbours up and down the street. Not surprising then that the McEvoys were first to arrive. 'Has the shindig started yet?' said Mrs McEvoy in a shrill excited voice when Annie opened the door.

'Happy New Year,' beamed Jer, jovial Jer who wouldn't have to be pressed too hard to sing later on. Jer and Nance loved any kind of a hooley and the Townsend's New Year party had become a fixture in their calendar. Annie had a good idea who was coming and who wasn't and it dawned on her there would be no change from the attendance of twelve months before. Who could believe they were already on the threshold of 1916?

The invitation had been for half-seven but people seemed to think it wasn't seemly to arrive while the Townsends were still rushing to have everything ready. When Nance McEvoy's shrill laugh echoed through the house it served as the signal for Mattis and Plinny to make their way down the stairs and shake everyone's hands in the hall. 'David, you take the coats will you,' said Annie. 'Come on in here where the fire is, let ye. Sammy, put a shovel of coal on the fire, that's a good boy.'

They all followed her into the parlour where bottles of whisky, brandy, stout and mineral water crowded the top of the piano and gave the place a festive and welcoming appearance. A wheeled trolley held an assortment of glasses. Isaac was there poking the fire to get a flame. 'Happy New Year to yous all,' he said turning to face his guests. Then to David, 'Offer everyone a drink, lad. I'll have a double whiskey meself.' When David handed him his drink he held the glass up to the gas mantle as if to marvel at its golden translucence. 'You can't beat the Irish whiskey,' he said to Jer McEvoy who stood trying to decide what his opening drink should be. 'Sure maybe I'll have the same as yourself, Isaac. It won't do me a bit of harm.'

When the door knocker sounded again Annie nodded at Becky who went out to see who was there. Annie guessed it was her sister who always arrived with a cream cake in a cardboard box tied with a decorative ribbon, and when she heard the shrieks of the younger children she knew she had guessed right. Rose came into the parlour to greet everyone before heading for the kitchen to see what needed to be done.

Guests were now being welcomed in quick succession. While new arrivals were being led into the parlour the knocker would sound again and someone would say, 'You get it will you.' It fell to the youngest family members, Sammy and Poor Ruth, to perform this duty.

John arrived. Annie heard him talking to the children in the hall. When they ushered him into the parlour he explained that he had inveigled a younger colleague to fill in for him at the barracks. John was no stranger in Orkney Street. He had been a regular caller ever since he landed in the capital and came to regard his brother's family as a sort of home from home. Annie recognised his collar as one she starched for him the week before. He looked good, she thought, in his suit and wearing a dark tie she hadn't seen before. He was a different man altogether without the stiff police uniform. It was easier for everyone to forget his position as a sergeant in the Dublin Metropolitan Police. Annie loved the way he got on with the children and they with him. Tonight he would enjoy his role of putting people at ease and keeping things flowing.

After a decent interval had elapsed Annie raised her voice and said, 'Time for a song.' She looked across at Jer McEvoy, sitting next his wife near the piano. 'This is a new one,' Jer said placing his whiskey glass on the piano top. 'I only just learned it.' Someone said, 'Hush,' and silence fell on the room.

'Give me a note,' he said.

Annie sat down at the piano and sounded a chord and then he was off.

My feet are here on Broadway, this blessed harvest morn... But oh, the ache that's in my heart, for the place where I was born...

The tune was a mournful one and there wasn't a whisper as the guests allowed themselves to wallow in the lament of the exile for his native sod. They expected the song would go on and on as was the nature of such ballads but whatever shuffling developed during the third or fourth stanza ceased when Jer dropped his voice to a whisper and sang,

My mother died last springtime, when Erin's fields were green... The neighbours said her waking was the finest ever seen.

Isaac drew out a voluminous linen handkerchief to blow his nose. No one dared say shush for Isaac's eyes were not the only ones growing moist as Jer reached the concluding lines of the sad verse,

For here I was on Broadway, with building bricks for load...

When they carried my old mother... Down the old Bog Road.

Jer had signalled for all to join in the concluding words which they did with gusto.

He allowed David to top up his glass, saying it was just what he needed after his effort.

Mrs Mattis cried out, 'I call on David here to do his recitation.'

David pretended not to know what she was talking about but a silence had fallen on the room and Annie said, 'Come on David, let's have *Sam Magee*.'

David put down the bottles he was using to top up people's drinks and, blushing, began in a low voice,

There are strange things done in the midnight sun, by the men who moil for gold,

The Arctic trails have their secret tales, that would make your blood run cold,

The Northern Lights have seen queer sights, but the queerest they ever did see

Was the night on the marge of Lake Lebarge I cremated Sam McGee.

'Oh, the Lord save us,' said Mrs Mattis out loud. 'Let him go on,' said Plinny, clearly fascinated. 'Speak up, son, so we can hear you better.'

Encouraged, David resumed his tale of a promise made to a dying friend, of a frozen corpse strapped to a sledge for endless miles over snowy wastes till the narrator comes at last upon the means to carry out his undertaking.

Some planks I tore from the cabin floor and I lit the boiler fire,

Some coal I found that was lying 'round and I heaped the fuel higher,

The flames, they soared and the furnace roared, such a blaze you'll seldom see,

As I burrowed a hole in the glowing coal and I stuffed in Sam McGee.

It was a long-drawn-out recitation but apart from the occasional gasp there was silence throughout as David's audience remained riveted right to the final line. Even before the applause died down Annie struck up a jig on the piano while her children went to the kitchen for the sandwiches they had prepared. Isaac threw open the double doors to reveal the dining room table with its plates of food. It was agreed all round that a bite to eat wouldn't go amiss at this stage and the music was suspended so that family and guests could get a little something inside them. The sound of rain against the window grew more insistent as everyone circled the dining room table peeping inside the sandwiches before making their choice. Annie heard a knock on the door and went into the hall to find Sammy had got there before her and Hannah was standing on the doorstep. 'Golly, you're drownded, Aunty Hannah,' said Sammy.

'Take this, Sammy,' Hannah said, handing him her umbrella. Sammy stepped outside to give the umbrella a good shake before placing it in the umbrella stand just inside the door.

'Oh Hannah,' said Annie, 'we weren't sure if you would be in Dublin. Come on in won't you and meet the people.'

People had started to drift back into the parlour and Annie said, 'You all know Isaac and John's sister. She's come up for a couple of days.' Hannah's eyes moved around the room in a circle of acknowledgement. John offered her his chair and Becky brought her a cup of tea. She sat holding the saucer just below the level of her chin and the tea-cup poised before her lips.

Now that the music had been interrupted, the room buzzed with the rise and fall of conversation. Annie noticed John chatting with his sister, asking how she was getting on with the farm.

'Don't talk to me,' she said. 'I'm run off my feet. This is the first time in ages I've been able to get away.'

'How's Jude? I presume he does all the heavy work. Wasn't that why you married him?' John was smiling as he said this but his sister was in no mood for jokes.

'If farming was all that congenial, John, it's a wonder you took yourself off for the cushy life of a bobby.'

There was silence for a while. 'I suppose you're right, Hannah. I wanted something more – more exciting.'

'Well I hope you got what you were looking for on the streets of this city.' He would have known she was talking about the police putting down the street demonstrations during the big lockout. Annie, who was eavesdropping, knew John had been confined to barrack duty on the day of the riots. She admired his forbearance when he simply said, 'Can I get you a little something, a drop a sherry or port?'

'I'm perfectly fine, thank you.' Hannah wasn't easily mollified.

Annie's attention shifted to where Isaac was repeating his conviction that the war would soon be over. 'The Huns don't have the manpower,' he was saying. 'They'll never match the strength of the Empire. Another couple of months at the most and the whole thing'll be history.'

'I seem to recall you saying them very words last year, Isaac.' Jer McEvoy must have felt on sufficiently good terms with his next door neighbour to risk making him eat his words.

'Listen here to me, Jer. The Irish regiments could have done the job on their own if it wasn't for them traitors McNeill and Hobson and their Irish Volunteers.'

'But sure most of the Volunteers followed Redmond. There's a hundred thousand of them fighting in France.'

'I'm telling you, Jer, crowds of them is refusing to sign up. Fine patriots that lot. Ashamed of themselves they should be.'

Annie, watching, saw Jer and his wife exchange a knowing glance. She wondered if Jer had seen David training with the Volunteers in the Park. If so, they must now realise that Isaac knew nothing about it.

John had moved away from his sister and was now engaged in serious discussion with Plinny, whether about policing or philosophy or politics Annie had no idea. Her children were in the kitchen probably finishing off what was left of Rose's cake. She had no wish to break up the flow of conversation but seeing that it was nearly eleven and the time was flying she stood up and clapped her hands for attention.

'Now that everyone has eaten, it's time for a little more entertainment before we sing in the New Year. I therefore call on my good friend, Mrs Mattis here, to give us all the benefit of her lovely voice.' 'Hear, hear,' said a number of voices. Although protesting she had no voice it was clear Mattis didn't need much persuasion. She yielded under pressure saying, 'What would yous like me to sing?'

'We'll leave it up to yourself,' someone said and there was general agreement with that.

'Alright, then.' She raised her voice to a comfortable pitch and began to sing.

'Oh, you'll take the high road, and I'll take the low road, and I'll be in Scotland before you,

For me and my true love will never meet again, on the bonny, bonny banks of Loch Lomond.'

The room fell silent before the sweet voice of the plump little woman from Mayo.

No one took any notice of Annie as she slipped out through the dining room door into the hall. She made her way through the kitchen to the scullery which was in darkness. She didn't bother to light a candle but closed the door behind her to sit there in the gloom. She rose just once to open the back door and look out at the rain, still lashing down as if to wash away everything that was real, every kind of memory, everything that might recall that terrible day when she was just seventeen. She wasn't being rational, she knew that. Mattis could have had no notion of what it might mean to Annie to hear that song again.

It was soothing here in the darkness near the open door. The sound of the water gurgling from the choked drain, flooding across the cement yard to seep away into the soggy grass brought her some comfort. And some small part of her was conscious of the irony, that the water that swept away her love so many years before sought now to soothe her sorrow and offer her a token of peace.

There was a movement behind her and Sammy placed his arm around her shoulder. 'Are you coming in, Ma?'

'Is there someone looking for me?'

'Father said to tell you it's nearly time. You better hurry.'

'Give me a hug, love.'

Sammy put his arms about her neck and squeezed. 'Why are you crying, Ma?'

'It's only the rain, child. Let's go on in.'

The countdown to midnight had already begun. *'Eight, seven, six...'* Everyone was standing. Annie pushed herself in between David and Becky. *'...three, two, one, MIDNIGHT!'*

'Happy New Year, everybody.' It was Isaac giving the cue for everyone to turn to their neighbour, grab their hands or throw their arms about their neck and say with easy joyous optimism, 'A very happy, happy, nineteen hundred and sixteen.'

A wave of cheery goodwill swept through all there, family and neighbours. With the war certain to end soon, 1916 would mark the beginning of a new era of peace and prosperity. They formed a circle, arms around each other's waists, and began to sing,

'Should auld acquaintance be forgot... And never brought to mind?

Should auld acquaintance be forgot... And the days of old lang syne.

For auld lang syne, my dear... For auld lang syne,

We'll take a cup of kindness yet... For the sake of auld lang syne.'

Though a smile lit everyone's face there was the occasional glisten of a tear as memories crept back of days gone by and sorrows never quite forgotten.

Everyone trooped to the front door to hear the bells of all the churches ring out in glorious cacophony but the rain drove them back inside before anyone could start claiming they could tell the different churches from the sound of their bells.

People didn't stay long after that. The McEvoys only had to slip next door and they were home. John would be back at the barracks in a quarter of an hour on his bicycle. Rose was within walking distance of her lodgings on Infirmary Road and insisted she was perfectly safe on her own but she gave in when David said he would walk her home.

Annie offered Hannah David's bed if she wanted to stay over. At first she declined saying she was staying with an old school friend on Berkeley Road and the friend would be expecting her back. But Annie persisted saying David would be glad to sleep on the parlour floor. He believed that sleeping on boards did something for your physique.

***

When Isaac came upstairs Annie was already in bed with the blankets drawn up over her head. 'People were beginning to wonder where you disappeared to,' he said as he got undressed.

'I felt a bit dizzy. The sherry must have gone to me head. I opened the back door to let in a bit of air.'

'You could've got your death.'

'I'll be grand in the morning.' As her husband climbed in beside her and blew out the candle she turned her back to him. Sleep had left her. *You could have got your death.* He little realised how close he was to the truth for she had been face to face with death before ever he knew her. She was thinking of an August day more than twenty years before when she was so full of the joys of life and love.

Thirty Six

Almost from the time she could talk she had wanted to teach and now her dream was about to be realised. It was the proudest and happiest day in her young life. The letter was dated July 30th 1892 and when her mother had read it she gave Annie the tightest hug ever as her young brothers and sisters jumped around the place with the excitement of it all. She couldn't wait to rush out of the house and all the way to the village to tell Rory her news. She knew he would want to be first to congratulate her. She called him out of his house and showed him the letter there on the street and he wanted to hug her, she knew he did, but he wouldn't chance it with his mother watching through the curtains. She could see that her achievement meant as much to him as anything he might have done himself.

On Saturday he called for her after dinner to say he was going for a walk and would she like to come? Annie begged her mother and she said, 'Alright, but be back here in an hour. There's a lot to be done around this place.' They strolled down to the lake shore and sat there on a big stone watching the swans ducking their heads in the water. Rory said, and he sounded kind of shy when he said it, 'I made this for you, Annie.' He put his hand in the pocket of his jacket and drew out a chain with a little wooden cross on it. Annie was amazed to see that the cross, with the figure of the Christ, the whole thing, was carved in detail out of a single piece of ash.

He leaned in towards her to fix the chain around her neck and when she said how beautiful it was he told her it had taken him hours and hours to carve it. 'I wanted to get it right,' he said. At that moment she felt so proud and privileged that this strange shy lad had made such a beautiful object for her and her alone.

***

From her upstairs bedroom Annie could glimpse the lake between the trees. A week or two after getting the letter from the training college she spied a boat on the water. She recognised it as Johnny Hoey's boat from the white stripe Johnny had painted from bow to stern. To anyone who asked he would offer his explanation. 'The pike is a most curious animal. Consumed with curiosity. So when he spots the white stripe he comes right alongside to explore. Almost jump into the boat if he could. That's why I do be able to catch 'em so aisy.' Johnny held the unofficial record for the largest pike ever caught on that lake.

What caught Annie's attention now was that there were two figures in the boat. She could just about make out which one was Johnny but with the sun on the surface of the water it was impossible to identify the second occupant. The puzzle was solved later that day however. Annie was coming back from her father's land where she had gone to count the cattle in the river field. It was her responsibility to make sure none of them had injured themselves on the barbed wire of the boundary. Coming through the village she saw Rory Reynolds walking towards her from the opposite direction. In his arms a fair-sized pike, its silver belly glistening in the evening sunlight.

'I was just going to ask your mother if she could use this lad for your dinner.'

'Will you look at the size of that boyo. Don't tell me it was yourself I saw in the boat with Johnny Hoey this morning. Is it into the fishing you are now?'

'Twas me alright.'

'Well you might as well come on home with me now and we'll

show me ma the fruits of your labour.'

Annie's mother was impressed alright and offered to give Rory a shilling for it but he wouldn't hear tell of taking money for it. It would spoil his luck, he said, and he might never catch another like it.

'So is it fishing you'll be from now on?' said Annie's mother.

'Johnny Hoey says I can take the boat anytime I want, now that I've got the hang of it.'

'That ould boat will be the death of someone yet.' said Annie's mother. 'That fellow leaves it lying out on the shore in all weathers. It's past needing repair.'

Later, out of earshot of her mother, Annie said, 'You might need some help if you're planning on doing any more fishing.'

'I'll not turn down any offers, Annie.'

'Many hands make light work,' said Annie, smiling.

***

Later, when the fields all about the countryside glistened with golden haycocks, Rory asked Annie would she care to go out on the water with him seeing as it was such a lovely day. Her mother wouldn't hear tell of it. Two young people seen alone on the lake in full view of fields and farmhouses for miles around would give rise to talk. Annie knew her mother's word was final, that it was useless trying to make her change her mind.

Annie said to Rory, why don't we invite some of the lads and lassies and we can have a picnic over on Inishee? She caught the moment of hesitancy in his eyes. She knew he wasn't a great mixer but she thought if she was there to help him out he would soon get over his own diffidence.

'Leave it to me,' she said. 'I'll organise the whole thing. You check with Johnny. I'm sure he won't mind letting you have the boat if you tell him you want to take a few friends across to the island for a picnic. Ask him how many does he think the boat will hold.'

She talked to the girls she knew and the girls talked to the boys. Kate Cussin was all for it and she persuaded Packie Smith, a lad who had begun to serve his time as a bricklayer with a builder in Granard and whom she was now touting as her boyfriend. Kate told Mags who promised to bring Jemmy Sweeney, a red-haired boy with a pimply face who lived a mile or two out the road.

On a pleasant Saturday morning they gathered at the spot where Nolan's land sloped down to the water's edge, the spot where Johnny Hoey was in the habit of leaving his boat half in and half out of the water. Its nose rested on a pebble beach in the shade of some scraggy bushes.

Tubs Turner turned up uninvited and nobody had the heart to turn him away. They couldn't bring themselves to say, 'You weren't asked, Tubs, go home.' They said he could come if he pushed the boat out into the water and sat in the stern to do the steering.

As Tubs tried to heave his hefty bulk into the boat it took many pairs of hands grappling with his pullover to drag him on board, almost capsizing the boat in the process. But the boat adjusted itself and found its own level in the water as they got the oars working and headed out onto the open lake. He turned out to be a useful navigator, Tubs. He knew he had to head straight out to find the deep channel before turning west and rounding a narrow point they all knew as Crow's Head beyond which lay the little wooded island where they planned to have their picnic.

Squeals of laughter rippled across the surface of the lake as they tried to get the hang of the oars and managed, almost in spite of themselves, to get the boat moving in the right direction.

Tubs sitting in the stern and handling the rudder was taking his job seriously, calling out directions for one side or the other to pull harder. Though the boat was low in the water at his end he had a look of deep satisfaction. He was doing a good job and he knew it.

Kate Cussin raised her voice in song. *If I ever go across the sea to Ireland,* she sang, *be it only at the closing of my day...* Though her voice was tinny her pitch was perfect and soon they all joined in and the sound of their voices carried across the water, a wave of song that might even have reached the now receding shoreline. The final strains of *Galway Bay* were marked by whoops of exultation. There was a silence then while they tried to think what next to sing and it was Kate Cussin who came up with the answer. 'I know what,' she shrieked, 'we'll get Rory to sing. Come on, Rory, it's your turn.' Rory blushed and said he hadn't a note in his head but the truth of the matter, as Annie well knew, was that he hated the limelight.

'Annie,' said Kate, 'can't you get your fella to give us a few bars of a song?'

Annie had never referred to Rory as her boyfriend but she experienced a secret stab of pleasure at this public linking of their names. Moreover she knew Rory had a good voice and she wanted everyone to hear it.

'Come on, Rory,' she said. 'Just a verse or two, that's all.'

Rory hummed a note or two to try to find his key. Stand up, stand up, someone shouted. Rory stood up, a little unsteadily on the uneven bottom of the boat. As he wobbled a sea of hands rose up to support him. Then he began, ever so quietly at first.

'Oh, you'll take the high road and I'll take the low road, and I'll be in Scotland before you;

For me and my true love shall never meet again...

At this point everyone felt the urge to join in and they belted out that final line, *...on the bonny, bonny banks of Loch Lomond...*

They all heaved to one side with the beat of the song and it was at that moment it happened. The boat tipped over and everyone was in the water. Annie's ears were filled with the screams of the girls, the shouts and curses of the boys. She felt with her feet for the bottom but there was no bottom there. She began to tread water using a skill she had picked up as a child in the deep pool on her father's farm, where the river slides over the smooth rocks to settle in a dark hole where generations had learned to swim.

It was that knowledge that enabled her to stay afloat and begin to take in the turmoil around her. She saw that one or two of the others had managed to get a grip on the upturned keel of the boat but she could also see that others were too far from the boat to use it for support. The screams were growing fewer now as she felt something hard push against her shoulder. She turned her head to see the oar which Rory was clinging onto and using to keep himself up.

'Get a hold of this, Annie,' he shouted. 'You take it, I'll grab onto the boat.'

'Alright, so. Hang onto the boat and don't let go. I'll try to get help.'

Using the oar beneath her body for buoyancy, Annie kicked her legs out behind her and began the hopelessly slow progression towards the nearest part of the shoreline.

***

She awoke in her bed to find everything about her a blur. She had no idea how long she had been there. There had been hazy figures coming and going, her mother certainly and probably her father and some others who kept fading in and out of her consciousness. She learned later that they had kept her in bed for the best part of a week. She had missed most of the funerals.

Rory's funeral was last since his body hadn't been found until several days after the tragedy. They allowed her watch from an upstairs window as the hearse went by, drawn by four black horses tossing their heads in haughty dismissal of the grieving all around them.

The hearse was followed by a couple of pony traps since Rory was to be buried with his father's people across the county boundary in Longford. She caught a brief glimpse of his coffin with white carnations at its foot. Her hand went to her neck, feeling for the cross and chain he had given her. It was still there.

It was at that moment it came back to her, something that had eluded her since she woke from her semi-conscious state. She heard Rory's voice again, that sweet baritone of his. And the words of his song, *for me and my true love will never meet again,* and she saw again how his green eyes had locked with hers for one sweet moment as he sang the words *my true love,* for he must surely have intended the words for her. What he could not have known though, was the tragic truth that lay within the words, the awful accuracy of the prediction, *will never meet again.*

She knew now the true extent of the feelings he must have had for her all along. Something akin to the strange unfamiliar sensation she herself experienced the day he came to the school to pick up his baby sister, when he admonished her in his own hesitant way, *festina lente.* It was the moment when she first knew he was special. Only now when the hearse bearing his coffin had passed out of sight at the bend in the road did she finally and fully understand the depth of her loss.

Later, she saw his name in black and white in the Freeman's Journal. Under the heading, A Tragic Drowning, a brief report listed the names and ages of the deceased:

Kate Cussin, aged seventeen years and two months; Patrick (Packie) Smith, aged sixteen years and ten months; James Sweeney, aged fifteen years and eleven months; Rory Reynolds, aged seventeen years and eight months.

Years later she was to ponder the fact that of those who survived, Mags O'Shea and Tubs Turner were both to die before their time. Mags would die giving birth to her first child, a boy who later went into politics in America. It seems Tubs Turner was never the same after the events of that terrible day. He left home before the end of the year and ended up on the streets of London where he was found frozen to death in the bitterly cold January of 1902.

Thirty Seven

Isaac could hear his sister moving around. Why she had to get up so early on New Year's Day he had no idea. The rest of the household was sleeping off the effects of the party last night. It must be she wanted to say goodbye to her friend on Berkeley Road before heading off home, back to her husband. She was in the kitchen when he went down. She was fully dressed. 'Up early,' he said. 'Did you sleep well?'

'I didn't sleep well at all, if you want to know.'

'Why not? Something bothering you?'

'You could say that.'

He looked at his sister. He had a feeling there was something she wanted to say. 'What is it, may I ask?'

'A letter came from Adam.'

Isaac stopped slicing the loaf and sat back, looking hard at Hannah standing at the gas-stove with her back to him. 'Just before Christmas,' she said.

'What does he want? Did he say where he is?'

'He doesn't know Father is dead. Can you believe that? Our brother doesn't know his own father is dead. And he thinks you're at home running the farm. I'm out of me mind with worry. The notepaper was belong to some hostel or other in Birmingham.'

Isaac tried to take all this in. 'Have you got it with you, the letter I mean?'

'It's at home. There's things in that letter that don't make one bit of sense. You can tell he's bitter. Very bitter. Something about being banished. It's not true, Isaac. Me poor father was asking for him on his death-bed. It broke his heart, the way Adam just disappeared off the face of the earth. The very last thing he said, me father, *tell Adam I'm thinking about him*.'

Isaac didn't answer. His sister put a plate in front of him, eggs and rashers. He didn't feel like eating. She sat facing him.

'At least he's alive and now we know where he is,' she said. 'It's time someone tried to find him, make contact. It's a sin the way he's ended up, our own flesh and blood.' She paused and Isaac could see she was getting more worked up. 'You and Robert with your secure well paid jobs and your sister left behind running the home place. Put to the pin of me collar I am to keep things going. A crying shame, it is.'

'Isn't the farm paying its way?'

'If you think I wanted to be tied to a farm for the rest of me days it shows how little you know me. It's not the life I wanted. Far from it. If it wasn't for Jude working his backside off, pulling and dragging with the sheep, I don't know where we would be.'

'You married a good man. He's a fine sheep farmer, Jude.'

She didn't answer and turned her eyes away from him.

'What are you going to do, Hannah? Will you answer that letter?'

'There was no proper address. It looked like Salvation Army notepaper. More to the point, what are you going to do? You were the last one he talked to, remember.' Her eyes were fixed on Isaac. 'He must have said something that day, why he was running away. None of us ever heard what really went on between the two of you.'

Isaac dropped his eyes, flicked some crumbs off the table. He wondered how much she really knew. He worried about what was in that letter. Had Adam mentioned a previous letter, the one Isaac had burned before anyone else could see it? He studied his sister's face and knew she was trying to see inside his head. She wasn't going to let the matter rest and he wondered what can of worms she was going to dig up.

Poor Ruth had come in while they were talking. God knows how much of the conversation she had been able to make out. The girl probably knew far more than was good for her. Hannah asked her would she like to come to Wicklow when the lambing was over. Poor Ruth nodded and smiling she mimed picking up a lamb and cuddling it against her breast.

'Don't you forget now,' said her Aunt, 'after Easter. That's the best time.'

***

As he left the house Isaac told Annie that he might be late home. The lads would want him to go for a drink or two afterwards. She didn't grudge Isaac his day at the races but she hoped to God he wouldn't overdo the drinking bit. They had seen enough of his outbursts whenever he arrived home plastered. Hail-fella-well-met to his drinking buddies, a devil to his wife and children.

The twins had their day planned as well. Becky had a big hockey match, with Graysons up against Pims in the final. As team captain she was determined to bring home the cup.

'It'll be a great feather in your cap, Becky love. Nothing would make Mr Grayson, Senior, happier.'

'Fingers crossed, Mam.'

'What are your plans, David? The Volunteers, I suppose.'

'We've a long route march, Mam. Assemble outside the Blue

Coat School and then out along the Quays and on to Lucan. Back through The Park and finish at the band stand.'

'Disband at the band stand?' said Becky. 'That's a good one.'

'Your father still doesn't know you're in the Volunteers,' said Annie. 'He'll blow his top if he ever finds out.'

'He doesn't have to know everything,' said David. 'What he doesn't know won't bite him.'

'Just as long as you're not shooting with real guns I suppose there's no harm done. What about your Auntie Hannah. Was she asking any questions?'

'About what?' said David.

'Well, about religion, for example.'

Becky laughed. 'No. I think she's given up on that one. We're too crafty for her now.'

Annie got on well with Hannah. Give her too much rope, though, and she would be running your home and family before you knew where you were. She had arrived on the doorstep the minute she heard each of the children was born. She saw to it that they were all baptised in the Church of Ireland. Annie, however, had been one step ahead of her each time for she made sure the children were taken the day after their birth to be baptized in Gardiner Street church. She marvelled at the thought that her four must be the only practising members of the two main churches at one and the same time.

***

Graysons didn't reopen until Monday. There was post waiting for Becky when she arrived at her desk. It was a card with a French stamp.

There is good news at last. I'm on my way out of here since I got a scratch on the knee and they're sending me back to England to get better. I'm in a place called Boulogne waiting for a ship to Folkestone. I was given home leave but I don't know when it will be now. I will write again as soon as we get to England. All my love, Eamon.

This was great news. It couldn't have been better. All her prayers had been answered. Eamon had suffered a minor injury which meant having to leave the war-front. Nothing else mattered right now. It could only be a matter of time till he was well enough to get that week's leave he had been granted.

Thirty Eight

He could scarcely believe his eyes. Two men crippled, one sprawled across a beautifully built dog-cart, semi-conscious, his legs hanging over the sides, the other, his arm bound up in bandages, dragging the little cart behind him. They moved between the lines of waiting men right up to the gangplank where a medical orderly lifted the man from the dog-cart and carried him in his arms aboard the ship.

Despite the biting pain in his right knee, Eamon stood and waited in line. He watched the seriously wounded arriving on every conceivable mode of conveyance, from motor trucks to wheelbarrows. The lines and lines of walking wounded seemed to grow with every passing minute. The whole operation was organised like a well-oiled machine. One ship had just pulled away from the quay and another had moved in to take its place.

As more wounded men climbed down or were helped down from the backs of trucks they were made to form the beginning of another queue. Looking around he tried to take it all in. There were hundreds like him, still able to walk and stand. They stood and waited their turn to be called forward to board the boat. A truck arrived and drove right up to the gangplank. Stretchers were lifted off by the ambulance corps and carried onto the ship. He noticed a forward movement as his line began to board.

He attempted to place his right foot on the ground but even with his crutch for support the pain made it impossible. As he tried to move forward in the queue, his crutch went skew-wise and he found himself stretched on the cobbles. Helping hands and arms helped him into a sitting position. He looked up to see the pretty face of a young girl looking down at him. She had come from nowhere, a vision, like one of those *aislings* his teacher had talked about so long ago. The girl was like something in a painting. On her head a white bonnet, tied beneath her chin with a blue ribbon. Her white cotton dress reached almost to her ankles. She must have seen him fall.

The girl said something in French but he had no idea what it was. Neither did any of the other men. She just laughed at his confusion and dipping her hand in her bunched up apron took out a packet of French cigarettes. She gestured for Eamon to share them out before she moved away down along the line, handing out cigarettes as she went. Other women in traditional costume moved among the waiting soldiers offering them solace in the form of a smile and a much longed for drag on a cigarette.

Eamon took a couple of cigarettes from the packet and placed one in his neighbour's mouth and one in his own. And even though his neighbour's arm was in a sling he somehow managed to light a match, cup it in his good hand and hold it to the cigarette in Eamon's mouth till it began to glow with a comforting redness that promised ten minutes of blissful intoxication. 'Thanks, pal,' Eamon said.

'Not a bother,' he answered in a Scottish accent. That's the thing about this war, they were all in it together, English, Irish, Scots and French, shoulder to shoulder in the effort to drive Jerry back where he came from before he got it into his head to make a grab for two islands to the west.

He felt more relaxed now as the soothing smoke filled his lungs and he took the time to look up and down the lines of crippled and wounded soldiers whose ranks continued to grow with the arrival of more ambulances and lorries. He saw heads swathed in bandages with mere slits for eyes, mouth and nostrils. Two stretcher bearers came by at a trot carrying a poor unfortunate with a bloody space where his face should have been. He doubted that poor devil would make it to an English hospital. As they rushed him on board the gangplank was raised and the ferry pulled away from its berth to be replaced by yet another. By the time his turn came to board he was fit to drop from pain and fatigue.

As the ship pulled away Eamon could see the activity on the quayside below. The wounded were still arriving, a non-stop stream of hurt and damage. Beyond the port were the little streets of Boulogne with people going about their business. Streets with stalls, carts with merchandise, women with shopping baskets, barely aware, it seemed, of the death and devastation being wrought less than a hundred miles to the east. On the quayside the girls in their pretty traditional costumes continued to move along the lines of wounded men dispensing their small acts of mercy. He thought of Becky.

If things had gone as planned he might have been back in Dublin by now, enjoying a welcome five days away from the front. He could have been with the one person he cared about most in the world. They would have been talking about the future, their life together after the war, dreaming of a nice little cottage where they would raise a family and be happy forever. For months he dreamed about it, ever since he first set foot in France. He wanted to tell her stories of the war and how they were still holding the line against the Jerries. About brave men who gave their lives for the sake of the people whose lands had been over-run by the German hoors. He must be careful not to let her think he himself was in any danger. He didn't want her tormenting herself with that kind of worry. Now all that would have to wait for here he was on a ship bursting with casualties, on his way to a hospital somewhere in England.

He looked at those around him. Some in little groups, chatting.

Others too shocked to talk. Those on stretchers left to brood alone on what lay ahead minus a leg or an arm. He decided there were two ways of looking at everything. He could look on the jagged piece of metal that had banjaxed his knee as a shitty thing to have happened or he could choose to see it as a free pass out of hell. He was on his way to a place of safety with no need to feel guilty at leaving his buddies behind on the front line. He had earned his reprieve. Instead of those five days he was expecting, it would be five weeks at least before he was declared fit for service but sooner or later he would be back in the trenches.

He now knew that talk of a short war was pure rubbish. He had seen no big battles although the French had made a crazy attempt to break through just up the road. But his unit had been bogged down in absolute stalemate since arriving in France five months ago. All they did was shell each other from safe positions behind the lines. He had gone out on night patrol, cutting the Jerries' barbed wire and checking that their own had not been banjaxed by the Germans. He wondered why they couldn't just agree to leave each other's defences alone. It could save a lot of trouble. Mainly though it was a matter of waiting and watching. And dreaming of home.

**

It was the ward sister who let slip the bad news. The doctors had found not just one piece of shrapnel but several. A piece of metal at the back of the right knee, they decided, was better left alone. If they tried taking it out, they could make things a lot worse. He would have to learn to use the leg, however awkward and painful that might be. Other pieces of shrapnel in his thigh were to be taken out and he should be back on his feet in a couple of weeks. He asked the sister what his chances were of getting back to the fight. 'That's a matter for the army medical board to decide,' she said.

He knew now he was going to be left with a limp. That depressed him. Men who limped were the butt of other people's mockery. He remembered how he jeered the men back from the Boer war, old soldiers with missing limbs dragging themselves around on crutches. A source of fun they were, called cruel names to their faces and mimicked behind their backs.

In his brighter moments he told himself to stick to the exercises he had been taught to make the limp less noticeable. He might even be declared fit enough to be sent back to the battlefield. That's what he really wanted for in spite of the hardship and danger of the war there was something there that appealed to him. Something to do with comradeship in the face of danger. He didn't want to call it patriotism but there was something about standing your ground against the common enemy.

Eamon asked one of the nurses, a girl from Carlow, how long he would be there. 'Not much longer,' she said. 'You'll be going to a convalescent home to recover.'

'Any chance you could get me a Christmas card for me wife?'

She was back in half an hour with pretty card that had *A Jolly Christmas* emblazoned across the front. Later she came back and said she would post it for him.

***

Ashdown Castle,

January 21st, 1916.

Becky my love, you can see from above that I have been moved. They sent me by train from the Lincoln hospital to this place in Derbyshire.

I'm living in a reel castle with turrets and all. It is owned by a

Duke and Duchess who want to do something for the war and they let their home be turned into a sort of nursing home for the injured soldiers. I would have said their home is their castle but I hear they have another home on one of them grand streets in the middle of London and probbly a few more if truth were told.

A few of the nurses here are reel posh. One is the daughter of a duke and the other ones talk like they have a marble in their mouth but they are nice all the same.

We have physical jerks first thing in the morning and the middle of the afternoon. The whole idea is to get us fit to go back there. To France I meen. It is doing me good all right. That old knee is a lot better than it was. I can jump and trot and the pain is not neerly as bad as it was.

Doctors come in every week and they ask you questions like how are you doing and they write it down. We all know what they are trying to find out, are you fit to fight. I keep saying I have never felt better. I feel a right cheat ambling around in the castle grounds while the lads in the trenches have to put up with you know.

Say a prayer Becky that they'll let me have a week at home before I go back to France, for my poor heart is yerning to see you again even if it's only for a few days.

Give my regards to David and tell him I hope he is enjoying the long marches with the volunteers but tell him from me not to take that Eddie Kent too serious. Tell him France is where the real action is if he wants to come on out. He is the only reel pal I ever had and I would never have met you if it was not for him. Tell him that, wont you.

I cant wait to get your letter.

Your one true love, Eamon.

When Becky read the letter she didn't know whether to feel happy or sad. Happy in one way, sad in another. At least he wasn't going to die on her. Her big worry was his constant going on about wanting to get back into the thick of it. Hadn't he done his bit? Why would he want to go back and risk everything they had planned and hoped for? But it was typical of the Eamon she knew. If there was anything going on he wanted to be in the thick of it. He wasn't the sort to sit on the side-line. Now that Larkin was gone off the scene there was plenty of work for those that wanted it. The future never looked so bright.

That evening before leaving the office Becky sat down to answer Eamon's letter.

My darling Eamon,

I just got your letter and I am real happy to hear you are doing so well. I envy you living it up in a real castle. There's no doubt about it but some people have all the luck. Seriously though I'm glad you're away from all the goings on in France.

You say you want a week at home but why only a week? What you should be wanting is a lifetime at home, not just a week. Okay I know you can't just turn on your heel and walk away. I realise you must wait to be discharged, but for God's sake Eamon will you stop telling them you're better or they'll want to send you back. How can you with the metal still in your knee?

Have sense, love, and use your head. Make the most of your time in the castle, there is no rush. When you're good and ready I want you back here in your Becky's arms where you belong, do you hear me?

Love and kisses, Becky.

Ps. David is drilling every week. He loves it but we all have to make up excuses so my father doesn't find out. I think it's real silly them Volunteers but I wouldn't say it to him since it seems to be what he wants. B.

Thirty Nine

All these chaps had one thing in common. They all fought on the western front and ended up with something missing or, like Eamon, something lodged where it couldn't be reached. He got to know some of these men better than others. A lot of them were of no further use to the army and were waiting for the day they would be discharged from the castle and return to civilian life.

He was thankful his injuries were not so bad as to keep him from going back to the front. So too was Manning from Nottingham who had a bullet dug out of his left shoulder. He signed up for active service the minute the recruiting posters began to decorate the walls and lamp-posts of his home town. Nick Manning wore wire-rimmed glasses which gave him the look of a bookie's clerk and sure enough it turned out he had worked as a clerk in a Nottingham Tobacco Importers, yet had never smoked a cigarette in his life, an achievement which left Eamon gasping.

'How come an Irish Paddy ends up with us bunch of Limeys?' Manning asked him. That's when Eamon realised the others, nearly all of them, belonged to the Nottinghamshire and Derbyshire Regiment. It made sense then that all these chaps had been sent up here to recuperate. How and why he himself had ended up with this bunch was a mystery but he wasn't about to complain.

Eamon remarked on the generosity of the gentry. 'You must give them credit, I mean handing over their house like this—. '

Manning snorted. 'Squaring their conscience, more like. Rich folks like this lot have influence in high places and you can take it from me, lad, they know how to use it.'

'I don't get you,' Eamon said. 'Use it how?'

'You've never seen a duke or a duke's son mucking it with the rank and file, now have you?'

'I suppose you're right, Nick. Them class of people is used to giving orders. It's how they're brought up.'

'They know how to give orders all right. But did you notice how they keep their command headquarters well back behind the lines. No danger any of them boys is ever going to take a shell in the neck. But that's not what I'm talking about. What I'm talking about is the way some of them make sure their boys are never going to find themselves in the danger zone. Up in the trenches? Not on your nelly. No, a nice safe cushy job as Aide de Camp to some general or other. And how do you think that's organised? By pulling strings, that's how. All part of the rich boys' club.'

'I don't know about that, Nick. I seen some fine officers put themselves in danger for their men and pay for it with their lives. I seen it meself.'

'Some of them, I grant you that. I'm talking about the posh families with influence at the top. And I mean *the top*. Do you get me?'

By the beginning of March most of these fellows had got some indication of where they were going when they left The Castle but Eamon was left guessing. Impossible to get a straight answer. He figured the doctors couldn't make up their minds whether he would ever be fit enough to go back into military service. He was constantly admonished by cheery nurses to be patient and enjoy the rest. It was useless trying to explain that he had never been one to enjoy rest. He had to be up and at it.

In mid-March something happened which gave Eamon a great sense of expectancy. An officer of the Sherwood Foresters arrived at the Castle and began to do the rounds of the rooms where the men were relaxing, reading or playing draughts. He was accompanied by an orderly who carried a sheaf of papers in his hand. As each man stood to attention and gave his name and rank the orderly handed a page to the officer who then told that individual when he was expected to report for duty. It was happening at last, a big clearing out of all the men deemed fit to leave. Eamon's spirits rose. He knew for a weeks that he was as fit as he would ever be.

'Private Eamon Brennan, Sir, Second Battalion, Dublin Fusiliers.'

The officer seemed taken aback.

'Dublin Fusiliers, is it? I didn't expect to see one of you chappies here. Well, we'll have to make enquiries then, shan't we? See if they want to have you back there or what. All right, Private Brennan, you've been passed fit for service. Expect to hear in a day or two what we intend to do with you. Rest assured you're not going to be left twiddling your thumbs much longer. What do say to that?'

'Yes, Sir.'

The officer and his orderly passed on to the man nearest Eamon who was already on his feet waiting.

Eamon couldn't believe his ears when he heard his old battalion had been disbanded and the remnants absorbed into the Eighth. Somehow in the reshuffle he had been forgotten about. The result was that when his fellow patients were moved to regimental headquarters in Nottingham Eamon went with them. Shortly after that he was formally accepted as a private of the Sherwood Foresters. It was a situation he was not entirely unhappy about since he had grown to know and like these men with whom he had shared almost ten weeks recuperating in The Castle.

His chances of getting the home leave that was coming to him were now higher than ever.

Forty

The Easter sun filling his room with dancing light filled David with an inexpressible sense of hope and resurrection. As he swung his feet onto the floor, he looked at Sammy's sleeping form in the other bed and smiled. So much for rising at dawn to see the sun dance!'

Sammy was sound asleep and breathing heavily. Something made David place his hand on his brother's brow. He noted how hot it felt and wondered if he should strip off the blanket leaving just the sheet to cover him. Then he thought better of it.

He didn't expect anyone else to be up this early. His mother had attended the Easter Vigil in the church so she was entitled to her lie in. He could hear his father snoring and hoped to be out of the house before anyone was awake. As he rustled up a quick fry for himself Becky came into the kitchen in her pink nightdress.

'I heard you moving,' she said. 'Is there something on?'

'Easter parade, didn't I tell you? All the Dublin contingents is out this morning. With the sun shining it's going to be spectacular. Come on down later and see me marching, why don't you?'

'Funny, but I've never seen you marching. Maybe I'll toddle along and see can I spot you with your rag-tag army.'

'Nothing rag-tag about it. The whole city will be out watching us. It's big. I'm not sure where we're marching. Maybe Sackville Street, maybe College Green. We never really know till we get there.'

'Got your uniform?'

'It's in the bag there. I'll put it on in the shed and slip out the back.'

'We don't want Father to know, do we? ' Becky said. David remembered Sammy, sweating in his bed.

'Listen Beck, could you take a quick look at Sammy? He feels very hot in the bed.'

'Will do.'

'Come 'ere,' he said as she opened the back door to let him out and he gave his twin sister a warm hug of appreciation.

Becky waited till he went into the shed before easing the door closed. Then she went to get dressed and walked the short distance to Hickeys. Early mass-goers were drifting across from the church and she was glad to have got the paper before the shop filled up.

She rarely bothered with mass now since the way she was treated by the priest who made her feel like an outcast. Occasionally she went with her father to St Paul's and sometimes with her mother to the chapel, but if there was any way out she preferred to avoid church altogether and sit in the parlour reading the paper beside the window.

Becky looked again at what she had just read, trying to make sense of it. David had just left the house filled with excitement at the prospect of marching in the Volunteers' Easter parade. Yet here was a notice in stark black and white calling off all manoeuvres.

Owing to the very critical position, all orders given to Irish Volunteers for Easter Sunday are hereby rescinded, and no parades, marches or other movements of Irish Volunteers will take place. Each individual Volunteer will obey this order strictly in every particular.

The notice was headed *Order of the Day* and signed by someone calling himself *Chief of Staff*. David was going to feel very let down. It was hard to make sense of it, calling everything off at the last minute. She heard her mother coming down the stairs and going into the kitchen. She heard the tap running and the kettle filling but there wasn't a geek from Sammy who was usually first one up. She followed her mother into the kitchen to tell her what David had said about their little brother.

'Would you run upstairs love and see is he making any move at all.'

Sammy had thrown aside the sheet and lay there in his nightshirt. She felt his brow. He had a temperature, no doubt about that.

'How are you feeling, Sammy?'

'Terrible.'

'Let me cover you up. You've got to keep yourself covered or you'll get your death.'

Her father came into the room to see what was going on. She told him Sammy was running a temperature. She noticed a look of concern on his face. He was a man who didn't often show his feelings. He said nothing and went back to his room to get dressed.

At the breakfast table they talked about the sick boy. 'Let him stay where he is,' Annie said, 'it's the place for him.' Isaac said nothing and his silence showed he agreed. Poor Ruth went racing up the stairs to hold her little brother's hand and wipe his brow.

David arrived home for his dinner. In front of his father he said his club had hurling practice again in the afternoon.

To Becky he whispered that the whole thing was a mystery. When he got to the Green he found only a handful there, fellows like himself who hadn't seen the notice in the paper. Eddie Kent was there with a face like thunder, telling anyone who showed up they might as well go home again.

She could tell he was disappointed and downcast. 'Don't let it get you down, David. Don't you have the hurling to fall back on?'

Late in the afternoon a young man with an incongruous looking ginger moustache came to the door asking for David.

'Is it about the hurling?' Becky said. 'Because if it is he's already above in the park practising.'

'It's not the hurling,' said the young man.

She had the distinct impression he was not about to reveal any of his business so she said, 'What'll I tell him then?'

'Tell him Eddie says it's on.'

'What's on, may I ask?'

'Tell him he's to report tomorrow morning before half ten. And bring all his gear.'

'His team has a match in the morning.'

'I'm only passing on the message. Just tell him will you?'

'Okeedoke.'

Forty One

He had to fight his way through to get anywhere near the bar. Always the same on a Bank Holiday. Working men didn't get too many chances to spend a full morning or afternoon, or both, in the company of other men, to have a leisurely drink and discuss at length the things that matter. Things like dogs, horses and the price of the pint. This Easter Monday morning was no different. Along the length of the bar men on tall stools caught up in animated conversation, with much backslapping and friendly jostling. Between the bar and the back wall where the battered wooden tables were fixed fast to the floor, it was standing room only. A fair number of the drinkers had been forced out onto a grassy patch at the back where a majestic chestnut watched over the customers with a sort of proprietorial interest.

It's to this open space Isaac pushed his way as soon as he had a foaming pint glass in his hand. It was a relief to escape the creamy haze of choking smoke that spread in layers below the ceiling before finding its way back into the lungs of men who seemed oblivious of its presence. Out here too, he found that the main topic of conversation was the jumps racing at Fairyhouse, with confident predictions being thrown around about the favourite's chances in the big race while others were only too ready to throw in their pennyworth with their misgivings about the hardness of the going or the jockey's inexperience over the sticks.

He heard his name being called and turned to see the grinning face of Charlie Ward, his old friend and mentor.

'Ah, there y'are, Isaac, old pal. How're you doin'? A great day for the races, what?'

'Are you going yourself?'

'Ever know me to miss Fairyhouse? We've a cab lined up outside, meself and a few of the lads. We can just about squeeze you in.'

'I wish to God I could, Charlie. I've been looking forward to it all week but me young lad's at home in bed with the missus looking after him. She would have me life if I took meself off for the day.'

'Jaze, I'm sorry to hear that. Did you call the doctor?'

'I called by his house but he's gone to Fairyhouse like everyone else.'

'Christ, Isaac, but that's a damn shame. Well anyway, meself and the lads is going to see if we can get through.'

'What you mean? Get through what?' Isaac took a first frothy sip from his glass.

'Did you not hear? A shower of Sinn Feiners has the road blocked at Cabra, whatever the hell's got into them.'

'Bloody Sinn Feiners. I always said they were up to no good.'

'You're damn right they're up to no good. I hear tell they shot a couple of bobbies who tried to move them on.'

Isaac's beer dribbled down his chin. 'What are you saying, Charlie? John's stationed up there. Didn't you know that?'

'Sure maybe it's only a rumour. You know the way these things lose nothing in the telling.'

'Are you sure they were shot, them police?' Isaac was worried.

'I'm only repeating what the cabbie told me.'

'I'll have to get up there and see for meself what's going on.'

'I shouldn't have opened me big mouth. I'm sure it's just talk, Isaac.'

Near the front of the pub three cabs were drawn up by the pavement, the horses' heads immersed in nose-bags while the drivers lounged and chatted, waiting for their fares to appear.

'What's this I'm hearing about trouble in Cabra?' Isaac tossed the question at the three cabbies.

'Are you talking about the bobby that got shot?' said a wiry little fellow, black hair plastered across his pate with oily cream.

'I just want to know what happened.'

'What you so worried about? You wouldn't be a Peeler yourself, would you?'

'Did you see what happened?'

'I was on me way out to Ashtown to pick up a fare. A regular client, you understand. Anyways, I sees this gang of fellas with rifles blocking the road. Shinners, I could tell, be the get-up of them. Well the next thing I sees is two policemen arriving on the scene, like they want to ask the Shinners what the hell they think they're doing, blocking the public road an' all.'

Isaac didn't interrupt. He wanted to hear every detail.

'I heard the leader fella telling them bobbies, *clear off with yous now before I have to make yous.*'

'One of the bobbies, he does something kinda stupid. He draws his baton as if that was going to be any use to him against fellas with rifles. I heard a shot and the baton goes clattering onto the road. The poor bugger is doubled up holding his chest. The second bobby made a run for it. He took a bullet as well, but managed to keep going until someone opened their front door to let him in.'

'Can you describe them for me, the policemen? Isaac tried to control his voice.

'I wasn't exactly writing down descriptions if that's what you mean. One of them looked a bit like yourself. You know, mousy hair, same build. Could be your brother, if you had one.'

'Drive me up there.'

'What you take me for? Them Shinners is mad as hatters. No, sir. You can walk if you want.'

Isaac felt Charlie Ward at his elbow. 'You would only be wasting your time, old pal. The injured bobbies will be gone out of there by now. Why don't you go on home and see if they heard anything?'

'You're right, Charlie. I promised the missus I wouldn't be too late.'

He wanted to take a look at Sammy, keep an eye on him. Of all his children Sammy was the one closest to his heart. He said goodbye to Charlie and headed for the narrow gap in the wall that opened onto the back road of the park. He turned for home, walking beneath the chestnuts and sycamores, and in a few minutes found himself at the gates of the Police Depot. He decided on the spur of the moment to drop in and see if anyone knew what was going on.

There was a police sergeant on duty in the gate-house. Isaac repeated what he heard about Cabra and asked him to check. The man's movements were slow and ponderous. It was useless to try and speed things up. He was at the mercy of this slow-witted sergeant who saw no sense in exerting himself. The man fumbled in his jacket pocket for the stub of pencil. He put the point of the pencil to the tip of his tongue. 'Now then, what did you say your name was?' He was determined to write everything into his dog-eared notebook.

'Townsend. My brother's Sergeant John Townsend, stationed in Cabra. I only want to know if he's alright.'

The sergeant went into the next room where Isaac could see a telephone fixed to the wall. He watched him take the phone from its hook and start to dial. With the earpiece to his ear he began to rattle the cradle with his fist. He replaced the earpiece for a moment before trying again.

'Hello! Anyone there?' he shouted into the mouth-piece. Isaac turned his back on this sad pantomime and gazed out over the parade ground. He recalled how he and Annie would take the twins up here on a Sunday morning to watch the recruits being put through their paces. The trainee policemen drilling on the open square in full public view while the police band blasted out one of Souza's military marches. And when either of the twins caught a glimpse of their Uncle John among the boyish faces they would shout, *There he is, over there, look,* and they would raise squeals of joy and excitement.

'There's no-one there.' The sergeant wore a satisfied look on his face.

'What do you mean *no one there*? There's always someone there, for Christ sake. There has to be someone there to answer the bloody telephone.'

Isaac could hear his voice rising, could hear the anger and despair in his realisation that something was wrong. John had said the station was never left unmanned. It's why John had his own room and bed in the upstairs part of the barrack.

He quickened his pace as he headed for Orkney Street and home. With the grace of God Sammy would be out of the bed when he got there, back to his usual perky self, pestering everyone with his incessant chatter and questions. He needed to know little Sammy was well. And he needed to know his brother was safe.

Forty Two

While he guessed that most of those he left behind him in the trenches no longer existed in this world, he had a hunch that the armies of the British, French and Commonwealth must be due for a breakthrough. Call it optimism if you like but the more Eamon thought about it the more he wanted to be in there at the end. Yes, he wanted to get back to the fight and help finish off them Huns.

First though, he wanted to see Dublin. He had been promised furlough, still had his notice of leave with its official stamp. His injury and long months of convalescence had got in the way, but now that his knee had healed up, more or less, he had reason for hope.

He was saddened to hear that his own battalion had been so reduced that it had to be disbanded – the handful of survivors who could still hold a gun shared out among the various battalions of the British Expeditionary Force in France. The Sherwood Foresters, with whom he now found himself, were being held in reserve. When the word came for them to mobilise he would know for certain that the final push was on. All the lads felt the same way about it.

Most of his pals in the company had gone home for the Easter weekend. Eamon plucked up enough courage to present himself before Captain Dexter and ask if it might be possible to get a few days at home in Dublin. The captain laughed and asked him didn't he think he was asking a bit much. Travel to Ireland at the army's expense for the sake of two days with his folks? Did he really think that was a reasonable thing to expect?

Eamon pulled a crumpled sheet of paper from his pocket and held it out towards the officer who took it saying, 'What's this, Brennan?'

'It's notice of furlough, Sir. I was getting ready to go home on leave when I got injured, Sir.'

The captain gave it a quick glance and thought for a few moments. Then looking straight at Eamon he said, 'I believe you've been through a bit of bother with that knee of yours. Tell me this, old chap, how's it shaping up? I take it you're well able to get around?'

He was doing his level best to cover up the limp, especially around any of the officers. So adept had he become at hiding it that he developed a way of walking, as close to a normal stride as made no difference. If there was any chance the battalion was to be sent into action he wasn't going to be left behind.

He watched the captain scribble a few details in his notebook. 'We'll see what we can do, Private Brennan. Nothing definite mind. It depends on developments.'

That's as far as he went but it gave him some slight reason to hope that he might see Dublin sooner than he thought, a chance to see the bride he left behind when he boarded a troopship at the North Wall nine months before. He missed her then and he missed her still. His sweet, sweet Becky.

In an almost empty barracks, he found himself at a loose end. There were some tattered novels left lying around and he tried to read but soon found it too much of an effort struggling with unfamiliar words. There were a few others with no homes to go to either and they occupied themselves at the billiards table or, tiring of that, the darts board or the gramophone.

On Easter Monday he asked permission to go downtown with Ronnie Grimes, a Yorkshireman who for reasons he didn't want to talk about, had no one belonging to him. Dressed in mufti they headed for a pub to drown their misery. Emerging from their third pub a few hours later all their worries had fled. The world was at their feet. They were ready to run the Jerries out of Flanders all on their own.

'Let's go find a pair of birds, matey,' said Ronnie, leaning against Eamon for support. It took a while for the suggestion to sink in. Eamon had never considered himself a saint. He never had much truck with priests or religion. But a struggle was going on in his mind all the same. Ronnie's suggestion sounded just the ticket, to round off the night with a couple of girls to cheer them up and put them in the right mood for France. More than tempted, there was yet something inside Eamon holding him back. Of course, he knew what it was. It was a sense of honour, of commitment. If he did this now, how could he ever look Becky straight in the eye?

'Come on, mate. I'll warrant it's that little girlie you left behind in Dublin that's bothering you. You've my solemn word, Eamon, she'll never hear a squeak outta me. So how about it, old boy? I've a few bob left in my pocket, enough to treat the two of us to a good screw. Get rid of all the pent up—. What you say?'

Who would ever know? Yet he couldn't bring himself to do it. He had waited this long for his Becky and he loved her too much to two-time her now. Soon they would be back together again even if only for a couple of days.

'I love you Ronnie, you're a great mate. Off you go and get yourself a girl. You deserve it. I'll see you back at the barracks.'

'Aw bollix, Eamon, you're after taking the good out of it. Some other time then. Let's go home and sleep it off.'

On the next corner a paperboy had tied a placard to a lamp-post. Large black type screamed, *Dublin Riots. Troops On the*

Streets.

'Wonder what that's all about, then?' said Ronnie.

'Nothing to get worked up about, Ronnie. If it isn't another lockout then it's a case of too much porter in their bellies. Dear old Dublin. Nothing ever changes.'

Back in barracks the place buzzed with excited rumours. An order had come from Command HQ for the battalion to ready itself for deployment abroad. They were on twenty four hours notice to move.

All next day the preparations went on. Eamon was handed two packs. One was a ration of dry biscuits, enough for a couple of days, the other a supply of ammunition for his Lee Enfield.

Forty Three

David found Eddie Kent already there, at the main gate of the Green, smartly turned out in his Volunteer officer's uniform. He had arrived with some of the men who had left their bicycles at his house to march in from Kimmage.

David locked his own bike inside the railings out of harm's way. The twenty or so men already there greeted his arrival like a gift from God. 'Glad you made it,' said Kent. 'We're going to need all the men we can get.' David was puzzled by his serious tone until Luke Feeney whispered, 'I called to your house yesterday. Did your sister give you the message?'

'You told her *it's on.* You didn't say what's on.' 'Today we strike a blow for Irish freedom,' said Feeney gripping David's arm. David looked around at the puny band that was set to take on the might of the Empire and decided Feeney must be having him on. However when Kent started issuing instructions it looked as if Feeney might be right.

There was something about Kent. Whenever David found himself in the presence of his tall slim commander he could sense the earnestness of the man. When Kent delivered one of his pep talks, which he did at the start of every training exercise, he always began in Irish. Then, after five minutes, he switched to English, for he must have known that most of these fellows understood little of what he was saying.

It was well known that the brothers in O'Connell's, where he went to school, were devils altogether for the Irish. He called himself *Kant* which David could only assume was Irish for Kent. It must have been the Christian Brothers who imbued him with his mission to set Ireland free from English rule. They got their boys to sing songs like *A Nation Once Again*, and *Who Fears to Speak of '98?*

Almost from the day David had been assigned to Kent's command he was taken by the man's belief in the absolute righteousness of the cause, not just a political cause but a Godly one as well. He liked to say things like *for Faith and Fatherland*, linking nationalism with the Catholic faith. For David there was certain logic in that. His mother constantly admonished him to stay loyal to the *One True Church*, outside of which there was no salvation.

When Charlie Burgess, who was meant to be second in command, had not shown up by half eleven Kent took the decision to set off without him. By this stage their numbers had grown to close on forty. German rifles were handed out, with a handful of ammunition for each man. 'These few bullets won't go very far,' David muttered to himself as he counted them into his pouch. Maybe they would get fresh supplies if they were needed.

In front of a growing crowd of gawkers they lined up in fours and when the order came to move off David knew they were not the most impressive contingent that had ever marched down Grafton Street. A policeman on duty at the corner of South King Street held up the traffic for the time it took them to march past. As David went by, the DMP man gave him a wink which he returned. In the spirit of the bank holiday, pedestrians spilled onto the roadway and were reluctant to move aside as the small band of Volunteers approached. However Eamon kept his head high and his mind on their noble objective, to wrest their country back from under the rule of a foreign government.

Nearly everyone along the way turned and looked as the Volunteers marched by. There were some who jeered but for the most part people seemed to enjoy the spectacle. It provided a nice little diversion for families out enjoying the sunshine on this Easter Monday morning. Well-dressed families from the suburbs made encouraging if slightly patronising comments. A man with the cultivated tones of Rathmines called out, 'Nice show chaps.' It appeared that a display like this was just the sort of entertainment these people had been looking forward to and it served to add a little colour to their day out.

As they swung around into College Green, past Trinity College and the Bank of Ireland on their right, a couple of Army officers in smart uniforms, swagger sticks under their arms, stopped and smiled indulgently. They didn't seem to fear any threat from a bunch of young chappies playing at being soldiers. Beyond Christchurch Cathedral, though, the comments of the bystanders became a little more earthy. 'Go home yous bowzies.' David hadn't expected this kind of hostility. But then he had never marched through here before. These southsiders were a very different tribe to the friendly folks who populated his own beloved Stoneybatter.

Suddenly they were passing St Catherine's. He heard his father's voice reminding him. 'Never forget, boy, where you were baptised. St Catherine's Church of Ireland on Thomas Street.' There it was now, on the left, the very church where he and Becky were welcomed into membership of their father's faith. But for David, St Catherine's meant something even more significant. He was treading on the spot where a great Irish martyr had met his death, for outside St Catherine's, a hundred years ago and more, Robert Emmet had swung on the end of a hangman's rope. How many of the others marching alongside him knew the significance of this spot?

Further along the street they passed roadside stalls smothered in second hand clothing, with hopeful shoppers milling around and ruffling through the goods in search of a bargain. They barely lifted their heads to give David and his companions a second glance.

At a fork in the road they branched off to the left and David began to wonder where exactly they were heading. He soon found out, however, when the command rang out to halt. The marchers came to an orderly standstill and awaited the next order.

'Face left.' They swung around to find themselves looking at double doors, one side open and the other closed over. Through the open part he could make out a variety of buildings with roads running in different directions. A sign in large lettering read, South Dublin Union. Home and Hospital for the Destitute of Dublin.

Suddenly the command came to charge and all the men made a dash to get inside the open gate before anyone should think of slamming it shut. Once inside they waited for further orders. Four of the larger buildings were to be seized and occupied. The men understood what was involved since they rehearsed battle manoeuvers such as this many times. Eight men were detailed to set up an outpost in a part of the grounds that commanded the Rialto gate, while other squads were sent to set up garrisons in various parts of the hospital complex.

'You fellows follow me,' Kent said pointing at David, Feeney and three others. They ran towards a solid looking three storey house at the junction of two roads forming an L-shape. They found the front door locked and, without bothering to knock, began to batter the door with rifle butts. When this failed they used their boots to kick it in. The lock yielded and the door swung open.

In a downstairs room two women in nurse uniforms looked frightened as Kent stormed in and said, 'How many of you in here?'

'Upstairs three, I think, maybe four, I'm not sure. They'll be fast asleep.'

'Tell them to get out of here as fast as their legs will carry them. Get a move on, let you, there's no time to hang around.'

The two nurses couldn't take their eyes off the rifle and without another word made for the stairs.

A few minutes later young women began to appear, hastily dressed, dishevelled and sleepy looking. As they moved towards the door one of them said, 'Ye ought to be ashamed of yourselves barging in on the nurses' home like a crowd of thugs.'

For answer, Kent motioned with the rifle towards the open door. There was no mistaking the message and they set off at a smart pace in the direction of the main hospital buildings.

'Search the place, lads, and make sure everyone's out.'

Once they were certain the building was empty they secured the door and set about smashing all the glass in the windows, before barricading both windows and doors. Downstairs they made use of whatever furniture they could find, tables, chairs, desks, cabinets, anything that could be relied on to stop a bullet. Upstairs they used upended beds and mattresses. Eamonn Kent kept saying it was only a matter of time till the army arrived.

Before the army got wind of what was going on Charlie Burgess arrived with twenty or thirty more men. Burgess was the sort who would have gone around to the men's houses and dragged them out of their beds if necessary. He would have considered it his bounden duty to rouse as many Volunteers as possible and let them know the rising was going ahead. Every man who could use a rifle was going to be needed. He must have been furious at the cancellation of manoeuvres the day before.

Burgess took charge of the nurses' home and David was happy to serve under him at a time like this. He was the most driven man David had ever come across, convinced that the only way the English would leave Ireland was at the point of a gun. After Kent had gone off to inspect the other garrisons under his command the very first thing Burgess did was to check out the internal barricades. He made no attempt to conceal his contempt for what he found. At one window he tugged the arm of a chair and the whole assemblage began to topple. 'Call that a barricade?' he snapped. 'It wouldn't stop a swarm of flies never mind a swarm of bullets.' He made them start all over while he watched and barked orders. Then he decided the stairs should be barricaded as well. If the British succeeded in penetrating the ground floor the defenders would retreat upstairs.

It wouldn't be too long now till the military got word of the situation in the Union. All it needed was a telephone call to the nearby Richmond Barracks. Chances were they had already been told there were armed men in Volunteer uniforms occupying buildings and threatening staff.

Burgess fumbled in his bag and drew out a folded flag which he opened up in front of the men. It was all green and bore the words, *Irish Republic*. He handed the flag to David with exaggerated reverence and ordered him to find a way onto the roof and set it up.

'This here house is Command H.Q.,' he said. 'The flag will make that clear.' David attached the flag to a broom-handle and found a way onto the roof where he tied it to one of the chimneys. As he stepped back to admire his work a bullet slammed into the brickwork of the chimney just where he had been standing. He threw himself down behind the parapet and began to crawl back in the direction from which he came. This was the first shot since they took over the complex and it was aimed at him, David

- 265 -

Townsend, Volunteer. He wondered if he should feel privileged at being the target of the first shot fired in anger, the first solitary precursor of the battle to come.

When Kent arrived back from his tour of inspection he found his way in through a back door concealed by shrubbery. They could see at once there was something amiss.

'Everything okay over there?' said Burgess, referring to the Marrowbone Lane garrison.

'Our boys came under attack before they could get anywhere near their stations. You've never seen the likes of it.'

'You're saying the British were waiting?'

'Hell, no. The British we could have handled. It's the plain people of Dublin I'm talking about. They're out in their droves, attacking our lads, trying to chase them out of the area altogether. Paddy Egan was forced to abandon one building altogether. And the women are the ringleaders. Cursing, spitting, punching, kicking. Some of them have their sons there in army uniforms, back from the war.'

'They're rabble, Eddie. Why didn't you tell the boys to ignore them?'

'You weren't there, Charlie. You should've seen it. One crazy old fellow tried to wrest a rifle off one of our men. They had no option but to shoot him.'

Burgess gave a bitter laugh. 'So this is the noble nation we're fighting to deliver from under the heel of John Bull. Are they worth it, Eddie? Are they worth it?'

'Pat Pearse says they'll thank us in years to come. Maybe he's right and maybe he's wrong.'

David was disturbed by what Kent had reported back. What meaning did it all have now, the high-flown speeches of Pearse and the other leaders? Where was the point in winning freedom for low types who lived only for the Dependents' Allowance, the money they got from the government while their men were in France fighting for the Empire? People for whom talk of a new nation rising on Celtic foundations was a pile of baloney. People who had nothing but contempt and hatred for those whose noble aspiration it was to lift them out of slavery.

There must have been a small gate through the wall on the Kilmainham side of the grounds. Willie Cosgrave had been tasked with covering that area with his garrison in the Storeroom but soldiers were spilling in under cover of trees and bushes without being seen or shot at by the defenders. Then, when the firing started it seemed to come from everywhere at once. It was as though a silent signal had sounded for the attack to begin. It seemed to the men in the Nurses Home that their garrisons throughout the hospital grounds were under simultaneous attack.

Kent and Burgess now had to acknowledge a major weakness in their position for they had left a number of buildings undefended, mainly those with bed-bound patients. They cursed the hundreds of Volunteers who failed to show up. With full battalion strength they could have given the army short shrift. As it was, the enemy was probably making good use of the hospital corridors to creep ever closer.

David, Feeney and a handful of companions took up their positions, one man at each of the upstairs windows. David had formed a loop-hole between two mattresses, just above the window ledge on which the barrel of his rifle rested. Eddie Kent came by with individual advice for each man. To David he said, 'Don't waste your ammo. Hold your fire till you're sure of your target.'

So David stopped firing and scanned the spaces between buildings. After a while he spotted a fleeting movement as a

Tommy made a quick jump to clear the space separating two structures. The jump could not have taken the soldier more than two seconds. As David watched, a second jumper cleared the gap. He took aim at the space and waited. He estimated the distance at something over a hundred yards. At the first intimation of movement he squeezed the trigger and saw a form stagger and fall.

'You got the bugger,' said Feeney from his position at the next window. 'Must be a good feeling, Dave?'

Forty Four

They lied to Isaac. Not for the first time did Becky conspire with her mother to keep the head of the household in the dark about David's movements. What they knew and Isaac did not know was that David had not slept in his bed last night. If his father got any inkling that David had not come home he was bound to make a connection with the trouble that had broken out in town. God knows things were bad enough as it was with Sammy sick in bed, running a temperature and no doctor to be had.

Mattis and Plinny had been downtown yesterday and came back full of talk about buildings being taken over by Sinn Fein and shooting breaking out between Shinners and soldiers. They swore black and blue they saw dead bodies on the street. It would have been too much for Isaac to take, that a son of his could be caught up in that kind of anarchy. If he suspected his eldest son was with the Sinn Feiners there's no knowing what he might do when he got his hands on him. So they let him think David had left early for work in case he found any of the streets blocked. Hearing that, Isaac approved. 'It won't take the army too long to round up that crowd of hooligans. They ought to be shot, every damn one of them.'

Isaac left home at half seven on the dot to allow ample time to get to work by eight. Before he left he took a look at Sammy in his sick bed. Then he put his head in the kitchen door. 'You better send Poor Ruth with a note for Considine to call.' 'Goodbye, Father,' Becky said. 'Mind yourself,' Annie called after him. They waited until they heard the door close behind him.

'What are we going to do, child?' Her mother sounded

worried.

'I'm going to find him and get him home.'

'You think he's really mixed up in it?'

'Sure what else, Ma? They were supposed to have manoeuvres on Sunday. Then they were called off. Suddenly they're back on again. It's plain as a pikestaff there's something going on. He told me he had to report for a march at the Green. Next thing we hear the Volunteers are shooting at people. Becky wiped her eye with the back of her hand. 'I can't believe it, Ma. He's not like that, David's not. Sure you know yourself he wouldn't hurt a fly.'

'I know that, love, but you never know what way their minds are turned when they get caught up with them sorts.'

'I'm going down to the GPO. That seems to be the hub of the whole thing.'

'You'll be late for business.'

'I'm not going in today. Graysons will get on fine without me.'

As Becky put on her coat her mother threw her arms around her. 'I'm sick with worry, love. Just get him home here before things gets any worse.'

'Take it easy, Ma. You'll make yourself sick fretting like that.'

'You're right, child. The whole thing would be a lot easier if we had a telephone in the house but your father has set his face against it.' Becky had heard her father question why he should pay for a telephone when Dodd at the back had one they could use anytime they wanted. It would have been easier too if the trams were running but not a single one had come near the Park since yesterday afternoon. Otherwise she would have taken the tram to Donnybrook where Shires were building to find out if her brother had made it to his work. With the trams off the road people were left with no option but to get around by bike or on foot.

When she set out on her search Becky didn't even think of it as a search. She thought that she might run into him along the way and that they would walk back together. Whatever it took, though, she was going to find him. Being his twin laid a special responsibility on her shoulders. *Oats and Legions*. The oath of allegiance they had sworn to each other as little children was something the years had done nothing to erode.

She met some people who told her the rebels were inside the GPO, that they had smashed all the lovely new windows and were shooting at any soldiers who came within their sights. Her worst fear was that David had got drawn into it. The very idea of him getting hurt or hurting someone else she found too terrible. She offered a prayer to the Virgin Mother begging her to keep her brother safe.

Turning into North King Street she heard the distinct sound of gunfire and every step she took seemed to bring the firing nearer. Each sharp crack of a gun was answered by a volley of shots in return. Already it was clear that the closer she got to the centre of town the closer the firing seemed to be. She took some courage from the sight of people going about their business as if it was nothing more than a fireworks display down along the river.

All that changed when she reached the corner of Church Street and saw a small crowd of people in a knot on the pavement. Coming closer she heard a woman's desperate wailing. Pushing her way through to see for herself the cause of the commotion she saw a pram with a baby's blanket soaked in blood. A young woman hysterical with grief clutched a baby to her face while an older woman tried to take the child away. In the split second that Becky caught a glimpse of the baby's face she knew it was dead.

'What happened?' she asked.

- 271 -

'That bastard of a soldier shot the child,' said a woman pointing behind her. 'Galloped past on his horse and shot the poor innocent little thing in its pram. Out and out savagery,' she said. Becky remembered seeing a mounted cavalry officer galloping on up towards the Broadstone. She found it impossible to imagine that he or anyone else could have deliberately shot and killed an infant in its pram. But when she looked again at the dead infant her head began to swim and she leaned against the wall to quell the churning in her stomach.

Unable to get the hysterical mother to release the dead baby from her grasp the crowd began to escort her along the pavement, maybe taking her back to whatever room she called home. Becky stayed looking after them, her head still swimming, trying and failing to make sense of what she had seen.

She was startled by the tinkling of broken glass on the pavement and looking up she saw the muzzle of a rifle appear through a window close by. It let off a volley of shots at some target she could not see. People were dashing for shelter wherever they could find it. She tried to squeeze herself against a closed door. She realised the doorway she was up against was the entrance to the Father Matthew Hall where she took Poor Ruth and Sammy to see the pantomime after Christmas.

Someone moving past tugged at her sleeve. 'Get yourself out of here. The Shinners is inside the Hall.' The street was soon deserted as people realised they were in the middle of a battle zone. She retraced her steps and turned right towards the city centre. Battle or no battle she was determined to get to Sackville Street where it seemed the rebels had made their headquarters. She had to satisfy herself that David was not there with them. And she wanted to check on Aunt Rose who worked in the cake shop across from the GPO.

Everyone she met had a word of warning about not getting too close to the area around Henry Street. This was new to her, the urge people had to talk to everyone else. Total strangers exchanged the latest rumours or dished out warnings and advice. A middle aged man caught her by the sleeve to warn her that the City Hall was in the hands of Sinn Feiners and that the military had started to shower the building with bullets. Just getting across Capel Street you could be taking your life in your hands, this man said. How right he was Becky discovered when she reached the corner of Mary Street and saw the body of an old man lying in a pool of blood in the middle of the road. People stared at him from the shelter of shop doors, yet no one made any attempt to go near him.

As she made to reach the dead or dying man she was pulled back. 'Who is he?' she asked the woman gripping her arm. 'Poor oul' Larry Heskin,' said the woman, who despite the heat of the sun wore a black shawl about her shoulders. 'Blind since he was little. He only wanted to cross where he crosses every day. We tried to warn him but he kept going.'

'Is he dead?'

'The Lord rest his soul.'

'Amen,' said Becky.

'What's taking you up there?' said the woman nodding towards The Pillar.

'I'm looking for me brother.'

'You won't get far, then. The soldiers is stopping everyone from passing. '

'They might let me through. I have to try.'

'Well best of luck to you, so.'

The road at the corner of Jervis Street was blocked with a barricade manned by soldiers. As she came closer she could see

- 273 -

people being turned back and was not surprised when the officer in charge asked for her pass and hearing she had none said, 'Sorry love, no pass, no go.' He was pleasant enough about it, almost apologetic, but of course he had his duty to carry out which was to let no one through unless they had a legitimate reason.

On Great Britain Street she met a straggling group of shawled women and ragged children, arms full of fashionable clothing and fur coats. A little boy about Sammy's age ran over and shoving a handful of Rolex watches at her said, 'You can have one for a tanner, missus.'

'Sixpence for a gold watch? Where did you get them anyway?'

'The jewellery shop is all smashed in, missus. You want to get up there quick, missus, or there'll be nothing left. Everything's getting robbed.'

She didn't know whether to laugh or cry. These people with their stolen booty seemed so happy, so unashamed. There wasn't a policeman in sight. The dispossessed were taking possession of their city for the first time in hundreds of years. Yes, she decided, she was happy for them. Something told her their moment of triumph would be brief, so let them make the most of it while it lasted.

On Sackville Street she saw the looted shops for herself and saw that they had indeed been stripped. Even the mannequins, even the cash registers, anything that wasn't fixed to the floor was gone. Street urchins played with golf clubs, men stood on the roadway fitting on dress suits and top hats, while a woman with unbelievable strength dragged a luxury armchair behind her. Such glee, such abandon.

Just past the Gresham Hotel she saw a horse with military trappings lying dead in the middle of the street and a well-dressed toff poking it with his walking stick.

'Up the Republic,' shouted a woman. 'No more peelers and good riddance too.' Uncle John was a policeman and she was glad he didn't have to see this.

In front of the Post Office was a space where few were willing to venture. From time to time a bullet ricocheted off the fluted pillars of the newly renovated building. Becky looked up and saw an army sniper on the roof of the Hammam Hotel, apparently ready to pick off anyone attempting to enter or leave the GPO.

As she watched she was surprised to see a white flag emerge from a side door of the GPO and after a long pause a woman stepped out into Henry Street. She had on a long blue dress under a white apron with a large red cross on the breast. Holding the white flag aloft she started across the street, pausing at the base of the Pillar for a few moments as if taking stock of her situation. She then continued to the corner of Earl Street where she stood looking up at a shattered window on the first floor and waving her little flag.

From where Becky stood on the plinth of the underground convenience she saw the side-door of Noblett's drawn inward and a man in the uniform of the Citizen Army quickly ushered the young woman inside.

What was going on? Could it possibly be that the rebels in the GPO were about to surrender? It seemed incredible but still it gave rise to a desperate hope in her heart that all the madness and mayhem would soon be at an end.

She had no interest in the politics of it, nor in the rights and wrongs of those who had decided to take the law into their own hands. Her sole interest was in locating her brother and making sure she got him home safe. She decided to wait and see what was going on with the rebel nurse carrying a mysterious message from the Volunteers on one side of Sackville Street to the Citizen Army on the other. However long it might take for the woman to appear again, Becky was determined to be there when she came out.

She could hardly have been waiting more than ten minutes when the door opened and the woman with the red cross on her breast stepped out onto the pavement. The door slammed shut behind her. It was time for Becky to make her move. She darted the fifty yards or so across the junction and grabbed the nurse before she could move away.

'Is it all over then?' she said.

The woman, a few years older than Becky, turned to see who had addressed her.

'Is the trouble over?' repeated Becky.

'The trouble, as you call it, is only starting. We'll keep it up till the country rises behind us.'

'I thought you were going to call it off.'

'I brought a message from Commandant Connolly for his men to move into the Imperial Hotel next door. There'll be no giving in till they blow us to pieces.'

'I'm looking for me brother. He's a Volunteer. I thought he might be in there, in the GPO.'

'What's his name?'

'David. David Townsend.'

'Townsend?' She seemed to consider for a moment.

'No, I haven't come across him. Is there any chance you could smuggle some ammo down to us? We're in for the long haul and we'll need all we can get our hands on.'

'I'm just interested in finding where David is.'

'What battalion is he in?'

'Battalion? I've no idea.'

'Who did he train with?'

Becky wracked her brain. She never paid much attention when David recounted his training activities.

'He usually trains in the Park – in the Furry Glen. Does the name Kent mean anything? Eddie Kent?'

'Eamonn Ceannt,' said the woman. 'That'll be the Fourth Battalion. I'm not sure where they're deployed. Could be the Four Courts, or maybe the Union.

'Thanks so much. I'll try both.'

'Good luck with your search but don't try to take a Volunteer away from his duty to the nation.'

If she succeeded in locating her twin brother that's precisely what Becky had in mind. To drag him away from foolish notions of duty to the nation and get him back home to the safety of his family.

She decided to head for the Four Courts, less than a mile away along the Quays. But first she had to go by the DBC to see if Aunt Rose was alright. Passing Clery's she picked her way through the pieces of plate glass that littered the roadway. The looters had gone, though, for there was nothing left to take. At that moment she wondered if the nation really cared a hoot who held the reins of power.

She arrived at the DBC to find that it too had been cleaned out. Every last cake and sticky bun taken away or more likely wolfed down on the spot. Chocolate and cream walked into the floor. The locked doors had been smashed in but the place was now deserted. Aunt Rose should have been in there behind the counter dealing with her customers but there was no sign of her or any of her staff. It added to her worries, yet she had to keep going. David was uppermost in her mind and she was determined to find him.

Every bridge along the river was guarded by soldiers with fixed bayonets. No one was being allowed to cross. All vehicles were being searched. At Capel Street Bridge she came upon some sort of commotion that made her stop and watch. A horse-drawn cart had been halted by soldiers. Apparently they had discovered a cache of ammunition concealed inside a milk churn and two men were standing on the road with hands behind their heads while the soldiers decided what to do with them.

As Becky moved closer she saw an officer step up to one of the men and shoot him in the temple. As the unfortunate man fell his companion attempted to make a run for it. He didn't get more than ten paces when he was brought down by a rifle bullet in the back. For the second time in a single day she had witnessed sudden violent death at close quarters.

Access to the area around the Four Courts was cordoned off by military barricades and Becky realised she had no choice now but to return home by the safest route she could find and report to her mother all that she had seen and heard.

Tomorrow she would try again.

Forty Five

Isaac was in no mood to take advice from some half-wit English Tommy. The stupid fool stood in his way, to stop him getting across the bridge.

'I have to get to work,' he said, trying to keep his temper under control. 'I've used this bridge every day for twenty years.' He hated the menacing way the soldier kept pointing the bayonet in his direction.

Another soldier came over to explain. This one pointed at the Mendicity Institute on the opposite side of the river. 'Them blasted Shinners is all 'oled up inside there, Sir. They been shooting on and off for the past couple of hours.'

'What about the unfortunates that sleep there, the down and outs?'

'All turfed out on the side of the road, Sir, every bleedin' one of 'em. Shinners doesn't give a shit about anyone but themselves, Sir.'

'There's no shooting that I can hear,' Isaac said and made to wheel his bicycle between the two soldiers. The two straight away stood in his way to block him and the points of their bayonets came dangerously close to touching his chest.

'You'll not risk your life on this 'ere bridge, you won't,' said the first soldier, the dim looking one.

'You might as well go home,' said the second soldier. 'All the bridges is closed.'

He was left with no option but to do as they said and head

back home. There was no question of getting to work today. He wheeled his bicycle up the slope at Blackhall Place, cursing both army and Shinners who between them had brought the city to a standstill, messing up the lives of ordinary citizens like himself. He didn't know how he was going to cope with the long day stretching before him. Then he remembered Sammy and thought it mightn't be a bad thing if he was there when the doctor arrived.

'Back already?' said Annie, as Isaac pushed open the front door and wheeled his bicycle into the hall. She didn't ask him why but it was obvious with the present state of affairs. 'How's Sammy?' he said. For answer she shoved Sammy's nightshirt at him. 'Feel it,' she said, 'it's soaked. I've just given him a dry one and I don't know how long that will last either.'

'Did the doctor come yet?'

'I'm just after sending Poor Ruth up to his house with a note to say it's urgent.'

He wheeled his bicycle through to the back garden and came back into the hall to hang up his coat. At that moment Poor Ruth arrived back panting. She had run all the way to the doctor's and back. She signed for Annie that the doctor was out but his maid had scribbled a message on the back of the note. *He is run off of his feet.* Annie handed the note to Isaac. He scrunched it in his fist and threw it on the floor. He felt in foul mood. With nothing to read, for no papers had reached the shop, he wondered how he was supposed to fill the rest of the day. He went into the parlour and collapsed onto the sofa, despondent.

The house seemed oddly quiet. David must somehow have got to work, though how he managed to get through the military checkpoints was a puzzle. And Becky?

'Where's Becky?' he called out. 'Did she go to business?' Annie appeared and sat herself down on one of the armchairs.

'Grayson's is closed,' she said. 'Most places is staying shut till the trouble is over.'

'A bloody disgrace what them thugs is doing. Shires must be still working if there's no word from David, although how he managed to get there beats me.'

'Becky's gone down town to see if Rose is alright.'

'If your sister has an ounce of sense she'll keep away from Sackville Street. The DBC will survive without her. And the same goes for Becky. She would be better off at home looking after her sick brother.'

When the doctor had not shown up by mid-afternoon they sent Poor Ruth with another note, this one explaining that Sammy was *pouring sweat* and they were getting worried.

Isaac set off to seek solace with men who shared their woes and their triumphs in the dusky seclusion of Cotter's pub at the bottom of the street. He would stay there till it was time for his tea. If there was any solid news to be heard this is the place you would hear it.

***

It was half six when Isaac let himself in through the front door. He had a good appetite for food, now that he had his fill of porter. He heard the low voices of Annie and Becky. When he opened the door into the kitchen his wife and two daughters looked up but there was no sign of food. It struck him with an extraordinary clarity then that he hadn't laid eyes on David in the past three days. Looking at the women he could tell from their expressions that there was something they were hiding.

'Where the hell is David?' Already a vaguely defined suspicion was eating into his brain. Could there be any connection between his son's absence and the havoc on the streets of the city? He stared at Annie and Becky in turn, searching for whatever their eyes might betray. When they each in turn looked away he knew there was something going on that he ought to know about.

'Where's David, I asked. Have yous all suddenly gone deaf?'

Poor Ruth looked straight at her father and they all turned to face her, the totally deaf girl who knew more about what was said and done in that household than any of its hearing members. What she knew, though, she kept to herself.

It was Annie who spoke. 'Becky here is after spending the whole day looking for her brother. She thinks he might have got himself sucked in.'

'What do you mean *sucked in?*' he snapped. 'Are you trying to tell me he's mixed up with that gang that's terrorising the life out of decent people? Is that what you're saying?'

Becky began to say something but trailed off.

'Speak up girl, I can't hear you.'

She looked at the table as she spoke. 'He trains with the Volunteers. Yesterday morning he said they were going on manoeuvres. That's all I know. When I asked for him at the GPO they never heard of him. I'll try again tomorrow to see can I find him and get him home.'

'By God, when I get me hands on that brat—. *Volunteers* me arse. Them's the crowd that wants nothing to do with John Redmond and he asking for decent men to go fight the Germans. Hanging their heads in shame they should be, not terrorising the ordinary decent citizens of this city.'

He left the kitchen for he couldn't trust himself to keep calm and made his way upstairs to the one person in this house with whom he had any sort of understanding. Sammy opened his eyes when Isaac sat on the edge of the bed. 'How're you feeling, Son?'

'I'm alright, Father. Just a bit hot.'

'That's a good sign. You'll soon be up and about, as right as rain again.'

'I don't like being sick.'

'I want to get you something when you're better. Something nice. Is there anything you would like?'

'A jaunt in Dodd's truck.'

'The new one?'

'His new Ford Pickup. He promised me but then he forgot.'

'I'll remind him. He won't forget again.'

Sammy smiled and closed his eyes. Isaac stood and looked down at his sick little son. Sammy was the only one in the family he could count on for unquestioning loyalty. The child hadn't asked for much. Isaac would have a word with Dodd about it.

Forty Six

The flag David had risked his life to set up on the roof drew streams of bullets but it must have provided a poor target because the gunners on top of the Royal Hospital soon began to focus their fury on the windows and doors of the Nurses' Home, command HQ of the Fourth Battalion.

All through Tuesday morning they kept up the barrage they began the evening before, spraying the building with non-stop deadly fire. The noise was deafening as a stream of bullets lashed the walls and windows like a deadly hailstorm. David was awake and back at his post. A mattress thrown on the floor of the basement is where he had gone to snatch a few hours' sleep.

Kent and Burgess agreed that the machine gun fire heralded something more serious, most likely an assault by infantry advancing from different angles. Yesterday there were signs of activity inside the boundary wall but they had succeeded in forcing these troops to maintain their distance. The relative quiet was not going to last, though, and they knew it.

Another man took David's place at the window as Charlie Burgess led him down into the basement where two laundry baskets rested on the floor. With the lids thrown open David saw that one was packed with rifle ammunition, the other with homemade bombs. Burgess lifted out one of the bombs and prized open the lid. Inside was an explosive mixture put together by some amateur scientist within the ranks. It seemed to be a mixture of household and industrial chemicals. The smells were familiar but hard to place. Stuffed inside the can was a small package of nuts, bolts and screws. David shuddered at the sight of the shrapnel. Anyone caught by one of these devices could hardly hope to survive.

Although David was no stranger to canister bombs having been shown how to use them at a training camp in Ashtown, the second-in-command was intent on giving each of his men a quick refresher course. There were two types of bomb. One had a short length of fuse to be lit before it was thrown. The other was more sophisticated and made use of a percussion cap, doing away with the need for a lighted candle standing by.

Burgess told David to take a fresh supply of ammunition for his Mauser rifle and handed him four of the improvised bombs. 'These are for when it gets close up and ugly,' he said. The way he said it gave the impression he relished the prospect.

David could see that this was what the second-in-command was expecting, an assault from inside the building. Burgess believed that somewhere in the maze of buildings, soldiers were already pushing their way through doors, walls, obstacles of every kind, to get close enough to force the rebels into submission.

The army now had machine guns set up at different locations around the grounds. You could tell from the angle of fire. Bullets sliced off the walls forcing David and his mates to move around on all fours to avoid getting hit.

As darkness fell and the intensity of the attack eased Charlie Burgess made a point of congratulating the men on their dogged defence. 'Two days gone and not a scratch on one of you.'

'That's right,' said Eddie Kent. 'A handful of men have held off the mighty empire of Britain. Feel proud.' Neither alluded to the fact that the infantry assault they had predicted had not materialised. But then, who knew what tomorrow might bring?

Praise from their leaders put the men in buoyant mood and when Kent said he was going over to check on the distillery in

Marrowbone Lane, Luke Feeney piped up and said, 'Don't forget to bring us back a bottle of whiskey, Commandant.'

Kent said, 'I'll see to it you get a distillery after the revolution, Feeney.'

When Kent returned an hour later he was smiling. He plonked a bottle of whiskey down on an upturned crate and said, 'Fill your mugs lads, we've cause to celebrate.'

The good news turned out to be twofold. For a start the Headquarters of the Provisional Government in the GPO was holding off a superior force and reports from garrisons throughout the city were equally positive. Even though a company of Connolly's men had failed to take the Castle, the Volunteers had occupied the City Hall and their presence there overlooking the Castle was crippling the Government's response. The second piece of good news was that Seamus Murphy in Jameson's had been reinforced by Conn Colbert, bringing the garrison up to well over sixty men and women.

'Something else I heard,' Kent said. 'All the lights are out, gas and electric. Our couriers are able to get around without being seen. So Pearse and Connolly are fully informed on everything that's happening in the city.'

The bottle of whiskey was shared out and the men were in cheerful mood as they prepared to settle down for the night. Two brothers from Pimlico were assigned to the night-watch and David looked forward to a good sleep. Before he slept, though, he thought again of his family and the pain his absence must be causing. He thought of Becky, his faithful twin who had promised to stand by him through thick and thin, though he doubted she would ever approve of the undertaking in which he was now engaged. That thought alone tore through him.

He thought of Sammy, his ailing brother, and it tormented him that he had no way of knowing if the little boy had recovered or was, God forbid, even sicker than when he had last set eyes on him on Monday morning. He thought about his mother and father, how frightened they must be, hearing about all the people being killed. That he was quite prepared to lay down his life in a noble cause is something they would never understand. Nor could he really expect them to.

And when sleep overtook him the dreams he dreamt did nothing to comfort him.

Forty Seven

Becky was determined to make contact with the rebels in the Four Courts. If she hung around the back streets she was bound to see someone going in or coming out. To the incessant sound of gunfire she picked her way across the broken cobbles of Smithfield and into the laneways behind the Capuchin friary. Something she had not noticed yesterday was the desperation on the people's faces as they went from shop to shop with empty cans in search of a drop of milk for the tea. And it wasn't just milk. She saw the same fruitless search for bread and meat. The shops were already cleared out and waiting for fresh supplies which were unlikely to arrive as long as the shooting continued.

'Them bloody Shinners.' She heard the same complaint outside every shop she passed. 'They ought to be ashamed of themselves.'

'I better give you double,' the milkman had said when he called this morning. 'The way things is looking I won't be here tomorrow.'

Becky couldn't count the number of women lugging bags of flour and meal. A queue had formed outside a miller's premises. Two nuns came out holding the bunched up corners of a sheet between them, with what must have been several stone of flour. 'We spent all day yesterday baking,' said the younger nun when she saw Becky staring.

'Have yous any bread left over?' said a toothless old woman with rippled skin.

'Come on up to Stanhope Street and I'll find you a loaf or two.'

'Ah, God bless yous and keep yous.' Her watery eyes lit up and her mouth formed a gappy grin.

The amazing thing was the number people out and about in spite of the constant crack, crack, crack of rifle fire and the answering volleys of machine guns. She noticed though that they kept close to the walls and when they needed to cross the street they did so at a smart pace.

Traversing the back lanes she knew so well she emerged beside the Capuchin church where David often got early mass on his way to work. He even joined the Third Order and told her earnestly how it would help him lead a more spiritual life. He was never done talking about Father Maurice and what he learned from that priest's lectures. It struck her now that if she could find this Father Maurice there was just a chance he could throw some light on David's whereabouts. Without thinking, she entered the church grounds and made for the door that looked like it might be where the friars lived.

A youthful looking priest appeared and shook her hand. Fr Maurice.

'I'm looking for me brother, Father. The Ma and Da is sick with worry.'

'Your brother? Do I know him? What's his name?'

'David Townsend. He's in the Third Order. He's always talking about you.'

The priest's eyes lit up at the name. 'You must be his twin sister then. I'm sorry, but I've forgotten your—'

'Becky, Father.'

'Yes, of course, Becky. So David's missing, is that what you're telling me?'

'He joined the Volunteers, Father, and I think he's with them now. I thought you might know something.'

'Never a word to me about anything like that. All we talked about was Church teaching on socialism, communism—. Tell you what I'll do. I'll call Fr Aloysius down this very moment. If anyone knows it'll be him.'

She waited in the hall, sitting on an austere oak chair while the priest set off in search of his confrere. Five minutes later he was back with Fr Aloysius. This older man took Becky's hand and with gentle eyes asked her for details about her brother. 'His name's David Townsend, Father. I was heading for the Four Courts to find out was he inside.'

Fr Aloysius grasped his long white beard repeating the name several times.

'Becky, dear, I was more than an hour in the Four Courts this morning. If your David was in there I'm certain I would have met him.'

Another disappointment. Another blank wall. Then she remembered what the Cumann na mBan nurse had said to her in Sackville Street. Eamonn something – Fourth Battalion. She repeated this now to the priest and immediately his eyes lit up. 'If your David's with Eamonn Ceannt, then he's with the men who've taken the Union.'

Becky couldn't suppress the catch in her voice as she tried to express her thanks. 'I've got to get going,' she said.

'Hold your horses there, child. You're not thinking of trying to get in there, are you? The army won't let you within an ass's roar of the place. Especially if you've any connection with the men inside. The Army's plan is to cut them off, surround and isolate them. I'm going up there myself this afternoon but I've a special pass to get through the cordon.'

'But I have to see him. I have to talk to him. Oh, Father, I'm so worried.'

'I'll tell now what you'll do. Why don't you go on home with yourself and wait until I have some definite news. If your brother's there, I'll tell him about your concern and ask God to bless and protect him. The way things stand it's the most I can hope to do. Off with you now and I'll see you back here at seven. God go with you my child.' The priest was probably right. There was nothing more she could do. For now she would make her way home and let her father and mother know the worst.

Approaching the horse trough at the top of Manor Street she saw a woman walking ahead of her. She was in a Red Cross uniform which seemed to be straining at the seams. From the woman's build and walk it had to be Hetty Kane. She quickened her stride so as to catch up.

'Hetty!'

'Oh, hello Becky! On your way home from business are you?'

'You look tired, Hetty. Were you on duty?'

'I'm fit to collapse. I've been on without a break for the best part of two days.

'With the fighting you mean?'

'We've an emergency hospital set up on James's Street.'

'James's Street? But that's where David is. In the Union.'

'Walk home with me, Becky, and tell me the whole thing.'

When they got to Oxmantown Road Hetty brought Becky into the parlour and asked her mother to put on the kettle. 'Me mother's making us a cup of tea.'

Though five years separated them they knew each other well. Hetty was often summoned to the Townsend household to provide first aid when any of the children grazed a knee or needed a wound dressed. She had covered Becky's own childhood cuts on more than one occasion.

'So you were up in James's Street, Hetty? Have you heard anything about David? He's inside the Union with the Volunteers.'

'Sweet Jesus! Are you sure?'

'There hasn't been sight or sound of him since Monday morning. Now I'm told he's with the Fourth Battalion. You haven't come across him, have you?'

'The only ones I've come across are the wounded from both sides. We're doing our level best with no medical supplies worth talking about. If I haven't seen David it's got to be good news.'

'What about the poor chaps shot dead? What about them?'

'They're still in the grounds. The VAD people have seen the bodies. Mostly soldiers. There's hardly ever a let-up in the fighting. Our boys go in at dusk to bring out the wounded. The dead they've had to leave behind. They lie where they fell.'

Becky buried her face in her hands and Hetty leaned over to place a hand on her shoulder. 'I'm sorry, pet. I let my mouth run away with me. I'm sure David's fine. He was always able to look after himself, amn't I right, Becky?'

Becky wiped her eyes and a look of resolute determination took the place of her tears.

'Are you going back tomorrow? Because if you are I want to go with you.'

'You won't be let. You need an army pass to get through the check-points.'

'Where can I get one?'

'The Royal Barracks. Tell you what you'll do. Take my old Red

Cross uniform. I can't squeeze into it any longer. Here, I'll go and get it.'

Hetty's mother came in with a cup of tea and a couple of biscuits on a side plate and put them down on a low stool.

'That'll keep you going,' she said.

'You shouldn't have bothered, Mrs Kane.'

'How's your family keeping, Becky?'

Becky just had time to say, 'Fine, they're fine,' when Hetty came back with the uniform and Mrs Kane said 'Tell them I was asking for them,' and slipped back out the door leaving the two younger women together.

'Wear this in the morning. Call for me at nine and we'll head for the Barracks, the two of us.'

Becky hugged first her friend and then the uniform. 'I'll try it on the minute I get home.'

Forty Eight

"I don't feel well, Mammy."

Annie looked at her ailing son lying listless in his bed. The expression on the little face was one of misery. 'Show me where it's sore, love.'

Sammy put his hand to his neck. 'I can't move me neck, Ma. It hurts.'

'Where else are you sore?'

'I'm sore all over me.'

Annie raised the child's nightshirt to look at his chest and for the first time noticed the rash.

It was now Wednesday and there was still no doctor, in spite of Poor Ruth calling to his house several times yesterday.

Isaac said he would go himself after dinner. 'I'll make bloody sure he comes.'

***

The doctor's maid answered the door and told Isaac the doctor had just come in after his morning rounds and that there were people waiting to see him when he finished his dinner.

'Tell him Isaac Townsend is standing here in the hall. Tell him I'll not budge out of here till he comes back with me to see the sick child.' He made no effort to keep his voice down and the maid glanced over her shoulder as she realised she had left all the doors wide open.

Dr Considine appeared behind her, wiping his fleshy lips with a linen napkin. He was a stocky man, about Isaac's own age. 'Ah, Mr Townsend! If you wouldn't mind taking a seat in there I'll come with you the minute I finish this mouthful.'

Isaac was getting somewhere at last and sat stiff and upright in the waiting room to be stared at by a fashionable lady with a fox fur thrown around her shoulders. Some twenty minutes passed before he was called out to the hall and found Considine adjusting his bicycle clips, apparently ready to go. 'You lead the way, Mr Townsend. I'll be right behind you.'

***

'Tired and sleepy you say?' Considine addressed the question to Annie. 'And the light hurts his eyes?'

She murmured an affirmative to both questions wondering what he was going to say next. The doctor took one more look at the little boy before giving his verdict. 'He'll have to be got to the hospital. There's a lot of meningitis around and while I couldn't be one hundred per cent sure I wouldn't want to take any chances.' Considine was a man of few words, but right now he had said more than enough to cause a ripple of terror in her breast.

***

Isaac would never hesitate to ask Harry Dodd a favour. Dodd was the most obliging man you could find the length and breadth of the country. There wasn't a thing he wouldn't do for you if it was in his power to do it. In a sense they inherited Dodd and his business when they moved in almost twenty years ago. As well as his main occupation, fixing motorcars, he was hoping to set up a haulage service with the new pickup he acquired before Christmas.

Dodd kept on working as Isaac telephoned every hospital on the Northside. The guts of a truck's engine lay strewn all over the floor. With his head under the raised flaps, he appeared to be in his element, but he must have heard each time as Isaac requested an ambulance to be sent out and heard as each time Isaac said, 'Too bad,' and hung up.

'No luck?' he yelled from inside the engine compartment.

'Every bloody ambulance is out on the road. No let up at all. There's people being shot all over the city. That's what they're telling me. The whole place is gone mad.'

Dodd extracted himself from the truck's engine and wiped his hands on an oily cloth.

'I feel terrible about this, Isaac. You know yourself I would do anything to help the wee fella. Anything on God's earth that was in my power to do. But you know what would happen to the new Ford if I took her out on the road.'

Isaac knew. Every vehicle the Shinners could lay their robbing hands on was being commandeered for the barricades. 'Listen Harry, I know you would be the first to help if you could at all. Don't even think about taking the truck out. I'll take him, the wee lad, meself. He's light as a feather. I can carry him no bother. It's only a short trot down to the Richmond.'

He waited while Annie put a clean dry shirt on her sick son before wrapping him in a warm woollen blanket. She held open the front gate to let them through. At the corner he looked back to see his wife and daughter still there, dabbing eyes, watching him carry Sammy to where he would be properly looked after. He stopped outside Mulligans to adjust Sammy's weight on his shoulder. He inhaled the warm comforting smell of men and porter that seeped between the swinging doors. As he changed Sammy's position the little lad began to mutter and mumble. Spasmodic movements of his arms and legs. On his flushed face a look of terror. In his fevered imagination he struggled with some unseen danger. Something, maybe, that happened here at

Mulligans Pub in Stoneybatter.

**

Kipper was Sammy's best pal. He lived in Kirwan Street and Sammy always walked home with him in case he was waylaid by the Stanners. Stanners were kids who went to the nuns' school and they knew that Sammy and Kipper went to St Pauls. Sammy looked on himself as Kipper's bodyguard.

Today was Wednesday, market day, the day when cattle came streaming down Manor Street on their way to the North Wall. Good cowpokes were always in demand. Ever since he saw Tom Mix in the picture house, Sammy had made up his mind to be a cowboy. 'You should've seen them Indians falling off their horses all over the place,' Sammy said. Kipper said he saw that picture himself although Sammy hadn't spotted him there on Saturday. But Kipper was allowed go to the Volta on his own anytime his granny gave him tuppence for the wooden seats.

They argued a bit about who should be Tom Mix before Kipper gave in and agreed to be one of the Indians. 'Only for this time. Then it's my turn.'

The herds had been passing through Cowtown since early morning. The evidence was everywhere in the form of watery animal dung coating road and pavement. When they reached Mulligan's they found themselves among a crowd of Stanners. Since Mulligan's was half way between the two schools this is where they nearly always met them. And this is where Sammy and Kipper kept their invisible mounts tethered, ready for a speedy escape. Their horses, Acorn and Pal, were well up to the task for they had been taking part in this dangerous game for the best part of six months.

Today, though, there was a distraction. The Stanners were gathered around a shiny new Ford truck parked by the kerb outside Mulligans. Boys and girls, all fascinated by this up-to-the-minute vehicle. They tried the door handles but found them locked. They leaned across the door and tried to turn the steering wheel. They rubbed their fingers over the glass of the headlamps. The girls admired themselves in the side mirrors.

'It's a 1915 Ford,' said Kipper, 'This year's model.' He pointed at the bulb horn mounted on the driver's side. 'Did you ever see anything like that?'

'I would love to give it a go,' Sammy said. 'Well why don't you?' said Kipper. Then all the Stanners started squealing, 'Give it a blow, why don't you?'

Sammy hesitated until someone shouted, 'I dare you,' and they were all going, Cowardy, cowardy custard, stick your head in mustard.

There was no way out. Sammy hoisted himself onto the running board and taking a quick look to make sure the coast was clear, he squeezed the round rubber bulb so hard that the blast made two old ladies jump with the fright. Right then the doors of the pub swung open as an angry looking man burst out. He held a stick in his hand. The kids scattered in all directions. Sammy had no time to whistle up his horse, Acorn. Before he could jump down, a strong hand gripped him by the shoulder. He caught a glimpse of Kipper hiding in a shop doorway – a case of every man for himself. Terrified of what was going to happen him, Sammy struggled and kicked, but no matter how he twisted, the man was too strong for him. 'Keep away from that truck unless you want a crack of this stick.'

The voice! Sammy knew that voice and as his captor swung him around he found himself looking into the face of Mr Dodd from the back lane. Dodd released his grip and his features softened. His voice too, as he said, 'So you want to drive the new pickup, Sammy Townsend?'

'I'm real sorry, Mr Dodd, I only wanted to try the horn.'

'Is that all? Well I think we can do better than that. I'll be taking her out to Blanchardstown the week after next. Maybe you could come along for the ride. What would you say to that?'

'I'll have to ask me Ma.'

'I'll handle your Ma. You leave the whole thing to me. Now off home with you before your mother has a search party out for you.'

'Thank you, Mr Dodd.'

**

Isaac eased his son onto his other shoulder and got going again, down through Stoneybatter in the direction of Brunswick Street. Several times more he was forced to stop and readjust the boy's weight and say some soothing words into his ear.

'You're alright, little fella. Not far left to go now. Then you'll be tucked up in a nice cool bed before you know where you are. You want to get better don't you?'

As they reached the corner of Brunswick Street, Isaac heard the crack-crack of gunfire. It was coming from the other side of the river, somewhere close to the brewery, and it came home to him for the first time how foolish and dangerous it would have been for him to try and get to work any day this week.

Soldiers with rifles and fixed bayonets surrounded the main entrance to the Richmond, a thing he had never seen in his life before. He soon discovered why. Before he could get Sammy safely inside the building, a horse-drawn ambulance came through the gates, the horses' hooves clanging on the cobbles. He found himself being pushed aside as a stretcher was lifted out and carried at a trot through the hospital doors. In those few moments he saw enough blood on the man's uniform to realise that this young Tommy was in need of urgent medical attention.

***

Isaac stood awkwardly in the centre of the ward watching as two nurses deftly placed the sick child on a narrow bed and eased a starched sheet up over his supine body. He was aware of the pervasive antiseptic smell and the silent movement of the white-robed figures between the beds. A beam of pale sunlight, slanting down from a high window, fell across the little lad's closed eyes.

As he made to approach his sleeping son one of the nurses blocked his path.

'It'll be better for him if you don't hang around,' she said.

'Can't someone tell me how he is?'

'A doctor will get to him sometime. You can imagine how busy we all are.' Her hand was on his arm and he sensed himself being propelled towards the door. On the way out he paused for a last backward glance and saw that his son had sunk into a deep sleep.

In the corridor he met an older nurse with an air of authority about her.

'Is there anywhere I can wait?' he asked her. 'I'm not leaving here till I know what's happening to me young lad.'

'You'll find a waiting room at the end of the corridor, on the left.'

'I saw a soldier being carried in. He looked in a bad way.'

'He's one of many. We've a couple of bobbies as well.'

Isaac realised that he had forgotten about his brother John. At the same time he was sure that if John had been badly injured he would have heard about it.

'My brother's a policeman. He might have been shot. I have to...'

'Well now, Mister, I really don't think that would be…'

'Where are they, the policemen? I want to see for meself.'

'They're in Room 13 but no one's allowed in—'

Isaac was already halfway down the corridor. He found Room 13 open with a uniformed DMP man sitting on a stool just inside.

'I'm looking for Sergeant John Townsend. He's my brother.'

Without stirring from his stool or uttering a word, the policeman pointed to one of the two occupied beds. Isaac saw John sitting up in his bed, a broad grin on his face. He didn't look like a man who was about to expire.

**

They waited, mother and daughters, barely touching their food, watching for Isaac to come home. It was now nearly seven and he was gone since half two. 'If I knew he was going to be that long,' her mother said, 'I would have taken meself and Poor Ruth down to the hospital to see what's going on.' Becky didn't know what to think but if her father was hanging on with little Sammy in the hospital, afraid to leave, it didn't look good. Yet she would not allow herself give voice to such thoughts. Instead she put a brave face on it, trying to bolster the others' hopes with comforting platitudes. 'He's in the right place now,' she said. Poor Ruth betrayed what they were all thinking when a tear rolled down her cheek and she made no effort to hide or wipe it.

Becky went to the parlour and with the light outside beginning to fade she pulled from inside her blouse a crumpled piece of paper. It was headed *Normanton Barracks, Derby* and dated April 17th, 1916. She read it when she found it on her desk on Saturday and she had read it many times since. The same few sentences saying so much and yet so little. Eamon had been attached to the Sherwood Foresters since his own battalion was split up. He had been promised a few days at home before his company went back into active service. Any day now, he wrote, they would be together again, if only for a few days. *I can't wait to see you, Becky my love. Eamon.*

Reading those few sentences for the tenth time she was frustrated by his lack of detail. *Typical*, she thought. The whole thing was vague in the extreme. However, she allowed herself to hope that the bit about leave in Dublin was more than just wishful thinking. All she knew now, though, was that her man was left kicking his heels in some English barracks she had never heard of.

Sitting there in the fading light she heard the booming of cannon and wondered which of the rebel strongholds was coming under fire from the big guns. She threw herself face down on the sofa, seized with the sudden realisation that the three individuals she loved most in the world were now, in one way or another, in grave danger. Eamon, if his new regiment was sent to the front line in France or Belgium, which from his letter seemed a near certainty. David, with his naive notions, allowing himself to be sucked into a violent conflict which had already cost innocent people their lives. And Sammy. Surely God would never be so cruel as to take her innocent little brother away from them. From the depths of her soul she begged God above to spare all three, her two brothers and the man to whom she had given herself in a secret ceremony.

Suddenly she remembered Fr Aloysius. The clock on the mantelpiece told her it was too late now to go back to Church Street. Tomorrow, with God's help, she would get close to the South Dublin Union where she believed David must be.

Poor Ruth put her head around the door and beckoned her to join them in the kitchen for the rosary. In the absence of their father, who could never see the point of endlessly repeated Hail Marys, they knelt down, the three of them, on the cold tiles and prayed more fervently than they had ever prayed before that this present nightmare would soon be a mere memory.

Forty Nine

As the first rays of sunlight crept across the Liberties and down into Kilmainham, David and the other men in the Nurses Home remained on full alert. The all-out assault they had expected hadn't materialised. On the contrary, what he found when he awoke on Wednesday morning amazed him. He looked out onto hospital grounds that were as innocent as the gentle flower beds and open meadows of the Phoenix Park across the river.

It turned out to be no illusion. The rifle fire had for the most part ceased. There still came the occasional burst of fire from the machine gun emplacement on top of the Royal Hospital but it was sporadic, more to serve as a reminder that they hadn't gone away. It became clear, though, as the morning progressed that the bulk of the attackers had withdrawn. It was as if the army had given up and decided to leave the rebels to their own devices. 'John Bull's up to his tricks,' Charlie Burgess muttered. 'Mark my words, they're up to something.' Burgess wasn't going to be lulled into any false sense of security.

Any movements they detected were of small groups of soldiers retreating towards the boundary in the direction of Richmond Barracks. Still, they couldn't afford to let their guard down. Who knew what trickery was afoot? The sporadic sound of shooting from their outposts in Bowe Street and Marrowbone Lane pointed to continuing duels between British snipers and their own men.

In the afternoon two women in Red Cross uniforms appeared, walking towards the rebels' Headquarters. Eddie Kent ordered his men to hold their fire – as if anyone would dream of shooting unarmed nurses. He opened the door as they came up and asked them what their business was. They explained that they were given clearance by the Army to arrange for the removal of dead bodies.

'No one's been hurt in here, thanks be to God,' said Kent. 'But I'm going to tell you now where the other posts are so ye can take a look for yourselves. Then come back before you leave and let me know what you found.'

The two later came back as requested and were able to tell Kent that all his Volunteers were alive, although three had injuries needing urgent treatment.

'Right so. See if ye can get those fellows to the hospital.'

Before leaving, the nurses passed on some interesting information which Kent shared with his men when they were gone. 'Most of the casualties they're treating are ordinary people shot in the street. The British are acting like brutes, picking off men, women and children. They know they can't dislodge us so they're taking it out on civilians. That's why it's up to you men to give them a taste of their own medicine and show them no mercy. The other thing I found out is that they've decided to hem us in and just sit tight. They think they don't need to do anything else once they've got us surrounded.'

'Well, they've another feckin' think coming,' said Charlie Burgess. 'Our job is to stop them moving troops or supplies anywhere within a mile of here. That's what we've been doing and that's what we'll keep on doing.'

It was only when the sun was low in the sky that the first of the stretcher parties arrived. Then the macabre little processions began, dead soldiers being carried from their final engagement to their final resting place. David watched from his vantage point the same pairs of VAD men return again and again until he lost count of the number of corpses being taken away. He hadn't realised just how many had been killed in those initial assaults as the army made their futile attempt to storm the rebel strongholds.

Fifty

'Of all the hare-brained ways of getting men to France this must be the daftest.' Ronnie Grimes was in foul mood.

'It would drive you mad,' agreed Eamon. 'We could have been in Folkestone by now instead of hanging around these Liverpool bloody docks.'

'It's what I hate about the effin' army. They tell you nothing,' said Grimes.

They arrived the previous evening after a tiring train journey from Derby, only to be told there was some kind of mix-up and the boat had sailed without them. They were marched off to an old run-down barracks on the outskirts of the city to be billeted there for the night. No sign of the officers in that dump of course. You could be bloody sure that they found themselves a posh hotel downtown. 'We had better get used to it,' Eamon said. 'It doesn't get any better in France.'

'What makes you so friggin' sure it's France? Suppose they ship us over to that Emerald Isle of yours? You would fancy that, what?'

'Now that you mention it, I wouldn't say no.'

'Can't wait to get your arms around that little girlie of yours, what?'

Eamon smiled. He had shown Grimes Becky's picture.

When the company at last marched aboard the ship Eamon had a strange feeling that maybe Grimes' smart crack about going to Ireland might not be so wide of the mark. Liverpool and Dublin had close links. Dublin was a short sail away across the Irish Sea. It was only when the boat left the quayside and set its course that it became obvious they were not heading South at all but West. Dublin it was then. There was unrest on the streets of his own city. He knew that. The papers were full of it.

***

They lined up on the pier at Kingstown, ready for the seven mile march into Dublin. They were handed sandwiches before they docked but these were soon eaten and the men were still starving. As he waited for the order to set off, Eamon watched several pieces of field artillery being hoisted off the ship and at that moment it seemed certain that the Germans must have landed and that was why they were diverted to Dublin. That idea filled him with a sense of pride like nothing he had ever experienced. He was elated, too, at the thought of passing through the places he knew so well on his way to face the invader. He marched with a palpable sense of relief, having been cooped up in barracks for so long.

At Blackrock a remarkable thing happened. As they marched down into the narrow curve of the main street, people came out of the shops to line the pavement, putting down their shopping baskets to clap and cheer as the soldiers passed. Nothing like this had ever happened in his life before. He was so proud. The men marching either side of him knew he was Irish, and here they were, his own people, showing their appreciation for what he and his mates were doing in Flanders and whatever it was they were there to do in Dublin.

A few miles further on, the same thing happened. Outside the RDS, fashionably dressed people heading for the Spring Show. They, too, stood and clapped only this time their shouts of encouragement were mixed with words of warning. 'Watch out for yourselves, boys,' one woman called. 'Those murdering

Shinners are all over the place. Keep your eyes peeled. They're on the roofs.'

He tried to take in what that woman had said. *Murdering Shinners*, she said. She meant Sinn Fein, of course, Griffith's followers who were always preaching peaceful means. It didn't make sense. He remembered when the Volunteers had split and he had opted to go with John Redmond's crowd while David had stuck with the dyed-in-the-wool nationalists. When the war started he heard David say something he didn't understand. *England's difficulty is Ireland's opportunity*. He hoped against hope that his best friend had managed to steer clear of whatever was going on in the city now. Becky had confided in him how uneasy she was about David getting so caught up in the patriotism game. But that was his decision and as far as Eamon knew there were no hard feelings between them. They had each done what they thought was right.

Marching down Shelbourne Road they heard more shouts of encouragement. 'On with yous, lads, and give them Shinners a taste of their own medicine.'

A shout from the roof of a house and Eamon looked up to see a soldier give a quick wave before ducking back behind the parapet with his rifle in the firing position. As they came closer to the canal, there was smoke in the air and the acrid smell of burnt-out buildings. At Beggars Bush barracks the wide gates swung open as though someone had been expecting their arrival. Once inside, Eamon experienced a great sense of relief and contentment, not just because the long march from Kingstown was over, not just that. He had an overwhelming sense of being back home at last in *dear old dirty Dublin*.

Fifty One

She dressed in the Red Cross uniform Hetty Kane had given her, the long sober skirt, the matching jacket and white blouse. Hetty had said the shoes didn't matter. Her mother told her as she ate her breakfast that her father hadn't come home. They worried about what his absence said about Sammy's condition. Her mother couldn't stand the not knowing and said she was going to the hospital and taking Poor Ruth with her.

'I would go myself except I arranged to meet Hetty at nine,' Becky said. It was Thursday morning and she still hadn't found David.

Hetty was waiting and together they set off for the Barracks using the shortcut through the married quarters and coming out onto Arbour Hill minutes later. They found a small queue had already formed outside the office. People were chatting among themselves, only too ready to share with each other why they so badly needed a pass.

Behind the desk sat an officer, listening intently as each applicant made their case and only occasionally querying their bona fides. When it was Becky's turn she told him she had volunteered for the VAD and that Hetty was there to vouch for her. The officer gave her a curious look which seemed to last forever. However the Red Cross outfit did the trick for he didn't ask for any more questions before half-turning to the sergeant bedside him, muttering, 'Sounds genuine enough.' The NCO asked Becky for some details which he wrote into the blank pass and rubber stamped with the words 'Official Passport.'

Once they produced their passes they'd no trouble crossing the river at Kingsbridge where a sympathetic soldier said in a Wexford accent, 'Watch how yous go, girls, no one's safe up there.' Hetty had just been telling Becky how the Saint John's Ambulance Chief of Staff had been shot dead as he bent over a casualty.

At the same moment that they arrived outside the church hall now serving as a first aid hospital, a car pulled up bulging with blankets, sheets, pillows and mattresses, collected, the driver said, from houses in Inchicore.

'We won't have enough there,' Hetty said. She asked the man to help herself and Becky carry the stuff inside and then sent him off to look for more.

Becky didn't mind the physical work even if it couldn't be further removed from her typing duties in Graysons. Looking about her at the injured people moaning on mattresses around the walls she was glad she was here for it was clear that every extra pair of hands was needed. Two doctors aided by a few medical students did what they could for the dying and injured. Only one of the doctors, it turned out, had any surgical experience and even he was attempting procedures he had never done before.

All that morning Becky moved around from one patient to the next, dabbing their brows with cold water, finding an extra blanket for those that shivered and whispering a word of comfort in the ears of those frozen with fear. While Hetty was highly qualified in First Aid, Becky had no training whatever.

Yet in these extreme circumstances she was expected to perform like a nurse, standing by while a man's chest was being opened to find and extract a bullet. 'Hand me that needle,' the doctor said, nodding towards a jumble of instruments. She handed him what she thought he wanted and watched as he stitched up the opening in the man's chest. The patient grasped

Becky's hand and the sheer pressure of his grip conveyed the degree of pain he was forced to endure.

For the first time in her twenty years Becky felt she was fulfilling some real purpose. That man would probably recover which was not the case with another man stretchered in, his waistcoat soaked in blood. This man had stopped his motorcar at a military checkpoint. He stepped out of the car and went to raise his hands in the air when he was blasted by a jumpy soldier. The doctors were now fighting to stop the bleeding and save the man's life but with little hope of success. They called for a motor ambulance to take him to Steevens' Hospital but who knew if it would ever show up?

Becky had been working all morning, right from the moment she arrived and helped to bring the bedding in from the car. She had been dashing around at the beck and call of the Red Cross and VAD people who seemed to take her presence there for granted.

By one o'clock she was fit to drop. She was ravenous, but since she forgot to bring any food she was forced to accept some of Hetty's sandwiches. They sat in a room at the back where water was being boiled in a giant saucepan. The streets outside were the scene of a fierce gun battle raging between the army and the rebels. As long as this intense shooting continued there was no question of anyone stepping outside to bring in the wounded. They were all confined to that little first aid hospital until the firing subsided. What they would find waiting for them then was too frightening to imagine.

Becky's head filled with dread. It was only now she remembered what it was that had brought her here. David was just down the street with the rebels in the Union. If only she could talk to him, make him see sense, get him to understand the futility of it all. Young men killing each other for some vague notion of freedom. Several times she felt the urge to go rushing across the street and, ignoring all shouted warnings, fly to him and drag him away from all the madness. It was an illusion — she knew it was — that there was anything at all she could do to change the course of events.

She thought of Eamon and as she did she thanked God that he was well away from all this. France could hardly be worse and though she knew it was the oddest of thoughts she was grateful that her young husband was destined to fight the Germans in Flanders rather than having to fire on his own countrymen in Dublin.

In the early evening the guns fell silent, except for the occasional crack of a rifle. This was the moment the VAD men had been waiting for. They ran with their stretchers across the street and hugging the houses on the far side made for the gates of the Union. They must have known the risk they were taking but most of them were either Red Cross or Saint John's Ambulance Brigade, possessed of a keen sense of service to their fellow men. As Becky watched them disappear into the hospital grounds she was surprised to see two friars go in with them.

Waiting for the first of the casualties to be brought in, Becky found a telephone in a back room that worked by dropping a penny in the slot. She telephoned Dodd's garage. Dodd was able to tell her that her mother and Poor Ruth had come back from the hospital and looked very put out. Little Sammy was under twenty four hour watch. In fact it was *touch and go*. She wasn't sure if these were Dodd's words or her mother's. All she could say was, 'Thanks, Mr Dodd,' before she hung up.

She came back to find feverish activity. The triage system they were using involved moving the critically injured down to Steevens' Hospital by any means available, even horse-drawn cabs and carts.

Only one of those taken to hospital was a Volunteer, barely

conscious and unable to speak. She saw him wheeled away on a hand-cart. Most, though, were civilians, people going about their daily business, whether targeted deliberately or victims of a ricochet bullet, who could tell? Hard not to suspect that some had been picked off at random by a sniper on a rooftop.

As dusk fell and the sound of sporadic gunfire eased off for the night, two friars arrived, intent on offering spiritual comfort to the injured. Becky recognised the long white beard of Fr Aloysius before he recognised her.

'Becky, dear, I didn't know you were in the Red Cross.'

'I'm only trying to lend a hand here, Father.'

'I've some news for you, Becky. Step over here so we can talk.' He led her to an alcove and placed a fatherly arm on her shoulder. 'I've seen your brother.'

Tears welled in her eyes. 'He's all right, is he? Tell me, is he safe?'

'He's safe, Becky. I told him you were scouring the city for him.'

'You did? And what did he say?'

'He said he's sorry. He's really sorry. He doesn't know how he'll ever face you again.'

'Oh Father, how could he possibly say that? How could he? Just as long as he's safe nothing matters.'

'There's something he has to tell you. Whatever it is he's very put out about it, I can tell you that much.'

'That's pure nonsense and he knows it. We've never kept anything from each other from the time we were little.'

'I heard his confession before I left. They're a brave bunch of lads in there, fighting for what they believe in. Commandant Ceannt says they'll fight to the last man. There's a nobility about

- 314 -

that man Ceannt. I can well believe him when he says he's ready to give his life for the cause.'

Becky burst into tears. This was not the kind of talk she wanted to hear. The priest placed a hand on her head and said, 'We can only trust in the merciful Lord to bring your brother home safe to you.'

'Oh, Father!'

Later, when the friars had left, she told Hetty she was too upset to carry on.

'You head off home, Becky, and see how you're feeling in the morning.'

Fifty Two

Inside Beggars Bush barracks the air was alive with news and rumours – all kinds of stories flying around. Eamon was stunned to hear that the Volunteers had taken over the GPO and placed barricades at key points around the city. As he sat down with his starving mates at the mess table to gulp down the sandwich and soup put in front of him, the stories kept changing, the reports and rumours ever more incredible. The woman dishing out the food felt the need to add her own tuppence worth. 'Did yous hear the Germans is in Cork? Came off a ship, they did.'

'You can't be serious.'

'As God's me judge. Sure everyone knows the Shinners is hand in glove with the Germans.'

She was talking about his former friends, the boys he had marched and drilled alongside for the sheer glamour and excitement of it. Things started to come back to him. Like David telling him what Pearse had written about the need for blood to be spilled. *Blood sacrifice*, he called it. He thought then that no one in their right mind would pay any attention to that kind of guff. Now it seemed Pearse was holed up in the GPO with a bunch of Volunteers, shooting at ordinary soldiers like himself. It was hard to make sense of it.

He listened with disbelief when he heard about the army pensioners, harmless old-timers, targeted as they walked back to Beggar's Bush at the end of their weekly route march, mown down by rebels on Northumberland Road. And he was depressed to hear that his comrades in the Foresters had come under attack just around the corner from where he now sat. Young fellows with little or no training, felled as they tried to make it across the canal bridge. If he ever had doubts about it before, he was convinced now that Pearse was a madman.

Eamon felt a sharp tap on the shoulder. He looked around to find a corporal called Walker with a sheet of paper in his hand. 'You Brennan, you Chapman. Report for duty. On the double.' He joined a band of men being assembled to escort a consignment of ammunition to Kilmainham on the western flanks of the city.

He had only minutes to scribble a note for Becky to let her know he was back in Dublin. He still had her last letter which arrived just before he left Derby and now he took the envelope, crossed out his own name and address and wrote instead, *Becky Townsend, c/o Graysons Builders Providers.* Then on the inside of a cigarette carton he wrote, *I am back in Dublin at last and I can't wait to see you I don't know when but pleese god soon, sooner than you think. Yours xxx, Eamon.* The woman who was serving his table looked at the address and said 'I'll see that she gets it, Ducky.'

He found himself assigned to the advance guard. He prayed that their route along the South Circular would keep them well away from the carry-on in the city. Emerging from the barracks they wheeled left along Haddington Road. Five minutes later they were walking with the canal on their right. Their speed was determined by the pace of the two handsome shire horses drawing the heavily laden dray. The sight of swans among the reeds somehow confirmed for him that this was home. This was his own town, the city he loved. He soaked in all the familiar sights, the familiar smells. The sound of horses' hooves on the road and even the fresh smell of their droppings. The only thing that could make him happier now would be to see, by some miracle of chance, the face of his own Becky coming towards him along the canal bank.

At Leeson Street Bridge his sense of contentment was shattered by the sound of rifle-fire from the direction of Stephen's Green. Unmistakable, the distinctive thud of the Mauser. He had been there with David Townsend when they helped stash away the German rifles before the war broke out. He had carried one of those guns himself in the days when he and David drilled with the others. Now those same guns were being used against mates of his own. His detachment kept moving, ignoring the gunfire in the city centre.

Eamon was one of a company of twenty men walking on opposite sides of the road ahead of the horse drawn consignment. The pace was relaxed. The bayonets fixed on their rifles glinted in the spring sunshine. The trees gracing the pavements in this quiet respectable area sported fresh crowns of green and promise. You could smell the wallflowers in people's front gardens. Apart from some children who stopped their play to stare at the sight of the soldiers nobody gave them much notice. There was a marvellous sense of normality about the whole operation.

At Rialto the road curved to the right as it approached the narrow humpback bridge which carried traffic across a spur of the canal. He knew it well, this bridge, the Rialto Bridge. He loved the name of it, *the Rialto*, exotic and strange, and the sight of it now brought back a day in his childhood, when they had taken the tram out here on a Sunday afternoon to picnic on the canal bank and watch a slender barge, laden with barrels of Guinness and drawn by a single horse, drift by on its lazy way to the midlands.

As he reached the top of the bridge his gaze fell on a canal boat drawn up against the bank, its cargo of peat being unloaded onto the grassy quayside. He admired the rhythmic movements of the men who tossed the hard black sods from the boat to where some boys built them into sloping stacks against the next downpour of rain.

A peaceful scene and not the sort of place you would expect anyone to take a pot-shot at you. But when a bullet ricocheted off the granite parapet a yard from where he was at that moment he knew someone had tried to kill him. Someone firing from a complex of buildings over to his right. You could see the entrance up ahead at a curve in the road. From where he was it looked like a hospital but why in the name of God would anyone start firing from inside a hospital? They must know it would become the target for return fire.

Two officers came up, one of whom was Captain Martyn, a man whose bravery on the battlefield he heard men talk about. The other was Captain Oates, the colonel's son. They had orders from the colonel to enter the complex and clear it of snipers in order to get the convoy safely across the bridge. Eamon was one of the squad to be sent in. They got inside the grounds by scaling a wall and taking shelter behind some outbuildings. From there they began their advance through the grounds darting from one building to another while trying to pinpoint the source of fire which became more intense now that the rebels had spotted the incursion.

Captain Oates passed the message along that he had identified the rebels' stronghold, a residence of some sort, possibly a nurses' home. By concentrating the attack on this building they could tie up the rebels long enough to let the convoy clear the bridge. There were now up to fifty or sixty Foresters in the grounds, more than enough, Eamon reckoned, to dislodge these head-bangers who imagined they could hold off the British army.

For some reason he thought of David Townsend and prayed that he had the good sense to keep out of it, away from such a madcap escapade. With the thought of David came the thought of Becky. The quicker this was over the sooner he would get to see his girl again. He had missed her so badly in the past ten months. Now at last they were going to be together again. Somewhere in this town Becky Townsend moved and laughed and longed to see him.

He watched as Captain Oates assembled an assault party. What came next was reminiscent of something he had witnessed too often in France. At the shrill blast of the captain's whistle this party made a dash towards the rebel stronghold. They were hemmed in by the buildings on either side and fully exposed to the rebels' fire. They ran into a withering blast of bullets, cut down without mercy until the remaining few scattered, seeking shelter wherever they could find it. Eamon could see no sense whatever in such a tactic. Where was the point of forcing men to rush to their deaths with no chance at all of reaching, much less breaching the target? He hoped the officers would not attempt a repeat performance.

He was summoned by hand signals to a meeting in a yard out of sight of the rebel headquarters. He was relieved to hear there would be no further attempts to rush the building in a frontal attack. The new strategy was to get in from the side. There were passages linking the buildings and this is how Captain Martyn planned to get close to the rebel HQ. Martyn needed a dozen men for this operation. Any more than that and they would be getting in each other's way. He cast his eye around the group, passing over some and pointing to others. To his credit the captain knew each of his men by name. He also knew the ones he could rely on to put up a good show. And so it went. 'You, Private Jennings, you, Private Stone. Corporal Walker.' One by one the chosen men moved to the captain's side. And finally, at the very end, Eamon heard his own name called. 'Private Brennan, over here, please.'

Eamon was now part of the assault party detailed to penetrate the rebels' headquarters and retake the building.

Fifty Three

'Don't relax, lads, don't relax.' Charlie Burgess was jittery. There was very little activity all that Thursday morning. Just the occasional bullet winging its way in over the barricades and slamming into wall or ceiling. Each bullet altered the pattern of pock-marks that decorated the rooms facing the front. Charlie remained convinced that the relative inactivity of the morning was no more than a ploy to lull them into a false sense of security. It looked like he was going to be proved right when they heard a sudden exchange of rifle fire from the Rialto end.

Eddie Kent took the field-glasses and crawled out onto the roof to see what was going on. He came back down with the news that the outpost guarding the western approaches was under sustained attack. He had set up that position to block any attempt to bring in reinforcements at Rialto. Now he realised that those men were exposed and outnumbered.

'They can't hold out,' he said. 'Eight men against God knows how many. They'll have to get out of there. Let's hope they can manage it safely.'

He handed the glasses to David and told him to go up on the roof and report back on any development.

Once out on the roof it gave David a feeling of grim satisfaction to see the flag he had erected lifting defiantly in the afternoon breeze. Though the fabric was ripped by bullets it was still there announcing to the nation that the fight went on, that the Provisional Government of the Irish Republic still held sway. It was good to feel that he, David Townsend, was playing his own small part in this great venture.

In the midst of these thoughts something at the Rialto end caught his attention. He focussed his binoculars on the low building, little more than a shed, from which the defenders had been firing. The glasses showed how flimsy this building was and from where he lay, four or five hundred yards away, it seemed to offer no protection.

The movement that caught his attention was what looked like a white handkerchief attached to a broom handle coming through a window. There was no mistaking the intent of this flag. It was an offer of surrender and David felt sick in the pit of his stomach. Not that he blamed those comrades, caught as they were in a death-trap. But the possibility of surrender had never been entertained by either Kent or Burgess when they took control of the South Dublin Union.

He reported what he had seen to Kent and saw the commandant shrug his shoulders as he said, 'Well, this is it, men. This is the big one. They're coming to get us.'

Within a short space of time the place was teeming with soldiers. They darted from building to building, seeking vantage points from which to fire on the rebel strongholds. Soon it became obvious that they were setting up a concentrated attack on the Nurses Home. They seemed to think that if they knocked out the rebel HQ the rest would be just a matter of mopping up.

It began with raking fire from the Royal Hospital. Bullets slashed the front of the building, side to side like a devil's whip, lash after lash of deadly burning lead. And yet the men inside stuck to their positions, each with his rifle at the ready, waiting for the coming infantry attack.

Eddie Kent spoke to each of them in turn. 'Hold your fire till you hear me shout and don't shoot unless you've a man in your sights.' David and the others assured him they could hold the building against any offensive. With the barricades in place, the place was impregnable and with plenty of ammunition they were confident they could stop any attack.

A whistle sounded from the direction of the army positions and straight away a body of men sprang out of hiding and made a furious dash towards HQ building. David picked his man, pulled the trigger and watched as the soldier fell and lay motionless where he fell. The next man he picked was already within yards of the building. He too came down. Everywhere they fell like ninepins and the attack fizzled out as soldiers began to falter before turning to make a dash for shelter.

A cheer went up in the Nurses Home. For David, the thrill of putting down a much stronger force was like the time he put the ball over the bar in the last minute of the hurling final to make his club county champions. Indescribable. All those gruelling weekends of military training in the Furry Glen had paid off. Each man knew exactly what to do when the moment came. They had stopped the enemy in his tracks. Looking through a slit in the barricade he saw the bodies of their attackers lying lifeless on the cobbles.

'Will they try again?' said Feeney.'

'If they want to commit suicide,' said David.

Kent came around to congratulate his men. 'Stick at your posts and stay alert.'

There was, however, no repeat attack. It must have been obvious that rushing the building could never work. It remained now to be seen what they came up with next.

'I'm going up on the roof to suss out the situation,' Kent said.

'Keep your head down for Christ sake,' said Burgess. 'We don't want to lose our commanding officer.'

'You needn't take me for a fool.' Kent grabbed the field glasses and disappeared. Ten minutes later he was back down. He had observed small parties of soldiers slipping behind the rebel strongholds. It could only mean one thing. They were trying to get in through undefended parts of the hospital and work their way close to the rebel positions on the inside.

'It's not good,' said Kent. 'We can't stop them if we can't see them.'

'They'll not get in here,' said Burgess. 'All the doors are barricaded.' He raised his pistol and fired into a heavy filing cabinet pushed up against an internal door. 'Let them try coming through there and they'll be sitting ducks.' Some of the men, though, were muttering amongst themselves. 'Room to room combat,' said Feeney. 'We never got no training for that.'

'Just take it as it comes,' said David. Kent went from man to man checking that each had a supply of canister bombs and knew how to use them.

During the next hour there was a distinct edginess in the tiny garrison as they waited and listened. Eventually they heard a series of dull thuds, carried to them through the walls as though from a distance. The pattern of sounds corresponded to the blows of a heavy hammer and confirmed the Commandant's analysis of the new tactic. As the minutes dragged by the thudding sounds came closer as yet another wall was breached.

Then there was a long silence as though the intruders were preparing for a final push. David tried to imagine what it would be like when soldiers came pouring into the rebels' stronghold. He didn't fancy the idea of such close up fighting, of looking into another man's eyes as you tried to kill him and he tried to kill you.

They heard muffled shots. It sounded like they were shooting into a blank wall. Then the wall shuddered from a blow on the other side. Flakes of plaster began to litter the floor. It was only minutes now before the beginnings of a hole would appear. The stairs leading to the first floor they had barricaded on the first day, which meant that the lobby was divided in two. This barricade of desks, bookcases and other wooden furniture reached nearly as high as the first landing. The opening at the foot of the stairs was designed to be blocked quickly and with minimum effort. It gave the defenders a distinct advantage since they could fire down on anyone in the lobby.

'Up the stairs, everyone,' said Kent. David stopped on the landing where he had a commanding view of the lobby. He could see the widening hole and expected that at any moment a large chunk of masonry would topple onto the tiles making an entrance for the attackers. He saw Burgess fire several shots through the opening to let them know what to expect. There were shouts from the other room and the hammering stopped. Something rolled through the hole, something he recognised it as a hand-grenade seconds before it exploded.

In those two seconds he had dropped down to avoid injury but Charlie Burgess beside him gave a yelp of pain and grasped his shoulder. Blood seeped between his fingers. 'The fuckers got me.' He grabbed onto David for support. 'Get me out of here, man.' With the help of others David dragged the Second-in-Command around the turn in the stairs, out of sight of the hall. Then he went back down to the viewing point Burgess had been using. Shadows showed movement on the far side of the opening. Then came the blow that knocked in a huge chunk of dried out brickwork which broke in pieces as it hit the floor.

Time to use one of the bombs. David threw his device over the barricade, aiming it to fall beside the gaping hole. It exploded as it hit the floor. He and those near him ducked down to avoid the shrapnel pinging against the wall above their heads or burying itself in the barricade inches from their faces. The response was swift. Another grenade exploded at the bottom of the stairs. Too close by far. He moved to join his comrades on the return. With grenades rolling across the floor they could no longer keep the lobby covered. Burgess, propped against the landing wall, was shouting, 'Don't let the bastards through. Shoot the first bugger that sticks his head in.'

'I can see nothing with the dust,' David said.

'Just keep the blasted hole covered, that's all.'

He doubted the hole was big enough to let a man through but he crept down a couple of steps to get a better look. What he saw surprised and frightened him. A soldier who had managed to get a leg through was attempting to squeeze head and shoulders in next. David waited until the bulk of the man's body was almost through. Then he raised his rifle and fired at the too soft target. The soldier uttered no sound as his body sagged. 'That's the way to do it,' said Burgess and further up the stairs other voices raised a cheer. He relished the acclaim of his mates, proud to be the one who stopped the enemy in his tracks.

***

'That has to be their command centre,' said Captain Martyn, indicating a green flag hanging limp above a three storey building at the far side of the complex. We're not going to take it from the front. The best way in is through the long building that butts onto it. Once inside we can work our way along. It's our best bet.'

'Excuse me, Sir,' said Edwards, a tall earnest looking lad with thick lenses. 'It's for all the world like a hospital ward.'

'If it's the patients you're worried about, they've a better chance with us than they'll get when the Huns arrive. Think of that, lad. We'll root out these trouble-makers whatever it takes.

Don't forget they've been armed by the Germans so we know what side they're on.'

Martyn divided his band into two groups. 'Edwards, Roberts, Payne, Grimes and you Brennan, you five come with me.' Eamon could barely conceal his pride at being picked to go with the captain. Corporal Walker was detailed to take the rest of the men and explore behind the buildings to see if there was another way in.

They made use of the cover provided by the machine gun on the Royal Hospital to make a dash for the entrance to the nearest building. They smashed in the door and found themselves in a hospital corridor. Nurses stood blocking the doorways that led to the rooms where patients lay. Fear and anxiety was evident on their faces. Behind them the sick and indigent of Dublin cowered beneath their blankets praying their nurses could save them.

The captain must have seen their apprehension. He announced in a loud voice that no one was going to get hurt. Just so long as everyone stayed where they were, he would have this whole thing under control in no time at all. One of the nurses, tall and authoritative looking, stepped out into the corridor to face him. 'Can't you see this is a hospital? You've no right to be here. These poor people are in danger of being shot in their beds.'

'I repeat, you stay in your rooms and no one gets hurt.'

'No one gets hurt, is that what you're telling me? No one gets hurt, is it? So what about Nurse Keogh, shot by your men, and she only doing her duty, tending to a dying man?'

'I'm so sorry to hear that, Ma'am, believe me.'

'And what about the old woman over in the asylum who got a bullet in the face as she sat in her chair by the window?'

'A stray bullet? It can happen, unfortunately.'

'There'll be no stray bullets if you turn around now and take yourself and your men out of here.'

'Stand aside nurse, we have serious business to do here. Come on men, follow me.' He pushed past her and the others followed. Eamon felt uneasy about where he now found himself. This was not the sort of war zone he experienced in France. He knew now where they were, where this battle was taking place. It was the South Dublin Union. He knew *The Union* and knew the fear it inspired amongst the city's poor, the fear that when old age and illness at last caught up with them they would find themselves faced with the shameful prospect of dying in *The Workhouse*.

He worried for these people now, hundreds of helpless men and women trapped in these old buildings while a full-blown battle raged all around them. He had thought Flanders was hell. Now another hell had burst open its gates in the heart of his own native city.

Their way was blocked by a locked door. They used a heavy trolley which they ran at the wooden door until it gave and swung open. They found themselves in a store room with a single door leading to the outside at the back of the building. A solid wall appeared to block any further progress. However fortune was on their side for the store held a variety of tools including spades, hammers, crowbars and, as luck would have it, a single pickaxe.

Beneath the plaster was a wall of brick which they attacked with vigour, taking it in turn to wield the pickaxe. The old brickwork began to crumble and their efforts were at last rewarded when a point of light came through from the other side. They worked with renewed vigour until at last the hole was big enough to allow passage into the adjoining building. The captain motioned for silence as he listened to see if their efforts had drawn any unwelcome attention. Though the sound of gunfire carried through the walls from a distance they heard no human voices and the adjoining building seemed deserted.

First through was the captain with revolver in hand. When he confirmed that the place was deserted he beckoned his men to follow. In the centre stood a wide table on which were piles of papers, cardboard files and ledgers. Against the wall stood three filing cabinets, a wooden drawer left open with an open file sitting on top. All the signs were that the place had been abandoned in a hurry, little wonder seeing that the windows at the front were shattered and the floor littered with broken glass. The walls were riddled with bullet holes. The occupants must have fled through a door opening to the back. A second door appeared to link this office with the next building. That building had to be their target, the house the rebels had taken over to use as their headquarters.

Sounds reached them from the storeroom they had just left. Captain Martyn signalled silence and they waited, guns at the ready, eyes focussed on the gap through which they had come. They heard shuffling and muted voices before someone came close enough to the opening for them to recognise the uniform of a Forester. Martyn whistled a low signal and got a similar tone in response.

The bulky figure that wriggled through into the office turned out to be Corporal Walker and he was followed by four others. They had come through a walled vegetable garden and found the door to the storeroom unlocked. There was now an officer and ten men, separated from the next part of the complex by a door which no one had yet tried. They stood with their guns trained on the door while the captain turned the handle and drew the door silently inwards. After a minute's wait Martyn went through signalling the others to follow.

They found themselves in a corridor with windows looking onto the back. At the other end, a door. All the indications were that this door led to the rebels' stronghold. They could expect it to be heavily barricaded.

As before it was the captain who approached the door to turn the handle and test the lock. He didn't seem surprised to find it locked but what puzzled Eamon was the fact that the handle was rusted and stiff as though the door hadn't been used for a very long time. Martyn signalled Ronnie Grimes to use the crowbar. The jamb of the door splintered as the locking mechanism burst. Nine rifles stood ready to pump a hail of bullets into anyone who appeared in the opening.

What met their gaze, however, was a dusty decaying wall hidden for years behind the locked door, bricks barely bound by crumbling mortar and blanketed in spiders' webs. The dull thud of a bullet burying itself in the other side confirmed they were right up against the enemy. 'Well boys,' said the Captain. 'We've come this far and we're not going back. Anyone handy with a pick, what?'

His gaze rested on Walker who was holding the pickaxe. The corporal stepped forward and struck a few blows at the wall. Pieces of broken brick fell about his feet. As he continued to rain blow after blow it became clear that the wall was thicker than they expected. Behind the bricks was a layer of concrete. He handed the pick over to Chapman, bigger and even burlier than himself. When it was Eamon's turn he realised his efforts were making little impression. He wasn't used to this type of physical labour. Others took his place.

Eventually a hole appeared as the point of the pick burst through. Immediately, two or three bullets came through from the far side. They had a welcoming party waiting to receive them! 'I'll pass them my calling card,' said the Captain, 'just so they'll know it's a friendly visit.' He drew the pin from a grenade and rolled it in through the hole. Seconds later the blast rushed back at them through the hole.

With the hole growing wider the pick swinger was in mortal danger and had to work while pressing himself against the wall. Even with the men taking turns it still took another half hour before the hole was wide enough for a man to get through. The captain called a halt. 'Five minutes, lads,' he whispered, 'then we go in.' He sent another grenade into the rebels' stronghold and again the explosion was deafening. Someone swore in the other room.

He began loading and checking his revolver while the men did the same with their Lee-Enfields. Bursts of rifle fire sounded on the other side and bullets continued to come through.

'Right, men,' said the Captain, his voice low, 'it's time to go in. 'A few grenades will give us the cover we need.' Eamon looked around at the other young faces. Two of these boys were only eighteen. None had war experience as he had. Some hadn't finished their basic training. They had barely been shown how to fire a gun. He thought he saw fear in their eyes as they waited. He and Walker were the two most experienced men in the group. Walker stepped forward indicating he would go first. The captain nodded approval.

Unexpected thoughts flashed through Eamon's head. He thought of Becky. Coming over on the boat from Liverpool he dreamed of meeting her, had imagined all the things he needed to say to her and all the things she would say to him. So much to tell her, so much to catch up on. They would have so little time together, even assuming he got permission to leave his unit for a few hours. Now everything was upside down. With the whole town in the grip of an insurrection it looked like his unit would be kept on high alert until the trouble was put down. And there was no knowing when that would be.

For now though, in this present moment, he wanted to carry the thought of her with him as he scrambled through the narrow gap separating his unit from the rebels on the far side of that wall. He watched the captain take a hand grenade from his belt, draw the pin and count four seconds before flipping it through into the next room. They froze until they heard the explosion and felt the blast of hot air that rushed back at them. They heard, too, a cry of agony from the other side that acted as a signal for Walker to go through.

The corporal turned sideways, put his right leg through, then his right arm, then his head. At that point he seemed to be struggling. There was a shot and the corporal's body went limp. 'Too bad,' muttered the captain. 'Okay, boys, get him back in here.' Easier said than done. They struggled to free Walker's bulky frame and drag him back into the room. It was difficult and dangerous work. Stand in front of that hole and you could get a bullet.

***

David watched the enemy wrestle to remove the body of their comrade. His mates were making use of the lull to strengthen their defences. They rearranged the office furniture at the foot of the stairs to foil any attempt to follow them up onto the first floor. In five minutes the corpse had been removed and more of the masonry knocked out making it easier for the attackers to get through.

First came a stream of grenades, one after the other. The lobby was lethal with flying shrapnel. When the dust had subsided David could make out a man in officer uniform standing in the lobby, drawing the pin from a grenade and making ready to throw it over the barricade.

'Grenade!' he shouted. 'Down, everyone.'

The grenade struck the top of the barricade and bounced back into the lobby. From his position on the landing David saw the officer bend down, sweep up the fallen grenade and without a moment's hesitation, lob it back over the top. 'Watch out,' he shouted, and threw himself down as everyone on the landing dived for cover. Burgess, injured, was unable to move and so took more shrapnel, new injuries. Some of the others had minor lacerations while David by some miracle escaped.

Burgess was in a bad state and the job was to get him up to the next floor and onto a mattress to assess the extent of his injuries. From the amount of blood, David thought he couldn't survive. 'Get back to your post, Townsend, and take these canisters with you.' It was Eddie Kent, determined not to allow the Army breach the barricade. 'Bomb the bastards to hell,' Feeney added.

Back at his post he saw four soldiers with their officer in the lobby below. They were dragging at the barricade, attempting to topple it. The officer had another grenade in his hand, sizing up the height of the barricade. Feeney appeared at David's elbow and grabbed a canister bomb out of David's hand. 'If it's bombs they want,' he muttered, 'here we go.' He lobbed the bomb over the top, in among the soldiers. The blast and the shrapnel had their effect. Stunned soldiers lay helpless on the floor as Feeney started firing. One managed to make it back through the hole. After him went the captain, dragging an injured soldier behind him.

'Let them go,' said David, for he couldn't but admire the English officer's bravery. A strange silence descended on the empty lobby. The scene of the battle was as peaceful as if there had never been an incursion. The enemy had been driven off with the loss of three men, two lying dead on the floor of the lobby and the one whose body had blocked the hole.

***

It took longer than expected to retrieve Walker's body and make the hole wider so as to avoid a repeat of that disaster.

Captain Martyn decided to lead the next incursion. First though, he would lay down a carpet of exploding grenades. He took grenades from the dead corporal's belt. 'When I go in,' he said, 'you all follow in quick order, Brennan first.'

They waited for the last of the grenades to burst before going through into the fog of dust. *You're with me, Becky, here goes.* Once through the hole, Eamon could see nothing in the haze, just a glimmer of daylight from above. He could just about make out the barricade dividing the room and heard angry shouts and swearing from the other side. He joined the captain in the space at the bottom of the stairs and was followed by more of his mates. They started dragging at the furniture that was blocking their way.

Martyn drew a grenade from his belt but before he had time to draw the pin something hit the ground at Eamon's feet. Hit and exploded in the same instant. There was a noise like thunder as his brain burned. Lights flashed and danced like sparklers in his head. Becky was there and she was smiling a smile more beautiful than he ever seen her smile before – radiant like an angel. Everywhere there were lights. The lights streaked like dashing stars and he rode up on them, up, up, until he imagined he was at the ceiling and looking down at the room with its dead and bloodied men.

Then he saw nothing.

***

When Kent came down to inspect the scene his first concern was to block off the hole bored by the attackers. If anything could be certain in a war like this, it was that they would be back. Now that they had penetrated the rebel stronghold, had seen the setup at close quarters, it was only a matter of time till they returned. And next time their strategy would be better thought out. He looked at the bodies of the dead soldiers. 'Get them out of here,' he said.

Two of the men dragged the corpses to the front door and waited while others took up positions at the windows to offer cover. Half dragging, half carrying, they got the dead outside and left them against the wall.

David helped Feeney retrieve the body of the man-in-the-hole, drag it face down out onto the pathway and turn it so that it was staring at the stars. Feeney hurried back to the safety of the building.

David delayed a moment, looking at the upturned faces of the dead soldiers. He tried to convince himself that what he saw could not be true for one of those faces was the blood -smeared face of his close friend, Eamon Brennan. The same Eamon Brennan who had set off eight months ago to fight the Germans in France. It didn't make sense. Brennan had written to Becky to say he was recovering from his injuries in an English hospital, that he would soon be back in the front line in Flanders. Flanders, not Ireland. But there was no mistake about whose body he was looking at now. They were shouting for him to get back inside. He hoped they wouldn't spot the moistening in his eyes. He turned his back on the only real pal he had known, the man he had only lately learned was the secret husband of his dear sister, Becky.

As he closed the door behind him he looked out and saw two friars approaching and recognised the familiar brown habit of the Capuchins. They came like an answer to prayer. Right now what he most needed was someone in whom he could confide, someone to share his terrible secret, someone to whom he could confess his overwhelming sense of shame.

Fifty Four

When she woke on Friday morning Becky knew there was something awful hanging in the air waiting to torment her. Things began to dribble back into her conscious mind. First David. Then Sammy. David she had spent two days trying to find before she was told he was with the Volunteers in the South Dublin Union. Sammy gravely ill in the Richmond. Her father and mother taking it in turns to go and sit by his bedside to watch his relentless decline. She remembered now that she hadn't laid eyes on little Sammy since he had been taken to the hospital. First thing this morning then, that's where she must go.

People she met along the way had a subdued look about them, defeated it seemed by the disaster that had overtaken them. The town they knew and loved was burning to the ground. From the steps of the hospital she could see a pall of black smoke hanging low over the city. Here in Brunswick Street you could get the smell, the sour sooty smell of burnt-out buildings.

Fresh casualties were being rushed through the hospital doors even as Becky watched. Inside the hospital the mood was sombre. In the corridor leading to Sammy's ward there was a grim silence. It was the brooding all-pervasive silence of death.

His bed was near the door and she picked him out straight away. His white face was to the ceiling and his eyes closed. For one horrible moment she thought he might have slipped away. She placed her fingers at his wrist and her hand on the cold brow. He opened his eyes and looked up at her. She bent low over him to give him a kiss. 'How are you, Sammy? Are you feeling better?' She detected a look of fear in his face.

'Does everyone go to purgatory when they die?'

She was taken aback by the strangeness of the question. 'If they've been really good they go straight to heaven.' She attempted a reassuring smile.

'Really really good? Will I go straight to heaven, Becky?' 'Of course you will, but not for a very long time yet. When you're an old man.'

'I heard two nurses talking and one said *it's a shame to see him go so young*. What does she mean? Am I going to die?'

'I'm asking the Little Flower to make you better. She's never let anyone down yet.'

'Will she know who I am?'

'I'll tell her you're my smart little brother, Sammy Townsend. She'll know you all right.'

'Will you tell her I don't want to die?'

Becky buried her face in Sammy's neck. 'You're not going to die, Sammy. I give you my word.'

'I'm real tired, Becky. I think I'm going to close me eyes.'

She stood beside the bed a long time, looking down at little Sammy's sleeping form. Then she bent to kiss his pale face. At the door she paused to look back at the slight figure in the bed. With the cuff of her sleeve she wiped her eyes. Yes, she would pray. Yes, she would storm the heavens. Yet a taunting voice told her that her prayers would lose their way among the uncaring clouds. Helpless in the face of fate she hurried from the hospital and made her way across the river to where her presence might serve to soothe some stricken soldier or wounded civilian.

***

She noticed a change. Things didn't seem as busy as yesterday.

The two doctors were nowhere to be seen. The medical students who had been helping out hadn't yet shown up. Mattresses around the walls had dead bodies and most of these were soldiers. She talked to Hetty, who never seemed to sleep. 'We were able to get most of the bad cases down to Steevens', Hetty said. 'And some of them that we treated were able to go home.'

'Where did these come from?' said Becky indicating the corpses that lined the walls.

'The morgue in Steevens' is full and the Mater's only taking bodies from the Northside. They've hundreds of bodies over there.'

'When were these brought in?'

'Last night. We arranged a ceasefire after you left and got them out of the grounds. All soldiers, no Shinners.'

No Shinners. Becky sighed with relief. She had been on the point of taking a closer look at the bodies to assure herself that David was not among them. Thank God, he was safe so far. When Fr Aloysius talked to him he was still okay. With that worry off her mind she asked Hetty how she could make herself useful.

'The least we can do for these poor devils is give them a bit of a clean-up. Most of them will be from across the water. It might be no harm to try and make them presentable before the army arrives to take them away.'

'Where will I start?' Becky was glad to have something to occupy her and get her mind off things. To stop her thinking about Sammy lying gravely ill in his hospital bed.

'Oh, there's a few more back there,' Hetty said, indicating the room at the back.

'Righto so, that's where I'll start.'

It was the same room where they boiled water for the tea. It had a tap and sink in one corner and a couple of gas rings with a saucepan sitting on top. Above the sink there were shelves with cups, saucers, jugs and spoons. There was no other furniture — just four bare white walls. She found hot water in the saucepan and used it to wet some cloths. Under the sink she found a sponge which would come in useful. Four corpses lay on trestle-tables, all in army uniform.

She dampened the sponge and decided to begin with the body in the corner.

Four bodies. She would start with the body in the corner. She had seen so many dead bodies in the past few days. It was hard to believe you could become so inured to death in such a short space of time.

She would start with the body in the corner.

There were already bodies in the streets on Wednesday when she set off on her odyssey in search of David. *Start with the body in the corner.*

Dead soldiers, dead workers. Dead women, dead children. This war had thrown up its healthy harvest of dead. All the dead who had paid with their blood for other men's noble dreams. In fifty fear-filled hours she had come to know the sweetly smell of the freshly dead. *Start with the body in the corner.*

She took her damp sponge to his brow, the brow of the body in the corner. She stared at the face and saw there the face of her boy, her man, her soldier, her lover, her husband.

For the body in the corner was his. *His was the body in the corner.*

Her screams brought people running. She pointed. They looked. She tried to speak, to tell them – explain. She pointed and they saw a dead soldier. She screamed again and they gave their arms to support her. Sweet oblivion washed over her then and she yielded to its merciful embrace.

Friday, the twenty eighth of April, 1916. The day that changed her life forever. The day her future died.

Fifty Five

David was on lookout on Saturday evening when he saw two nurses walking towards HQ. He called Eddie Kent and Kent said he would talk to them.

'Have yous got anyone hurt in there?' one of them said.

'I've a man with a bullet in his side and an ugly wound in his shoulder. He's going to need treatment but there's no way he'll agree to leave.'

'Can we come in then and dress it for him?'

'Hang on a minute.' Kent left the nurses waiting in the lobby and went upstairs to talk to Charlie Burgess. Burgess was reluctant, maybe doubting the women's competence, but Kent overrode his objections. The nurses were brought upstairs to where the wounded officer lay on a bed, his eyes closed, in obvious pain. David went up with them to see if he could be of any assistance. They were both Red Cross but revealed that they were also in Cumann na mBan, in sympathy with the rebels.

They spent some time cleaning and dressing the wounds, watched by David and one or two of the others. Once finished, they said they had some interesting news. There were persistent reports that the GPO and the Four Courts had surrendered the previous day. 'They were seen laying down their guns at the Parnell Monument.'

Charlie Burgess gave a roar and tried to raise himself despite the obvious pain showing on his face. 'It's lies,' he shouted. 'Get out of here will yous with your lies. No Volunteer ever surrenders. We'll fight to the end, every one of us, to the last drop of our blood.'

In the face of his anger the nurses beat a hasty retreat. Eddie Kent, however, followed them outside to get more details. Not only had Pearse signed the surrender, they said, but he issued orders for all commanders to follow his example and lay down their arms. They had heard all this from some Cumann na mBan women who were in the GPO up the moment they had been forced out by the flames.

When the nurses were gone, Eddie Kent called his men together. 'It seems General Headquarters was forced to surrender but I can't see any of the other garrisons giving up so easily. Not De Valera in Boland's Mill or Tom McDonagh in Jacobs. I can't see it happening. I can't talk for Connolly's crowd in Stephen's Green. I know nothing about them. I never trusted that Citizen Army — always thought they had their own agenda. Anyway, you can take it from me lads we won't be giving in so easy. Are yous with me, boys?'

His answer was a loud cheer.

'That's what I wanted to hear, lads. David, I want a word with you.'

David followed the Commandant to the back door. 'I want you to make your way over to Jamesons. Find Conn Colbert and tell him I sent you. Ask him what he's heard and what he plans to do. Then come straight back here to me.'

'Right, Sir.'

'And keep to the shadows. We don't want anyone taking pot shots at you.' He passed David a handgun.

***

Conn Colbert remembered him right away, remembered the evening David arrived at the recruiting office saying he had a row with his father and had nowhere to go. 'Did Cathy look after you alright, David?'

'She let me stay a couple of nights till my own sister came looking for me.'

'Where would we be without sisters, what?' A boyish grin spread across Colbert's youthful face. It was hard to believe that this chap, not much older than David himself was commanding the Jamesons Garrison with sixty to a hundred men and women under his command.

David explained why he was there, that Commandant Kent wanted to know what they should do when they got Pearse's order to surrender. Colbert suddenly looked serious. 'What does Kent think? I can't see either himself or Burgess giving up so easy.'

'What'll I tell them?'

'Tell them I'm going to sit tight and see how things work out.'

David waited to see if the boyish looking leader was going to elaborate on this. 'Sit tight?' he said.

'Just tell them that,' said Colbert and David understood he wasn't going to get any more on the subject.

Fifty Six

There was a stranger in Sammy's bed. Isaac looked around for a nurse but there wasn't one to be seen. He went back out to the office.

'Me young lad's been moved. He was below in the men's ward but he's not there now.'

'Moved? Do you know where?' She was a slip of a girl, sparkling with the excitement of life. Probably new in the job.

'Can you find out where they're after putting him?'

'Your name, Sir?'

'Townsend.'

She opened a ledger and drew her pencil down through the names beginning with 'T.' Then she heaved the book shut and looked at Isaac.

'Will you take a seat over there and I'll see can I find out for you.' She headed off, leaving the reception desk unattended. After what seemed like an age she arrived back with a nurse who asked Isaac who had he come to see.

'Sammy Townsend, me own wee fella.'

She looked at him thoughtfully before she said, 'Is there anyone else with you?'

He was about to say *open your eyes woman* but gave her a blank stare instead.

'Things is hectic at the moment,' she said, 'I'll show you a more comfortable spot to wait.'

She led him to a small room furnished with a couple of soft armchairs. On a low table lay a copy of the London Illustrated News with an artist's impression of a burning Dublin. Twenty minutes passed before the door opened and two nurses came in, one mature and grave looking. This one said, 'You know about your little boy, don't you? I mean his sad passing.'

Isaac turned the phrase over in his head. *Sad passing*. What could that mean? Sammy was very sick, and that was sad. But *passing?* What was that? *Sad passing*. He had heard this somewhere before. In church – that was it – in church after old Essie Noble slipped on the frost and cracked her skull.

'No,' he said, 'it's Sammy Townsend I'm looking for. My little son. I was here with him yesterday. I only want to see how he's doing. I won't be staying long.'

The younger nurse came over and laid her hand on his arm. 'He's in the mortuary, Mr Townsend — your son Sammy. I'll take you down there now if you would like to see him.'

He followed the nurse down a long cold corridor and across an open yard, his mind a maelstrom of emotions. There, inside a bleak building apart they had left his little son, all that now remained of wee Sammy Townsend, his greatest hope for the future, nothing now but a lifeless remnant.

***

When Isaac told his wife she began to cry — quietly at first with silent sobs. And when the sobbing turned to a heaving that threatened to choke her she slid down onto a chair, holding the edge of the table for support. Not knowing what to say or how to deal with his own grief he went into the parlour to sit alone with the awful anguish that enveloped him.

***

Poor Ruth came in from the back garden to find her mother in the depths of desolation and knew without being told that she had lost her little brother, that she would never again play with him, sit and read with him, keep up with his every new move in chess, decipher his stories of hair-raising escapades with Kipper Warrick or frolic with him as they ploughed the drifts of Autumn leaves for chestnuts.

***

They found him lying in a flimsy night-shirt on a marble slab with a loose sheet thrown over his body. His eyes were closed, his features rigid. There were other bodies on other slabs but those they hardly noticed. Annie placed her hand on his forehead in the same gesture she had so often used when drawing the blankets up over his sleeping body. Poor Ruth held his cold hand in her soft warm grasp and bent her face against his unresponsive cheek.

Annie had wanted to be here when Becky arrived not knowing what had happened. They ought to be the ones to break the news to her and then they would weep together, mother and daughters, over their unspeakable loss. Annie looked at the clock and stood up. She signed to Poor Ruth that they ought to wait for Becky in the lobby.

As they got up to go, the door opened and a woman in nurse's uniform came in.

'Ah, there you are, Mrs Townsend. I was hoping to catch you. I'm Sister Willis, by the way.'

Annie and Poor Ruth took her proffered hand in turn.

'I can't tell you how sorry I am at your loss. Such a sweet little boy and he with his whole life ahead of him. A terrible waste.'

'The Lord's ways are not our ways.'

'I came to tell you I was with him last night only an hour before

God took him. He was awake and wanted to talk so I sat beside him and asked him if he was happy. His face lit up on the spot. "I'm going to the angels," he said. I was so taken aback I hardly knew what to say. "What does that mean?" I asked him. "I saw them, the angels, and they're going to take me with them tonight, so they are." And his little face was radiant. To tell you the truth, I could barely hold back the tears.' Even now as she spoke, a tear glistened in her eye and neither Annie nor Poor Ruth, who was following every word, had the slightest doubt that she was telling the truth.

'Thanks be to God and his Blessed Mother,' Annie said as a wave of consolation swept over her. She was more at peace now for she knew it was a message from above that the Matron had brought her. 'He's with the angels,' she said to Poor Ruth and Poor Ruth nodded and managed a brave smile.

Fifty Seven

Becky awoke to a terrible sense of loss, a gaping void that nothing would ever fill. She felt empty, drained, the life sucked out of her. She had told no one but Poor Ruth and sworn her sister to secrecy. Her sister and brother were the only living souls who knew about her marriage to Eamon. She would share her grief with her mother, but not yet. Her father she could never—would never—tell. He had forbidden her to have anything to do with Eamon and was never going to understand her loss, much less forgive her flagrant flouting of his wishes.

Both her parents were up early and when she came into the kitchen they told her that her father would go first to the hospital to check on Sammy and that Annie and Poor Ruth would go down later. Becky said she would go to the First Aid centre in the morning and visit Sammy in the afternoon. 'There's talk the fighting is nearly over,' she said. 'They're handing up their guns, some of them.' Her father didn't comment. He had too much weighing on his mind, she thought.

When her father had left for the hospital Becky went straight to Piggery Lane to commiserate with them on Eamon's death. If they hadn't yet heard she would have to face the brutal task of telling them their boy was dead. Had they even known he was in Ireland, in Dublin? As she walked across the uneven cobbles to the decrepit cottage with its crop of weeds growing out of the roof she saw a piece of black crape pinned to the door. They knew! The curtains were drawn closed. Absent, the normal hustle and bustle of noisy children with their squealing and squabbling.

When her knock was ignored she pressed the latch and pushed

in the door. She stood in a darkened space, immersed in a sea of sobbing. The father sat in his corner, his stoic face staring at the dying coals in their coating of grey ash. Opposite him the mother, her arms about her eldest daughter. Mrs Brennan turned a tearful face towards Becky. 'I suppose you heard,' she said. Becky threw her arms about the neck of Eamon's grieving mother. Two women sharing the depths of loss and despair, one the devoted mother, the other the grief-stricken bride.

'When did you hear?' Becky said. 'Last night an officer came to the door. He said they're bringing him up to Marlborough Barracks and we'll be able to see him today.'

'I saw him last night at the First Aid Centre. I wiped the blood from his face.' She wanted to say how brave and manly he looked. She wanted to say how proud they could be. She wanted to say—.

'I loved him so much. So much.' Her tears flowed then and mingled with those of Eamon's mother. So little in common they had, yet so much.

Fifty Eight

Isaac felt isolated and alone. All around him in the pews were husbands and wives, parents with their families of children, grandparents and babies — family groupings of one kind or another. He sat alone, for now with little Sammy gone, none of his children showed the slightest interest in coming with him to Sunday Service. He must accept at last that his wife had won the battle for the minds and souls of her children. Sammy alone had stuck by him, stayed loyal to the end. Now he was alone and isolated — defeated. With Sammy dead he had nobody.

Isaac stood with the congregation as they rose to sing.

Abide with me, fast falls the eventide; the darkness deepens —

How had it come to this that he had so alienated his family? How had he failed? What sin had he committed that God should punish him so? The congregation took their seats as the Reverend mounted the low wooden pulpit. He cleared his throat before intoning his text.

Therefore if thou bring thy gift to the altar, and there rememberest that thy brother hath ought against thee, leave there thy gift before the altar and go thy way. First be reconciled to thy brother, and then come and offer thy gift. Matthew Chapter Five, Verse twenty three.

Rev. Maunsell closed the book and placed his two hands on the sides of the lectern.

'Love for our brother goes far beyond our immediate family,' he said. 'It embraces the whole of humanity. In times like this it behoves us to remember that we are commanded to love even our enemies.' He went on to speak of bitter disputes that wreck harmony between neighbours, petty squabbles that lead to major rifts. And he spoke about the differences that can arise within the family itself, growing out of all proportion until they become intractable. Isaac shifted in his seat, glancing at those around him to see if they noticed his discomfort.

The Reverend's words made him think. Not only had he alienated his eldest son but he harboured within him a darker crime which he could reveal to no one. How he envied the people who in biblical times heaped their sins on the head of a goat and drove the condemned animal out into the desert, there to perish and their guilt with him.

How easy too it was for the Catholics. His wife could whisper her sins in the ear of a Roman priest to be told to *go now and sin no more*. What a boon it must be for them to be so easily shriven.

Isaac was at a cross-road. His eldest son had thrown in his lot with a murderous gang of outlaws while the rest of his family had been turned against him by his duplicitous wife. Things were coming to a head. Something would have to happen — what exactly he had no idea.

***

Annie saw how hard her husband had been hit by Sammy's death. He moved around the house like a man who carried an intolerable weight. You couldn't help but feel sorry for him. Gone the bluster and arrogance. Gone the overbearing attitude to his wife and children. He was like a stricken animal trying to make sense of a senseless world.

This morning he hadn't said much over his breakfast before going back upstairs to get himself dressed in his church-going suit. He left the house like a man in a daze, without a word.

Late into the night she had lain awake. She had a lot to think about. She thought about the randomness of death, the way it struck where it willed and swept up whoever it fancied. Yesterday as they stood beside Sammy's body in the morgue Becky had confided in her another tragic loss. Through her tears she told her mother how she had married young Eamon Brennan before he left for the war, and how she had discovered his dead and bloodied corpse at the First Aid station on Friday. Doubly bereaved, her daughter, doubly inconsolable.

Annie found it hard to make sense of what had befallen them. They were supposed to accept all such trials and visitations as the will of God. And God had his reasons whether we understood them or not. She had always accepted God's will precisely because it was His will. Three times she had lost the babies she carried in her womb, real living children she had come to know and love even while they lived and grew within her.

Annie thought it was only right and proper that she go with Isaac to see little Sammy where he lay in the hospital morgue. She waited outside St Paul's for him to come out after the service. He seemed surprised to see her. 'You could've met me there,' he said, 'in the mortuary'. 'We ought to arrive together,' she said.

***

'I can arrange to have prayers said before he's moved,' the matron said. 'A clergyman — or a priest maybe?' The matron was being remarkably thoughtful even if she seemed unsure about their religious affiliation. Annie looked over at Isaac but he indicated he would leave it to her. 'Thank you, Sister, it's so kind of you but we would rather just say our own prayers ourselves.' It was the safest course. There had been too many rows over religion in the past. Now Sammy's death was helping to put things in perspective.

'How about a coffin?' Matron said. 'I can fix that for you if you want. We got a supply in to cope with all the deaths in the past week.'

They accepted her offer and she left them alone in the morgue with their son's remains, alone in the vaulted space, apart from the stiffened corpses of the dead waiting in silence to be moved out and make room for those who would shortly follow them into the silent ranks of the departed. Annie could see that her husband was put out by talk of coffins and graves and burial for his little boy. She knew it from the way he left her to do all the talking. He was never like this before.

Coming out of the hospital they bumped into Annie's sister on her way in. Rose's face glistened with her tears. 'I got your message last night,' she said.

'We're just after coming out of the mortuary. He's like a little angel.'

'That's where he is now, with the angels,' Rose said.

'We're on our way over to the undertakers, to make arrangements,' Isaac said. 'Call up to the house after, why don't you?'

In Queen Street they found the door open and Bourke in his office. 'Open on a Sunday, Mr Bourke?' Isaac held the door as Annie came in. 'Busy times in this line of work,' Bourke said. They told him their business and he expressed his sympathy. 'All hearses is booked up for the next week,' he said. 'Never in my born days have I seen so many funerals. Queuing up on the road outside Glasnevin they are. You might be better off making your own arrangements, like a lot of folks is having to do. How about Mount Jerome? Seeing as you're Church of Ireland, I mean.'

'Right so,' said Isaac. 'I'll ask Harry Dodd if he can help us out.'

***

Through Stoneybatter and Manor Street he walked beside her

but said not a single word. In silence they arrived at their own front door. They knocked but no excited Sammy came charging through the hall to open. Poor Ruth in her silent world could not know they were there. When Becky came down the stairs to let them in Annie noticed her face was damp with weeping. Her daughter bore within her a double grief yet she was solicitous for her mother and father. 'Go in there to the parlour let yous, and I'll bring yous in a cup of tea.' Poor Ruth came in and gave each of her parents a long loving hug but Becky took her away and they retreated to the kitchen to leave their parents alone together.

Annie sat facing her husband. Never since she had first known him had she seen him like this. The fight had gone out of him. He was a shaken man. They sat together in the front parlour, something they never did. But this was not a normal day. There is nothing normal about a day when you've gone with your husband to take a long last look at your youngest child. In an odd way Sammy's death made her feel closer to Isaac than for many a long year.

'Did I ever tell you where this little cross came from?' she said. He looked up, snatched out of his torn thoughts by his wife's voice. He had a distracted look on his face as he struggled to relate to what she had said. 'Did I ever tell you about this wee cross?' she repeated. He looked across and saw his wife's hand at her neck, fingering an object attached to the light metal chain she always wore.

'I never paid much heed to it to tell the truth.'

'I got it from a young lad I knew.'

'You never told me that before. Who was he?'

'A lad I courted in the country. You wouldn't have known him.'

'In the country?' Isaac pondered this for a while. 'And you're still wearing it? He must have been something, that lad of yours.

- 355 -

What is it anyway?' His interest was aroused. 'It's Jesus on the cross. He carved it himself.' 'But you gave him up? Or was it he gave you up?'

'God took him. This is something to remember him by.' She held up the little crucifix for him to see. He looked at it in an absent sort of way but said nothing. She wanted him to know. The time for secrets was over. The time had come to tell her story. She had kept it from him for too long.

'I should have told you about it before now,' she said. 'A wife should have nothing hidden from her husband.'

'You never told me because I never asked — I suppose that's the truth of it. You seem intent on talking about him now.' She fondled the little cross with reverence and affection. She noted a spark of interest in his eyes. 'I'm telling you now because there's nothing to hide. It's all water under the bridge in any case. His name was Rory,' she said. 'Rory Reynolds.'

And she told him it all, from beginning to end, right to the moment she saw from her bedroom window the hearse with Rory's coffin disappear around the bend in the road, taking her love away from her forever.

They sat in silence a long time each lost in their thoughts. She felt all the better for having told him about her first love. How he received her story she didn't really know but she got a good inkling of his reaction when he said he too had a confession to make. She straightened in her chair wondering what in God's name was coming.

Then Isaac revealed for the first time what it was that had been troubling him all these years and the misery he had endured having no one to confide in or not finding it within himself to confide in anyone.

Fifty Nine

It was a long story and Annie refrained from cutting across him as he talked lest he should change his mind and withhold from her the true depth of his despair.

Isaac told her how he had heard their father entrust Adam with the task of taking the cart into town to collect the sacks of barley seed. He saw his older brother nodding with barely concealed impatience and wondered about Adam, that he seemed unable to display the slightest enthusiasm for their father's new enterprise.

Traynor had arrived the day before with his team of horses to turn the sod. It was a morning when a hard frost spread the grass with a carpet of crystal. It was a sight to be savoured, the brown earth bursting upwards in all its fertile freshness, a flock of squawking rooks swooping in behind the plough. It was a scene that spoke of promise and renewal. As they watched the plough team plodding up and down the expanse of the Six Acre and saw the sod rise and turn before the blade, they knew their father was deadly serious about this project, that there was to be no turning back now. Yet Adam had muttered to Isaac, 'It'll never work. A mad notion it is, to be sowing barley here. He should've stayed with the cattle.' 'Father's no fool,' Isaac said. 'When he gets his teeth into something he'll stick with it. You know yourself how stubborn he can be.'

Jacob Townsend had been galvanized for weeks by his new plan. The distillery in Enniscorthy was in the business of turning local barley into the finest malt whiskey. And sure as anything the demand for that spirit was never going to wane in this drink afflicted country. That's what he told his wife and children. Esther, seeing his enthusiasm, perhaps catching a little of it herself, went along with the idea. After all it was only the Six Acre they were going to plough and they would be finished trucking with the cattle and all it entailed.

***

Coming into town Adam allowed the mare slow to a walking pace. His thoughts were on change and how change was about to affect his life. Ploughing, sowing and reaping all meant more work. The sheep would still have to be looked after. Cattle were easy. Turn them into a field and let them alone to feed and fatten, then sell them off when they were good and ready. With sheep you were never finished, what with the dipping, the shearing, the worming, the lambing. All this would still go on as before. What Adam saw ahead of him was the worst of all worlds, double the work and double the trouble.

These were the thoughts that troubled his mind as he spotted two old friends chatting in the Square. Drinking pals of his. Chaps he had known since he started coming into town at weekends to escape his taskmaster father. They waved now when they saw him and he shouted, *How yiz doin'?* before taking the mare to a spot where he could tie her to a rail.

The bank was busy but Adam had barely taken his place in the queue when a door opened on his right and Barrington stood framed in the doorway beckoning him over. The bank manager had everything ready, the notes already bound with rubber bands and a little paper bag filled with coins. Barrington was careful to count them out in front of Adam so there could be no question of any mistake. He placed the money in a cloth bag with a purse-string top which he drew closed.

'My advice, Adam, is to go straight round to Merritt's and get the money off your hands. That way you'll have no worries about anything going amiss.'

The seed merchant's was locked up when Adam arrived outside. A sign in the window said that owing to the sad demise of Mrs Merritt the premises would remained closed until two in the afternoon. Just as well then he had the extra cash in his pocket for he was hungry and Nash's Hotel would provide him with something to eat and a pint of porter to wash it down.

As he crossed the Square to Nash's he saw his drinking pals coming towards him. They were both out of work, proper paid jobs being hard to come by. Since he was planning on having a bit of lunch he might as well ask them to join him — no point being mean about it. Nash's always did well by their diners. Their bacon-and-cabbage was renowned among farmers and townsfolk alike. The beer, his pals agreed, was first class but they couldn't go on accepting his generosity. He insisted, though, for he couldn't bear to see them so totally skint through no fault of their own.

Julia-Ann collected the empty glasses and gave the table a wipe of a wet cloth. The big clock behind the bar told Adam it was not yet one o'clock. There was still an hour before the seed shop reopened. 'We'll have the same again,' he said. As he loosened the string on the cash bag and drew out a gleaming guinea coin the eyes of his companions widened. It was a near certainty, Adam thought, that neither had ever seen so much money in one place in the whole of their lives.

***

By six o'clock it was pitch black in the yard outside.

'What the hell's keeping that fella?' Jacob said making no attempt to hide his irritation.

'If he's not home soon Isaac should go for him.' Esther sounded worried.

Two hours later her unease had turned to real concern. 'Let Isaac go for him,' she repeated.

There had been nights when they heard Adam crawling to his bed in the early hours, but those were times when his work was done and he was free to spend time with the boyos in town. This was different. He had been dispatched on a mission and should have had the seed home with him well before tea. Yet Jacob refused to let Isaac go. 'I'll deal with him in the morning,' he said.

In the morning there was no sign of Adam and it was agreed that Isaac should take the pony trap into town and find his brother. At the bend in the road Isaac looked back to see Hannah at the wicket gate standing with her arm about her mother's shoulder and holding little John by the hand. He understood their worry and hoped Adam would have some reasonable explanation to offer.

As he turned into the Square the first thing he saw was the mare tied to a rail. She was still hitched to the cart and a nosebag hung slack and empty beneath her head. He jumped down, and throwing the distressed animal an armful of hay, released her from between the shafts. He asked some locals if they had seen his brother and soon the names of various drinking establishments cropped up. One man had seen Adam in the Castle Arms the previous evening *standing drinks all 'round.* Someone else told him to go down to Fagan's straight away and he was sure to find his brother there. Isaac felt the anger rise within him as he set off in the direction of Fagan's Bar. He found his brother slumped in a corner on his own, a bleary, amused look on his face, in his hand a half-finished pint of Murphy's Stout and beside him a tumbler of spirits.

After several attempts to elicit some answers from his drunken brother Isaac gave up the effort. He ordered Adam not to budge till he got back. To the barman he said, 'Look at the state he's in. He's not to be given another drop, do you hear me now?'

In Merritt's Seed Merchants the cashier swore there had been no sign of Adam. The sacks of seed were ready and waiting out the back but of course they would have to be paid for up front. Back in Fagan's there was no trace of the money on Adam's person. Nor could he offer any coherent explanation of what had happened. When Adam saw the anger on Isaac's face he started to cry. However his tears cut no ice with Isaac who determined to get him home as soon as possible to face his father's rage.

**

Everyone rushed outside as Isaac drove into the yard but what they saw astonished them — Isaac on the cross-plank driving the mare, with an empty pony and trap following behind. Young John took charge of the horses and Isaac went inside to tell what he had found. They listened with disbelief when he said he found his brother in a drunken stupor, with no trace of the cash, the savings put aside with such effort, the money on which the future of their farm depended.

'I'll bate that good-for-nothing blackguard within an inch of his life,' said Jacob. All next day he was like a demented man, kicking things out of his way, muttering to himself, swearing under his breath. When he said anything at all it was to curse the blight on the family that was his first-born. Nor did he make any effort to hide what he intended to do with Adam. 'I'll flay the hide off of his back. And after that I never want to lay eyes on the brat again.'

However his anger lost its edge and at Esther's prompting, he agreed to offer an olive branch of sorts. They would invite Adam to come back home on the understanding that he would work to pay off the debt. In the event that he was unwilling to do so the farm would pass to their second eldest, Isaac. That was the solution Jacob and Esther came up with between them.

Isaac was to be the peace envoy. Once again he would travel into town, dig out Adam from wherever he was skulking and put his father's conciliatory offer to him. If Adam came back home no more would be said about the escapade, he would work the farm to pay off what he had squandered but with no guarantee the farm would be his in the long run. That was the price he must pay for his gross irresponsibility.

***

Adam attacked the sandwiches like a ravenous dog. Only when he had satisfied his hunger did he ask the all-important question.

'What's he saying, me father? He must be raging. What's he's going to do to me, did he say?'

'I'm not sure I can repeat what he — .'

'Tell me for God's sake, tell me.'

Isaac took his time. He waited till the fear showed in his brother's eyes.

'He's in a black mood, I can tell you that. A bloody bad black mood.'

'How am I going to face him? I'm scared in me boots, I tell you.'

'He's not going to let you away with it. I saw him getting the shotgun off the top of the dresser.'

'The gun? Oh Christ, you're making this up.'

'As God's me judge, Adam. Why would I tell you a lie? He says no court in the land will blame him. Maybe I shouldn't be telling you this. Maybe he'll simmer down after a while.'

Isaac watched his older brother dig his knuckles into his eyes.

'What else did he say, Isaac? Do you think I can ever show me face again?'

Isaac's eyes never left his brother. He took in the pleading in his brother's expression, the fear in his brother's eyes. He took his time. He was getting to the crunch and he wanted it to hit hard. 'I don't know whether I should say this or not,' he said.

'Just say it for God's sake.'

'He swears you're no longer his son. He's written you off. As far as he's concerned, you don't exist.' Adam seemed to struggle with this before a hint of understanding appeared in his eyes. 'You mean my inheritance, don't you? He's writing me out, that's what you're trying to tell me, isn't it?'

Isaac nodded and looked away. He couldn't bear to watch as the last vestige of hope drained from his brother's face. Yet he experienced a strange thrill for he was certain now his older brother would never go back to face their father's anger. He had succeeded in convincing Adam that there was no future for him on their father's farm.

They moved then to discussing the merits of different cities, whether there were job opportunities in Dublin or whether the money was better in Liverpool. Before they parted, Isaac made Adam promise to write and let him know how he was getting on. If there was anything he could do, he said, he would not let him go short.

They shook hands and then on an impulse Isaac put his arm around his brother's shoulder and drew him close in a brotherly hug.

Sixty

Birds sang in the grounds of the South Dublin Union, responding in the way of birds to the bells of Christ Church ringing out a message of normality to a city opening its eyes on a kind of uneasy peace. The Volunteers in the South Dublin Union heard no firing all that Sunday morning. There was something creepy, unsettling, about the stillness in the air. War and the sounds of war had drifted away to some lost realm of history.

David had never heard Kent and Burgess argue before. Now he listened amazed as the row raged in an upstairs room. David guessed the argument concerned the message he brought back from Conn Colbert in the distillery. Colbert had said he wanted *to sit tight* and see how things worked out.

'What kind of a feckin' answer is that?' Charlie Burgess was saying. 'I don't give a shit what Pearse and Connolly do. If them sleeveens want to throw in the towel that's their own business. We're not budging out of here, full stop.'

'I never said anything about throwing in the towel, Charlie. '

'Well why don't you get over there and tell that runt Colbert to stop talking through his feckin' arse?'

The men listening outside the door could see no point in the argument. Eddie Kent had no notion of surrendering—that was obvious—any more than Charlie Burgess had, or indeed any of the men in that building had. Yet they were fascinated by the depth of emotion aroused in their leaders by news of Pearse's surrender. But Kent and Burgess were men like other men and their reactions were nothing if not human.

When the altercation between the two men had tailed off Kent emerged and called his men together. 'I'm going over to Marrowbone Lane,' he announced. 'I need to find out what they've heard and what they intend to do. I can assure you lads that no one here has any notion of giving up. Why would we give up when we're winning? When they tried to shift us out of here we sent them scurrying like scalded rats. Yous can take it from me, lads, there'll be no surrender.'

But before he left the building a messenger arrived from Colbert to say Tom McDonagh had arrived and wanted to talk to Kent.

'McDonagh's supposed to be with his men in Jacobs,' Kent snapped. 'What's he doing over here?'

'I don't know, Sir, but he wants to talk to you.'

'I better get over there and find out what the hell's going on,'

They could hear Burgess shouting something from his sick-bed upstairs but Kent ignored him and slipped out the back.

Time dragged as they waited. The men grew fidgety and the belief grew that things were at a critical stage. When Eddie Kent came back over an hour later it was to confirm their worst fears.

'Okay, lads, it's over.' He avoided looking any of them in the eye. 'We're the last garrison holding out. The rest of them have thrown in the sponge.'

He went up then to face the injured Burgess with his decision. Burgess' roar could be heard throughout the building. 'Do what you want, Kent. I'm not budging.'

Eddie Kent left him there attempting to struggle to his feet and came back down to address his men in the lobby. 'I'm Commandant here. You men take your orders from me. Now go get your things. We leave in five minutes.'

Then he sent one of his men to find Willie Cosgrave, commanding another building, with orders for him to take his men to Marrowbone Lane. As David went to follow the others out the back door, he caught a last glimpse of Charlie Burgess on the landing, leaning against the rail for support. 'They can come to get me, fellas, but they'll never take me alive.' In his hand he brandished his revolver, symbol of his defiance.

They trailed Kent in single file through the shrubbery, dragged open an ancient wooden door on its disintegrating hinges and one by one passed through the narrow opening onto the canal bank. In silence they followed their leader, each man lost in his own thoughts, until they came to an iron footbridge beside where the Guinness barges lay sleeping in a tiny harbour. On the opposite bank people pushed prams or walked their dogs in the Sunday evening sunshine. Not one glanced in their direction as they came to a halt at the steps of the bridge.

'Okay, lads, this is it,' Eddie Kent said. 'We join our comrades in the Distillery and wait for the army to come and take us. Or we use this last chance to walk away, blend with the strollers and make our way home to kith and kin. I'll not judge anyone either way. I'm going to cross this bridge and wait three minutes. Each man of you must decide for himself.'

Kent crossed the bridge and walked on a few paces before he stopped. The men looked at one another, each waiting to see what the rest were going to do. First to make a move was Luke Feeney. 'Well lads, prison's not for me if I'm to have any say in the matter. I might be a rebel but I'm not an eejit. Live to fight another day I always say.' With that he skipped up the iron steps, crossed to the opposite bank and headed off in the direction of the Rialto Bridge. He was followed by young Fitzgerald from Phibsboro who had a widowed mother to think about. David looked around at the rest before he spoke. 'Okay, boys, who's for doing the honourable thing and sticking with the commander?'

No one answered but when he crossed the bridge to join Kent on the other bank, they followed him one by one.

Sixty One

Isaac heard Hannah stirring. The alarm clock said six. She had always been an early riser, Hannah. She had dropped everything and come to Dublin the minute she got his telegram. He knew she would, that she would want to give whatever assistance she could. He himself had slept badly, troubled by the thoughts that haunted him — thoughts of guilt and inadequacy. Guilt at the wrong he had done to his own brother and inadequacy in the way he failed to win the love and respect of his eldest son. He got himself dressed.

Hannah had made tea and she poured him a cup. 'Have you done anything about the funeral?' she said. 'Funeral? I don't know whether you could call it that. Dodd is going to collect the coffin from the hospital and take him over to Mount Jerome. Me and Annie is going with him.'

'Who else is going, do you think?'

'I'll book a cab for yourself and Rose and Becky and Poor Ruth. I don't want anyone else there. I want it private.'

Hannah found a loaf and started to cut herself a slice. 'I found out where Adam is.'

'Adam?'

'That's who I said, *Adam*.'

'Where? I mean how did you manage —?'

'When that letter came before Christmas I got in touch with a firm of solicitors over there. They found out he's been in a hostel for down and outs for years now.'

'My God!'

'*My God* is right. You, Isaac, were the last one to talk to him and I've often wondered if we ever got the full story about what happened. Why did he run off like that, Isaac? Can you tell me that?'

'Who's to say why anyone does anything? Did you get an address? For the hostel, I mean.'

Hannah fished around in her handbag and produced the solicitors' letter. 'It's here. I'm thinking one of us ought to go over.' She looked straight at him as though waiting for his reaction.

'I'll go,' he said. 'Copy down the address for me. First we'll bury Sammy, then I'll try to find Adam.'

Hannah went off to visit her friend on Berkeley Road and Isaac went into the parlour to think over what she had told him. He heard Annie coming down the stairs and going to the kitchen. Then Becky and Poor Ruth came down and voices came to him in muffled whispers. He was alone. For years he had been an outsider in his own family. They talked together when he was out of earshot. When he was there the conversation dried up. Why were they so afraid of him? Was he really such a tyrant? He got on well with the men at work. They seemed to enjoy his company. Same thing with the regulars in Cotters where he always got a warm welcome when he appeared. Yet here in his own home there was a barrier, an invisible wall which he could not break down.

As for David, what was the cause of the fearful rift that had opened between them? His son was pig-headed, no doubt about that. But maybe he could have managed him better. He had dealt with his son the only way he knew how, the way his own father would have done, the way of the iron fist. There had to be authority in the family and the father was the one to exercise it. That was self-evident. All the same, he wished things could have been different. David was his son and no one on God's earth could alter that fact. For the past week his own son was in grave danger of being killed and there wasn't a thing he could have done about it.

He heard the raucous voice of Mrs Mattis in the kitchen. No doubt she had some gossip to impart. Probably glad he wasn't around to spoil it for her. When she was gone Annie came into the parlour with the morning paper open in her hands. She was followed by the two girls. It was like a delegation.

'Mattis just showed us this in the paper,' Annie said. 'It's a list of the men arrested. David's name is there.'

'Give it to me.'

Further Arrests. The headline jumped out at him. There was a photograph of men, a rag-tag bunch, being marched away between an escort of armed soldiers. Beneath the picture was a list of names with the addresses and occupations of those taken into custody. Annie pointed to David's name— *David Townsend, Carpenter, of Orkney Street.* She eased herself down onto a chair. 'Mattis said she spotted the name straight away.' The girls' eyes were on their father, waiting for his reaction.

'All over the papers,' he muttered and threw the newspaper down.

'They were taken to the Richmond Barracks,' Annie said. 'They're to be sent over to Wakefield.'

They sat in silence for a while before Becky said, 'I wonder would they let me talk to him?' Nobody answered but Poor Ruth was nodding her head as if to say *we can lose nothing by trying*. So the girls set off on bicycles for the barracks in Inchicore. They were gone a while before Annie broke the silence. 'When are you going back to work? The fighting's over by all accounts.'

'Time enough for that next week,' he said.

'You mean you're taking another week?'

'We've got to bury the wee fellow tomorrow. Then I'm heading for Birmingham. Hannah was just telling me she tracked Adam down to some class of hostel. I'm going over to bring him home.'

'When are you going?'

'I'll get the boat on Wednesday morning.' He could see her looking at him. She must be wondering what had come over him. He felt different within himself. He felt like a man in a trance. And it must be obvious to her—to them all—that something inside him had died.

***

As they came close to Richmond Barracks, Becky and Poor Ruth saw a mob of people, women mostly, milling around a pair of high iron-barred gates. They parked their bicycles and joined the crowd, trying to squeeze their way through to the front. They were jostled and pushed by others trying to do the same.

On the cobbled yard inside the gates stood the prisoners, or some of them, watched by the soldiers standing around with rifles and bayonets. The soldiers didn't seem unfriendly – if anything they were well disposed towards the men. The women on the outside were calling out the men's names, trying to attract their attention. In one or two cases a man got close enough to the gate for a wife or girlfriend to slip something into his hands. Then the men were told by the soldiers to move back and keep their distance from those outside.

Poor Ruth tugged at Becky's sleeve and pointed. Across the yard a dozen men were being transferred from one building to another. Among them was David. Becky called his name at the top of her voice. *David! David!* It was no good. Her voice was drowned out in the din and he was too far away to see her in the melee.

She turned to the woman beside her. 'Could you lend me a piece of paper?' The woman tore a page from a notebook and with Poor Ruth trying to shield her from the jostling she wrote a few lines. *Sammy is gone to heaven. Eamon is dead, killed in Dublin. My heart is broken. God watch over you brother and keep you safe. Becky.*

On the back she wrote, *For David Townsend.* When one of the prisoners came close enough to touch the hand of a girl who had called to him Becky pushed her note at him. He looked down at the name and winked. 'Righto,' he said pushing the note into his jacket pocket.

The girls mounted their bicycles and headed back home. Becky told her mother and father everything she had seen and heard. She had seen David but hadn't been able to talk to him. She spoke openly in front of her father. The time for hiding things was gone. He knew, as the whole world knew now, that his son had been one of those who had attempted and failed to overthrow the rule of England in Ireland. She told them what she heard people saying, that the men would get long sentences and be sent to prisons in England and Wales.

'Did it look like he's being treated well?' her father asked.

'Yes, I think so.' It was a long time since Becky had heard her father expressing any concern for David's welfare.

Sixty Two

The weather had changed. In place of the warm sunshine of Easter week, a biting breeze swept the open expanse of Mount Jerome, across the bleak tomb-encrusted landscape. Here and there in different corners of the graveyard Annie saw little knots of people gathered around open graves as the coffins of their loved ones were lowered into the ground. It was a busy morning for the grave-diggers.

As one such group began to drift away towards the gate, Harry Dodd called the gravediggers over to lower Sammy's little coffin into the grave. Watching them as they did so were Annie and Isaac, standing together, Becky with her arm around Poor Ruth, both attempting to stifle tears, as well as Hannah and Rose. John had told Isaac he was on duty but that he would be thinking of them all. Mattis was there too, having made her own way to Harold's Cross. She said Plinny would have given his right eye to be there but had no choice but to go to work.

Once the gravediggers had lowered the coffin they said they had another funeral to attend to and moved off to where a hearse had just pulled up. 'We'll lave them shovels and yous can make a start with the filling.'

They handed over their shovels to Isaac and Dodd for them to start throwing the sticky clumps of clay in on top of the wooden box that held the wasted remains of little Sammy. Isaac looked at Annie where she stood with her rosary entwined in her fingers. She knew he was waiting for her to say some kind of prayer by way of farewell. So she said, *May the souls of the faithful departed, through the mercy of God, rest in peace.* To which everyone said, *Amen*, except Poor Ruth, busy with some private words of her own. As the first shovelful of stones and soil thudded onto the lid of the coffin, she raised the fingers of her right hand to her chin and signed, *Goodbye forever, little brother.*

They walked back slowly towards the gate, Isaac's Sunday shoes caked in muck, and when they got to where Dodd had parked the truck, just inside the gate, Isaac handed Becky the money for a cab to take herself and Poor Ruth back to Orkney Street. He invited Hannah, Rose and Mattis to avail of the lift if they wished. Hannah said she would travel with them as far as town. She wanted to get back to Drumboley as soon as possible. Rose, too, said she would take the lift as far as the quays. Mattis accepted the offer to get home by cab. Annie climbed into the front of the truck and again found herself wedged between her husband and Dodd.

There was little conversation until they came to Patrick Street, busy again with street traders at their stalls, selling fruit, fish or clothing. Right next to the Cathedral was a little park. 'That's where they surrendered,' Annie said, pointing at the park, where mothers were wheeling prams and children played on the grass between beds of tulips and wallflowers. 'How do you know that?' Isaac said. 'Hetty Kane told Becky. She said this is where David's lot handed over their guns. St Patrick's Park.'

The subject of David was now out in the open. No need any longer for pretence and denial. Just as the city tried to make sense of what had befallen it, they too would have to unravel the train of events that had changed their lives in the past ten days. No longer was there any need to hide things from her husband or fear his moods. Their son was in the hands of the military and would have to pay the price for his actions.

Still, she hadn't told Isaac the full story. Hetty Kane had called around yesterday and told Becky she had seen lines of prisoners being marched between columns of soldiers down Thomas Street and James' Street on their way to Richmond Barracks. 'Did you see David by any chance?' Becky asked her. 'Yes, and he looked over when I called his name. Then he was gone.' 'How did he look?' 'He had a sort of determined expression, in spite of the foul abuse they were getting from the low types that came out to jeer.' Hearing that, both Annie and Becky had felt a sense of pride.

When they got back to Orkney Street Annie stood back as Isaac tried to make Dodd take some money. 'To cover the petrol,' he said. But Dodd wasn't having any of it. 'Look on this as a promise fulfilled, Isaac. I assured the wee lad he could have a drive in the truck and somehow or other it slipped my mind. Today he got his ride—.' Dodd's voice trailed off and he looked away. They both knew that Sammy had got his first ever lift in the new 1915 Ford Pickup, in a wooden casket carried in the back like so much cargo. His first jaunt turned out to be his last.

When the cab arrived half an hour later they saw Mattis and Poor Ruth getting out. Annie let them in. 'Is Becky not with you?' she said. 'She decided to report for work in Graysons,' Mattis said. 'She didn't have to do that,' said Annie. 'They would have understood.'

Mattis made her way up to her own rooms and Poor Ruth made tea for her parents who were sitting in the parlour. Annie wondered what was going through her husband's mind. Most likely he was thinking of his two lost sons, the one he had just buried in a newly opened grave in Mount Jerome and the one heading for incarceration in an English jail.

'There'll be people out there,' she said, 'that'll admire and respect them Volunteers, and our David too, for what they done. We should be on our knees this minute thanking God that he came through it without a scratch even if he has to do time in jail itself. He's got nothing to be ashamed of and neither should we.'

He didn't answer and Annie chose to interpret his silence as a small sign that he was coming to see another side to the story, willing now, perhaps, to acknowledge his son as his own. For there was only one son left to him now, with the little boy he adored already growing cold in his grave.

***

Everyone wore a smile in Graysons, especially the bosses, who seemed to have shed years in the week they were forced to keep the shutters down. Now it was all go. Calls for building materials were pouring in. They had doubled their orders to the suppliers. It seemed they would never get their hands on enough sand, cement, timber, glass, to keep up with demand. Destroyed and damaged buildings meant work for builders and boom time for those who supplied them.

Mr Grayson, Senior, noticed Becky back at her desk and asked was she alright. She told him she had lost her little brother to meningitis, that she had buried him this morning. 'But you shouldn't have come in, my dear. We can manage. Go home, Miss Townsend and be with your family. Your mother and father must be heartbroken. I insist.'

'Thank you so much, Mr Grayson. Alright, I'll do as you say and go on home.' 'Convey my condolences to your people. It must have been a terrible time for all of you.'

Just how terrible he couldn't have known. She mourned her dead brother and she mourned her dead husband. The one she could mourn openly while the other she must weep for in the secrecy of her heart. For nobody here knew, not her workmates, not her bosses, that she had married Private Eamon Brennan the week he left for France in July, 1915. Her friend Patty overheard her conversation with their employer and the word spread amongst the rest of the staff and many of them made a point of commiserating with her on her loss.

As she tidied her desk to go home she found an envelope hidden under a sheaf of papers. She recognised the writing immediately. It was a note from Eamon enclosed in an envelope she herself had addressed to him in Derby. Inside she found a torn cigarette carton with a hastily scrawled message, *I am back in Dublin at last and I can't wait to see you, I don't know when but plees god soon, sooner than you think maybe. Yours xxx, Eamon.*

She shoved the envelope and note into her handbag and then, in spite of her best efforts, she burst into tears.

Sixty Three

As the cab moved away in the direction of the port Isaac caught a glimpse of Annie, Beckie and Poor Ruth on the front door step, waving him off. He pondered what the cabbie had just told him, that one of the ringleaders had been shot this morning in Kilmainham Jail. 'A chap be the name of Pearse. They're saying he's half-English. What do you make of that?' Isaac didn't know what to make of it. He still couldn't make any sense of anything that had happened during the past ten days. It was like his whole world had turned upside down, inside out.

Now he was setting out to find his brother Adam, to try and bring him home, but without any clear idea what he would do with him if Adam could be persuaded to return. But he knew he could never live with himself if he didn't at least make the effort, for his sin still weighed heavily on him.

At the Metal Bridge the cab swung right onto the bridge and crossed to the other side. Looking out, Isaac could see that the North Quays had been blocked off and the traffic diverted. Further along, at O'Connell Bridge, he saw for himself the wrecking balls working all out to bring down the teetering facades on Bachelor's Walk and Eden Quay. He saw crowds of scavengers picking over the ruins of a devastated Sackville Street. At Butt Bridge he began to worry he would be late. 'I don't want to miss the boat,' he shouted at the cabbie.

'Keep your hair on, Mister. This ain't one of them new-fangled flying machines.' At that point, however, they had passed the Custom House and the traffic began to move again. He relaxed and sat back.

As he caught a first glimpse of the Liverpool boat at its moorings they ran into another delay. Just ahead, a contingent of over a hundred men was being marched towards the docks between two lines of armed soldiers. As they overtook the marching men he stuck his head through the cab window to get a better look and saw they were Sinn Fein prisoners. Lining the route were men, women and children, cat-calling and spitting in the direction of the Shinners.

The hostile crowd attempted to break through the line of armed soldiers but they were held off and driven back by levelled bayonets which here and there drew blood. He heard swear words seldom encountered outside the darkest alleyways. He had no doubt at all that if these hooligans succeeded in getting their hands on any of the prisoners they would tear the flesh off their bones. It was odd to think that the soldiers protecting the Shinners from the fury of their own people were the very ones they had been doing their damnedest to kill for the best part of a week.

Isaac paid the cabby who was eager to get away before either himself or his cab suffered any damage. It scared Isaac to think that David could easily have been one of these prisoners but casting his eye over the group he could see no sign of his son. Arriving on the quayside, the prisoners were led behind a wooden barricade where police stood with batons drawn. Some persistent thugs attempted to follow them and blows were exchanged between police and attackers. One burly brute was laid low with a crack on the head from a police baton. Even as the prisoners were funnelled up the gangway and through an opening in the ship's side the mob surged again and again in their direction.

Isaac stood with other passengers on the quayside watching the disturbance. One by one the prisoners disappeared into the bowels of the ship. Then he saw him. It was David – his own son

David – standing in line at the foot of the gangway, waiting his turn to board.

'David!' he shouted, but his voice was lost in the commotion around him. 'David!' he called, louder this time. No response from his son who had begun to make his way up. Isaac was seized by a sudden urge to run towards his boy, hug him to his chest, tell him he was sorry for everything, that things could be different from now on. He ducked under a heavy rope and began to run towards the prisoners.

Get back there, you! Several shouts at once. A soldier swung around to face him, the look in his eyes a mixture of apprehension and aggression. He pushed the barrel of his rifle sideways against Isaac's throat. David, on the gangplank, seemed lost in his own world, a million miles from the turmoil around him, intent on escaping the abuse and insults of his fellow citizens.

'It's my son. I need to talk to him. Just a word. Please!'

'Step back there, Sir, right now and you won't get hurt.'

At that moment David turned to look down and their eyes met for the briefest moment before he disappeared through the opening. Isaac felt like sitting down there on the quayside and weeping. Instead he dragged himself back to where a group of regular passengers had been watching the whole scene.

***

The ship's siren sounded as she moved into mid-stream before turning about with much churning of white foam. Then with an almost imperceptible movement she began to glide towards the river's mouth and Dublin Bay. Isaac made his way up onto the topmost deck.

Behind him now lay Butt Bridge, O'Connell Bridge and all those other bridges that spanned the Liffey, all the way back to where the river caressed the sloping meadows of the Phoenix Park. In the distance he saw the diminishing outline of the Wellington Monument. It was a strange unsettling feeling to see all the familiar sights slide away. How must it be for those who leave these shores to seek a new life across the water? How must it have been for Adam, all those years before when he thought he had no choice but to seek a new life for himself in a foreign land?

As they moved past the grimy, smelly, gasworks at Ringsend he saw the nearby coal mountain and the line of carts queuing to carry coal to the various coal-yards along the quays. It occurred to him that no matter how much coal they moved, the mountain would always stay the same, always replenished by the next coal-boat to arrive from England. The men who drove the drays would in time pass on and be no more, but the shiny black mass that kept the city's fire's burning and its town gas flowing, would be there forever, the eternal mountain, always different, always the same.

It reminded him of John, solid and dependable in his black police uniform. He had talked to his brother in his hospital bed where he was treated for the wound he suffered at the hands of the rebels. He was impressed at how forgiving John was, how he harboured no bitterness but instead made excuses for those who had shot him. 'They have a dream,' he said. 'They're only following their dream. If you don't mind me saying so, Isaac, you've been far too hard on young David. When all's said and done, they're the only ones we have, our family. Without family we have nothing.'

He thought now about John's words. There were times he had been harsh, a bit too harsh. If he had gone easy on David things might have turned out different. Maybe that was Annie's secret, how she managed to get them all on her side.

If only he could find a way down to where the prisoners were being held he would tell David there was a place for him when he came home. It was never too late for them to start afresh on a new footing. But while he and David were travelling on the same boat they were a world apart. David was under guard below decks on his way to an English prison while he himself was trapped in a prison of his own making.

The Irish coastline was fast fading in the distance. The sharp cone of the Sugarloaf stood against the morning sky. The next peaks he would see would be those of the Welsh mountains. Isaac had never felt so alone. One of his sons lay lifeless in the damp clay of Mount Jerome while the other was caged in the bowels of this very ship.

As for himself, his only hope of redemption lay in the mission he had set himself, to find and rescue his brother from the degradation to which he, Isaac, had condemned him. Perhaps he might at last make atonement for the crime that had lain heavy on his heart for over twenty years.

He used his handkerchief to wipe away the sea-spray that misted his eyes.

About the Author

PJ Connolly lives with his wife Joan McKenna on the Dublin/Wicklow border. His previous novel, *The Priest's Wife*, is set in the Ireland of the 1970's.